A Place For Freddy

A Novel

Tim Naderson

© Timothy John Anderson 2016
First Published in Great Britain 2016

Published by Timothy John Anderson
Royce Close, Dunstable, UK

Dedication

This book is dedicated to all those who have helped me throughout my life. My parents, my family, and my ancestors, without whom I would have been unable to write this story.

I would also thank the Edwardian Territorials who served our country during the First World War. They left their diaries and letters for me to read and wonder at.

Contents

Preamble

Can you see that someone is lucky just by looking at them? Some are endowed with beauty, a charming smile, or wealth. Does that make them lucky?

Can you know that someone is lucky just by talking to them? How long would that conversation take to be sure one way or the other?

Some will profess to being lucky, while others in the same circumstances will see themselves as disadvantaged by life, to be unlucky.

The near miss while crossing the road, was it good luck, or a near disaster?

Optimism and pessimism may play a part?

Some are seen as lucky only by others with a better perspective, or with no perspective.

Does a person have to believe that they are lucky to make it be so?

Or, can a person be lucky and ignorant of the fact?

Can luck be measured?

I pondered this matter while I again read Freddy's opening paragraphs:

My name is Frederick Scott, and I am a very lucky man, or so I have been told. I am not so sure.

I have lived a mostly ordinary life, which is now nearing its natural conclusion. Along with many of my generation there was a time when we knew that the fate of the Free World depended on us and we did not let it down. We faced the challenge and triumphed, though many of my friends fell by the wayside and they were not with us at the end of the journey.

I know that I have been lucky, in many ways. I was born into a loving family and enjoyed a good education. I have always benefitted from excellent health, and now that I am in my ninety-second year I am free of most of the frailties of old age that have marred the lives of my friends and acquaintances. My mind is crystal clear and yet it is at times very troubled. None of those who know me are privy to my innermost thoughts, I keep them to myself. This is the source of my distress. I need to be free of these thoughts before I go to meet my maker.

I would like to tell a story, and I hope that you will find it interesting and stay with me until I have told you everything. In writing my tale I hope to put my mind at rest before my body finally fails me and is put to rest in its turn.

Though it is my story, it is not only about me. It is about my generation. It is about those, who, like me, fought the Kaiser War and endured.

It is about telling the story of those who cannot tell their own story, for they are gone.

Would I, could I, agree that Great Uncle Freddy was a lucky man?

Chapter 1

I have always had a soft spot for Freddy. As a youngster my mother and father often took my brother Tom and I to visit Freddy in his flat. I think they felt sorry for him as he seemed to live a spartan life in comparison with our own. His flat was above a shop that sold wool and dress patterns. The building had been owned by Ted, one of Freddy's chums from the old days who had died in the 1960s, leaving Freddy as a sitting tenant. Ted had apparently allowed for Freddy in his will, bestowing on him the right to stay in the flat for the rest of his life, rent free.

The flat was entered through a door alongside the shop, off the the High Street. My father had a key and we usually let ourselves in, Mummy calling, "Freddy, it's only us!" as we entered. He would invariably meet us on the landing, beaming, and dressed in his tweed sports jacket and tie, though with his old and faithful slippers on his feet, threadbare, and with the stuffing bursting out.

I never saw Freddy outside of that flat. It seemed to me to be his whole world. It was always tidy, in a male sort of way, but dusty, and with neat piles of old newspapers and books on nearly every surface. The wall displayed photographs from Freddy's past. One was of a group of men in old fashioned military uniforms, sitting and standing in front of a wooden building. Some of the men looked older, others were fresh faced, young, but something about them looked strange, uncomfortable. Another was a less formal group of similarly clad young men, their arms around each other's shoulders, and holding glasses. One of them, a big man with a big face, was wearing what looked like a bonnet. All were smiling, as if at a celebration. On his sideboard were a few items of bric-a- brac, odd items that did not seem to go together, yet somehow seemed of the same period. At one side of the room was a table where Freddy ate his meals. I always puzzled as to why there were usually two places set, though I never knew Freddy to have any visitors other than my family. Over all hung the heavy sweet smell of tobacco smoke, Erinmore Mixture, which Freddy would stuff into his pipe and light, and relight, as he talked to us.

I became fascinated as a small child watching the ritual and unchanging preparations for Freddy's pipe smoking. Firstly he would put his hand in his right pocket, rummage around absentmindedly, then shift his weight in his chair and rummage through his left pocket, all the time continuing to talk. After a minute or so of fruitless searching, he would look to the mantelpiece where invariably his pipe would be, carefully placed on a shiny circular brass ashtray. He would continue to talk as he eased himself out of his armchair (the brown leather one with the split seam above his right shoulder) and reach up for the pipe. He would sit down again, fingering the pipe, turning it this way and that, his fingers absentmindedly probing the bowl. Eventually he seemed to notice that the bowl was empty (he always knocked the ash out into the coal scuttle at the end of every smoke) and start searching for his beloved Erinmore. Of course, it was always in the same place, but Freddy went through his routine of exploring first the right pocket, then the left pocket of his jacket before once again reaching up to the mantel and discovering the yellow and red tin next to the brass ashtray where he always kept it.

There followed the ritual of opening the tin with a decisive twist, the extraction of a carefully measured right hand pinch of tobacco into his left hand, which he then rolled between his hands after closing the tin and returning it to its position on the mantel. He would then carefully pour the tobacco into the bowl of the pipe and tamp it down with his thumb. While the rolling was taking place the room would be infused with the

7

sweet smell of the mixture. Next, Freddy would search for his matches, right pocket, left pocket, mantelpiece, as before. He would push open the box, extract one match, strike it, and apply the flame to the pipe in one easy and much practised action.

Then the mupf mupf mupf sucking on the pipe as the tobacco caught and glowed. Freddy would throw the match into the fireplace beside his chair, again in a practised but almost absent minded way.

He would then continue the conversation with us without seeming to pause, puffing away until the bowl was exhausted, at which point, without hesitation he would stand, knock the pipe against the scuttle in the fireplace, return the pipe to the ashtray, and sit down, all without comment. It seemed an automatic and unvarying routine.

In fact, his life seemed to be automatic and unvarying.

I never knew him to go on holiday. He never went out, as far as I could see, and apart from reading newspapers and books, I knew little of his interests or opinions. He always wore the same jacket with its leather elbows, shirt and tie, the one of dark blue with zig zag red stripes.

As a child visiting his flat Freddy was always welcoming, seemingly pleased that we had come to see him. He would always have a white paper bag of pear drops on the table beside his chair. He would invite my brother and I to take one each, and at the end of our visit he would give the bag to Tom with a wink, while my mother was out of the room, and say, "Mind you share these with your sister." My mother and father knew of this, of course, but never objected, even though they restricted sweets for Tom and I to special occasions. It seems that visiting Freddy was included in this category.

After my graduation, Freddy asked me to help him to write his biography. Tom was probably better placed to do this than I was, but as I grew into young adulthood Freddy and I came

8

closer, while Tom seemed to drift away from the family routine, eventually moving to London to work as many of our generation did. In any case, I did not have a job to go to until the autumn and felt a little flattered that I had been asked to do this, and a little intrigued to find out more of the man who had been a part of my youth.

So, it came to pass that I sat with Freddy to start talking about his life. The year was 1987, and I was a 21 year old, some seventy years younger than Freddy. The age difference did not seem to matter, rather I think that it made our discussions easier. I was on the brink of true adulthood, at the start of my exploration of life, and Freddy was nearing the end of his time here. We looked at life from both ends, he looking back, me looking forward, maybe to discover some truths that would help me as I grew older.

I knew that Great Uncle Freddy was the youngest child of my Great Grandad George and Great Grandma Sarah. My grandfather was his older brother, also George, as my father was George in his turn. I have always been intrigued as to why with so many Georges my brother ended up as Thomas.

I had known that our family had been in the same town for generations. The family business was as merchants. We bought grain and other agricultural products and exported them. We also imported timber from Scandinavia, and more recently Russia, and sold this to local companies involved in construction and agriculture. We had made a comfortable living, despite regular forecasts of doom and gloom. Over the previous three centuries and more we had established the family name in the forefront of East Anglian society.

Both Tom and I had been educated at Fishers, the private school in the middle of the county, as had many of our relatives, including Freddy. This had advantages as well as disadvantages. I went when they had only just opened up to admit girls, so going there was something of an experiment for me and the three other girls in my year. Tom, however, had to stand up to comparison with my father, his father and countless other Scotts who had haunted the corridors and dorms since the 17th century. At least Fishers gave all of us something in common. At one time or another we each had been schooled in the same way in the same classrooms and on the same sports fields as everyone else.

Fishers was a great experience. Being located in a small town, really no more than a big village, it was free from the vices and distractions of a city or town. The pupils were known to the villagers, and any misbehaviour or adventure was sure to be reported, in detail, to the staff. In general, we were well behaved, and rarely clashed with local people. In many ways life there turning into a teen, then a young adult, was idyllic. The big skies always seemed to be clear, nature was going about its business all round us. The nurturing and considerate staff kept us well and busy, and taught us to think on our feet, to think independently.

Tom had gone up to Cambridge and read law, while I had decided to buck the family trend and went to Nottingham to read history, without any real idea of where I wanted this to take me in life.

Chapter 2

It was a warm and humid Wednesday in late July 1987 when I went to see Freddy. I had called him on the phone and agreed to talk about writing up his life story. I had not really thought too much about it, I had no real idea of how long it would take or even how to start. Being at a loose end it seemed a good idea to spend more time out of the house and keep myself occupied while waiting to start work later in the year.

The weather had been dry for some weeks, with growing concern about the lack of rain and a possible hosepipe ban, and the effect it might have on the harvest. It had turned humid, though, and a storm was promised that would break the drought and freshen up the air. I took the bus into town as I had no car, and walked the half mile from the Millfleet to Freddy's end of the High Street. As the weather was hot, and I did not expect to be out very long I was wearing light clothing, just jeans and a T-shirt. Even then I could feel my skin and face starting to perspire as I walked up the street, closed in as it was by shops whose glass frontages reflected and seemed to focus the sun's rays. I began to wonder whether I should be going to see Freddy on such a day as this when I could have borrowed a car or Tom's scooter and gone to the coast with friends.

I arrived at the flat and let myself in. Just as Mummy did I called out, "Freddy, it's just me, Kate." as I started climbing the stairs. It was a little cooler inside, but just as humid, and the air was just a little more dusty and stagnant than usual.

When I reached Freddy's door I gently knocked, but he did not answer or come to the door. Using the keys I let myself in. Freddy was slumped in his usual chair, fully dressed, tweed jacket and tie, with a newspaper on his lap and his hands hanging down outside the arms of his armchair. At first I was tempted to turn round and go home, but decided instead to go to the kitchen and get a glass of water.

I returned to the sitting room and sat in the armchair opposite Freddy and gulped half the glass, then sat back and tried to cool off a little. Freddy was absolutely still, and the thought flitted through my mind that maybe he was ill, or worse. His steady, shallow breathing reassured me that all was well.

I took the time to study his face. It was the first time that I had seen him in repose, and I was able to look at him directly, without embarrassment to either of us. He was a small man, maybe no more than five seven tall, with a face that was a little pasty looking, but not really wrinkly, certainly not for a man in his early nineties. His hair was more white than grey, shining bald in the middle, but with a thick curtain of hair from his temples round to the back of his head. His ears peeped out from beneath the curtain, with a crop of curly white hairs clustered around his earlobes and lower ear. His white moustache hid his upper lip.

Despite his years, Freddy did not wear glasses, though there were a pair on the mantelpiece. I had never seen him wear them, but I supposed that he maybe wore them to read his paper.

His face was oval, with a benign countenance, at the same time serious looking, but with a hint of humour. His nose was prominent, not overly large, and of a pleasant shape.

I sat looking at Freddy for maybe a full half hour. My mind wandered a little, and drifted off to ponder other things. Without being aware, I fell into a doze, or at least a state of semi consciousness, vaguely aware of where I was, neither asleep, nor awake.

An hour must have passed before I became aware that Freddy was looking at me. How long this had been I had no idea, but neither he nor I seemed to feel awkward in being in the same room but not speaking. As I surfaced, I muttered my apology. "Sorry, Freddy, you were asleep when I arrived and I just drifted off, in sympathy, perhaps."

Freddy did not acknowledge what I had said, but just kept looking at me, not in an intense way, but almost absent-mindedly, as if he were also thinking about something else.

A minute or so later, he said, quite quietly, "Right then, young lady, let's get down to business. I have some papers here that I would like you to read."

"Can I get you a tea or some water?" I said, "You must be ready for a drink."

"Why yes, a cuppa would do nicely. You know, you remind me of another girl I once knew, though her name was not Kate. Constance was her name, we called her Connie. She was just as pretty as you, and headstrong. She knew her mind, and let everyone know so!"

This surprised me, I had never considered Freddy having lady friends, he always seemed to be the confirmed bachelor type. "Tell me more, Freddy, she sounds interesting."

Freddy just smiled, "You will hear more of Connie in due course of time, in the meantime, I need that cuppa, and you need to read my notes."

I went into the kitchen, boiled the kettle, and brought Freddy his tea, and one for me.

In the background there were muffled voices, the sound of the occasional car, and footsteps on the pavement down below. Freddy's sash window was open halfway to let in some air, and the sounds of the town intruded gently.

Freddy said, "Are you still sure that you want to help me? You can change your mind if you want to. There must be many better things a young woman like you could be getting on with. There must be younger men than me that you should be spending your time with."

"No, it's OK. I am happy to help if I can. I think I would rather be with you than with some of the idiots that seem to be attracted to me. I have only ever found one boy that I liked enough to look forward to going out with, but he was spoken for. I did not want to double cross or upset his girlfriend. She and I were good friends, and her friendship was worth keeping. I suppose that Mr Right will come along at some point, but he has yet to make an appearance!"

"Good girl. I know that you will find the right man. I think I understand about personalities and character, and you will make the right decision when the time comes. You have a lot of your Grandad George about you. He was the sensible one in our family. He never made a bad decision, he always seemed to know what was the right thing to do, when to do it, and how to do it."

"I never really knew Grandad, he died when I was only about four or five. I do remember him cuddling me and bouncing me on his knee. He had white hair like yours, only a bit more of it! He also used to tell me stories at bedtime, though I cannot for the life of me remember any of them."

"Yes, he was an affectionate man, and he was good at stories, because he had need to. I will tell you more about him later, but he was a good man, a great patriot, though these days patriotism seems to be out of fashion. Except with the right sort of people, that is. I always wanted to be more like him, but I never could be."

"You were younger than Grandad, weren't you? How much younger, and where did Great Aunt Sissie fit in?"

"George was the oldest and Sissie was older than me. I was the baby of the family. I suppose that I was able to get away with murder. My mother and I were very close. I think that by the time I came along the other boys were starting to be more independent. Sissie was destined to be awkward and difficult and my mother and her used to clash. I was the co-operative one. I liked to spend time with Mamma, while the boys and Sissie were happy not to."

"You said the boys, but I thought there was only you and Grandad?"

Freddy paused, looked away for a brief second, then slowly explained, "We had another brother, Edwin. He died in the war. He was more like George than I was. If he had lived I am sure that he would have done great things, like George did. He was very calm and organised. He used to help me with sorting things out if I ever got into trouble. When we went tree climbing, for instance, he would be the one to climb first, then tell me the best way to climb up and how to get down again, He would have made a good father, he was kind and considerate. I loved him, and I think that he loved me."

"How did he die?"

"It's in my notes," Freddy said, brightening a little, "but he died doing the right thing. He was a hero, my hero, and I miss him, a lot."

"OK, I look forward to hearing more about Edwin, but I am surprised that Grandad never mentioned him."

"It was just the way in those days. Many children died, and in the war there were so many that we just accepted that they were gone and we had to carry on."

Chapter 3

7th August 1914, King's Lynn.

The day had started out cool and humid after an early morning shower, but as the daylight grew the sun appeared and a warm day was in promise.

In the North End the families were abroad to welcome the fishing boats back into port with their overnight catches, quickly preparing them for market. Groups formed as rumours spread that there had been naval actions and sinkings off the east coast. Men from the town had left two days previously to join the Royal Navy as reservists, and their families were understandably concerned that bad news may be on the way. Or, possibly, good news of a British naval victory. Some men were serving on their own boats as navy patrols in the German Sea, but they had no information to add.

One among them was sure that his son was safe. Thomas Hastings, a father of six girls and a son, also Thomas.

Thomas the son would normally have followed his father into the fishing fleet, but he had not been able to overcome his seasickness, despite going out on the boat from the age of twelve. The father had reluctantly let his son stay on land, firstly apprenticed to be a rope maker, and later when he married Daphne, the girl next door, son Thomas had gone to work on the railway. In order to supplement his wages Thomas had attested into the Territorial Force and now had two sons and a beautiful daughter of his own. At the age of twenty eight he was content with his lot in life.

But Thomas the father was up early that Friday. His son had received his mobilisation orders from the drill hall three days earlier and had spent the intervening days working hard to get his equipment ready so that he would be ready to march out with the Norfolk Volunteer Artillery Brigade. The day had arrived, and young Thomas Hastings was now at the Artillery drill hall on Purfleet Quay with the rest of the gunners and officers. The gun teams of the battery were being drawn up on parade so that the dignitaries, and the ordinary folk, could say their goodbyes and wish their men well as they marched off to fight the foe.

The atmosphere was jolly and almost celebratory. The rush to mobilise following the declaration of war had been long enough ago for preparations to be completed. Along the pavements were stalls set up selling toffee apples and sweetmeats. Many people had made placards which they held above their heads, with signs which said such things as 'We are proud of you all' , and 'Give the Kaiser a good bashing!'.

One group that were notable by their absence were the town's small congregation of Quakers. They had not yet had time to consider their position on the war, and by default had not been able to support or decry the actions of the Crown.

On The Millfleet a dais had been erected, and on the other side of the road the town band was playing joyfully patriotic tunes.

Ten o'clock came, and the men, officers, families, and well wishers were standing around in groups waiting for the march past to begin.

The mayor was in one group, in discussion with Colonel Howard, the commanding officer of the brigade. The men and guns were now fully ready and lined up on The Millfleet. Howard was a solicitor in his civilian life, a magistrate, and a councillor, with a reasonable aspiration to be the next mayor.

Another group had formed around the local engineer, and self made businessman, William Mann. He was accompanied by his sister, Florence, and his daughter Constance. William Mann's wife had died soon after Constance's birth, so his sister had become his housekeeper and had brought up Constance as her own. Constance had an older brother, Walter, who was with the Norfolk Regiment, Territorials, at their drill hall. They had also been through the process of mobilisation and they in their turn would be marching out on the morrow.

William Mann's private secretary was James Newman, who was parading with the guns. Newman had finished checking his men and their equipment. Everything being in order, he felt able to join his father who was standing on the pavement, looking on with a mixture of satisfaction and concern. James was his only son, and at the age of thirty nine showed no sign of settling down with a wife and children, which Newman senior thought ought to have been the correct thing. "Well father, I think we are ready, what do you think?" said the younger man.

"You may be, but I am not sure that I am. At least this time you should be away for a short time, I am told that it will all be over before the end of the year, and we will be able to get back to normal life again." he replied, "Then you can settle down for good. Your mother was not happy when you volunteered back in '99, and she worried about you all the time you were away."

The Scott family also formed a cluster on the pavement. The two boys, Edwin and Freddy, resplendent in their lieutenant's uniforms were being fussed by their mother, with sister Sarah looking on with amusement. "Now, Edwin, I want you to look after Freddy, he is still very young and he needs you to keep an eye on him, or he will get into bad ways."

Mr Scott looked on with pride. As a prominent local businessman having his three sons in uniform at this time (the eldest, George, was serving with Walter Mann and was at the drill hall at that moment) would prove that his family were doing their bit for the country and the town. The unfortunate part was that the chosen enemy at this time were the Germans. Unfortunate in that a major part of the business was trading timber, agricultural products and machinery with their German partners in the Baltic. But, the war was going to be short, and they would be able to pick up the threads quickly again once the war was over. The harvest was not yet in, and when it was he was sure to be able to get good prices as wars always drove up prices. "Right, you two youngsters, I want you to do your duty by the country. Make sure that you do not let me down, do what your officers tell you to, and make me proud of you."

Edwin and Freddy exchanged a knowing look and without prompting both faced their father directly and threw up a smart salute. "Of course, sir, you can depend on it!" exclaimed Edwin, with a little more humour than he intended.

Mother Scott joined in, "I know you Edwin, you will lead young Freddy astray if given half a chance. I have asked your brother George to keep an eye on both of you, and Buster will as well. I want you to consider signing the pledge while you are away. I know the problem that drink can be for young men like you. You must not let me down with any women either, just think of me and Sissie when a girl is giving you the eye."

Sarah, known in the family as Sissie, looked on with a smile, knowing that mother's words would be acknowledged then ignored by both her brothers. She looked away and caught sight of the Manns standing a few feet away. She was friends with Constance, they were at school together, and shared an impish sense of humour. She eased away from her family group, and put her hand on Constance's elbow, encouraging her to turn. Giggling, she said, "Connie, do me a favour, please?"

"What can I do?"

"Mamma is worried about the moral fortitude of Edwin and Freddy while they are away. How would you feel about going over and giving the boys a peck on the cheek for good luck?"

A fleeting sign of enquiry came on Constance's face, then a smile, "Yes, as long as you do the same with Walter tomorrow when he marches off. Is that agreed?"

With that the two young women edged back to the Scott family group, coming up behind Mrs Scott, facing the brothers, who had noticed the conversation without understanding. They were used to the two girl friends getting up to mischief. Sissie was a tomboy, achieving this despite the efforts of their mother to turn her into a young lady. While Sissie dressed well, her temperament was always to undermine any attempt to restrain her natural exuberance and rebellious nature.

As Mrs Scott drew breath, the two young women stepped forward, and Constance said directly to her, "Mrs Scott, I would like to make a present to Edwin and Freddy, may I?"

Somewhat taken by surprise, Mrs Scott stood back and said, "What? Oh, it's you, Connie, yes, yes, please go on."

With that, Constance stepped up to Edwin, put her hands on his shoulders, and brushed his left cheek with her lips, stood back, and said, "Edwin, I wish you well as a soldier. Please do your duty, and come back safely."

Edwin blushed, but said nothing, taken aback by this sudden and unexpected attention. He had not before considered Constance in a romantic way, and was not sure if he was the subject of another of his sister's pranks, or whether he should take the affection on face value, or not. He quickly resolved that the sight of him in uniform, and he being an officer, that he should behave appropriately, especially in view of his mother's recently expressed concerns. "Why, thank you Connie. I will make sure that I do my duty fully and considerately."

Constance then turned to face Freddy. "Freddy, I will not leave you out, you also need my best wishes and affection." With that, and before Freddy could react, she had kissed him as well. Freddy also blushed, this being the first kiss that he had ever received other than from his mother or sister. He felt a strange headiness, without knowing why. For a moment he looked directly into Constance's eyes and saw something he had not before realised. Her fragrance lingered, and a warmth covered his cheek. Constance was a woman, not just Sissie's friend.

James Newman marched smartly over to address William Mann, "Please excuse me, Miss Florence, Mr Mann, I would like to beg your leave, if you please."

Mann replied, a little gruffly perhaps, "Yes, it must be time for you to go. Come back soon, if you can. We have much to do. Write to me when you get to where you are going and I will let you know what we need. I have been approached by the War Office and I am thinking of engaging for war contracts, but I am not sure yet what we can do for them. Let me have your views when you have settled in and know what might be of utility to the Army."

"Yes sir, I will certainly do so, and goodbye Miss Florence, please wish me well. I will value your correspondence if I may be of service to you as well." said James.

"Godspeed, Mr Newman, I will write if I have need of advice." replied Florence, offering her hand for James to shake.

With that, Newman saluted, about turned as if on parade, and marched off to the guns. There he saw the battery sergeant major, Barry Evans, who had just finished fussing around and checking the men's appearance, for the umpteenth time. "How are things, sergeant major?"

"Fine, fine, we are all ready for the speeches to begin, sir!" replied Evans.

The adjutant, Captain Christopher Chilvers, came across to the two men. "Right, I think that it is time we got everyone mounted and ready for the march past. Can you two get the men together, I will get the Battery Commander to round up the young gentlemen and let the Mayor know that we want to get started."

"Righto, Kit." replied Newman, while the sergeant major nodded, saluted, turned and went off in pursuit of the men. Chilvers found the battery commander with the mayor's group behind the dais. "Sir, the men are mounting up ready for the Mayor's address, are you happy for the officers to join them for the march past?"

Major Philip Mount, the battery commander, turned to look at Chilvers, nodded, and turned back to the lord mayor, "Right, Mr Mayor, all seems ready to go, may I ask you to ascend the steps and say a few words?"

The mayor did as he was bid, made a brief speech wishing Godspeed to the men in uniform, and the wish that they would all come through a brief and successful war safely. With that the gun teams moved off, with Colonel Howard at their head on his favourite hunter, followed by the other officers on their chargers, the harness and tackle creaking and sparkling in the sunshine, the wagon wheels rattling as the passed over the cobbles. When the parade reached the bottom of Millfleet they wheeled right and trotted down London Road, past the South Gates, and carried on to South Lynn station where they loaded the guns, limbers, wagons, stores, and equipment onto a specially arranged goods train. The men then sorted themselves into the carriages, second class for the men, first class for the officers. At five minutes past two in the afternoon, exactly to schedule, the train steamed out, across the Great Ouse and into the Fens towards Lincolnshire.

Chapter 4

15th July 1987, King's Lynn.

Great Uncle Freddy and I spent the rest of the afternoon reading through his diaries from the First World War.

"Uncle Freddy, there are a lot of acronyms in your diaries. What do they mean?" I asked.

"The Army loves to use them and soldiers just get used to them, without thinking about it, I suppose. Which ones are you talking about?" he replied.

I looked through a few pages and wrote down some of them and gave the list to Freddy.

"Ah, BC, that stands for Battery Commander, the officer in charge of a battery."

"What is a battery?"

"The artillery had a basic unit of a battery, with four or six guns, and about a hundred men to work them. The BC would be a major, and he would have a few more junior officers to help him, and NCOs, of course."

"NCOs?"

"Non Commissioned Officers, men with stripes on their arms, corporals, bombardiers, sergeants, and sergeant majors, though sergeant majors were warrant officers as well."

"It all sounds complicated." I said.

"Yes, it is until you get used to it all. This next one, brigade. Can be two things, actually. An infantry brigade was three or four battalions of infantry soldiers, about four thousand of them altogether. An artillery brigade was a few batteries working together, sometimes three batteries, sometimes four or more. An infantry brigade commander was a brigadier, while an artillery brigade commander was a colonel. Now, division. Yes, division. Infantry and artillery brigades would be organised into a division, commanded by a major general. As well as the infantry and artillery brigades there would also be engineers, service corps troops, cavalry and other bits and bobs of units to make up a balanced formation that was self sufficient in the field."

"I am confused already!" I said.

"Yes, don't worry, you can ask me again whenever you forget what I have said. Right, you have written OP here. OP stands for observation post. This was where the artillery officer, or any soldier for that matter, was placed in order to look for information or targets. Sometimes it was a proper bunker with a window or slit to look out from, sometimes it could just be where a soldier had decided to stop and observe something or other. In the artillery we found that we had to put our guns in positions, the gun line, where they could not be seen or shot at by the Germans. As they could not see the enemy either, we sent officers forward to a position from where they could see the Germans and could send information to the guns as to where to shoot."

"By radio?"

Freddy chuckled, "No, we did not have wireless, at least at first. We used flags, semaphore flags, or I have even heard of heliographs being used, but not much. Soon after the war started they gave us field telephones and miles of telephone cable so we could lay the wires between the gun line and the OP and speak to each other that way. The problem was, of course, that the cable would get broken so we would be unable to communicate and the signaller would have to go out, find the break and repair it. A bit dangerous when the shells were flying! They did use wireless, but the equipment was big and heavy and not suitable for our level in the army. Later on, though, they did use wireless more and more, but we never had any where I was."

"So the gun line was where the guns were, what about the wagon line, and the horse lines?"

"When the guns were in position for firing the horses that had drawn the guns were taken back to a safer area, to the horse line. In open warfare this could be just behind the hill we were on, but in static warfare, most of the time in the Kaiser War, the horses were kept two or three miles to the rear. The wagon line was where the ammunition and supply wagons were kept, usually close to the horse lines."

"Thank you, Freddy, I think that is clearer, and I know that HQ is headquarters."

"Yes, HQ is where the commander was most of the time, with his signallers and staff officers, though our divisional commander, General Trubshawe, spent more time in the trenches than at his HQ! He was a rum old boy, there's no doubt about that!"

"Uncle Freddy, I am surprised. I thought that as soon as the war had started that they sent you to the front. I see from your diaries that you went off to Lincolnshire for quite a long time."

"Yes, that is right," said Freddy, "looking back it was the right thing for us to do. The Territorials were a home defence force, so we knew that our job was to defend the country from invasion. First off we went to defend the east coast if the Germans tried to invade. Most of us did get more than a little frustrated to be twiddling our thumbs while the fighting went on in France. Looking back, though, we would not have been much use to the army. Our guns and so-on were out of date, we did not have all the horses and transport that we needed, and some of us were too old or too unfit to fight." Freddy explained.

"So, how long was it before you got to France?" I asked.

"We sailed in late March '15, and we were sent to Belgium for a few weeks to get used to things at the front."

"Belgium? I thought the First World War was fought in France." I said.

Freddy explained, "The British Army fought in both countries. At first we went to Belgium where the British had ended up after the opening battles, and as the war moved on the French asked us to take over more and more of the line. We took over sections of the line from time to time until we reached the River Somme. In fact, I spent a few months the other side of the river, on the southern side."

"Have you ever been back?" I asked.

"Yes, we did a charabanc tour back in, I think, '32 or '33, I can't remember exactly. Several of us old sweats thought it would be a good idea to go back. The government had been building monuments to the various battles and so on, and the war cemeteries had been more or less completed, so we went back to see what we could see."

"And what did you see?" I asked.

"Well, the charabanc that we had kept breaking down, so we saw a lot of the roadside, and if we were lucky it broke down near a village and we could while away the time in a bar."

"What about the monuments and so on?"

"They were, are, I expect, very impressive. But we only had time to visit France and Belgium, we never got down to Italy, I have never been back there." said Freddy, a little wistfully.

A sudden thought came to me, and without really considering it I said to Freddy, "Why don't we go there together, you and me?"

Freddy looked at me, looked at the fireplace, then back at me. "How would we get there?" he asked.

"I don't know," I said, "but it can't be impossible. Would you like to go, because I have a few weeks before I start working, and it might be a sort of holiday for both of us."

"Mmm, yes, I think I would like to go, especially with a pretty girl to look after me!"

"I can be your companion, and you can be my chaperone!"

So, having agreed to taking a trip to Italy I took some of Freddy's diaries to read and went back to Saddlebow to read them and talk things over with Mummy and Daddy. I had suggested to Freddy that he write an explanation for each word or acronym that would be unfamiliar to most people and include this as a glossary at the end of his memoirs. This he agreed to do after we came back from the trip.

Mummy was against us going, of course, but Daddy was surprisingly positive about the idea. He suggested that I take his MGB and drive Freddy around. That way, he said, we would be able to come and go as we wished, and I could take Freddy wherever he wanted to go. Being Daddy, of course, he also gave me a large amount of cash to pay for the expenses, saying, "Here is enough cash to make sure that you and Freddy can eat and drink your way across the Continent in style. If you want you can regard it as a loan against your inheritance when Mummy and I pop our clogs."

So, a week later, arrangements having been made, and the MGB coming back from the garage fully fettled and with a new set of tyres, I drove into Lynn, parked, and went to Freddy's flat.

When I arrived he was packed and clearly excited.

He had just one slightly battered suitcase, which I picked up for him and we went to the car, got in, and we were off!

As we drove down to Dover to catch the ferry Freddy told me all about his time in Lincolnshire before he was sent to Belgium.

Chapter 5

25th January 1915, Market Rasen, Lincolnshire.

Outside the weather was bad. Sleeting rain and winds from the east, cold, and uninviting. Inside the farmhouse that served as the officers' mess for the Brigade a fire was burning in the grate, radiating a meagre warmth and flickering light across the room. A small group of officers sat around the fire on the bum warmer talking quietly. A general air of gloomy depression was in the air.

Philip Mount's voice cut above the low burble of conversation, "I hate this weather! Riding is no fun and the damned foxes seem to know that we will not be out and about."

"Well, Philip, I am more concerned that the men are getting a bit forlorn. Many of their tents have been letting in the weather, and the lack of action is affecting their enthusiasm, we really need to get a better task than waiting for the Hun to invade. In my opinion he will never do it, so why are we still here?" said Kit Chilvers.

James Newman turned to face Chilvers, "I am sure we will get our chance soon. I hear that some of the Kitchener battalions are being made ready to go to Flanders. We are better trained and prepared so the War Office should be looking to get us sent out soon, just be patient. I know from the South Africa campaign that when they need us they will get things moving, and moving fast. It's obvious."

Buster interjected, "Yes, but by then we will have lost our edge. Another factor will be that the War Office will have to get us to sign up for Imperial Service, those that have not already signed up, that is. Philip, have you had any correspondence on this matter yet?"

Mount turned to look at Buster, "No, and I hope we do not just yet. There will be plenty of time for young bloods like you. You know that Kitchener really does not like us Territorials. I don't think he trusts us to do what he wants after your lot deserted him after hostilities finished in South Africa. He prefers to have people that he can control, not people who can exercise free will like that. In any case, I am happy to stay here, as Milton wrote 'Thousands at his bidding speed. And post o'er land and ocean without rest: They also serve who only stand and wait.' Well, we are serving just by waiting our turn. As Territorials we joined up to defend England, not to go and fight the King's enemies in foreign lands. That job is for the Regulars. If they need us they will come knocking on the door, until then, let's just enjoy ourselves as best we can."

At that point the door opened and some of the storm accompanied Edwin Scott into the room.

"Aha, the wanderer returns!" Buster called, "How is the old town, young Scott? I presume the Hun airships missed you?"

"What awful weather! Yes, the Zeppelins missed me alright, you have obviously heard about the raid. Though we were at Saddlebow we still heard the bombs exploding, and the Zep passed directly over us. I understand that most of the bombs hit the railway station and the docks, which must have been what they were after. I went down there with my father the next day, and it was a bit of a mess, to say the least. Anyway I am glad to be back here with you fine fellows." Edwin said, "Any news of the call to action, yet?"

"No, none as yet, but it can't be long now I'll wager." stated James Newman, "Was there no action against the Zeppelin when the raid happened?"

"Nothing that I could see or hear, I think they have the skies to themselves. We are defenceless, as far as I can see." said Edwin.

"I will write to Mr Mann and suggest that he look at building a carriage for our guns that would allow them to fire at high elevation. With their high muzzle velocity they should be able to get a shrapnel shell up to the same height as the Zeppelin. If we can sort this out we may be able to get a better role as anti Zeppelin artillery. At least that way we might see some action instead of sitting on our backsides here in the middle of the countryside. I will write to him this evening. At least then I will feel that I am doing something for the war effort rather than sitting in a field out here." said James, clearly determined to do something. He uncoiled his lanky frame from the bum warmer, nodded to Mount, and left the room.

Freddy went up to his brother and asked, "What news of Mamma and Papa? How are they getting along?"

"Fine, fine, though Mamma is clearly missing her little boys. She sent a parcel for you, Freddy, and one for George. I will take it over to him tomorrow. She also reminded me to stay away from the local girls and hard booze. Just to respect her wishes I bought a bottle of whisky in Lincoln while waiting for the train, fancy a drop?"

"No thanks," replied Freddy, "I don't have the taste for it. I am happy with my cordial, thank you. How is Sissie, it must be difficult for her being alone there with Mamma?"

"She is doing alright, I think, she gets out of Saddlebow as often as she can and spends time at the Mann's. I went over there and she and Connie were as thick as thieves. Connie's aunt Florence has them both helping her to raise funds for soldiers' comforts. She said that she would make sure that some will come our way soon. Though she did say that they were going to give priority to those boys actually in the war rather than us lot sitting in the marshes here. None of the ladies seem to be very impressed at us having to stay in England while the real war is happening across the water. Actually I agree with them, to be honest, civilians in Lynn have seen more action than we have what with the Zep raid. Even Papa has said that next time they come over he will be on the roof with his shotguns and have a pot shot at them. I am sure he will see action before we do. Between you and me, I am thinking of asking for a transfer to another unit. They are sending out reinforcement drafts all the time to make up for casualties, and I am sure that I will be of better use to the War Office over there. To be frank, I am getting somewhat bored with our role here!"

Freddy brightened and said, "Well, Edwin, why don't we both do that tomorrow. I do not think that Philip would be happy, but we could ask Kit Chilvers to help. As a regular he will know the best way to go about things, he has all sorts of contacts."

Edwin replied, "Actually I am not sure that would be a good idea for you to request a posting as well as me. Philip may be prepared to lose one officer, but if two of us get posted he might raise objections. After all, he has to keep the battery up to scratch and losing both of us would upset his applecart. Let me speak to Kit in private tomorrow and see what he thinks can be done, then we can decide what to do."

Freddy said, "Right, agreed. I think some of the men are getting a bit restless as well. Hastings came to see me when we heard about the Zep raid, his family is split between the docks and the railway so he was concerned for their safety. Could you go and reassure him tomorrow? He is a good man, very keen, and hard working, I would not want him to lose heart. When we do get to Flanders, we will need him and the others like him."

"Yes, of course I will. I did enquire at the police station and I think all of our families are safe, I had better pass that on to Philip and the BSM so they can let all the men know." said Edwin. Going to the fireplace and turning to Philip Mount, he said, "Excuse me, please, Philip, I have information from the police in King's Lynn about the casualties from the Zeppelin raid last week. It seems that all our families were unaffected, would you like me to pass this on to the BSM so he can reassure the men?"

Mount looked across at Edwin, with a quizzical look, not seeming to take in the information, his eyes narrowed, then comprehension came, "Oh yes, they have let me know, I had a telegram from the rear party a couple of days ago. Yes, all right, tell the BSM that all is well at home, I am sure that he will be pleased to pass it on." With that he turned back to Buster and continued his monologue on the joys of steeplechasing.

Edwin and Freddy exchanged glances, Edwin raised an eyebrow, and Freddy grimaced. Edwin left the mess, back into the rain that had eased a little and marched briskly over to the barn where the sergeants had their mess. Knocking at the barn door, he called, "BSM, may I come in? I have news from the home front."

The door opened and Sergeant Leman stood in the entrance, he saw Edwin, then stood back and motioned him to enter. "I am afraid the BSM is not here at the moment, sir, he is in the mens' lines checking the state of the tents, he is concerned that some of them may be getting wet. He should be back soon, would you like to come in and have a drink while you wait?"

"Thank you, Sergeant Leman, that would be good, it is somewhat inclement out here." Edwin moved further into the barn and saw that most of the battery senior NCOs were there. As he joined them they stopped talking and turned towards him. Leman said to the the assembled crowd, "Make way lads, we have a lost sheep here who needs to find shelter. Young Mr Scott here has just returned and has some news for us, so pin your ears back. Before you start, sir, can I get you a wet?"

Edwin smiled, "A bottle of beer would be nice, thank you."
At that moment the BSM came back through the barn door,
shaking the rain from his mackintosh. Seeing Edwin, he smiled
and said, "So you are back from your travels, young sir, how
are things?"

"I am fine, sergeant major, I came over to let you know
about the air raid on Lynn. May I go ahead and tell the mess?"

"Of course, please do."

Addressing the group Edwin said, "As you will know by now
the Hun decided to mount a raid on our town. He came over
in a Zeppelin airship and dropped several bombs. It seems the
target must have been the docks and the railway. Some say that
they were after the King at Sandringham, but all the bombs
landed on the town and most of them missed and fell on
houses. There was one bomb that hit the docks. The police
have told me that four people were killed and a dozen or so
injured. However, all our families seem to be safe, and I spoke
to Sergeant Bowles at the drill hall and he will send us a
telegram if further raids occur. Please let all the men know
what I have just told you, and if any of them have concerns to
let their officers know. We will try to get as much information
as possible from the authorities in Lynn, and Sergeant Bowles
has been tasked with keeping in contact with the police. He will
stay with the rear party for the foreseeable future and will sort
out any issues with families for us. Any questions?"

"So, old man Bowles has seen action before we have! Would
you believe it!" exclaimed Leman, "Mind you, he is so deaf
and dopey he probably slept through the raid and had to be
woken up to find out what had happened."

Edwin replied, "Well, as far as I can see Sergeant Bowles has
been very busy with running the drill hall, what with them
recruiting a new second line brigade, and having all sorts of
odd bods turning up and needing attention. They have also
used the drill hall for a Kitchener brigade, so it is bursting at

the seams and old Bowles has lost what hair he had left. So be kind to the old gent, if you will. Actually, on that note, the rumour is that the Kitchener battalions will be going to the front before we do. Apparently Sergeant Bowles saw some tropical uniforms in a delivery to the Kitchener brigade, though no-one was expecting them and they assumed that as usual they will get orders after the goods have turned up. The K men have also been issued with one of the new 18 pounders and are training with that. They seem to be getting the new stuff before we do!"

Evans nodded, and said, "Well, that may be so, but we have these old 15 pounders and we know how to work them. I am sure that we can do anything with them that a bunch of Johnny come latelys can do with newer guns. What we need to do is make sure that when the call comes we are ready and able. That call will come, soon, hopefully, and then we will need no excuses."

That evening the rain eased and Edwin, Freddy and Buster decided to walk down to the village pub. The air was cool and damp after the rain, and there were many puddles in the lane that led from the farm to the village.

The pub was full when they arrived, with the log fire in full force. Buster went to the bar and asked the others over his shoulder what they would like to drink. Edwin opted for cider, while Freddy asked for a cordial. They received their drinks and retreated to a corner where they could talk.

Freddy asked Edwin, "How did your visit to the sergeant's mess go?"

"I think they were glad to hear good news, but I rather think that they had already had the news about the raid. They seemed to be more worked up about the lack of information about what the War Office wants to do with us. There are rumours of the Kitchener men being sent abroad. Apparently someone has seen tropical kit being put into stores, so they may be off to India or Basra, or even Africa. Anyway, it seems that some of them may be off before we are."

At that moment the outer door opened and George Scott came in with Stephen Sansom. Buster saw them and waved at them over the heads of the people sitting down. George acknowledged the wave and came over after he and Stephen had achieved a full glass.

"Well Buster, thanks for looking after my two brothers, I hope that they are not annoying you, too much at least." said George.

"No, they have been working hard and keeping their noses clean, at least as far as I can see. How are things with your lot, George?"

"Well, probably like you we are getting more than a little bored with kicking our heels here when we should be out in Flanders, but I think things may be about to change. Apparently they are going to formally concentrate the division and have appointed a general to command it. I understand that his name is Trubshawe, doesn't mean a lot to me, but if we get a general, it must mean that we will be getting ready to go into action, doesn't it?"

Edwin and Freddy paid attention.

"Trubshawe? Sounds a bit familiar but I'm not sure I know him. Any more information?" Buster asked.

"Apparently he served in South Africa and won a medal at a place called Paarderberg. He is an Infantryman, and has a couple of brothers who are generals as well. They come from a military family it seems. Anyway, the rumour is that we will get official orders to concentrate in a week or so, and this General Trubshawe will then probably want to come round and give us the once over to make sure that we are up to scratch."

Buster nodded and added, "What about the Imperial Service complication. Presumably we will have to volunteer for service overseas. I am not sure that all our men will be up for that, a few of them have become a bit windy. One of them, a chap called Hastings came to me this afternoon concerned that his wife and children might be bombed by the Huns and saying that he was not sure he should not be at home with them. I suppose that if a few like him did not sign up for IS we would get some reservists or K men to make up the gaps?"

"Yes, I am sure there will be a few, after all we have some older men here who may not make the grade in any case. I am sure the War Office has a plan. Whatever they decide we will just have to work with."

"How long before we find out, do you think?" Edwin asked George.

"Not sure, maybe a couple of weeks I would think. From what I hear they need more divisions over the water, and soon. The Territorials should be able to field about a dozen divisions, and a few brigades have been formed and are on the way already, our time can't be far away."

2nd February 1915, The Horse Lines.

"Well, Sergeant Leman, how are the beasts this morning?" Freddy asked.

"I think that some of the nags we received last week have ringworm. Luckily we have kept them separate as they may have infected the others. I have reported the situation to Lieutenant Chapell, the veterinary officer, and he should be here this afternoon to see for himself. If it is ringworm we will have to keep any infected animals apart and clean any tackle that has been in contact with them. I have seen this before on a farm in Welney when the ploughmen were not good at keeping the beasts clean. We should be able to sort it all out in a couple of weeks, though." Leman said.

BSM Evans added, "At least we are getting up to strength with horses now, even if the standard is a bit variable. I am not sure where the beasts are coming from, but some of them are in poor condition. But, if we look after them and feed them up, hopefully we will be all right in a week or two."

Freddy, "Yes, a mixed bunch all right, but we should be able to sort them into reasonable teams. I understand that the rumour is we will need to be ready to go by the end of this month. Have you heard any more, BSM?"

"Nothing so far today, sir," said Evans, "but the rumours are getting stronger. I expect we will get official orders soon if something is going to happen."

"My brother is in the Norfolks and he says that he saw tropical kit go into the stores last week. He says the rumour over there is that they are bound for India or Africa, what do you think, sir?" asked Leman of Freddy.

"Well, whatever is decided for us I am sure that we will be able to do our duty well, unlike the dockers. I hear they have been threatening to strike, for more pay, just when people like us are risking our lives for the Empire!"

"Yes, I have an uncle on the docks and the rumours of a strike are in the air all right. Mind you, the dockers have always been in a difficult line of work. Feast and famine with the owners having the upper hand. My uncle had an argument with the charge hand a year ago and did not get any work for months after that. I suppose that now the dockers have the upper hand they will make hay while the sun shines. A lot of them have signed up for the army and there are not enough of them left to work the ships." said Leman.

"Well, that may be the case, but in times of war we all need to pull together." said Evans.

James Newman then arrived, "Morning Freddy, BSM, Sergeant Leman, how are we all this fine morning?"

Freddy saluted Newman and said, "It looks as if we may have some ringworm, James, the veterinarian has been notified and should be here today."

"Right," said Newman, "I am sure that Sergeant Leman and the BSM can handle this. I have just heard that the rumour about the division forming are right, and General Trubshawe will be round to inspect next week. So we had better get ourselves sorted out to set a good first impression. The Adjutant has given a list of kit to the BQMS that will be arriving later this week. Apparently all the stuff we have been waiting for will come in by rail and we will have to collect it from the station. We will have to sign up for Imperial Service as well. Only about fifteen of the battery are already signed up, so we will need to persuade the rest to sign the forms so we can go as we are."

"How did Mr Mann respond to your ideas about using our guns against the Zeppelins?" Freddy asked Newman.

"He thanked me for the idea, but said that he has been contracted by the French to assemble aeroplanes, so he is busy converting the works. The problem is that there is a lot more wood involved than metal, so he has had to try and find men who have woodworking knowledge. He is a resourceful man and I am sure he will manage to do it, even though I will not be there to help him." said Newman.

"Maybe you would be of more use to the war effort if you were back at the works rather than in uniform." said Freddy.

"Maybe," replied Newman, "but my die is cast, as it were, and we have work to do!"

10th March 1915, Battery Office.

Major Philip Mount was due to give orders and Captain Kit Chilvers had assembled the officers and senior NCOs in the office. An air of expectation and excitement was in the room.

Rumours of their heading for the front had strengthened and they all expected good news from Mount when he arrived.

Freddy was standing by the window keeping a look out for the battery commander's approach. A low burble of conversation pervaded the room.

Freddy straightened, turned to the room, and said, "Right-o, the BC approaches!" The room fell silent.

Mount came through the door a little more assertively than was normal for him, with a pinched look on his face. He was accompanied by a lieutenant wearing the badges of the Royal Army Medical Corps.

"Right, chaps, I have had orders this morning that we are to be ready to go at the end of the month. Captain Chilvers will be issuing written orders, but for now I will take you through the outline. The division is being formed, and we will be the first battery of the first brigade of artillery. The Suffolk Brigade will be the second brigade, and a howitzer brigade will be joining the division to bring the artillery up to establishment.

As Territorials, we are not currently obliged to serve outside the home country, so all soldiers will need to sign the form agreeing to Imperial Service. In addition, some of our men may not be fit for overseas service and Lieutenant Benefer here will be carrying out medical inspections of all ranks to see who will not make the grade. Mr Benefer has been posted as the Brigade Medical Officer, so you will be seeing him around on a permanent basis from now on. Please make him welcome in the normal manner."

Benefer nodded, and made a weak smile, not being sure what being made welcome 'in the normal manner' might mean.

Mount continued, "It has been confirmed that the GOC will be Major General Trubshawe, who comes well qualified. He had a distinguished record in the South African War. Those of you who were in that war may know of him. General

Trubshawe will be inspecting the division on a unit by unit basis next week, details to be advised. We will need to be on top form for that, brass polished, leather oiled, and the equipment and horses in top form. General Trubshawe was an infantryman, so as gunners we will need to be on our mettle to impress him. He has been in Flanders commanding a brigade. He was in at the beginning last August and kept his brigade together throughout. They did very well. General Trubshawe will be coming back to England to take over our division this week. Right, the adjutant will be issuing written orders after this meeting, are there any questions, gentlemen?"

Buster asked, "Yes, sir, do we know where we will be sent?"

Mount replied, "No firm details yet, but I believe that it will be somewhere in Flanders."

Newman asked, "What will happen to anyone who fails the medical or does not sign up for Imperial Service, sir?"

"They will be left behind and will be posted to a unit that is remaining in England. Anyone who refuses IS will be posted as far away from their home as possible! Make sure your men know this and persuade them to sign up. We need all the trained men that we have."

"Will we be getting newer guns? The old ones we have are clapped out." said Edwin.

"There is no information about that." replied Mount, "I know the 15 pounder is an old piece, but it can still do good duty. It served us well in South Africa, did it not, Buster?"

"Well, it has been improved a bit," agreed Buster, "but the new 18 pounders are better."

"Sir, We still have some deficiencies in uniform and tack," said BSM Evans, "will these be made good before we go?"

"I imagine they will," said Mount, "the BQMS has a list, please make sure that it is in the hands of Brigade tomorrow and let me have a copy. Make sure the BQMS knows of any deficiencies before then. Captain Chilvers can follow up when he goes to div HQ later this week. If that is all, please go and collect the written orders and brief your men. Medical inspections will be posted outside this office today. Good luck to us all."

With that Mount put on his cap and left the office, leaving Benefer to introduce himself.

Lieutenant Robert Benefer was not an impressive figure. Short, slight, and bespectacled, he reminded Freddy of his Latin master. Benefer also lacked the required moustache so beloved of the soldiering profession. He looked older than his twenty six years.

Freddy went up to him and offered his hand, "Welcome, I am Freddy Scott, the youngest officer in the brigade, how come you have been posted to us?"

"Well, I only volunteered in September and they put this uniform on me and taught me how to march." he responded, "This is my first time with a brigade, it's all a bit new to me."

Freddy was a little taken aback, but continued, "Well never mind, I am a bit new myself, only joined a year ago, but I did spend time in the OTC at school. Let me introduce you to the others."

With that Freddy took Benefer and introduced him to each of the others in turn. BSM Evans arranged to provide a nominal roll for the battery and went off with the doctor to make arrangements for the medical inspections.

Freddy, Edwin, Buster and James left together and chatted as they crossed the yard towards the lines.

"What do you make of the news?" Edwin asked.

"Well, at least we are to leave this awful place." said James, "I am fed up with the cold and rain, and feel the need to do something more productive and exciting. I am happy, though this Trubshawe chap needs a bit of study. We need to work out just what sort of a general he is."

"Yes, when he comes for the inspection I am sure he will let us know what he expects of us as well. The new doctor seems a strange cove, not exactly a soldierly figure." said Edwin.

"He is a bit unimpressive to look at," said Freddy, "he seems to have drawn the short straw. I am sure he is as patriotic as the rest of us, but next to some of the farm boys we have on the guns he will look like something the cat dragged in."

"Never judge a book by the cover," said James, "some of the bravest men I know look pretty ordinary. Once we get into action we will see if he is up to it or not. In the meantime we have work to do."

Freddy said, "Right, if I may change the subject, it occurred to me that maybe I should make a will, just in case sort of thing. What do you think?"

Edwin chuckled, "Well, as it stands, neither you nor I have much to leave to anyone, except our mess bills. I would not worry about that just yet, Freddy."

Buster added, "Well, as I have a wife and children, I have already made a will. I think it might be a good idea for everyone to think hard about it, if only to concentrate your mind on not needing one. Speak to the adjutant, he can advise you better than I can."

Buster veered off to go to the horse lines, while Freddy and Edwin continued towards the gun park and their men.

"What should we do about a will, do you think?" Freddy asked of Edwin.

"I think we should nominate each other as beneficiaries, and if we are both killed, then George to get whatever we have."

"What if he is killed as well?" asked Freddy.

"In that unlikely event, Sissie can have anything that is left."

With that they parted and went to their duties

20th March 1915, The Officers' Mess.

The officers were taking afternoon tea. Buster and James Newman were in discussion.

"What do you make of Philip being binned? Though he is not the most keen of soldiers, I thought that they would at least let him into the front line." said James.

"Well, in my view he was well past it. He seemed to be more interested in hunting foxes that in hunting the Hun. It is probably better all round that we get a more up to date BC. After all, Philip was almost fifty, and unlikely to survive the conditions at the front for more than a few weeks before he would come down with pneumonia or something like that. I am just wondering who will be posted as the next BC."

"Well, you and I are not that far behind him in age, are we, but at least we know what it is like to be on campaign. Though South Africa was warmer and drier than we can expect in Flanders. I wonder how far from home they will post him? What impression did you get of the General when he inspected us?" said Newman.

"He seems a nice old chap, but maybe like Philip his best years may be behind him. I did rather expect someone looking more like Kitchener, but Trubshawe looked a bit more like a railway clerk, though he certainly knew his stuff. He asked all the right questions when he saw the gunners, I think he even impressed BSM Evans, which is saying something. You know, Evans has been around a long time, started as a boy soldier, a trumpeter, I think, and he has seen service in India and Africa, I think he even fought in the Zulu Wars, he has seen more action than you and I ever will," responded Buster.

"The doc found eleven of our men unfit, including Philip, and we have another dozen who have not signed up for IS, what is going to happen to fill the gaps, do you think?" said James.

43

"Who knows, we may get some reservists I suppose, or a few of the K men. I understand that Kitchener's recruiting drive has been very successful and some of them might have some military experience. Kit is looking into things and division say that they are hopeful of bringing us up to numbers before we leave here."

Benefer came over to the two men, "Sorry, but I overheard you talking about the medical inspections. There are a couple of the men that I am concerned about."

"Such as?" asked Buster.

"Well, most of the younger men are in good shape, but some of the older men with families might not be too happy to go. I had gunner Hastings say that he is concerned about sailing to France as he gets sea sick." Benefer stated.

"What about young Trumpeter Kent? He is only fifteen, but will be sixteen in a few weeks, and is keen to go with us." enquired Newman.

"It's up to the adjutant, but if we just keep quiet I am sure we can keep him with us. He is very keen, I know, and once he is in the field it is unlikely that anyone will claim him back. I know his father is keen for young Kent to do his bit." said Buster.

Just then Francis Chappell, the veterinary officer, came in and spoke to the adjutant, "All your animals have the all clear on the ringworm, and are free from any other conditions, now. Your BSM and Sergeant Leman have worked wonders with them, Kit."

Kit replied, "Thank you, Francis, yes, Leman is a good livestock man, we are lucky to have several farm boys in the battery, they know about animals."

"Yes, they are good men, just keep an eye on them, please, to make sure they keep up the good standard. Plenty of ointment and keep the tack and harnesses clean." With that Chappell turned and left.

Buster stood and said to the room, "Who is game for a trip to the village hostelry this evening? As this may be our last opportunity for some relaxation let's make a night of it."

Most of those present nodded their agreement.

After following the by now well trodden path to the pub, the officers settled in to a night of drinking, joined by George Scott and Stephen Sansom. George and Stephen had also been hard at work preparing for the journey to Flanders.

George said to his two brothers, "Now that you are about to become real men I think that you should start drinking like real men. To this end he produced a bottle of whisky, pulled the cork, drank a mouthful from it, and passed it to Edwin. Edwin hesitated, then wiped the neck, and drew a small mouthful of the liquid, screwing up his eyes as he did so. He wiped his lips with the thumb and forefinger of his left hand, grimaced, and handed the bottle to Freddy. Freddy looked at the bottle for a few seconds as if making his mind up, looked at George, then slowly raised the bottle to his lips. The bottle did not pass the horizontal as he took a small sip, swallowed, gagged a little, then passed the bottle back to George.

George said, "Now we are brothers in blood and brothers in whisky. Here's to us, may we all do our duty well and come back safely!"

Edwin replied, "I hope that Mother does not find out about this, you are supposed to be looking after Freddy and me, and keeping us away from girls and drink."

Sansom reached over and took the bottle from George and said, "Well, we are not having any luck with girls, so having a drink is all right. As there are no fillies here we are still keeping away from girls **and** drink, it is the combination that is forbidden, not each in isolation."

George took the bottle back and offered it in the direction of Buster and Newman. Newman gave a brief shake of his head, but Buster grabbed the bottle and took a healthy swig and returned the bottle to George.

"To absent friends, and family." said Buster.

They all nodded, though Freddy was making swallowing motions as if he still had not been able to consign the whisky to his stomach.

Edwin said, "Yes, absent friends. I feel that we have already lost a few friends. With the BC being binned, and the shoeing smith being in hospital, and the men who failed their medicals, I am starting to feel somewhat bereaved already."

Newman said quietly, "The farrier, Corporal Watts, is dead, I am afraid. The head injury was worse than we thought, the doctor told me just before I left the office, and he passed this afternoon. There will be a funeral tomorrow, his wife is being brought up and we should go along and say goodbye. Watts was a funny old chap, but he had been with us for years. A great shame that he will not be coming with us, especially as he passed the medical and was keen to do his bit. When General Trubshawe notified us that we are going to Belgium Watts was quite excited, he said that he had relatives living there and was hoping to look them up, but it is too late for that now."

This news quietened the group for a few minutes.

"Let us drink his health, then." said Buster, grabbing the bottle from George and taking another swig. The bottle did the rounds several more times before the group by general agreement decided that it was time to return to camp.

In the morning Freddy woke with an unfamiliar sensation behind his eyes, something that he would later recognise as an alcohol induced hangover. Fumbling for his pocket watch he realised that he was already late for muster. Quickly dressing he made for the lines, only to be intercepted by the adjutant, "Well, good afternoon young Freddy, do you know the penalty for being late on parade? Come to my office in ten minutes."

Before the ten minutes were up Freddy was in the adjutant's office, looking ashamed and dishevelled. "Sir, I am sorry that I missed muster, I feel unwell and think I must be coming down with something."

Kit Chilvers eyed him with the faintest evidence of a smile, "I think that rather you are suffering from an excess of liquid refreshment last evening. Now, the way that I intend to teach you to moderate your drinking is by giving you extra duties. Do you accept my punishment?"

"Yes. sir, I do, and I am sorry for letting you down, sir." Freddy said.

"You have only let yourself down, young man. I need someone to supervise the cleaning up of the horse lines, BSM Evans will be pleased to see you there in five minutes. Take a shovel with you, there is a pile of horse dung to be moved."

"Thank you, sir, I will make sure that I do not miss any parade again."

25th March 1915.

"Well, BSM, are things ready for the off?" Chilvers said to BSM Evans at the edge of the field that had served as the wagon park and horse lines, and which now was empty apart from muddy wheel tracks and a pile of horse dung by the hedgerow.

"Yes, sir, all wagons are on the way to the station, the guns have already loaded and the carriages for the men will be there at eleven o'clock. The BQMS has completed his handover, so we are all clear from the site." The BSM replied.

"Let's get on then, BSM, our future awaits. I think we regulars have done well to keep these Territorials on the ball and ready to serve the King. A few last days at Larkhill then we will be on the way to the front. We have both been here before, haven't we? How are you feeling at the moment?"

47

"I am pretty chipper, sir. The Army has been my life since I joined up as a boy back in '77. If it were not for this war I would be getting ready to go into civvy street, so in a way I think the war is good for me. I am not sure I would know what to do with myself out of uniform."

"Yes, all of us old sweats are getting an extension for a while, and the war will end one way or another, but until it does, we will just enjoy ourselves. Let's get to the station before the boys leave without us." said Chilvers as he started toward the field entrance where their two horses were patiently waiting for them. They mounted easily, as ones practised in horsemanship over many years do, turned up the lane, and trotted towards the town, the station, and the future.

Chapter 6

23rd July 1987, Dover.

The drive down to Dover passed without problem. The MGB hummed along nicely. We parked on the dockside waiting for the instructions to start loading onto the ferry.

"Freddy, when you went off you sailed from Southampton, according to your diaries." I said.

"Yes, Southampton was the main port for transporting troops out to France, though other ports were used as well for leave and so on. When I came back on leave I landed at Folkestone, not that far from where we are now."

"You must have been excited to be going off, especially after the time in Lincolnshire."

"Yes, we were excited all right. Most of the men had never been out of the county, let alone going abroad to a completely different country. Of course, the older men, those with wives and children, were more mixed in their emotions."

"How long did it take?"

"We got to Southampton about midday, I think, and loading took most of the afternoon. We sailed the same night. Apparently they always sailed after dark, to avoid the submarines. We disembarked at Le Havre the next morning and after sorting out the men and horses we went by train to near the Belgian border, then trekked to the front line."

"Did anyone see you off?" I asked.

"Military movements were kept secret, of course, but a few people did get to know when we were to leave and came to see us off."

Chapter 7

29th March 1915, Southampton.

Southampton's East Docks were wreathed in a mist drifting from the Solent as the first train conveying the brigade slowly eased its way through the city and into the dockyard. A burst of steam escaped from the engine as the train groaned and clanked to a stop.

The faces of gunners peered from the windows of the carriages. A pause of a minute or so, then an RTO lieutenant and two sergeants with clipboards came alongside and shouted, "Come on, shake a leg, change here for Flanders and all points east!"

Men in khaki poured from the train as if they were commuters arriving at Liverpool Street Station on the 7.35 on any Monday. Their NCOs gathered them in groups awaiting further instructions. The officers climbed out from the first class carriage and stood around chatting while Kit Chilvers and BSM Evans went over to the RTO for clarification on what was needed next.

Having obtained written orders they returned to their respective groups and allocated dockside duties. Some of the men were sent down to the dockside to oversee the stevedores loading the guns, wagons, horses and stores onto the steamers. The officers were told to keep out of the way until five o'clock when they were to report to the RTO office on the dockside. The various groups moved off to their duties, the officers wandered off in the opposite direction to perambulate the dockyard, having three hours to fill before their next reporting time.

The working party led by Sergeant Leman were in high spirits. For some of them this was the furthest from home they had ever been, with the prospect of further travel exciting their interest. Gunner Jabez Brown was particularly buoyant. At nineteen, he was just old enough for overseas service, and he was keen to extend his knowledge through travel, even if it meant having to go to war to get it. His pal was Gunner Roland White, also nineteen, but a much quieter and reserved individual. They had met when working at a fruit farm near Setchey, the owner also importing fruit through the port of Lynn. They had become firm friends, and had joined up together.

"I wonder what is in our lunch bags." Roland said to Jabez, "The BQMS usually makes sure that we are well victualled."

"Well, we will find out soon," replied Jabez, "when Sergeant Leman lets us open them. I am fair famished, I could eat a horse."

"Keep it quiet, you two, we have work to do and I will let you know when it is time to eat." snapped Leman, "You young'uns do too much mardlin'. Keep your minds on what we have to do here on the docks."

They found the ship and there, drawn up on the dockside was their gun, limber, and GS wagon, with the horses still harnessed and the drivers standing beside them. "Right, get the horses unhitched, remove all the tackle, and secure everything for loading." shouted Leman, "We do not have all day to get this done."

The men went to it and within a few minutes the horses had been unhitched, the tackle removed and tidied into canvas bags on the GS Wagon. A group of dockers came over, and without much ado put strops and hawsers on the vehicles, and the horses were led away by the drivers under the direction of a crewman from the ship. They were led up a ramp alongside the ship and turning at right angles attained the open deck where they were secured. The vehicles were craned from the dockside, over the ship and lowered into the hold in an easy

51

and well practised motion. Once Leman's gun was loaded the men looked to him for a lead as to what to do next.

"Right, time for scran! Get your bags out and lets see what the BQMS has given us and who has got the Mason's egg." he said, and with that they eagerly opened the bags and peered inside. Now, it had become the custom in the battery that when food bags were issued as packed rations, it was usual for a hard boiled egg to be included, one for each man, as a simple yet nutritious part of a meal. BQMS Arthur Mason, however, had a mischievous streak and was wont to include one unboiled egg in each batch, the intention being to surprise the random recipient with a more liquid result from cracking the egg. Some men, knowing this, had taken the habit of cracking their egg in a way to avoid trouble if by chance they were the recipient of the raw egg. A few had taken to cracking their egg against a friend's head as a way of proving whether they were the (un)lucky egg man of the day. An early form of what we might these days call Russian (egg) Roulette.

Today, the lucky man was not in Leman's group, and a shout from another section indicated where the egg had landed.

In the officers' group things were more restrained. While the younger men were putting on a show of bravado, reflecting their excitement at the prospects of travel to a foreign land and seeing action, the older men were more measured, particularly those with wives and children. For those, like James Newman, who were older yet unfulfilled in family terms, the coming journey was less concern for their relatives than for conditions of the journey. James had suffered seasickness before while sailing back from South Africa in 1901. The memory of it for him was still clear, and he had no wish to experience it again.

James watched the stevedores with passing interest. It seemed to him that these men were highly practised in transferring all manner of loads from shore to ship, and he felt sure, in the opposite direction. While they were not a disciplined uniformed force as soldiers were, they did work constantly, each man seemingly knowing what his workmates expected of him and how he could make his contribution to the collective effort.

His reverie was interrupted when Freddy spoke to him, "I say, isn't that William Mann over there. I wonder what he is doing here, maybe he has come to make sure that you are actually going off to war."

James looked at Freddy blankly, then followed his gaze towards some warehouses set back a little from the quayside. There a small group of people stood in a loose circle, with William Mann immediately recognisable by his height, posture, and the stovepipe hat that he habitually wore when on formal business. James squinted to see a little better, and he saw that with Mr Mann were his daughter Constance, and his sister Florence. "He has probably come to say goodbye to Walter, he must be on another ship, the whole division is travelling over the next few days." said James, almost to himself.

"Shall we go over and say hello?" said Freddy, loudly enough for the other officers to hear.

Edwin looked across, and saw what Freddy was referring to, "Yes, let's, come on chaps." Edwin said to no-one in particular and immediately started a fast walk towards the Manns. Freddy was two steps behind him, followed by Buster, and James gave a shrug and then followed them.

As they approached Buster said loudly, "Well, by all that's right with the world it is good to see you, William. How are things with you and yours?"

William Mann, who had been facing his son, Walter, in conversation turned and, recognising Buster, gave a rare brief smile and held out his hand. Buster, James, Edwin and Freddy shook the offered hand in turn according to seniority as is usual in the military.

While William and Buster exchanged pleasantries, the others listened politely. After a minute or so Edwin had moved around to the other side of the group and touched Constance's elbow, indicating to her that he wished to speak to her away from her father. Constance smiled at him, and did as she was bid. She and Edwin turned their backs on the circle and slowly walked towards the buildings and away from the quayside. Freddy had been focussing his attention on what William was saying, but as it became clear that nothing of great import was in prospect, he turned his attention instead to Walter. He and Walter had been contemporaries at school, and though not bosom buddies, were familiar to each other as they had been in the same school house. Walter had been a good sportsman, while Freddy had not.

"Well, Walter, how do you feel about your family coming to see you off?" Freddy asked.

"A bit embarrassed, actually." he replied, "Our movements are supposed to be a military secret, but Papa obviously has information from his own sources. It is going to take me some time to live this down in the mess as no other officer has had a visit, though I am sure some of them might like one. How are things with your battery, everything going to plan?"

"I have no idea," Freddy replied, "all this stropping and lifting is a bit beyond me, but I have not heard anyone shouting too loudly so I expect things are well in hand. The BSM and BQMS seem to have everything under control. These docks must be seeing units come through pretty well every day, so they probably know all there is to know about loading ships. I am happy at the moment to just wait and see what happens. Fancy a wander about to see what else is going on?"

"Yes," said Walter, "let's do that, Papa will not miss me for a while as he can talk business with Buster and James Newman. I think there is another dock round the other side of these warehouses, lets go over there and see what we can see."

With that they wandered off in a different direction to Edwin and Constance. "Do you think you and your men are completely ready for the front?" Walter asked Freddy, "My lot have done a lot of training but there are still some things we can improve on. Musketry, for one thing. Do you know we did not get any ammunition for range practice until two weeks ago, and we have probably only shot off a hundred rounds per man. Some of them still cannot hit a barn door. The regulars will laugh at us if we ever have to face a Hun attack."

"Well, we have not done much musketry at all," said Freddy, "but we did get a good shoot with the guns on Salisbury Plain last week. The problem for us is not the men, we have got them pretty well drilled in firing, but the guns. The ones we have were obsolete ten years ago, and not as good as the new ones that the Regulars have. Even the Kitchener brigades are getting 18 pounders, and most of them have only been in uniform for a few weeks."

"We just have to make the best of what we can do. I just hope that the Hun gives us some time to settle in before he gets nasty with us." said Walter.

"Good God!" Freddy exclaimed as they came round the corner of a warehouse towards a dry dock. There before them in the basin was a ship much like the one they were going to be sailing on with an enormous jagged hole in its bows, twisted metal protruding at odd angles. "What on earth happened to that!"

"It hit a mine in the Western Approaches, five of my men are dead and three are missing." came a voice from behind them. They turned and saw a man in stained trousers and a worn reefer jacket, wearing a misshapen peaked cap, bearded, and smoking a pipe. "I assume that you young gentlemen will be sailing tonight, I hope you will have a safer passage than I did."

Freddy and Walter were stuck for words for a few seconds, then Walter replied to the seaman, "Yes, so do I. I am sorry to see your ship so badly damaged, are you all right yourself?"

"Aye, I am all right, but my ship is not as well as it should be. The dockies say they will patch her up and have me back at sea in a month. Until then I have no pay, though at least I have somewhere to sleep, in the mission. When you get over to France make sure you get a few Hun for me and my crew."

Freddy had stayed silent throughout the exchange, and the man turned and walked away before he could think of anything to say to him. He looked at Walter and said, "Goodness, I think that the war just got closer to us than I had been thinking. When you see damage like that," pointing to the ship, "you realise how dangerous things might be."

Walter nodded agreement, but did not say anything, he seemed to Freddy to be in deep thought. Wordlessly they turned along the side of the dock and continued walking, each inside his own head. As they reached the end of the dock, about two hundred yards along, a movement at the side of a building caught Freddy's eye. As he focussed he saw Edwin and Constance walking in much the same way that he and Walter had been. Realising that the sight of the damaged ship might not be suitable for a young lady, Freddy grabbed Walter's elbow and motioned him towards the other couple, heading them off before they could round the corner onto the dry dock.

Thinking quickly, Freddy said as he neared, "There is not much to see on this side of the dock, it is much more interesting where we were before. Walter and I were thinking that it is time that we got back to see if they are finished loading yet." While saying this he was making a motion with his head trying to indicate to an uncomprehending Edwin not to continue further on his present course. Edwin, trying to make sense of what Freddy was saying, said, "What on earth are you up to, Freddy, why are you twitching like that?"

Walter intervened on Freddy's behalf, "Connie, I think you should not go that way, I think it would be dangerous. We saw a sailor who told us things could be unpleasant, that is why we came this way."

"Two brave soldiers, off to fight the Kaiser and you are afraid of one sailor! Well I never, I always thought you boys had more in you than that!" said Constance, "I am not afraid. Edwin will look after me even if you can't or won't."

With that she strode determinedly around the corner and away from the three men. Edwin shot a look at Freddy and Walter, then marched after Constance concerned that he may lose sight of her. Freddy looked at Walter, and shrugged, "Well, if they get as far as that ship they will get as big a surprise as we did."

Walter nodded, "Connie never does the sensible thing, unfortunately, serves her right if she gets a shock. We had better get on and see what Papa is up to."

They walked for another five minutes back alongside the shed towards the loading dock. As they emerged from between the buildings they saw that the group was still more or less where they left it. Buster and William were still talking, though James Newman and Florence Mann had struck up a conversation to one side. As Freddy and Walter approached they parted and Florence said to Walter, "Where have you been, Walter, James and I were wondering what had happened to you."

Newman nodded his agreement, but said nothing.

Florence turned towards her brother and said, "William, the boys are back, and now Constance is missing. Where can she be? Walter, you stay here and wait until we have Constance back." This later sentence was said in a more stern tone than she used when addressing her brother.

"Actually Aunt, I know where Connie is, and I think that she will be back here soon. I saw her at a dry dock just behind

57

these sheds and I think she will not like what she sees there." As Walter was saying these words Constance and Edwin appeared from between the sheds. Constance was a little flushed, and Edwin appeared more agitated than was normal.

At this moment BSM Evans had arrived at the group, saluted, and said to Buster, "Beg pardon, sir, please excuse me Mr Mann, ladies, loading is complete and Colonel Howard wants to address the brigade before we embark. He has requested that all officers return to the dockside and parade with their men, in five minutes, sir, if you will."

"Thank you BSM, I will round up the young gentlemen and will do as you say." replied Buster, returning the salute. Turning towards William and Florence Mann he said, "If you will pardon us, it seems that duty calls. It is time for our last farewells until we meet again after we have beaten the Kaiser's men." With that he shook hands with Florence and William Mann, nodded to Constance, and opened his arms as he turned to indicate to the other officers to come away. Constance, in an apparent impulse pecked Walter on the cheek. Edwin, said, "Do the other heroes get a kiss from a miss as well?" and stepped forward towards Constance in anticipation. Constance hesitated, then put her hand on his shoulder and kissed his cheek. Freddy, again on impulse and not wanting to be left out, stepped forward and also demanded a kiss, which Constance smilingly supplied. In the background, and out of earshot of the others, James Newman said farewell to Florence, rather stiffly, and without any sign of affection by either party.

Constance then said, a tear in her eye, "Come back safely, my soldier boys, write to me and tell me how things are, please."

The artillery officers then followed Buster back towards the dockside loading area. When they were fifty paces or so away from the Manns Edwin turned and smiled back. Freddy and

James noticed this and also turned as they walked for a few paces then turned forwards again, as if determined to meet their future.

The men were already paraded in an open horseshoe, with each battery taking a side. Colonel Howard was to one side in conversation with the adjutant, Kit Chilvers, and a small group of officers from the brigade were at the far side of the parade. Buster's party marched smartly across the rear of the horseshoe to join the officers. The adjutant turned from Colonel Howard and called the parade to attention.

He stood them at ease, and then gave them instructions for the embarkation. Batteries were to put one third of their number on each of the three ships. He explained that this was for reasons of security. He also announced a number of other administrative details and warned that once aboard ship they were to obey all orders passed to them by their NCOs, who would, in their turn, receive orders from the crew. No smoking was to be allowed on deck, particularly at night in view of the submarine threat. He said that in the past week three ships had been attacked on this crossing and that their ships were to be escorted by the Royal Navy. He then called them to attention again, turned, saluted Colonel Howard. Howard then addressed the brigade.

Howard told them that the next morning they would be in France. They were to land in Le Havre and from there travel by train to Flanders where they would detrain and march to the front line. They were going to relieve a regular division, and would have three days to learn their duties there before the regulars were withdrawn.

He also warned them of the activity of spies. Once they were in France they should be alert for strangers taking interest in what they were doing. He said that it was vitally important to capture any spies as France was full of them and they were a danger to the British Army.

He finished by wishing them all well. The BSM then read out instructions as to which detachments were to embark on which ship, formed the men into corresponding groups, then instructed NCOs to march each group to its allotted ship.

Embarkation proceeded smoothly, and by sunset the ships were casting off and preparing to make way down the river and into the Solent. Slowly gathering speed the ships waddled into a ragged line and the Eastern Docks slipped aft. After fifteen minutes the banks receded and they started their turn to pass the Isle of Wight and into the Channel. Unseen by the soldiers on board two escort ships of the Royal Navy slipped their moorings in Portsmouth and took station on either side of the troopships.

On the main deck of Freddy's ship, a general cargo ship, the holds had been converted into huge dormitories with bunk beds and mess decks. The junior officers were sitting around on deck chairs, chatting and joking. On the bridge, the officer of the watch, the navigator, and the helmsman were at their duties, the pilot had been dropped off. General Trubshawe was on the bridge talking to the captain, who had felt it appropriate to invite the most senior officer to join him as the voyage began.

"I imagine that this is a routine event for you and your crew, captain?" said Trubshawe.

"Yes," replied the captain, "this way tonight, and we will return tomorrow night. It is a bit like I imagine a train driver might be, up the line today, and back down to home station the next day."

"Are you worried about Hun raiders? I hear that their submarines and minelayers have been active." said Trubshawe.

"A life at sea has many dangers, and the Hun is just one of them." said the captain.

"Of course, a man such as you must have seen much during your life at sea," said Trubshawe, "Please, don't let me detain you any further, you must have things to organise. If I may I will stay here for a few minutes with my thoughts and I promise to keep out of your crew's way, thank you captain."

"General, if you need anything please do not hesitate to ask, goodnight." said the captain as he turned to leave, "There is a small saloon next to my cabin which you are welcome to use." he said almost as an afterthought as he left, "Or there is the bridge wing that you may use, for fresh air."

The general nodded, opened the door beside him and stepped out onto the bridge wing. He stood looking out into the night, though there was nothing for him to see as the darkness had by now deepened to a misty, gloomy, murk. This was of little import for Trubshawe as his attention was more inside his head than on his surroundings.

His thoughts took him back to the time that he had sailed for South Africa all those years ago, when he was younger and more optimistic than now. He thought about his wife and family. He thought about the responsibility that the War Office had placed on him. It was a welcome extension to his service as he had been due to retire shortly after the war had begun, and now they needed generals with command experience. He remembered the emotion he had felt when the telegram had arrived, and the difficult conversation he had with Mary when he shared the contents with her. He recalled the retreat, for that is what it was, from Belgium, and the desperate fighting before Paris, and the advance back northwards as the front lines solidified the previous autumn.

Mary had, however, with her usual good nature, accepted the situation and had amended her plans and aspirations for a quiet retirement. Their farewell prior to embarkation was emotional. Mary had come to relish their time together, and now, just when they had been planning to write the final chapter of their lives the Kaiser had intervened. They had managed a few days together after his return from Flanders before he took up command of this new division of Territorials. This would be the culmination of his career. He could retire on a major general's pension rather than that of a brigadier. He would make sure that Mary would see the benefit of this.

Mary had no children to offer her solace, as their marriage had been fruitful in every respect except that of bearing children. The doctors had examined both of them and found no real cause of their inability to procreate. They had long ago accepted this fact, but the emptiness had been compensated for by activity. He in his care and the fellowship of soldiers. Hers in her work with the regimental association which looked after the old soldiers who had been unable to adjust to civilian life after their service had finished. However, the emptiness persisted, and for Robert Trubshawe his men had become his substitute for sons of his own. He had resolved, on hearing of the tremendous losses already suffered by the army, that he would command his division better than those generals who he had served under on previous campaigns. Such as in the Transvaal, where distain for casualties and good tactics had appalled him as a young man. In fact, as he thought of this he felt again the moment a Boer bullet passed through his left lung, deflating it and smashing his shoulder blade. He felt again the rising panic as he had tumbled face down into the bush and could not breathe, until pulled to safety by one of his men. He recalled being left out in the sun while the boer sharpshooters continued to shoot British soldiers, and the long painful ride draped over the back of a mule, after dark, and the final arrival at the dressing station where he was hastily operated on and sent back down river on a barge.

He felt the residual pain from his shoulder, which even at this distance in time had failed to resolve fully. He absentmindedly put his right hand to his shoulder as was his habit when the pain returned.

"Well, enough of that, I have things to do. Onwards, always onwards." he said in a low voice, to himself.

On the main deck Freddy and the others sat even though the evening clamminess made them feel a little chilly. Freddy would have preferred to retire to the saloon, but did not want to leave the company of his fellows, and he was sure that the others felt the same but did not want to be the first to suggest it. It seemed to be more manly and soldierly to suffer a mild discomfort. And, in any case, he reasoned that if they were sunk by a mine it would be better to be above decks where he could make an easier escape than being trapped below decks.

James Newman spotted the general on the open bridge wing above them, and said in a low voice, "Be aware, chaps, the general is just above us, be considerate in what you say in case he can hear us."

Buster and the others followed James' indication and nodded. "I suppose that now we have senior officers all over us we will have to watch our language." said Edwin.

Freddy added, "I am really looking forward to arriving in France, it will be my first time in a foreign country, has anyone been there before?"

Buster said, "Yes, I have been in Flanders before. We have trade with agents in Brugges and Lille, and I have been over a few times to negotiate contracts with them. Of course, they are occupied by the Germans now, so trade has stopped, but we can still communicate with them. Our agent in Holland helps keep the communications going and of course we hope that when the war is over we can start again. Flanders is similar to where we live, a few low hills, and the smell of dung everywhere. The people are all right though, mostly because we have a long history of trade with them. A lot of them have come across and settled in Norwich and Lincolnshire, mostly protestants getting away from the French. In fact, you could argue that we are on the wrong side in this war. We have more in common and do more business with the Germans than with the French. The King has more German blood than English, and the French are our historical enemies. It's strange how things work out."

"Ours but to do and die I suppose." added Edwin.

"Well that was about the Crimean War, and we were with the French in that one." said Freddy.

James added, "We found several Frenchies fighting for the Boers. As Englishmen it is better to regard all foreigners as potential enemies, until they demonstrate conclusively to the opposite."

Kit broke in with, "As a long serving regular soldier I have had to deal with many different King's enemies. I have learned just to take orders from above and make the best of things. Subjects such as friend or foe of the moment are way above my station. My advice is not to analyse things too much, just do what we have been trained to do, and that to the best we can do!"

"Kit, you have been at war before, what is it like the first time one gets shot at?" asked Freddy.

"Bloody frightening!" said Kit with some emphasis, "But you get over it very quickly. And after a day or so it becomes quite normal to hear rounds cracking around, though, of course, as gunners, if the range shortens too much we tend to pack up and beat a hasty retreat!"

James added, "But if the Hun has sharpshooters like the Boers then they can be a menace. We had men shot at the gun line at over a mile from the Boers, didn't we, Buster?"

Buster looked across, "Yes, it was bit exciting from time to time, but the air was much clearer in South Africa. In Flanders there will be more moisture in the air and visibility should not be good enough for long range sharpshooting, though there is always the chance of stray overs. My advice is to keep our heads down and keep under cover as much as possible. That is why we have seen all those pictures of men in trenches. I think that our best friends will be of the iron sort, our guns and our shovels."

Just then Trubshawe emerged from the passageway. Buster noticed him and immediately stood, surprising the others, who looked round towards where Buster's attention had shifted. "Please, do not get up, gentlemen. I apologise to you, but I overheard your conversations and thought that you might allow me to join you." Trubshawe said in a friendly tone. Freddy found another deck chair and held it for the general to occupy. "No, thank you, young man, but I prefer to stand. Please carry on, gentlemen."

The group stayed quiet for a few seconds, not knowing how to address a senior officer, and each wondering if the general had heard what he had said and would take exception to it.

Trubshawe felt the awkwardness, and to break the silence said, "I am sure that each of you has questions and concerns about what lies ahead for us. I would like to assure you that I have confidence that each and every one of us will acquit ourselves satisfactorily in the coming battles. I see that some of you have ribbons from previous campaigns, and you will know what campaigning entails. My advice to you younger men is to listen closely to the advice and instructions from the more experienced of us. Though we are going into a modern war, many of the lessons are as old as history. The essentials of war have always been the same, he who endures and has the will to win will overcome. And, of course, we have right on our side, which gives us the moral superiority over our foe. Make no mistake, though, he also feels he is in the right, even though we know that he is wrong in that assertion."

Colonel Howard had heard General Trubshawe speak and had arrived at the conclusion of what the general had to say.

He said, "General, I hope these youngsters have not been disturbing you."

Trubshawe turned to look at Howard, "No, they have been very polite and let me witter on. I think that you are lucky, colonel, to have men such as these under your command, please look after them for me." With that he nodded to the colonel, and made his way forward.

When he was out of earshot Howard said to the assembled officers, " I think it is time for us all to turn in for the night. We will be arriving in the early hours and will want to set a good example to the men by being up and about before we dock, ready for the proceedings. I wish you all good night, and good luck for the morrow, goodnight."

The officers then stood and in their turns said goodnight to each other and made their way to their cabins.

In the main hold, where the men were messing, BSM Evans was also holding court and offering good advice to the men of the battery who were aboard this ship.

"Hastings, how are you feeling? Any signs of seasickness?"

"No, not yet, sir."

"Are any of the rest of you feeling bad? How about you, young Kent?" Evans addressed the group as a whole. Receiving replies in the negative, he added, "Well, if any of you do start feeling sick my advice is to get up on deck and take good lungfuls of fresh air, that should sort you out. Bear in mind which way the wind is blowing or you might take a lungful of smoke from the funnel."

Trumpeter Harold Kent had successfully avoided the question as to his age that would have prevented him sailing with the battery. Though he looked his sixteen years, many of the other lads, though nineteen or more, looked very much the same age to the casual observer. He felt that going off with his comrades would be better than staying behind and working in his father's grocery shop. Though he got on well with his father and his mother, Harold was an adventurous lad, and saw the potential in seeing active service. He was sure that he would survive the war to return as a hero to his younger brothers. "Sergeant major, I met some regulars on the ship who are going back after leave. They told me that things were really bad over in Flanders. What do you think, sir?"

"Don't mind them, young Kent, they are just trying to frighten you. If it were that bad they would not be so keen to get back, would they?" Evans replied.

He looked around at the men. As they were in an enclosed space they were permitted the luxury of lighting, albeit dimmed. The men were sitting around on the deck or on bunks, in small groups and singly. Evans looked at them with affection. The Army was his life, and he had never married and, as far as he knew, he had no sons or daughters of his own. These men he regarded as his children. He knew that his duty was to obey the orders passed down to him, but his self appointed duty was to look after these youngsters as best he could. They were mostly farm boys, with a few shop workers, clerks and factory workers, and a sprinkling of more well to do scions of notable local families, some of whom had been posted in to the battery to take the place of men who had failed their medicals, or had not signed up for overseas service. He was satisfied, though, that overall they were a good bunch, and he was sure that they would make good when the time came.

"Right, time for lights out. Sergeant Leman, your section will be on duty at 4 o'clock tomorrow morning, make sure you wake me up first and get everyone else up and ready for the docking tomorrow. Get some sleep now, and God bless us all." Evans said in a low tone, and went to his berth.

Chapter 8

24th July 1987, Vlamertinge, Belgium.

Freddy had asked me to drive him to a small village called Vlamertinge, about an hour's drive from Calais. We found the sign to the Commonwealth War Graves Commission cemetery and parked the car outside. I helped Freddy out onto the verge. Despite his years, and the long time we had spent in the car, his eyes were bright and he moved like a younger man.

He had a list in his pocket of the graves that he wanted to visit. We found the grave register noted down the details for each of these graves and made our way around the cemetery to see all of them.

I was surprised at the size of the cemetery, there must have been around two thousand graves there, each with its identical headstone, clean and tidy, with roses and other flowers in front of each. It felt just like being in an English country garden.

Freddy spent a few minutes at each grave and told me something of each of the men buried there. Some were well known to him, some he only knew in passing, but all those we visited had served with him and he knew them.

When we had finished we returned to the car and Freddy said that there was just one more grave to see, near another small town further on. We drove there and followed the signs to the cemetery, which was through a farmyard and alongside a farm track. Again we took the register and found the entry that Freddy was looking for, and went to the grave.

I read the name on the headstone 'Second Lieutenant Walter Mann, The Norfolk Regiment.'

"Who was he?" I asked Freddy after a few moments.

"A friend," said Freddy, "we were at school together."

"Oh."

After paying his respects Freddy and I went back to the car and drove off towards France and our evening's lodgings.

"Freddy, tell me more about the graves we saw." I said as I drove.

"They were all men that I knew." he said.

"It must have been very frightening to have all those men being killed all around you, Freddy."

"It was, but not at first. The first year we had hardly anyone killed, or even badly injured."

"But all those graves?"

"The ones in Vlamertinge were much later, in 1917, in the autumn. Only the last one, Walter Mann, was in our first year. He was with the Norfolks, the infantry, in my division. He was unlucky." said Freddy.

"Getting killed is always unlucky, isn't it?" I said.

"Yes, it is."

A pause of several minutes passed, then Freddy said, "There is a lot of rubbish talked about the war, you know, Kate. I know the memory can play tricks, especially with age, but at first it was a bit of a lark. It only became more serious as the war went on. A lot more serious."

Chapter 9

3rd April 1915, Neuve Eglise, Belgium.

James Newman looked forward at the column in front of him. The four gun teams were immediately ahead of him, with the ammunition wagons at the front of the column along with BQMS Mason's GS wagons. Buster was at the head with BSM Evans, having been appointed battery commander at the dockside in Le Havre. They had been marching in column for about eight hours, and James was beginning to feel the effects of the saddle on his nether regions. Though he had dismounted often, to march beside his horse and ease the pressure on his backside, he was still discomforted. He was tall and had a spare figure, insufficient flesh on his buttocks and the lack of padding on the military saddle had led to pressure sores. He reasoned that a fleshier man, such as Buster, had a distinct advantage when it came to spending hours in the saddle. Especially those who had the social position and the opportunity to hunt, as he did not. Still, there were other things to worry about.

Trumpeter Kent was by James' side, also mounted, but seemingly happy with his lot. He had been whistling through most of the journey. James had decided not to mention his discomfort to anyone for fear of being thought too long in the tooth to serve alongside younger men.

The brigade had arrived at Le Havre early on 30th March, and had unloaded and entrained without problem. The train had carriages for the officers, flats for the guns and wagons, and covered wagons for the horses and men. The battery was accommodated on one train, with a few extra officers, men and horses from Brigade HQ.

The train had proceeded at a leisurely pace eastwards from Le Havre on the one hundred and sixty mile journey to Hazebrouck where they detrained. The rail journey took a total of twenty hours, an average speed of around eight miles per hour, with frequent stops for refreshments for men and horses.

Kent's voice broke through James' thoughts, "What do you think about that to do at Hazebrouck station, sir, when the French police arrested that man? He seemed quite ordinary to me, not like a spy at all."

James looked at Kent and said, "He was probably just a local man interested in what was going on, but the French police will know what is best. If he is in the clear they will just let him go later, and if he is a spy, well, they will probably shoot him."

"How will they decide, sir?"

"I have no idea, but they will. Spies do not always advertise their profession, and there are many people in France who have sympathies with the Hun, especially here in the North. I am sure the Hun wants to know how many troops are being sent to the British sector and will have his spies out and about. Anyway, it is for the French to manage security behind the front and we just have to trust them to get on with it." James said.

Just then James heard a sound that took him back several years. He stopped talking, cupped his hand to his ear, and concentrated. He could just make out the sound of gunfire in the distance. He looked at Kent while he continued to listen, then said, "Listen carefully, can you hear it?"

Kent cocked his head and also put his hand to his ear to catch the faint sounds of war. "Yes, sir, I do! Active service at last!"

"Yes, we can't be far from the front now, maybe two or three miles at most." said James.

The column moved off.

Further along Freddy and Edwin were riding alongside each other. Though they were meant to ride at the head of their sections, Freddy had become bored with this and had decided to move forward to the section ahead and speak to Edwin.

"I am glad to be out on the road after that train journey, Edwin, though it was fun at times it did rather go on longer than I thought it should." said Freddy.

"Shouldn't you be back with your section, Freddy, now we are on active service you should stick to the rules." said Edwin.

"There's no harm done, and I was getting bored back there. I was not too happy with the coffee that they gave us at the stop on the train, it tasted horrible."

"That's because it had brandy in it, silly. Haven't you had coffee and brandy before?" said Edwin, with a little snigger, knowing full well that Freddy had not developed a taste for any strong drink at all, especially as Mamma forbad anything more than sherry in the house.

"No, and I am not sure that I want to try any more. I don't see why people drink it, it tastes awful."

"I am sure that we will have to get used to many new things, including the food. They probably have different tastes over here, and like it or not, we will have to get used to it. When in Rome, and so on." laughed Edwin.

At that moment Edwin also heard the faint rumblings from the front line, and said, "Listen carefully, Freddy, I can hear gunfire up ahead, we must be getting close to the front."

Freddy, at that time more interested in his stomach than his duties replied, "That is all very well, but when are we going to eat? It has been hours since breakfast, and we have had nothing since. Corporal Ely kept the victuals flowing on the train, but since he has had to pack up his pots and pans we have had nothing."

"You are always thinking about your stomach, Freddy. Ely can't do much until we get to a stop, and I am sure he will produce his usual standard of food. I am never quite sure how he does it, but he is a real brick when it comes to scoff. If we are getting near to the front then a halt can't be far away. Just be patient." said Edwin, motioning to Freddy to stop talking by putting his finger to his lips.

A little later Edwin's prediction came true. The column halted and the BSM rode back down alongside the vehicles. He told everyone that there would be a one hour halt while the BC went forward to get orders and to make the best of it. Tea and sandwiches would be available at the BQMS wagon in fifteen minutes. He also said to make sure of full bellies as this may be the last opportunity before going into the line.

Freddy dismounted, tied his horse reins to a fence by the side of the road and went back to his section on foot. The men were in high spirits despite their hunger and weariness.

Sergeant Leman had already taken charge of the two gun teams and had split the men into two groups, one of these passing Freddy on their way to get food. The men nodded to Freddy as they passed, Freddy nodded back. When he reached Sergeant Leman he asked, "How are things, Sergeant, any problems?"

"No, all is well with us, sir, thank you. A bit tired perhaps, but looking forward to seeing some action, at last. Where do you think we will be setting up for the night, sir?"

"I have no idea, but I am sure that all will be well. The regulars we are taking over from will be glad to see us, I am sure. I understand they have been here in the line for months, all through the winter, so they should be glad to be getting a relief from us. You seem to have the feeding well in hand so I think I will go and get some grub myself. When the men have fed make sure they get some rest, this may be a long night if we have to go forward later." said Freddy.

"Right sir, I will do that. I hope that Corporal Ely has something nice for your supper." said Leman, and with that Freddy turned about and walked up the column until he found Ely who had set up a table with a cloth, and had bread, cold meat and pickles set out for the officers to eat. Kit and James were already eating there, and as Freddy arrived Kit asked him, "Every thing all right with your section, Freddy?"

"Yes, Sergeant Leman is always quick off the mark and has sent half of the men to feed and the other half will be along in a while. I see that Corporal Ely has come up trumps again, I am not sure how you do it." This last remark directed at Ely who had been busy rummaging in the mess wagon.

Corporal Benjamin Ely looked up at Freddy and smiled his thanks, and continued to rummage.

"That man is worth his weight in gold," said James, "I have every confidence that he will keep us well fed and watered. On campaign that is just what we will need. The worst of the winter weather has passed, I imagine, so at least we have spring to look forward to. It doesn't feel too cold at the moment. I just hope it does not rain too heavily until we have settled in to the position."

Kit added, "Buster should be back soon, and he will be able to tell us what is expected of us. My guess is that the regulars will be anxious to get away as soon as possible, so we need to be sharp when the time comes to move up into the line. Corporal Ely, please make sure there is some food left for the BC." he added, looking in the direction of the mess orderly.

Edwin arrived, and the four officers continued to chat as they finished their supper and the evening turned into night. The temperature dropped. "It might be a good idea to get some sleep, perhaps," said James, "We may not be able to get any once we start moving forward."

The officers dispersed to their sections awaiting instructions.

Buster returned to the column just before midnight. Ely had stayed awake to make sure that there was food and tea to drink. Then he packed away his kit while Buster briefed BSM Evans. "BSM, we will be moving forward by sections at one o'clock. The battery we are taking over from will be staying in position until tomorrow evening when they will withdraw, so we will have the benefit of a day's handover. Colonel Howard is already at Brigade HQ which is in the town. Our battery positions will be on the east side of the town in farmland, and the front line is a mile or so in front of us. Please ask the section commanders and gun numbers one to come here for orders in fifteen minutes."

Evans nodded, saluted, and went off as he was bid without comment.

When the orders group had assembled Buster went through the instructions for the relief, emphasising the closeness of the front line and the need for the operation to be completed without lights and as quietly as possible.

A few minutes before one a.m. guides arrived from the battery they were relieving, and on the dot of one the first section moved forward and into position some mile and half away. By first light all sections were in position and ready to begin their front line service.

As dawn broke Freddy was still awake. It had not taken long to get his guns into position in a barn, and the men settled into a heap of straw. The horses and wagons had then gone back to a wagon line a couple of miles in rear. The firing positions that the guns were to occupy were a little further forward, behind a hedge line. Freddy had been told that the coming day was to be spent reconnoitring the surrounding countryside and going up to the front trenches for familiarisation. At last light the guns of the other battery would be taken out of action by sections, withdrawn, and Freddy's battery of guns would be taken into position by the gun teams so that they would be in a position to offer SOS fire to the infantry by first light.

Freddy had a good look round the position where his section would be that evening. Later in the morning Buster called Freddy, Edwin, and James to be ready to go forward to the trench line at midday. At the appointed hour the four officers followed the BC of the outgoing battery. The route they had to take was somewhat circuitous, as the BC explained, most of their position was on a forward slope and therefore under continuous observation from the German positions on the ridge to their front, below the village of Messines.

The party firstly followed the bed of a stream that led south eastward, to the point where it passed a track, crossed the yard of a farm. At the far side was another track, which the BC warned them to cross with care as the Germans occasionally sent a burst of machine gun fire along it, and sometimes a shell or two. The track crossing had been screened with hessian, but this was useless against bullets and shells. They then were on the north side of the track, and went along another stream bed until they came to another farm, on the front line itself.

Freddy was surprised to find that as the land here had a high water table there were no trenches as such. The front line was a parapet of sandbags running across the fields from north to south. Here he met the infantry. At first sight he was not that impressed by their appearance. While he was still quite smartly dressed and mud free, except for his legs below the knees which were now thoroughly soaked and stained with mud, these soldiers appeared to be largely coated with mud. Their boots were caked, the legs and tunics of their uniform were spattered and torn, and their faces also were mud covered.

They gathered in a building which had been a farm house, but which now had largely been rearranged. The roof was gone at one end, there was a large hole in the wall facing the enemy, and all the windows and doors had been removed. He was amused, though, by some drawings on the walls that an English soldier must have drawn for amusement, mostly of caricatures of the Kaiser with somewhat ribald Anglo-Saxon titles. This was, he learned, was the forward platoon HQ, and the position for the battery forward observation post, which the artillery officers would take turns in manning through the hours of darkness. Buster decided that James would take the first duty there that night during the relief.

Freddy looked at the parapet running either side of the building and decided that it looked like a dangerous spot, which was confirmed by the outgoing BC, who told them that the infantry had taken a number of casualties from snipers. His advice was, whatever you do, never put your head above the parapet in daylight, use the observation ports that had been built in to the parapet. Even these had to be used with care as the Germans had them all located and could put a sniper bullet through them whenever they wished.

As the artillery officers were leaving after having a good look around, George Scott arrived with Walter Mann as part of the infantry handover. After discussion it was agreed that Walter's platoon would occupy the position that night and he and James would do the night duty together.

They returned to the battery position, again taking great care to follow the prescribed route. Throughout their journey to and from the line they had heard no gunfire at all. That was not what they had expected. The BC explained that on some days the Germans and the British would not fire at all, while on other days the Germans seemed to take great delight in 'brassing up' the position, without warning or apparent reason. His advice was 'just be very careful when out in the open.'

All went well with the handover, and that night the battery swapped position with the outgoing battery and by dawn the division was in position, though several officers and NCOs remained behind to complete the handover and help with any emergency that might occur.

After three days the new division was on its own. The Germans had been remarkably passive during the handover period and all units managed to settle in to the daily routines of life in the line.

Freddy did his share of night duty at the forward OP.

On the early morning of 22nd April the officers and men were about their duties when they heard the sound of much gunfire to their north, though their sector remained quiet. Later in the morning they smelt something strange, and eyes watered and throats became sore. The next day they learned that the Germans had released chlorine gas on the French positions near Ypres and had then attacked, but the line had been secured with only minor loss of territory. The BQMS came back from the divisional supply dump near Bailleul and reported that there were many men there in the field hospital suffering the effects of gas poisoning. Soon afterwards an order came round from division for improvised masks to be made from locally sourced materials, essentially a material pad with tapes to secure it over the mouth and nose, the pad to be soaked in urine before use. Though these were never used by the battery, most men recoiled at the thought of being gassed and having to protect themselves in this way.

Sergeant Leman came across a cow that had lost its owner, and asked Freddy and Kit Chilvers if he could keep it near his gun. As a herdsman in his civilian life he assured them that he would be able to do whatever was necessary. Though Colonel Howard was doubtful at first, he was persuaded to permit this arrangement when he was promised fresh milk for his morning tea.

Near to the gun line was the farm of Monsieur and Madame Grossemy. It became the routine for the battery officers to take lunch at the farm, with Madame Grossemy being helped by their one and only daughter, Roselyn. Roselyn appeared as a shy girl, never speaking in the presence of the British soldiers, merely doing her mother's bidding, bringing the omelettes and coffee to the table and clearing away. Freddy and the others speculated on what life for Roselyn might be like now that her two brothers were away with the Belgian Army. Monsieur Grossemy gave the impression of being very gruff and gave grunted orders to his wife and daughter, and rarely attempted to interact with the British, even though Buster and Edwin had reasonable facility in the French language. Freddy also tried to converse with the father and daughter to no avail, monsieur just ignored any approach with a shrug, and Roselyn just did her mother's bidding with no apparent pleasure or the reverse.

The officers decided that Roselyn was either a little backward, or very shy. In any event they gave up trying to communicate with her and instead satisfied themselves with the food and coffee that Madame provided, then returned to their duties.

As April developed into May the weather warmed and life became routine. Though there was occasional excitement when our infantry and the Germans exchanged fire, no real threat developed, and Freddy began to realise that being at war was not as bad as he had anticipated. In fact, he started to feel a little resentful. As the most junior of the battery officers he felt that he always had duties that were a little more uncomfortable or strenuous than his seniors, but resolved that in time this might change.

In early May Buster, by now well used to being BC, gave Freddy orders to lay a new telephone line between Brigade HQ and the forward OP. The existing line was to be duplicated in case of enemy action, as should this one be cut Brigade would need to have an alternative means of communication.

To fulfil this task Freddy was allocated Gunner Hastings and Trumpeter Kent. Hastings had been trained as a signaller and would do the technical work, while Kent, though younger, would carry the reel of cable and the pegs and other accoutrements needed to secure and conceal the cable.

They set off after breakfast, reported to the signals officer at Brigade HQ, secured the line to the exchange panel and followed the route given to Freddy on a map. As they passed the gun line they moved the cable into the stream that they used to go forward to the OP, using pegs, stones and rocks to sink the cable into the bed of the stream as they went. When they came to the part of the route where they would need to cross the track Freddy went ahead to see what arrangements were to be made. The signals officer had told him that the existing line crossed the track in a channel that had been dug across the track and backfilled. Freddy located the channel and waited for Hastings and Kent to catch up with him.

Freddy lay back on the bank of the stream and enjoyed the feel of the sun on his body. He could hear a skylark and looked skywards to see the tiny bird flapping and singing as if it had not a care in the world. At that moment Freddy felt as one with the world and envied the skylark for its ignorance of the war and its simple responses to spring. He started to drift into a reverie, and would have drifted into slumber if Hastings had not brought him back to consciousness, "Come on, sir, give a hand! We are struggling a bit here."

Hastings and Kent had completed their work in the stream bed and dumped the cable reel next to Freddy and slumped down on the track side next to him.

"It is getting warm, sir, can we take a break? My arms are tired." said Kent, his voice sounding more energetic than his words conveyed.

Freddy smiled at him, nodded, then sank back onto the bank. The three men then lay enjoying the warmth, the buzzing of a stray bee, the gentle rustle of the grass as a zephyr stirred.

After a few minutes Hastings, rolled over onto his side towards Freddy and asked, "Is this where we have to cross the track, sir, did you find the channel we were told about?"

Freddy opened one eye, took the blade of grass from his mouth, and sat up, "Yes, it's just behind us, I suppose we had better get on. I noticed that the hessian screen is a bit out of place. I will get a working party here tonight to fix it. We will have to be careful not to show ourselves as we lay the line across. Ready, off we go."

Hastings and Kent were happy to have had their rest, but were also looking forward to completing the task and getting something to eat and drink.

The two soldiers crawled out onto the track and with a shovel carefully dug the loose soil from the channel. They then brought the reel of cable across and carefully placed the line into the channel and started to fill the stones and soil back into the channel.

Crack! Crack! Crack! Crack!

The three were momentarily rooted to the spot then instinctively they fell to the ground and rolled into the ditch at either side of the track, Freddy and Hastings on the far side, Kent on the near side.

Crack! Crack! Crack!

Freddy had a sudden realisation, someone was trying to kill him!

Recovering his thoughts, Freddy said, "The Hun must be awake, I wonder if they saw us or were just firing randomly in the hope?"

Then they heard a metallic rustling sound coming closer from the direction of the Germans, and a shell exploded further up the track towards the gun line, about 50 yards from where they were laying. Another arrived, this time falling in the field behind Freddy, but still far enough away to be of no immediate threat. A few pieces of stone and dust fell on the track. They waited the arrival of the next shell, "Should we run for it, sir?" shouted Kent across the track.

"No, we should be safe enough here, wait until they stop and then we will have to continue with the cable laying. Stay there until I give you the word to come over." Freddy shouted back

After two minutes no further missiles had arrived, Freddy lifted his face and decided that it was safe to proceed. He said to Hastings, "Do we have the reel here?"

"Yes, sir, it's beside me."

"Right, time to go, then," said Freddy, raising his voice he shouted to Kent, "Kent, you can come across now, make sure you keep low and run like the devil!"

He could see movement on the far side of the track as Kent collected together his equipment and raised himself to a crouch, then leapt up and ran across the track. Just as he reached Freddy and jumped into the ditch there came another burst of machine gun bullets Crack! Crack! Crack! Crack!

Kent was giggling as he rearranged himself having gone full length onto the ground, Hastings started laughing and Freddy then also broke into laughter. They lay there, breathing deeply with fits of giggling for a few moments, not being able to control their emotions.

Hastings eventually broke the mood, "Bloody Hell, the bastards must be able to see the track."

"Yes," said Freddy, his voice a little shaky and higher in pitch than usual, "We will have to be more careful when we come back. At least we can say that we have been in action now!"

Hastings and Kent nodded, and prepared to continue their task, fortunately they were now in a stream deep enough to keep them out of view for most of the remainder of the cable laying task.

Freddy felt that at least now he could consider himself as a real soldier, who had survived an enemy attack, and had safely brought men under his command though the action. All three of them were in high spirits as they worked, joking and laughing as they progressed along the stream towards the OP.

On arriving at the building they met Walter Mann who noticing their demeanour said, "What is so amusing, Freddy, didn't you hear the shooting a while ago? The Hun seems to be on his toes today."

"Hear it! We were in it! We were up by the track laying this cable and he must have spotted us. It was far enough off line to miss us, but it was a bit exciting while it lasted." Freddy smiled.

"Well, all right, then, but we have seen some movement over the other side and have been told to expect a raid tonight or tomorrow. General Trubshawe will be coming down to have a look and says he wants to take a patrol out into no-mans land tonight. We are expecting him to arrive at any minute."

With that Walter offered Freddy and the two soldiers some tea, which they accepted and drank while Walter and Freddy looked through periscopes and Walter described what they had seen out in front.

Hastings had connected the line to the field telephone that he had brought along, and had tested the connection. "The line is working, sir," he said to Freddy, "we are through to Brigade."

"We had better warn them about the track being under observation, especially if the general is coming down. We wouldn't want the old bird being winged, would we?" said Freddy to Walter. He turned the call handle on the phone and a voice at the other end answered. "This is Second Lieutenant Scott at the first battery OP, please be aware that the track to this position is under observation by the enemy. Please advise any visitors to exercise caution if they are intending to visit."

The voice at the other end said, "Thank you, I will pass that on." Freddy put the receiver down.

At that moment he heard a voice that he recognised, Trubshawe!

Freddy tried to look busy and keep himself as inconspicuous as possible as the general entered the room. If it were not for his voice being recognised the general may well have been taken for a tramp, or itinerant. He was wearing an old mackintosh that was stained and torn, and tied around his middle with what looked like rope, and he was bare headed, his balding head showing its pink flesh, and his moustache was grey. His bearing was, however, that of a younger man, and he moved with an effortless gait. Freddy noted that his boots were muddy and his lower leg shadowed darker with damp. Freddy concluded that Trubshawe had arrived by the same route as himself.

"Right, young man," addressed to Walter, "show me where you saw activity this morning, I need to take a look for myself. I want you to take me out into no-mans land tonight and I need to see the lay of the land and see for myself what the Hun may be up to."

"Yes, sir, please come this way." said Walter as he indicated to the general to follow him outside and along the line. As they left Freddy heard Walter tell the general about his observations and they then passed out of earshot. Hastings looked at Freddy and raised an eyebrow. "Who was that, sir?"

"That, Hastings, was our divisional GOC, General Trubshawe."

"He looks like he sleeps under a hedge." said Hastings, "Is he really going out over there?"

"Well, as our chief I suppose he can dress how he likes." said Freddy, "He must be a game old chap if he has crawled down those streams like we did and is happy to go out on patrol."

Crack!

A single shot rang out. Freddy jumped at the sound, surprised that as an experienced front line soldier he reacted to it.

A shout went up from along the parapet. Corporal Rippingill rushed in, "Mr Mann has been shot!" and went past Freddy into another room then came back with a stretcher and rushed out again.

Freddy looked at him not quite believing what he just heard. He did not have the wits or time to gather his thoughts to stop Rippingill and question him, it happened so quickly.

Freddy went out to the back of the building and looked along the line and saw a group of four or five men gathered around a figure lying on the ground. This figure was twitching and arching his back. Freddy watched as the other men lifted the figure onto the stretcher and then, one at each corner they carried it towards the building in a crouching run. Part way one of the men at the back of the stretcher stumbled and the stretcher tilted and the figure, who by now Freddy had realised must be Walter, fell off. The men picked him up again and continued to crouch run towards the building.

The men put the stretcher down behind the building and Freddy could see that the right side of Walter's face was bloodied, his right eye socket was smashed. The stretcher behind his head was slick with bloody matter.

Rippingill applied a field dressing bandage to Walter's head, covering the gaping wound. Walter's face had gone grey. The blood had drained away. He was moaning.

Freddy felt nauseous. He felt the vomit rising in his throat. He turned away and wretched.

By this time Walter's sergeant, Baker, had arrived. He gave orders for four of the platoon to take the stretcher and go with him to get Walter back to the RAP. Freddy realised that this was over a mile away, and they would have to cross the track. Before he could say anything, Sergeant Baker had left and Walter was on his way.

Eventually Freddy gained his wits and said to Corporal Rippingill, "What happened, Corporal."

Rippingill looked at Freddy and said, "Bloody German sniper. Mr Mann was looking through the observation slit in the parapet and the general was looking through another one a few feet away. He was describing to the general where we had seen the Germans this morning when the bullet got him, right in the eye! Bastards! I think I know where he must be. Can you get the guns to fire at him, a bit of shrapnel up his arse will give him something to think about!"

"Damn." thought Freddy, I should have thought of that myself. Freddy went over to the field telephone and turned the handle. A voice answered him. Freddy said, "Forward OP here, we have just had a man shot by a sniper, may I have permission to fire the guns at the sniper position?"

"Wait a minute." replied the voice. Freddy could hear voices in the background, then the voice said, "Permission denied."

Freddy did not know how to respond to this information. He felt a rising anger mixed with nausea. He went outside and was sick again. He started to shake. His legs felt unsteady. He leant against the wall with his arms high and his head down.

Freddy remembered that he had Hastings and Kent with him, and for them, his own dignity, and the sake of the reputation of the Gunners that he needed to regain his composure. He took a deep breath. Then several more, and stood away from the wall.

What had seemed, just an hour or so before, to be a fine day for an adventure, had suddenly turned into a bad dream.

Freddy went back in to the building, and tried a smile, but it was a weak attempt, and betrayed his state of mind to the others inside.

Corporal Rippingill was swearing and muttering. Hastings and Kent looked sheepish and avoided Freddy's gaze.

At last Freddy said, "Right, we will have to go back to the battery, we have done what we set out to do, the line is working."

Kent said, "I wonder where the general is."

Freddy replied, "Probably along the line somewhere, lets go before he returns. We will only be in the way."

With that the three gunners collected their kit and left. The general was, in fact, with the infantry company commander, Major Wiley, discussing the military situation and commiserating over the wounding of Walter Mann.

The return to the battery was uneventful, they were apprehensive about having to cross the track, but succeeded in this without mishap. As they approached the gun line evening was drawing in. Freddy's mood had lifted a little. He noticed that there were primroses along the foot of the hedges, and as they came within earshot of his section he could hear singing. The gun crews had gathered around an area of grass that they used when not serving the guns. They were amusing themselves by singing. Singing not ribald soldiers' songs, but 'Nellie Dean'.

For a moment Freddy was angry, angry that these men could be so relaxed and cheerful when he had seen what he had seen earlier. Then he realised that they probably knew nothing of what had passed and were just doing what felt right to them.

The three men continued past the gun line and reached the battery HQ. There Freddy dismissed Hastings and Kent, and went off to find Buster, who was at Brigade HQ. Freddy found Buster in conversation with a new officer wearing the lapel badges of a chaplain. Buster introduced him to Gregory Fitzgerald, the newly appointed Brigade Chaplain.

Buster said to Freddy, "I know you have had a bit of a shock today. I think a chat to the padre here might do you some good, how do you feel about that?"

Freddy, who, though he generally attended chapel on Sundays, did not consider himself to be especially devout, or held much store in religion, nodded his agreement. "You know about Walter, then, is there any news of his condition?"

"I am afraid he passed before they could get him to the dressing station. I am sorry, he was a friend of yours." said Buster.

"We went to school together, but we were not all that close, though his going is a bit of a shock, I have to admit. His sister Constance is friends with my sister." replied Freddy.

Buster put his hand on Freddy's shoulder and gently moved him towards the padre. "Let me know when you have finished with chatting to Gregory."

There was an outhouse at the rear of the building, and that is where Gregory took Freddy. Inside were chairs and a solid wooden table. Gregory sat down and indicated for Freddy to do likewise.

He started with, "Freddy, I know you have been through a difficult day, tell me what happened, if you can."

Freddy looked at Gregory, as if trying to decide whether to expose his emotions, or to act as a soldier should. He chose the latter. "It was all straightforward, really. We had to lay a cable down to the OP. When we arrived there we spent a little time talking to the infantry in the line. One of them, Walter Mann, was shot by a sharpshooter and was taken away on a stretcher by his men. As you heard from Buster, he died on the way back."

"Is that all?" asked Gregory.

"Yes." said Freddy.

"Well, you seem to have got over it pretty well, we are after all in a war and men do die. Please, feel free to see me any time if you need to. And that goes for your men as well. Men react differently to the things that we have to do and see. If I can help you or any of them cope with their reactions, well, that is one of the things I am here for."

Freddy looked at Gregory, not sure how to respond. One part of him wanted to admit to being sick and getting confused and shaky, but another part wanted him to be a proper soldier, a man, who could take nasty things in his stride. He had noticed that Gregory had an accent, but could not place it. "Thank you padre, I will remember that and let you know if we need to talk to you. By the way, where do you come from, I don't think you are a Norfolk man?"

"No, no, I am from Ireland, County Wexford." replied Gregory, brightening a little.

"Are you a Catholic?" asked Freddy, not sure why he asked this, but in his life so far he had not known many Roman Catholics and had formed the view that most Irish were of that religion.

"I am ordained into the Church of Ireland, so no, I am not a Roman Catholic. Would that have been a problem?"

Freddy gave a small laugh, "No, not at all, I am not sure why I asked that of you, I suppose I made an assumption. But what makes a man of the cloth want to go and fight?"

"Well, my task is not to fight, but to help those who do. I conduct services for those of any religion and none, I comfort the wounded, and help to bury the dead."

"But I am not wounded, and you are offering me comfort, I suppose?"

"There are different sorts of wounds, are there not, and not all of them are visible to the naked eye. I know you have duties to attend to, but may I make a suggestion to you?"

"Of course," said Freddy, who had regained some of his usual demeanour.

"Some men find comfort in drink, some find comfort in women, but I have found that a good pipe works for me. There are no bad consequences in smoking a pipe, while the drink and consorting with loose women will lead only in one direction."

Freddy was somewhat taken aback, as he had little experience or desire for any of these things.

The padre continued, "Here is a pouch of my favourite tobacco, when you feel the need for comfort take a pinch and smoke it. I have found the act of preparing tobacco, filling a pipe, lighting it, and keeping it going, are a great antidote to the stress and strain of this life."

Freddy accepted the pouch and stood up to leave, "Thank you padre, I will bear in mind what you have said."

"One last thing, Freddy, do you think that Walter's family would like to know what happened to him? Could you write them a letter, do you think?"

"I had not thought of that. I know his family in passing, really, our fathers do business with each other, but apart from that I only really know his sister because she is a friend of my sister. In any case, would they want to know the grisly details? It was not a pleasant way to go, and the truth might not be what I could tell them."

"In that case, not telling all the truth may be the right thing to do. Imagine it yourself. If one of your family were to die in similar circumstances, wouldn't you want to hear from someone who was there and who could fill in the details for you?"

"I suppose so, but I am not sure that I can do it. I might upset them."

"Look, I suggest that you tell them that you were there when he was shot. That he died very quickly. And he was in no apparent pain. You should add that he was cheerful and doing his duty well, and that you are sorry to be the bearer of bad news. By the time your letter arrives they will already know he is dead. But, a letter from you will, I am sure, ease their grief and help them to cope better than if none of his comrades writes to them."

"I will do as you say."

Freddy left and went to seek out his brother. Edwin was with the BQMS. A delivery had been received from home with comforts for the troops, arranged by Florence Mann and a committee of ladies. There were a number of tea chests full of small packages, each one addressed 'For a Brave Norfolk Soldier.'

As Freddy arrived Edwin saw him and gave him a smile. "You have had a difficult day, Freddy."

"Yes, I have, but not as bad as Walter's. You have heard?"

"Yes, a great shame, I liked Walter, he was a very straightforward chap, his father will be very upset." said Edwin.

"And his aunt and Connie. The new padre has suggested that I write to them and let them know that I was there when it happened, though smoothing over the details somewhat."

"You should," said Edwin, "do you want any help in writing? We could do it together, if you like."

"No, I think I would like to do it on my own," said Freddy, "I need time to sort it all out in my own mind. Thanks for offering. By the way, the padre gave me some tobacco, he says a pipe of tobacco is his way of dealing with things, what do you think?"

"I have not met him yet, but I have no idea if it would work or not. Why not give it a try?" said Edwin.

At this point BQMS Mason joined in the conversation, "Pardon me for overhearing you, sir, but I agree with the padre. I like a smoke and I do find that it calms me down. I have a spare pipe you could try, if you like, I will get it for you once we have distributed these parcels."

"Right, that sounds good, Staff, thank you," said Freddy, "maybe one of these packages might have a pipe inside that I might be able to use, though I rather think that Miss Mann and the ladies of the town might not be in favour of such things."

"Most of them are married and will know what men need, I am sure that a few of them will have slipped a few nice things into the packages for us," said Staff Sergeant Mason, "wait a minute, there is a parcel here addressed to Mr Newman!" He picked up the parcel, pressed and squeezed it between his hands as if to try to determine the contents, "Must be from his father, or a secret admirer, perhaps."

"Probably from one of the ladies at the Mann Works, I would think," said Edwin, "I wonder if there is anything in here for me."

Freddy went to find his sleeping quarters. Ely had anticipated his return and had food and drink ready for him. After eating Freddy tried to sleep but found that his mind was still racing and he was unable to settle to slumber.

He went back into the mess in the hope of finding tea. The doctor, Robert Benefer, was sitting at a table writing in a leather bound book. Freddy nodded and grunted a greeting to him as he entered and went in search of the tea pot and a cup.

When Freddy had found what he sought he went to sit at the table. The doctor looked up at him and said, "Problems sleeping?" to which Freddy nodded. Robert leant down and picked up his haversack. From it he took out a bottle and two glasses, poured liquid from the bottle into the glasses and set one of them in front of Freddy. Freddy looked at it as Robert then took a small package from the haversack, unwrapped it, and poured a small amount of white powder into Freddy's glass, swirling the glass to dissolve the powder. "Drink it down in one."

"What is it?" asked Freddy.

"Whisky, with a sleeping draught."

"I don't like drink, especially hard liquor. In any case my mother told me not to."

"Well, I am in loco parentis in these matters Freddy, and I say it is what you need." said Robert, who raised his glass and emptied it in one gulp, "Down in one, Freddy."

Freddy unenthusiastically lifted his glass to his mouth, making a reluctant face as he smelled the whisky, and drank it down in one, but more slowly than the doctor had done.

He clearly did not enjoy the sensation of the alcohol passing his throat, but gulped and then replaced the glass. "I saw the padre this evening, and he says for me to avoid the perils of drink." said Freddy flatly.

"Well, he is entitled to his opinion, I prefer to rely on science," said Robert, "go to bed straight away, that powder will knock you out until the morning, good night."

Freddy, already starting to feel a little drowsy stood up and without comment went back to bed where he slept soundly until the morning.

Freddy woke up refreshed. He went into the mess and ate a hearty breakfast supplied by Ely, then sat down at the mess table to write to William Mann.

He was surprised that composing the letter came easily to him. In it, he said that he wanted to tell Walter's family the circumstances of his death, that Walter was fulfilling his duty at the time, that he died instantly, did not suffer, and was highly respected by his men and fellow officers. He said that Walter's family should be proud that he had been a loyal, diligent, and popular officer. Freddy added that when he was home on leave that he would be very happy to visit and answer any questions

93

that they may have. He wished William, Florence and Constance his sincerest condolences. He then passed the letter to Kit Chilvers who was responsible for censoring all letters, asking that it not be delayed due to the circumstances, to which Kit assured him that it would be delivered to the Manns the next day or the following day at the latest.

Three days later Freddy received a letter from Constance Mann thanking him for his letter, saying that his account of things had been a great comfort to her father, and asking Freddy to visit when on leave as she had many questions to ask him.

Some days after this Edwin was on night duty at the forward OP. It had been a quiet evening, with no interference from the Germans. A small patrol had been sent out from the British position to investigate the German wire and to see if a later patrol to capture a prisoner would be feasible. This first patrol was led by Stephen Sansom, and General Trubshawe went along dressed as a private soldier, though his years sat uncomfortably with this deceit. Corporal Rippingill had volunteered to join the patrol.

Edwin's task was to call up SOS fire from the battery if the patrol were to get into trouble or the Germans needed to be distracted. Once the patrol had started, Edwin concentrated on the ground beyond the parapet to ensure that he would be able to respond if need be.

Hastings was manning the field telephone. After the patrol had been out for a half hour Hastings indicated to Edwin that he wished to relieve his bladder, to which Edwin nodded his agreement, and Hastings went outside to fulfil the need.

When he returned, he told Edwin that he had seen a flashing light to the rear, which he was certain was a signal of some kind. Though it was not Morse code, or not that he could recognise, but the flashing went on for all the time he was outside. Edwin pondered what this could have meant. Telling Hastings to keep an eye and an ear out for action to the front, Edwin went outside and saw the flashing light for himself. He took a compass shot towards the light, and wrote down the direction in his note book.

Just then, a machine gun burst into life and bullets cracked overhead. The signal for the SOS was to be one red and one white Verey light. Edwin peered out, but no flares were to be seen. The machine gun continued with irregular bursts for another five minutes, but Edwin could not discern what was happening and return fire. He decided not to fire the SOS, but a thought kept nagging him, what if he had missed the flares? What if the patrol did not have enough time to fire them? Edwin sent a message to the infantry commander asking for orders, the reply came back to hold fire.

Three hours after the patrol had left it returned, but with a man missing. Corporal Rippingill had not been seen after the patrol started its return passage through the German and the British wire.

General Trubshawe and Lieutenant Sansom had a muffled conversation then went off to the company HQ leaving Edwin and Hastings in their room. The rest of the night passed without further incident, and Corporal Rippingill was posted as missing in action.

On his return to the battery the following morning Edwin reported to Buster, mentioning the flashing lights. The two men plotted on their map the direction recorded by Edwin and to their surprise the line they drew passed directly through Papillon Farm, the Grossemy's farm. Buster decided that this should be investigated. He gave orders for Edwin, Freddy, James Newman, Sergeant Leman and Gunners White and Brown to arm themselves with revolvers and rifles and to place themselves on the eastern side of Papillon Farm that evening and observe the farm for lights. If they saw signalling, they were to identify where the lights were coming from, surround the spot, and arrest or otherwise dispose of whoever they found there, arrest being the preferred option. If there were to be armed resistance then they should take whatever measures were appropriate to remove the threat.

As dusk fell the six men left the gun line and melted into the night. They had selected a spot to observe the farm which was in the lee of a haystack about four hundred yards from the farm, and between it and the front line. If there was a spy in the farm they would be signalling towards the Germans, and from their position here in the haystack they would be able to see it clearly.

Before they had left on their mission the officers had discussed the possibilities. Edwin had thought that maybe Monsieur Grossemy was a Kaiser sympathiser or maybe he had German blood in him. Though Edwin had to admit that as the farmer had hardly passed a word with the soldiers, and seemed not to understand English that the information he could garner to pass to the Germans might be very limited. He was certain, though, that the flashing lights from the farm led to the machine gunning of the patrol.

Freddy was not sure about anything, but felt quite excited by the prospect of catching a spy, something of a distraction from the more routine duties that had developed in the month or so since they had come to this area.

James Newman was more reserved in his judgement. He said that it was quite possible that information was being transmitted to the Germans by a spy, but that there could also be an innocent explanation, and that they should reserve judgement and act cautiously.

Sergeant Leman, a farmhand in his previous life, was prepared to go along with Captain Newman. Having lived all his life in the country he knew that things that looked normal in the day could take on a more perplexing (although he did not use that word) complexion at night. Sounds carry differently, and the dark often led to unreasonable fears.

At around midnight, when attention was waning, Gunner Brown nudged Sergeant Leman and whispered, "Sarge, look, there is a light, over there."

Leman felt around and made sure all the others were alert and whispered for them to look in the appropriate direction.

As they watched, a light flickered and moved as if dancing, then it disappeared for a few seconds, then reappeared in a slightly different position. It flickered on and off, occasionally being visible for a few seconds, then winking on and off for a while.

"There does not seem to be a pattern to it," said Freddy quietly, "I can't make anything of it."

"We should go and investigate more closely, come on." said James.

The eased themselves upright, then, James in the lead, they went in single file towards the light.

Though they were all familiar with the farm yard at Papillon Farm, the direction they were approaching it from was unfamiliar, with unexpected hazards. Firstly James tripped and fell into a ditch, resulting in a muffled curse from him and a very wet leg. Then they came to a barbed wire fence on which the top strand was slack, which made getting over difficult as it snagged their boots as they each tried to lift their leg over the fence.

Freddy struggled to restrain a giggle.

As they moved nearer to the farm they saw that the light was coming from the barn at the near side of the farm buildings. James, who everyone considered to be the leader of this patrol, indicated for Edwin and Brown to go to the left side of the barn, Freddy and Leman to go around to the right, and for Gunner White to go with him to the far side of the barn where he thought the main door would be. The two side parties were to prevent any escape, while he, James, would wait for a minute then enter the barn and deal with whatever he found inside.

The arrangements having been made, Freddy went off with Leman and felt his way along the dark side of the barn. Part way along he felt a door frame, and, feeling round it located the catch which he assumed would open the door when needed.

He reached out and touched Leman, felt down to his hand and guided Leman's hand to the catch, and whispered, "When we hear Captain Newman go in to the barn you open the door and I will go in this way."

Leman did not reply, but Freddy sensed him nodding agreement to this part of the plan.

Freddy found a crack in the door frame, and put his eye to it. What he saw inside confused him. He could just make out some of the details of the inside. He could see a lantern hanging by a nail on a beam, swaying gently and irregularly. He could also see a ladder leading up from the floor of the barn to a hay loft, and he could see the near edge of the loose hay was moving, but he could not see what was causing it. He looked back at the lantern and could see that there was no hand upon it, and therefore, he reasoned, it was not being used as a signal lamp.

Freddy heard a clunk as a door to his right, which he guessed was at the front of the barn, opened. He heard footsteps and rustling as James and Gunner White came into view, James holding his revolver and White with his rifle at the ready. Leman lifted the catch on his door, pulled it open, then Freddy moved into the barn, James looked at him, Freddy indicated to the loft with his revolver.

James waved his revolver to tell Freddy to climb the ladder, while he stood guard at the bottom, Leman and White standing away a little distance. Edwin and Brown had by this time joined them and Freddy again indicated the loft as he started to climb as quietly as he could.

As Freddy's head came level with the loft floor he saw the hay move, and a naked human foot! Taken a little aback by this, he paused, looked back down the others. James waved his revolver indicating that Freddy should continue. Freddy heaved himself up the last few rungs and knelt on the loft floor looking in the directions of the pile of hay.

In the half light he saw something that he did not at first understand, but which a more worldly wise person would recognise as the act of love, or, if not love, of lust.

He saw the back of a man, completely naked, moving his hips rhythmically. He also saw a hand on the man's right buttock, and another on his left shoulder. For seconds Freddy struggled to take in what he was seeing, though his instincts told him that it was not an immediate danger to him.

He stood up, and shouted in his most authoritative tone, "Stop! You are my prisoner!"

There was a flurry, as Edwin rushed up the ladder, and the naked man rolled to his right into the hay with a most surprised expression on his face. As he did so Freddy's attention was drawn to what this exposed. A naked girl! Freddy glimpsed her figure, immediately taking in the shape of her breasts and the dark triangle between her legs. The girl rolled to her right, away from the man, and reached into the hay, pulling her clothes toward her.

The man had gone into a crouched posture, his face away from Freddy and one hand held up, palm towards Freddy as if in a protective signal.

The girl, though, stood up to face Freddy, her clothes in her hand, and she stepped towards him. Freddy, despite the apparent threat had fixed his gaze on her breasts, which even in the poor light he could see confirmed her as a woman. She pushed Freddy with the palm of her free hand and shouted something that Freddy did not understand, but knew the meaning of. His sister, Sissie, had often used this technique to admonish him, though when she did so she was always fully clothed.

Freddy, felt uncomfortable, embarrassed, as he now understood that he had stumbled on something that he did not really understand, but instinctively knew to be private and not for him to see.

Freddy turned his gaze away to the man, who by now was trying to put trousers on, muttering and fumbling.

Freddy pointed his revolver towards the man and indicated with his other hand that he should put his hands up. Meanwhile the girl had finished pushing Freddy and had turned to Edwin in a similar attack, still showing no inclination to replace her clothes. She was still shouting, and Freddy glanced in her direction and noticed how her breasts moved as her arms shoved Edwin. Edwin had started to laugh, and James' head now appeared at the top of the ladder, "What on earth is going on?"

What he saw, from his position at floor level, was Edwin giggling and being pushed backwards by an angry naked woman, and Freddy pointing his revolver at a bare chested man with his trousers half on and half off. Taking in the situation quickly, James said, "Oh dear, I think we have interrupted things. Freddy, let that chap get dressed in peace, and Edwin, get that woman into her clothes and bring them both down the ladder." With that his head disappeared. Freddy could hear voices down below, then laughter.

Freddy put his revolver back into his holster, and offered his hand to the man to get him to stand up and dress. The woman had by this time calmed a little and was stepping into her dress while still shouting at Edwin. Freddy was drawn again to look at her breasts as they disappeared into the bodice of the dress, not sure why he was drawn to look, but feeling that it was important nonetheless.

Once the man's trousers were in place, and he had put on his shirt, Freddy pointed at the ladder and the man stepped across and started to descend, "He's coming down." Freddy shouted to the men below. The woman followed, still shouting unintelligibly at Freddy and Edwin. Edwin followed her, and Freddy started towards the ladder, then realised that he ought to search the loft in case there was something of interest there. This proving negative he also went down the ladder.

Gunner White said, "We should take them out and shoot them."

Leman turned to him and said, "No, I don't think so, they were not spying, they were doing what we all wish we could."

"I rather think you are right, Sergeant Leman, but who exactly is this chap?" said James, taking the lamp and holding it to the man's face.

Freddy had looked at the man, then the woman, and realised that he had seen her before, "Isn't that Roselyn, the farmer's daughter?"

Edwin added, "Yes, it is!"

Roselyn, whose normal demeanour was demure and uncommunicative, was now animated and vocal. She continued to shout at the soldiers, and stood next to the man. She was pointing in turn at him and at James, occasionally at Freddy, but none of the soldiers could understand what she was talking about. The man stayed silent, his eyes downcast.

"So, what do we do?" asked Freddy, to the group in general.

"Well, I do not think they are spies, so we have no need to arrest them, but we should deal with the lamp as it must be visible by the Germans. As for the young man, shouldn't he be in the army? I think we should take him in and find out who he is." said Edwin, "Agreed?"

James instructed Sergeant Leman to tie the man's hands together with a rope and to get Gunner White to hold the end of it while they took the man back to Brigade HQ.

James indicated to Roselyn that she should go, but she shook her head and took hold of the man's arm. James shrugged and then told everyone to leave the barn and extinguished the lamp. He then joined them outside and they made their way back up the familiar lane to Brigade HQ.

Reporting to Kit Chilvers James explained what they had found and suggested that they hand the man over to the Belgian military. Kit agreed, and made a telephone call. He was instructed that the man would be collected the next day. The girl would not leave, though.

Freddy, James and Edwin dismissed Leman and the gunners, and returned to the gun line. As they walked along the lane they discussed the events of the evening. "So much for spies, then. Just a young couple out doing what comes natural." said Edwin.

Freddy, being not entirely sure what this could mean just grunted. James said, "These country folk have a different way of doing, things, I suppose. What was Roselyn saying, I couldn't understand a word, but she did seem to be upset."

"It sounded very different, I can understand some French, but it wasn't what she was speaking, could it be German?" said Freddy.

"I took German at school," said Edwin, "it did sound similar, but not the same. Maybe it was just her accent, maybe she comes from another part of the country."

When they arrived at the battery Buster was there to meet them. "Had a good evening, lads?" he beamed, "Interrupting a tryst?" he chuckled.

"You know it was Roselyn from the Grossemy farm?" said James, "She was a very different girl this evening than is usual for her."

Buster shook his head, "I have a sister, a wife, and two daughters, and the way they change their behaviour still confuses me. It is one of the female's better features, keeps us chaps on our toes!"

"What about the man, I don't think I recognised him at all, and he said nothing. Could he be a spy?" asked Freddy.

"Well, I don't think being a spy needs you to get quite so close to the local population. Maybe he is a local lad avoiding having to join up, or a deserter. Who knows? Anyway, the Belgians will know what to do with them. By the way, I hear that Corporal Rippingill has come back in. Apparently his father was a game keeper at Sandringham, and he used to help out catching poachers. He says he decided to get the bastard who shot Walter Mann, so he sloped off from Sansom's patrol and hid himself near where the sniper fired from. The next morning the German arrived and Rippingill was waiting and got him. He had to wait until last light to come back in."

"Good grief, that's a story, no doubt about it!" said Edwin, "I should go down tomorrow and thank Rippingill."

"No need," said Buster, "they sent him back up for the doc to look him over. He is a bit bruised and knocked about. Apparently he got into a fist fight with the Hun and ended up stabbing him to death. You could go across to the Norfolk's RAP and see him, tonight."

Freddy and Edwin looked at each other, nodded, and Edwin said, "We will go straight away." They both turned around and went back the way they had just come down.

At Brigade they went to see Kit, who was still on duty, "Freddy and I would like to go up to the Norfolks, apparently Corporal Rippingill is with the doc being checked over. Buster said that he has been out in no-man's land catching a poacher."

"Yes, I heard that as well, he's a strange cove, that Rippingill. Get along and let me know when you are back in case you are needed." said Kit.

Edwin and Freddy reached the Regimental Aid Post after a quarter of an hour's walk, and found it in an outbuilding of another farm. The doctor was there with Rippingill, who was sitting in a wooden chair smoking a pipe, looking very calm and composed. In the lamp light Freddy could see that his right hand was bandaged and his jacket was open as the top few buttons were missing, and his right thigh was visible through a large tear in his trousers. He was bare headed, his cap was balanced on his knee.

"Please excuse us, Doc, but may we speak to Corporal Rippingill? We are from Buster Webb's battery, and the good corporal here has done us a great favour."

The medical officer nodded his agreement and indicted that he would be off to his bed, saying, "He's all yours."

"Tell us all about it, please, Corporal," Edwin said, taking the seat recently vacated by the doctor. Freddy settled himself on a wooden beam.

"Well, sir, it is very simple, really. I killed the bastard Hun that got young Mr Walter." Freddy was a little surprised that he had used Walter's first name, but did not make any response to this familiarity.

"I understand that you had to use your bayonet and there was a struggle." said Edwin.

"Nothing worse than I have seen before, sir, but he was a little runt of a man, and he didn't really have a chance. I knew where he would be because I found some cartridge cases. I hid myself behind where he would be. When he arrived and had settled himself I jumped him and stuck this knife into his belly and up under his ribs. My bayonet would have been too long, so I used this one." He reached down and produced a knife which was only a few inches long, "Then I grabbed his hair and pulled his head back and slit his throat. I held him down while he thrashed about. It was all over in a minute or so."

"What about your injuries? How did you get them?" said Freddy.

"I fell into a ditch and there was a coil of barbed wire down there that someone must have lost. It cut my hand and ripped my trousers trying to get untangled. I hid up for the rest of the day and then crawled back in at last light."

"You know you were posted missing?" said Edwin.

"Yes, I did not tell Mr Sansom what I was going to do, but the general knew."

"Did he, and he let you do it?" said a surprised Freddy.

"Not officially, of course, but he knew, and he wished me good luck. He is a strange man, you know, he gave me two bars of chocolate before we went out and said, "That should keep you going, Corporal." So he must have known what I was up to."

"Mr Mann was a friend of ours, we are very grateful to you for what you did. We will tell his family that he has been avenged, and let them know it was you who did it." said Edwin.

"I take no pleasure in what I did. It was a duty. It just had to be done. Please pass on my condolences to Mister Walter's father, but please do not mention me by name. My family have a history with the Mann's, and in a way I am just repaying an obligation to them, sir. Mister Walter was a real gent."

Edwin stood and shook Corporal Rippingill's hand, saying, "Thank you, we will do as you say, well done. If there is ever anything I can do for you do not hesitate to say."

"No need, sir." Rippingill said as Freddy also shook his hand, Freddy noting that the corporal's hand was still blood stained, large, warm, and firm.

Freddy decided that he liked Rippingill. That he wished to be like Rippingill. He was not sure that he could be, though.

The two young officers left the post and returned to report back in with Kit, returning to the gun line to get some sleep.

The next morning the battery was alive with the news of the previous night. Whenever Freddy arrived the soldiers would smile and nudge each other and enquire of Freddy if he was going spy hunting tonight, and if so could he take them along as they could do with a good laugh. The implication was that long absence from accessible female company increased their interest in coming across a young woman who might be comely and agreeable, both to the vision and the aspiration of the young men.

Freddy had to put up with this ribbing for several days, though he noticed that James and Edwin were spared.

The news about Corporal Rippingill was also abroad. Though many of the men knew of him, and his family, only by reputation. There were none of the Rippingill family in the artillery brigade, but over time the talk of his action meant that his reputation assumed greater dimensions than he would have liked, had he known, as in fact he was a modest man who knew his duty and did it without any reflection or compunction.

The following day Freddy was down at the forward OP. Edwin and James were in the mess enjoying a cup of coffee.

"Constance Mann has sent me a reply to the letter that I sent to her father," Edwin told James, almost in passing and as a way to start a conversation. James was his usual quiet self, and Edwin felt the need for conversation.

James looked up and asked, "What did she say?"

"She said they were grateful to Freddy for writing to them about Walter, she said it gave her father much comfort to know that someone who knew Walter was there, and that Walter did not suffer any pain."

James cut in, "But that is not true, is it? I understand that he was in a lot of pain, and it took him a long time to pass. If they could have got him back faster he may have had a better chance."

"That is what Freddy was advised to say to them, and I think it is right. Why give them more to worry about than is strictly necessary?"

"I have worked for William Mann for many years, and I have found that he prefers to hear the truth, however difficult. He would not be very happy if I had ever been less than truthful in my dealings with him."

"Anyway, Constance says they were comforted, and I for one will not be telling them what really happened. She also said that Florence had joined the VADs because of Walter. She wants to do more than knitting and collecting comforts. She says that bringing up Walter and Constance for her brother taught her a lot about nursing and organisation, so she is off to war. She wants to be sent out to France."

James had not received any letter recently from William Mann, and felt uneasy about that. He was used to advising William on business matters, and was worried that William may be finding things difficult without James to help and guide him.

"Do you ever worry about being killed, like Walter?" Edwin asked.

"Being killed? No, not really," said James, "but I do sometimes worry about the act of dying. If I am to go I just hope that it is quick and as painless as possible. I have no dependents so only my father will remain to mourn me, and he will not be around for ever either. In fact, he has encouraged me to serve in the Territorials. He says it shows our commitment to the country, and in a way, I think he may like me to make the ultimate sacrifice as further proof."

"Well, I do, worry, that is, but I also worry about flunking it if the time comes for me to be tested for real. I rather think that we have had it easy so far, and that more difficult times are round the corner." said Edwin, unusually serious.

James looked at him for a few seconds, then said, "I am sure we all worry about letting ourselves down. Some men do fail, and some do not. If my opinion is of any value, from what I know of you, you will do well. There are a couple of others who my experience tells me to watch out for, but you will be up to it."

"Such as?" asked Edwin.

"I will keep my opinions to myself. Just keep an eye out and make your own mind up who you can trust and who you can't. But, be prepared to give everyone the chance to prove themselves. Even those who fail once may not do so again, and those who do not fail in one situation may find themselves out of their depth in another. Take Rippingill, for instance, he did well to get that Hun, but even his courage may fail later." said James.

"Mmm." said Edwin.

Just then Kit Chilvers came in. "I say, have you heard the news about that chap you picked up in the barn? Apparently he was a deserter from the Belgian Army. They have sent him off for court martial. Apparently he was posted missing when the Germans captured Liege and he must have found his way down here."

"And the girl?" asked Edwin.

"They let her go, though the police may take her in later. Apparently she is not Grossemy's daughter at all. She lost her family up north when the Huns invaded and she just pitched up here. As all Grossemy's labourers had been called up they took her in. She does not speak much French, apparently, only Flemish, that must be why you did not understand what she was saying to you. She must have been trying to ask you to let

108

the young man go as she probably knew he would end up being shot if he was caught." explained Kit.

"Quite a story," said James, "I feel a little sorry for the chap, really, and the girl. They have probably lost everything, and what little they kept is now likely to go as well."

"Did the Grossemys know he was there?" asked Edwin.

"They say not," said Kit, "but who knows, not our problem really, it's for the Belgians to sort it out. We are here to help them sort out their differences with the Huns."

"I suppose it is people like that, poor little Belgians, that we came here to fight for." said Edwin.

"Ours not to reason why, but to do and die." added Kit, "By the way, Colonel Howard has had orders for a move. I think we will be here for a couple of weeks then a New Army division will be taking over from us. The colonel will be giving out orders in the next couple of days."

"Where will we be sent?" asked James.

"The thought is we will go further south. The French want us to take over more of the front, and we will probably be taking over from them somewhere further along. The details are still being discussed, apparently, and as the new divisions come over from Blighty we will need a bit more elbow room to fit them in." explained Kit.

"Whoever comes here is welcome to the place," said Edwin, "it's too damp by half, though with summer coming on things will be better, but I cannot imagine a winter in Flanders."

Kit's news came to pass. Colonel Howard briefed all his senior officers on the move and they in due course passed orders down through the brigade. In addition, they were to receive new guns. They would hand over the position to a division of Kitchener's New Army, mostly men who had volunteered in August and September 1914 and who had now been trained and equipped sufficiently well to take their place in the order of battle.

In late May these men arrived, full of enthusiasm and optimism. As they brought their guns into position they made disparaging remarks about the old fashioned guns that were being withdrawn. The outgoing men, though, felt themselves to be seasoned campaigners, and gave their best advice to the new arrivals, and bid them good luck as they trekked south, over the border and into France, crossing near the town of Armentieres.

Their trek then took them to the south west, arriving at the small mining village of Ferfay, where they passed two weeks in the warmth of the spring. There was a large ordnance depot nearby, and new 18 pounder guns were issued and the obsolescent 15 pounders were withdrawn.

While in Ferfay a reorganisation took place. Edwin was posted to Brigade HQ as they had found that they needed more personnel to man the HQ. Edwin was not entirely happy with this as he did not get on well with Colonel Howard, but Buster told him that he must go, but would come back to the battery if circumstances changed.

The Brigade had been lucky while they were in Flanders, there had been no fatal casualties in the artillery. At Ferfay this changed, and the first death occurred. Driver Sutton, of Brigade HQ, managed to shoot himself in the head accidentally while mounting his horse. He died immediately and was buried in the village cemetery.

The news came through that Italy had finally declared war on Austria and had therefore joined the Entente, though it would be another year before they joined the war against their old ally Germany. Corporal Benjamin Ely was very pleased to hear this news. His maternal family were Italian, from Padua.

In late June the Brigade started to trek again, this time to the south east, passing through the city of Arras and on further until they arrived at the small village of Hebuterne, which would be their home for the next twelve months.

Chapter 10

24th July 1987, Arras, France.

We drove down from Belgium to our hotel in Arras, just in the corner of the Grand Place. As we drove I reflected on what Freddy had told me as we drove along.

I had always believed that the First World War was an unending struggle with mud and death, but Freddy seemed to think that it was a bit of a lark, young men free from the normal constraints of home and having a good time.

Freddy dozed in the passenger seat as the MG thrummed its way southwards.

We arrived at the hotel about six, and after an hour unpacking and taking a bath, Freddy and I went out looking for dinner. We stepped out of the hotel into the square. There were still cars parked around, but preparations were underway for a market the next day. Stalls were in various stages of erection and setting out. Freddy and I turned to our right and went along the pavement.

As we walked I asked, "Did you ever come here during the war, Freddy?"

Freddy seemed to be lost in thoughts, so I let it go that he had not replied. I was beginning to think that maybe his hearing was deficient as we continued to walk in silence. We reached the end of the square and continued along the street and came into another square, Place des Heros. I saw the street sign, and said to Freddy, "Do you think they named this square after you?"

He looked at me blankly, looked up at the sign which I was pointing to, then smiled, "No, I do not think so. I only came here a couple of times, and I did not do anything heroic, though I did eat some dodgy oysters once. The last time I was here I think they called it La Petite Place, but I may be wrong on that detail."

To my eyes the buildings on the square looked as if they had been built at least two hundred years previously and had not been particularly well looked after in the meantime. They were of stained limestone, tall thin properties, terraced, each of a similar but slightly different style.

We came across a restaurant just near the City Hall next to an hotel and went in. We sat at a table and the waiter came over. He was young, unshaven, and slim. He smiled at me in a friendly way that young men reserve for young women, though he addressed his questions to Freddy. I sensed that in his mind he was trying to work out what the relationship might be between Freddy and me.

Freddy turned out to be quite fluent in French, putting my schoolgirl usage into the shade. The restaurant was almost empty, there was just one other table occupied when we arrived, with two earnest looking middle aged men in animated conversation. One was bald, spectacled, and rotund. He seemed to be the senior one, the other, younger, slimmer, and smoking, seemed to be trying to persuade the older man in some enterprise or other. They were wearing jackets, but no ties. Their exchanges went on without interruption throughout their meal.

Freddy ordered the local speciality, andouillettes, so I decided to have the same. We each had a pichet of wine, which Freddy ordered. While we waited for the sausages to arrive the restaurant started to fill up with locals as they finished their day's work.

Freddy commented, "I say when in Rome! A tip for your future travels, Kate. Always eat the local speciality and order the house wine in a pichet. That way you will never eat a really bad meal, at least on the Continent, and French restaurateurs will always have a very acceptable house wine. It will always be a reasonable price. Occasionally you will have a really memorable feast, though that will usually be because the people you are with are special."

"And is the company this evening special, Freddy?" I asked, a little mischievously as the wine was starting to make me feel light headed.

"Yes, of course, I suppose that is what I was saying in my clumsy way. Any meal with you is special. You know I value your company. You have always been special to me."

I could see that Freddy's eyes were moist as he spoke, I felt a little embarrassed. I looked away toward the bar where the young waiter was talking to an older man who was leaning on the counter with a glass in his hand. As I looked I caught a glance from the waiter. We smiled at each other, then I realised that he might take this as an invitation, so quickly looked back.

As I continued to focus my attention on Freddy I was aware that the waiter was still looking in my direction.

"So, Freddy, tell me about the first time you came here to Arras."

"Ah, yes, it must have been in the late summer of nineteen fifteen. I remember it being warm in a late summer sort of way. Our guns were in position to the south, near Hebuterne, where we will go tomorrow. The colonel needed someone to go to a lecture on something or other to do with ammunition returns. At that time of the war we still did not have enough shells, and every one had to be accounted for. A lot of brigades had got themselves into trouble because their daily and weekly returns did not tally, so instead of giving us more shells they seemed to be more interested in accounting for the paltry few that we did have. Anyway, enough of that nonsense, who did I come with? I seem to remember that we rode over together from division." Freddy looked away to the window for a few moments as he tried to remember something important. As he did so I shifted my gaze towards the bar without turning my head. He was looking again! I felt a little shiver run up my spine to my neck - stupid! I moved my eyes back to Freddy's face, feeling that my own was flushing a little..

"Ah, yes, that's it, I came over with Dobbin's cousin, Matthew, Matthew Holt. He was a studious sort of lad, and probably more suited to a lesson in accounting than me. He had come out to join us just after we arrived in Belgium and had been posted to one of the other brigades. Anyway, as we were acquainted we agreed to bunk down together on the course. We arrived in the early afternoon and reported to the HQ here. They sent us off to get fed and watered and told us to report back the next morning, so off we trotted and set about seeing what we could in the town."

"Was it badly damaged during the war? The buildings look as if they could do with a spruce up now."

"When we came here first it had some damage, but nothing like later on. The Germans had been through here early in the war, but had been pushed back out by the French soon after. The town was in range of their long range guns and a few shells had landed in the centre, but it was reasonably safe to be here. Later on, of course, it took a real battering and when we came here after the war most of it had been rebuilt. What you see now, though it looks old, is no more than fifty years or so. To their credit, the French decided to restore rather than rebuild, so the buildings were put back to how they were before the war."

Freddy continued, "So we wandered around the town, including this square that we are in this evening. The shops were all open, and restaurants aplenty. We ate our fill, then went shopping! I bought a few things for Mamma and Papa, and some lace handkerchiefs which I sent back to Sissie by post. I put a little note in with them telling her how things were going on. They had little hearts around the border, quite sweet, really. I don't know what became of them, but I am sure that they were appreciated. It was amazing that the French post offices were still open for business. Later on we were forbidden to use them for security reasons, but I must admit that I did occasionally break the rules and send things home by the civilian post office. Actually, the service then was better and faster than it is today! Incredible. My recollection is that it was a bit like any town in England at the time, not really what you might think of as wartime at all, apart from all the soldiers around. There were still a lot of French military around of course, though we had taken over the line from them several weeks before. I will tell you a bit about them later, some really surprising stories to be told. You know, the French can teach us a few things about dealing with adversity, they see these things very differently to us. I suppose it's because they were used to having their old enemy invading their country."

We continued to chat, Freddy becoming a little rosy cheeked as we finished our wine, me trying to avoid, unsuccessfully, glancing towards the bar. Freddy left the table to use the gents. While he was away from the table I looked around the restaurant at the diners. They were a mixture as you would find in any town anywhere in France. In one corner was an oldish lady, dressed with clothes that had been couture in their day, but which now looked a little shabby and grubby. Paying more than polite attention to her was a younger man, maybe in his forties, casually dressed, but hanging on her every word. A group of youngsters, more my age were, a couple of tables away, loud in a sociable way. At another table were serious looking business types. I pondered which group I would have been in at home.

I became aware of someone at my side. I looked up and the young waiter was there. A little startled, I did not speak for a few seconds, then he spoke in good but accented English, "You are English, yes?" I nodded. "Is that your father with you?"

"No," I replied, "my great uncle. We are here to see where he fought in the war, The Great War."

"Ah, the battlefields!" he said, "We have many English visitors for that purpose. If it were not for these English, our city would be very poor. You are very welcome to come here. I will be very pleased to help you if you need anything. My grandmother always told me of her affection for the English soldiers. She was here during the war. My name is Sebastian, Sebastian Leclerc." and he held out his hand. I shook it, just as Freddy returned, "I did not think it would be long before a young lass like you would find a younger man!" Freddy said with a twinkle in his eye.

Sebastian held his hand out to Freddy, another shake ensued. I said to Freddy, "Sebastian tells me his grandmother was in Arras during the war, maybe you met her?" I winked at him. Freddy looked at me blankly, then understanding dawned on him and he flushed a little, "Well maybe, but not in that way, young lady!"

"How long will you be staying in Arras?" said Sebastian as we left.

I looked at Freddy, he replied, "Two nights, we will be back tomorrow evening then will be driving on the next day."

"Then please come back tomorrow evening, I will ask my father to see you, he has some photographs from the war years and will tell you some stories that his mother used to tell him. Come back to the restaurant as my guest, please."

Freddy looked at me, and I looked at him. Such open generosity made us Brits feel a little awkward. I think Freddy wanted me to decide, and I was not sure my judgement was clear. I hesitated and then said, "Merci, Sebastian, vous etes tres genereux."

"Vous parlez Français , après tout. Jusqu'à demain, alors." Sebastian replied. I smiled at Freddy, he smiled back at me.

As we walked back to the hotel Freddy said, "What a pleasant young man that Sebastian is, and good looking I suppose?"

"Yes, very kind, and not what I had expected. I felt a little awkward because he kept looking at me from the bar. I thought he might be a bit of a creep, but it looks like he is OK." I said.

"It's a good job you have me with you to keep you on the straight and narrow. A young woman like you could have her head turned by a handsome stranger if she did not have a father figure to look after her, don't you think?" Freddy added.

Ignoring his jest I said, "Freddy, you never married did you? Did you never meet the right woman?"

Freddy said nothing for a minute, then stopped walking, turned to me, and softly said, "No, no wife or children, but I did meet the right woman, but it was not to be. She went and I lost the will. I never found anyone like her, and losing the chance for a family makes me very sad. I think I would have made a good father, certainly a proud one. I have made the best of being an uncle and great uncle, though, don't you think?"

"Yes, you have always been my special uncle, Freddy." We reached the hotel and went to our rooms, me a little flushed from the food, wine, feelings of fondness for Freddy, and thoughts of Sebastian.

Chapter 11

July 27th 1915, Hebuterne, France.

Brigade HQ had arrived in the village of Hebuterne ahead of the main body. A division on the move was an impressive sight, and Freddy saw columns of all sorts converging on the countryside to the west of Hebuterne. He was riding with his section, and on arrival at the rendezvous he dismounted from his charger and went to the head of the column to get instructions from Buster. As he approached he heard banter and laughter coming from the gun teams and in the warmth of the sun he felt that all was well with the world. He was even looking forward to getting back into the line. The days spent in reserve, re-equipping and training had become a little tedious to him and he now wanted to get back to the job of a front line soldier.

Buster had with him a French officer with whom he was in conversation. Freddy was aware that his schoolboy French would not be up to scratch in dealing with the allies, and he knew that Buster was more or less fluent. Freddy stood to one side and patiently waited for the other battery officers and the BSM to arrive. He became aware that the Frenchman and Buster were, in fact, conversing in English, and the Frenchman had an accent that Freddy was sure put him in London, or at least somewhere in the south of England.

When all were assembled Buster turned to his officers and introduced them to Lieutenant Armand Chaleyer, who had been appointed liaison officer for the handover period.

Buster gave instructions for the BSM to laager the wagons and await further orders, while the officers and two signallers were to go with Lieutenant Chaleyer to look around the HQ and communications centre. The horses were to be left at the rendezvous and they would go forward on foot.

The French Brigade HQ was in a house in the village, and it took only ten minutes for the group to walk there from the RV. Freddy was surprised that there were no sounds of war to be heard. Not a rifle shot, nor an explosion of any kind. As they approached the village Freddy could see no damaged buildings, all seemed to be normal, peaceful. There were men and women working in the fields, carts were moving along the tracks. The air was warm, and the sound of birds singing and insects buzzing and going about their natural business. There were butterflies all around, and Freddy's thoughts went back to his home in Saddlebow where as a nipper he had often gone with Edwin and the village lads to play in the fields and woods around the village.

In the HQ building they entered by a door and immediately descended stairs into a cellar area, where a low burble of conversation could be heard. The smell of bodies and French tobacco created an atmosphere in contrast to the bucolic scene outside.

Freddy looked around and met the eyes of some of the French soldiers and officers occupying seats at telephone boards and at a map table which dominated the central part of the cellar. They nodded at each other.

Chaleyer indicated the map to the Englishmen and then described the layout of the position to them, indicating where the German trenches were, where the French trenches were, and a host of details including the area of responsibility for the various batteries. Freddy noted that his guns would be two miles away in front of the village of Colincamps in a shallow valley out of direct observation from the German positions. The centre of arc would be towards the village of Serre behind the German line. After having a few minutes to study the map more closely Buster said that the party would now go forward to see the OP and the infantry trenches.

To Freddy's surprise they did not go back up the stairs and out into the village, but Chaleyer lifted a blanket on one side of the cellar and passed through into a passage, a tunnel, beyond. The Englishmen looked at each other, raising an eyebrow or two, then followed Chaleyer into the passage. Every ten yards or so a dim electric bulb lit the way and the men quickly became adjusted to the faint lighting.

They followed Chaleyer for what seemed hours but was in fact only a few minutes. The passage turned corners, left, right, right again until Freddy had his sense of direction blunted by the various twists and turns, but felt that they must be going in the direction of the front.

Eventually they came to stairs, which they ascended, and found themselves in another building, one where a wall was damaged and had no glass in the windows. They then passed into a trench which started just inside a doorway and passed out into the open. This section of trench was open to the skies, but the top was some three feet higher that any of the men as they walked along it. Freddy felt better to be in the fresh air, but more disoriented by not being able to see around him.

After following the trench as it twisted and turned for about a hundred yards Freddy noticed a high wall on the left above the trench, and in the wall were large ornate gates that Freddy felt must belong to a cemetery by their size and design. As this thought was going through his mind he heard what sounded like the ringing of a bicycle bell. He turned to Hastings who was immediately next in line and said, "Did you hear that? It sounded like a bicycle, but that must be impossible!" Before Hastings could say anything the bell rang again, and round the corner came a French soldier on a bicycle, cigarette in mouth and pedalling in a most leisurely fashion. As he passed the Englishmen, who without exception were open mouthed, he nodded and continued on his way, leaving a trail of pungent smoke in his wake.

The trench became a tunnel again, and after a few more twists and turns Chaleyer pulled back another blanket and they entered a room, similar to the first they had seen back in the village. A telephone operator sat at one side, and a table occupied the centre of the room. The lighting was again by electric bulb, a little brighter than in the tunnel section.

"Gentlemen, please make yourselves at home for a few minutes, I will go and find my commander, Capitaine Marc Duclaux." said Armand.

While he was gone the Englishmen looked around the room. "Where do you think we are exactly?" Freddy asked no one in particular.

"Underground in a French bunker." said Edwin, unhelpfully.

"Thank you, Edwin, that is obvious. I think we are in the funk hole below the forward OP. The Frenchies certainly seem to like their engineering. These structures are far more substantial than what we are used to." said Buster.

Chaleyer returned, with a smaller officer, who he introduced as Marc Duclaux. Chaleyer explained that Capitaine Duclaux did not speak English, so he would translate for them.

Duclaux then proceed to pull a map from his pocket, spread it on the table, and proceeded to speak very quickly, gesturing occasionally at the map, gesticulating, and not pausing for breath. After five minutes of this, he abruptly stopped, and without further ceremony, turned and left.

The Englishmen looked at each other and shrugged as one. Buster said to Chaleyer, "I am afraid that I did not catch everything that the capitaine told us, could I ask you to go over it all again, to make sure we have full understanding, please, Armand?"

"D'accord." replied Chaleyer, and proceeded to give a full and helpful briefing, and answered all the questions asked of him. Freddy formed the opinion that he would rather deal with Armand than his captain.

"If you have everything marked on your maps and no further questions let us go to the observation position and I can point out everything of interest to you." said Chaleyer, and led the way back out of the room. He lead them further along the tunnel to steps which led up, around a corner, and further up until they emerged into a space that had an observation slit at one end. There was only room for two people at a time to see through the slit. Chaleyer explained to each officer in turn what could be seen from the slit and the others stood back.

While Edwin was having his turn at the slit Freddy and James fell into conversation.

"They seem to have a very good set up here, don't they, James?"

"Yes, all very well organised, and the ground must be better drained here than Flanders, or the trenches would be full of water. If we are still here in the winter we will be much better off than the last position."

"That Duclaux is a strange sort, I got the impression that he was not happy to see us. I wonder what was eating him?" said Freddy.

"Not all the French are happy about having to rely on their old enemy. Maybe his family have a history with the English." replied James, "In any case he will be out of our hair in a couple of days and we will be on our own, so we just have to get on and learn the ropes as best we can."

When it came to Freddy's turn at the slit he listened carefully to what Chaleyer had to say and correlated everything he could see to his map.

"Over there, do you see a bushy topped tree and a ruined farm house, that is Touvent Farm. We had a big fight there with the Germans a few months ago and we took it from them to straighten the line. They were not happy, but have accepted the situation now." explained Chaleyer.

"Do the Germans cause you much trouble?" asked Freddy.

"No, not really, we have a 'let sleeping dogs lie' attitude to each other, they do not fire at us much, and we don't fire at them. There are Bavarians over there at the moment and they are a peaceful lot. Last year we had some Prussians, and they were always trying to start a fight, and came raiding and so on, but the Bavarians are all right if you leave them alone." said Armand.

"The position here seems well developed and very safe." said Freddy.

"Yes," replied Chaleyer, "we have been able to do a lot of improvements here, especially as the Germans are so quiet, but, if things change we will be ready. One thing that has helped is that their guns always seem to fire short. I am not sure why, but they do occasionally try to hit the village, especially if we make a lot of dust during the day, but the shells always land in the fields over there. We are not sure if they do it deliberately or if there is something wrong with their guns, but we are very happy with the situation. All the communication trenches to the infantry trenches are in tunnels so moving to and from the first line is quite safe, and all the infantry have bunkers like this to shelter in. I will take you down there when we have finished here. Any more questions?"

"No, thank you very much, Armand." said Freddy, then, "Actually I do have a question, why is your captain so…., so uncooperative?"

"Ah, it is just his way. He is the same with all of us, nothing is ever good enough for him. But he is a good officer. You know, his wife and children were in Belgium during the invasion and he has had no news of them since. He is very worried about them, of course, and will do anything to shorten the war. He gets frustrated that our colonel is not aggressive and is happy to leave the Boche in peace. If Marc had his way we would be at their throats every day!"

"Mm, I see, thank you."

"I am lucky, my wife is English and stayed in London when I was called up. I know that she will be safe there, not everyone has that same luxury, even here in France. We will be handing over to your Brigade tonight and I will be staying with you for another two days just in case you need any help or advice. Maybe we can have a drink together later?"

"Yes, I would like that, Armand, let's wait until the handover is finished and I will get some English beer or whisky, what do you prefer?" said Freddy.

"Whisky, please. We have pinard on the position here and I will show you where we store it. The poilus like it but it is not to my taste. I will make sure we leave it behind for you and your men to enjoy."

"Pinard? What is that?"

"Ah, you have not yet met pinard! You have not lived! Pinard is the wine that we issue with our rations in the French Army, rough as hell, but it keeps the men happy."

"We have rum for the same reason," said Freddy, "I do not like it myself, but the men enjoy getting it. It keeps them warm at night and it is supposed to give them courage and fortitude when they need it."

"Maybe we will try some of both and come to a conclusion, Freddy."

Freddy stepped down and Kit took his place.

Later the group retraced their steps all the way back to the morning's RV after visiting the infantry positions. Buster sent the officers back to their sections and went off to consult with Colonel Howard.

On his return Buster gave his orders. The battery would take over the positions occupied by the French battery of '75s'.

The French had six guns per battery, whereas the British only used four guns. The arrangements were that the French would withdraw one gun per section to be replaced by an English gun which would be laid on the SOS target and readied to fire if the Germans interfered with the handover. Then the French would withdraw their other guns and another English gun would take position, which would leave an empty position in each section.

BSM Evans and James Newman would supervise the occupation of the gun lines while Buster would be at the forward OP where he would call down the SOS if required. He was also keen to impress the French with the efficiency of his battery, or at least not to let down the infantry as they would be taking over at the same time.

At last light columns of men, guns and wagons emerged from the surrounding countryside and made their various ways into position. All went well with no interference from the Bavarians opposite. As a parting gesture Duclaux had instructed his gunners to retain 40 rounds per gun on their positions, and at his order, at one thirty in the morning the French gunners fired off these remaining ammunition stocks into the German front line.

Up to now the battery had been allowed only a few rounds per gun each day, and on most days they had not fired at all.

The English gunners had never before seen such a display as put on by the French gunners.

As per the plan, and despite their amazement at the amount and speed of firing of their French comrades, the Englishmen were in position to schedule and laid on the SOS targets as required. When the Germans retaliated to the French fire the position only held English gunners, the Frenchmen having made a rapid 'out of action' manoeuvre and were away.

As predicted by Armand Chaleyer, the German shells landed well short of any suitable target and no harm was done.

The newly arrived gunners were on their mettle, but no ground assault was attempted by the Germans, and at an hour after dawn they were stood down and BQMS Mason arrived with a hearty breakfast for the men.

The battery was now deployed and ready for anything in their new position on the Somme front.

Five days after occupying the position, General Trubshawe ordered that a trench raid be carried out. A company of the Norfolks under Major Hubert Watson were ordered to cross no-man's land, examine the German defences, especially the barbed wire, and if possible capture at least one prisoner.

The guns were at stand to in order to cover this operation, their role being to bring shell fire down on the German trenches as the raiding party withdrew. In the event the raid went well, no casualties were experienced, and two Germans were found in the trench, captured and returned with the raiders to spend the rest of the war in captivity. The German trenches were found to be only lightly manned, and the wire defences easily overcome.

As the raiding party withdrew the guns fired their SOS mission, firing five rounds of shrapnel each, a large amount for British guns at that time.

The men and officers of the battery now felt that their new guns had been adequately 'blooded' and that the division had passed its first real test.

Sergeant Leman had somehow come across three sheep, and requested permission to keep them at the gun line. The battery was occasionally host to a lone German reconnaissance aeroplane, and Leman reasoned that a few sheep in their field would help disguise the fact that it was occupied by the battery. Whether this would have fooled the Germans was never established, but he was allowed the keeping of the sheep. When Colonel Howard saw them on one of his rare visits to

127

the gun line he was not best pleased, saying that he was commanding a brigade, not a menagerie. He relented when told by Kit that the sheep would be useful to augment the rations which could become monotonous at times.

Time passed and the summer eased into autumn. The arrival of British troops opposite them rather upset the Bavarians. While they had become used to the 'live and let live' situation with the French, they found the British to be more aggressive and upsetting.

British trench raids spawned retaliatory German trench raids, to the point where every night at some point on the divisional frontage action of some kind took place. Often Trubshawe himself was present. He wanted to experience for himself the conditions on the ground and the state of training of the men.

While the officers on the spot tended to find Trubshawe's presence somewhat intimidating, the men generally appreciated it and took steps to look after 'the old bastard' as he become known, affectionately.

The ammunition supply situation did not improve, somewhat limiting the ability of the gunners to effectively support the infantry in their exploits. A high proportion of shells failed to explode, either due to faulty fuses or poor explosives. The main shell supplied was the shrapnel shell. This shell was designed to explode in the air and shower hundreds of spherical lead bullets at the enemy. While this type of ammunition had been designed during the days when armies faced each other in massed ranks and above ground, it was not very effective against troops dug into trenches and protected by many feet of soil.

The Brigade were notified that a training course was to be held in the city of Arras, some ten miles to the north, and they were to nominate one officer from each battery to attend. The course was to train these officers in a new accounting procedure. The Army had obviously decided that rather than provide more shells of a higher quality and efficacy it would be better to improve the way they accounted for the miserably small quantity of shells that they could supply. Such is the military mind.

Chapter 12

September 1915, Somme Region, France.

It was a sultry afternoon as 2nd Lieutenants Frederick Scott and Matthew Holt rode towards Arras past seemingly endless convoys of wagons and supply dumps. They were behind the gun line now, so even their own guns were just a gentle and occasional bark in the middle distance. In earlier times it could just as well have been two young bloods out for a ride with a summer thunderstorm in the far distance. As they rode there were high energy exchanges and laughter between them with easy silences in between.

"What do you think the food will be like in Arras?" said Matthew, "I need a good feed after our BQMS's grub. We really do need to find a better cook for my battery. I think the one we have used to work in a knacker's yard boiling up tallow, at least that is what the food usually tastes like. How about yours?"

"Oh, not so bad really. Most of our lads come from King's Lynn, so we have a good sprinkling of all the skills we need. The BQMS used to work in the Duke's Head hotel as maitre d'hotel and he knows the best ways to get things organised for us. Our mess servant worked in a restaurant as well and knows how to keep good food coming, he has never let us down. Our chief difficulty is that most of the drivers are used to town horses and not country draft horses. They are learning, though, but living outside with the beasts is a bit new for them. They are used to looking after their charges in proper stables and find it hard to work out in the open. Still, the weather is good at the moment. As for Arras, I understand that their speciality is a thing called andouillette, made up of cow guts. I rather think it sounds better than it will taste. We will have to see, we can always have an omelette as an alternative. I am more interested in the wine, they do not make any stuff locally, so we will have to see what is on offer."

A few minutes silence as the road continued in front of them. The soft clop clop of the hooves on the dusty dirt road, a gentle swish as a zephyr disturbed the long grass of the verge.

They reached a crossroads with a trough, and a calvary. Matthew reined in his charger and dismounted, "Lets give the nags a slosh and rest for a few minutes."

"Yes, good idea."

They led the horses to the trough and the beasts eagerly dipped their heads and drank their fill, nuzzling each other from time to time, as if in play and grateful for a break from the journey. The horses stepped a few paces and seemed to be happy to drop their heads and munch a few mouthfuls of the dry and browned grass.

Freddy and Matthew lay down near each other on the bank just above the trough. "How are things with your men, Freddy? Ours are getting a little fed up, 'tis the truth. Not much goes on most days, we only have a few rounds each day. The adjutant gets upset if we fire any of them. Anyway, he says it complicates his life trying to keep track of how many we have. I think he would be much happier if the war just stopped and we went home and he could close down his accounts. He is a bit stiff and not really military at all. I think the colonel gives him a lot of gip, actually."

"Yes, our lads get a bit bored from time to time," Freddy said without opening his eyes under his cap, which he had pulled down over his face to keep the sun off, "but our sergeant major really knows his stuff. He gets them to play football, or thinks up other competitions to keep up spirits. When we do get a fire task the gun subs really do go at it to be the first to report ready, and if they get to fire more than one round at a time they compete to see who can report 'rounds complete' first. Actually the BSM has a real sense of humour, which luckily our BC, Buster Webb, shares in the same spirit. The BSM is a keen man on playing snooker, which he played when he was out in India with the army. B Sub is called snooker sub because he has managed to get it crewed up with soldiers with colours as surnames. It's quite funny, but the men seem to see the joke and play up to it."

"Yes, I think I would rather be with your battery than mine. Buster seems a great character to work for. Did your firm have any business with him before the war?" Matthew asked.

"Yes, quite a lot. We used to export a lot of his stuff for him. He was trying to sell more in Germany, but I suppose that will have to start from scratch again after this war comes to a conclusion."

Another warm, humid, silent interval. Then Matthew enquired, "How are your brothers? Isn't George with the Norfolks? Why did he join the Infantry, he has to march rather than ride?"

Freddy thought a while, then responded, "George never told me that, I think it is because Papa used to be with the Norfolks, Edwin has more sense and is at our Brigade HQ, all he has to do is stand watch and make the colonel his coffee in the morning!"

"That does not sound like Edwin, I imagine that he tends to share his opinion with the colonel a little too often?"

"Yes, he does get a little fed up at times, and keeps saying that he wants to get back to the battery, but at the moment there is no room for him. The colonel values his presence despite his strong opinions. In any case, as there is not much doing at the battery currently he would not have any more to do if he did come back. I think he knows that he is better off where he is, and he gets more time to be out and about on his own running errands for the colonel."

Another pause while they dozed. The sun was lower now, and just starting to lose its force. Matthew heard the rattle of approaching wagons, and lifted his torso and leant on his elbow to watch the column as it threw up dust. He looked, without much interest, as the wagons passed by. The drivers, horses, and wagons were all the same colour from the chalky dust that rose from the track. When the tail of the column had passed, he stood, prodded Freddy with his foot, and said, "Come on lazy bones, there is adventure to be had. The ladies and restaurants of Arras await us!"

Freddy lifted the peak of his cap, looked around, sat up, rubbed his eyes, then stood and walked with Matthew the few paces to the horses. They mounted, turned the horses' heads up the track, and started to trot towards the city.

They were travelling parallel to the front and the occasional explosion far away to their right did not intrude into their thoughts. On approaching the outskirts of Arras they came across more and more military camps and dumps. A provost post on the approach to the centre required them to show their passes, and gave them directions to the HQ. They soon found themselves in among all sorts of people moving hither and thither, British military, French soldiers, and civilians all going about their business in a deliberate yet steady manner. They found the reporting office, signed in, and were then free to roam the city until the next morning. They left the horses at lines in the Grand Place after making sure they were fed and watered, then wandered off to find some diversion for themselves.

"Have you ever been here before, Freddy?"

"No, but I think all French towns are more or less organised on the same pattern. It will be easy to find somewhere to eat." Freddy said, convincing Matthew to let him lead the way.

They found themselves in La Petite Place, selected a likely looking restaurant, and went in. They feasted on oysters followed by andouillettes which were both cheap and seemingly the speciality as Freddy had thought. The restaurant was full of

133

British officers, and they sat and chatted between courses and after they had eaten their fill they continued chatting until the late hours.

Freddy found Matthew an easy companion. True, he had spent more time with Matthew's cousin, Dobbin, who was in the same form as Freddy at Fishers School, but they had much in common. Their families were close, the Holts and the Scotts had business links over several generations, and the boys had often played together during the holidays.

Freddy had enlisted just before the war having left school, while Matthew was a year younger and had left the OTC and enlisted as soon as war had broken out and had come out to the division earlier that spring.

"How are your parents going on, Matthew?" Freddy asked at one point.

"Fine, a little worried by having so many of us away at once, but more for the state of the business, I think. Papa has to find ways to replace the business we have lost, and I think if things do not get better soon he will have a nervous fit! Still, Mamma is a calming influence on him, nothing seems to perturb her."

"Yes, I think my parents are in a similar position, with George, Edwin and me all away. At least Sissie is still at home, but I rather think that she will eventually want to find a way to escape as well."

"Yes, I think so too, a lot of the girls at home seem keen to improve their lot by getting involved in war work. The suffragettes have been quick to see the advantage in men being away at war and filling their places. Papa has told me that they have their first woman drivers at the warehouse, though he is not too keen on it. Handling draft horses is man's work, though he says they are keen enough." Matthew said, lowering his voice in a conspiratorial manner, as if this news might have security implications, "How about your firm?"

"I get regular letters from Mamma, but Papa rarely writes to me. Mamma is more interested in letting me know about the garden and so on, but I suppose that girls will be getting involved. Actually, I am quite in favour of it. Sissie is a bit of a tomboy, as you know, and I think getting out of the house and doing something more physical will be to her taste. I rather think she will end up driving a motor bus or an ambulance. She liked spending time in Papa's car and even learning how to oil the engine and change tyres. Even now I am sure she is driving it around when she can. If ever I had to go on a journey by motor then I would definitely like to have Sissie with me!" Freddy stated.

"Doesn't Sissie have a friend that she is always thick with? What's her name?" Matthew looked down at the table as if searching his memory, "Connie, yes, is that her name?"

"Constance Mann, yes, or Connie, as we call her. Yes, a fine girl, more lady like than Sissie, much admired by my brother Edwin, I think he is quite sweet on her." Freddy replied.

"Why do you call your sister by that name?"

"Sissie's name is actually Sarah, but when she was born, after George, he called her Sissie and it stuck and we all call her that now. Sissie and Connie have been friends since they met at school, and with three brothers Sissie needs some female company I think to remind her what a lady should be like!" Freddy explained.

At the mention of Constance Freddy felt a warmth in his cheeks - maybe the wine, or the weather, he was not sure, but he felt embarrassment for no apparent reason that he was aware.

"So, we ought to get off to bed to be ready for the brainwork tomorrow," said Freddy, "we need to be sharp as pins to deal with what they have to tell us."

With a nodded agreement Matthew and Freddy stood, paid the patron and sought out their billet.

The next day progressed as they expected. A portly staff captain lambasting them for poor accounting, followed by a chief clerk explaining how to keep account of ammunition stocks and expenditure and the importance of accuracy. For two young men this was as welcome as a bout of influenza, but they stuck it out as best they could and completed the 'worked examples' without earning undue attention from their tutors. They were dismissed in the middle afternoon, and, not having to report back to their units until the next noon, they decided to make an evening of it.

First stop was a grocery store. Freddy had been asked by Corporal Ely to pick up some delicacies for the mess, some pickled walnuts, some oysters, some eggs, and a few other comestibles. Matthew tagged along with no particular aim in mind. Freddy arranged to pick up his purchases early the next morning so that the oysters would still be fresh by the time he reached the battery.

They returned to the same restaurant in the early evening and a similar crowd filled the tables. Some of the other officers on their course came along and they put some tables together so that the could all be seated together. They finished eating around nine and then continued drinking for an hour or so. As is traditional in the British Army it was considered bad form to discuss military issues at dinner, as well as a possible security problem. In any case, as young men with money and opportunity, as they drank the noise level rose and the conversation gradually became more boisterous.

Being in a large city, with civilian distractions and an almost peace time atmosphere, and with money to spare and little parental guidance, they were inclined to liven things up.

As eleven o'clock came and went the group began to thin out as those with further to travel on the morrow went off to get some sleep. By midnight, only Freddy, Matthew, and an artilleryman from a Scottish brigade, William, were left at the table.

"Well, I think that it is our turn to vacate the pub and be ready for the morning, do you agree?" Freddy said, in slightly slurred but understandable way, to no-one in particular, more as if expressing an internal thought.

William was sprawled across two chairs with his feet on one and his back at an angle on the other. "You English always finish too early, you have no stomach for grog, lets stay until the morning!"

"Well, young William," Freddy stated, though he was in reality about the same age, "you may be right, but you may be wrong. From your accent you are as English as I am, but I am not about to get into an argument with you, my good friend. I know when I have had enough. I bid you goodnight, and fare thee well on the morrow. May all your difficulties be small, and the adjutant never find you out!"

Matthew smiled at his friend and passed him his hat, which somehow had ended up on the floor. "You're right, Freddy, let's go and let William see in the dawn on his todd." William waved a hand towards the door, and raised no further comment.

As the two of them left the restaurant they entered a sudden darkness. They paused outside the door, just off the kerb, and stood for a moment or two to adjust their eyes to the faint light from the stars. All seemed very quiet, then just diagonally across the square they could see two people standing face to face, clearly having an altercation, about thirty yards away. One was taller than the other, and seemed to be more animated than the shorter figure.

Suddenly the taller of the pair grabbed the other and his voice grew in volume.

"Some things never change," said Matthew, "I imagine they have both had a little more to drink than they can handle, best to keep out of their way, I think."

Just then, they heard, and dimly saw, the taller figure strike the short one with a fist, knocking them to the ground. He then stood over the victim shouting and started to pull at their clothing.

Freddy said to Matthew, "If the provost sees that they will both be in trouble, we need to go over and calm things down." With that, he strode confidently across the square, saying as he neared the pair, "Come on, enough is enough, you will be getting into strife if you carry on."

The standing, ranting, man seemed not to hear Freddy and continued to shout at the now cowering figure on the ground. As he got closer Freddy saw that the recumbent figure was a woman, and the man standing over her was a soldier. He pushed the soldier away and put himself between them. The soldier staggered but kept his feet, a look of surprise on his face, and was suddenly less animated.

Matthew said in his firmest tone, "What is going on here?"

The soldier just looked at the two officers as if unsure what to do next. These clearly were two officers, striking one or both of them would lead to serious consequences if the provosts got involved, but his innate urge was to react aggressively. A bare few seconds passed while the three men each processed their thoughts differently, Freddy wondering what would happen if the soldier became violent towards him, Matthew wondering if he should say or do anything further, and the soldier weighing up his best course of action.

Matthew broke the spell, "Be off with you, and report to your officer tomorrow morning!"

The soldier responding to the words of command turned and went, disappearing round the corner and away up a side street. Freddy bent and offered his hand to the woman. He was surprised how light she felt as he helped her to stand. "Are you all right?" he said, not realising that being French, she would not understand.

"Merci, monsieur," she said "vous êtes très gentil. Je suis désolé."

Freddy recognised his error and said in his basic French, "Vous etes bienvenu. C'est mon plaisir."

The woman, in reality a girl of perhaps fifteen or sixteen, seemed to be surprisingly composed considering the event she had been through, "Je vais rentrer à la maison maintenant, s'il vous plait."

Matthew said, "We ought to go with her, didn't we? To make sure she gets home in one piece'"

Freddy agreed and said, "S'il vous plaît nous permettent de vous accompagner à votre domicile, mademoiselle."

She looked at both of them warily, as if not sure if it would be right to let them walk with her. Seeming to make her mind up, after a few moments she turned and immediately started walking. Freddy and Matthew fell into step with her and in a few minutes they reached her house in a side street. She knocked, and the door opened after a short pause. An older woman appeared and the girl quickly disappeared inside, the door closed, and the two men were left in the darkness of the street.

They retraced their steps into the square again, gained their bearings and headed off to their billet, passing the restaurant where William was still drinking.

The next morning they were up at dawn and on their way after a hearty breakfast, remembering to collect their victuals from the shops. They rode together in the early morning, the mist lifting as they left the city outskirts. At Sailly au Bois they parted, Freddy to ride on to Collincamps, and Matthew to Bertrancourt where his brigade was stationed.

As Freddy came towards the village he heard the bark of the guns about a mile away, at the end of the avenue of trees that extended south eastwards from the edge of the village. He stopped off at the wagon line just short of the village, dropped off the food that he had bought in Arras with the mess orderly, "We will have the oysters this evening, if you will, Corporal Ely, and I bought some small sausages for tomorrow, keep them safe, will you?"

Corporal Ely was an older man than most, having enlisted in the Territorials after returning from the Boer War. He had been a regular soldier and wanted to keep the fellowship that he had found in the army. He took great pride in running an efficient and caring mess for his officers. He was not a big man, maybe only nine stone in weight, short at five five, and now, in his late thirties was starting to lose his hair, though he tried to hide this by combing over his remaining sandy hair, which, in truth, was greying a little.

Ely had left the army and gone into business with his brother running a public house outside the railway station. They had developed a successful business catering for business travellers returning from London, reasoning that those who could afford to travel would want and be prepared to pay for, a better class of food and drink. He was proud of his achievements, especially that he had left school at thirteen to join the army and had no formal training. He was a resourceful man, hard working, and regarded his work looking after his officers as a vital military task. He reasoned that if his officers could eat well, drink well, and be well rested, they would be better able to do their jobs. His officers regarded him as a little fussy, but also a cross between a caring mother and a guiding father.

"I certainly will do that, sir." Ely replied to Freddy, "How was your journey?"

"Very quiet, thank you, and Arras was a pleasant surprise. Surprisingly peaceful considering how close the Boche are to the city. I am going to report back to the adjutant and should be back for dinner as usual tonight. Are the other officers eating together this evening?"

"Yes sir, we have a full house tonight."

Freddy rode over to the Brigade HQ just at the edge of Hebuterne, went inside the house and reported in to the adjutant. "How was the course, young Freddy!" said Kit, "Are we able to get a better set of accounts from First Battery now."

Freddy replied, "I hope so, but I will need to take Buster and James through the new system and see what they think."

"Righto, they will be back soon, let me know if I can help in any way, won't you?"

Freddy hung around for a while until Buster had returned, then introduced him to the new system. Buster asked a few questions and assured Freddy that they would change to match the new methods.

Freddy then went back to the wagon lines at Sailly where the mess was established, a couple of miles behind Hebuterne and out of immediate danger, though still within range of the heavier German guns.

During the night Freddy felt unwell, then was sick. Ely heard this and came to see what he could do to help. He asked what Freddy had had to eat while he was away, and after Freddy told him about the oysters and the andouillettes Ely nodded knowingly. "It's that peasant food they gave you, to be sure. I would never advise anyone to eat oysters at this time of year and this far from the sea."

Ely went and roused the doctor, who came and examined Freddy. Robert instructed Ely to make up some whisky in sheep's milk and give that to Freddy.

While Freddy was downing the beverage, Ely stayed with him, and the two men chatted.

"Thank you, Corporal Ely, I think that will stay down, at least for a while."

"Perhaps you will be more careful in future, sir, the French do not know much about hygiene, you know, you should be careful when eating with them."

"Yes, maybe you are right. Your family came from somewhere over here didn't they?"

"My grandfather was Italian, from Padua. He had to leave during the Risorgimento back in the 1860s. The Austrians were after him and he had to escape. Actually he told me that our family were originally from Austria and that we were not really Italian at all. My grandfather said that life in England was better than going back to Padua, so he just stayed, married my grandmother who was a local girl, and set up in business as a greengrocer."

"But weren't you in the Regular Army?"

"I wanted a more exciting life than King's Lyn could offer, and not go into my father's business, so I joined up as a boy and served twenty years. When I left, my brother wanted to start a restaurant so I joined him, but I enjoyed the soldiers' life so much I enlisted in the Territorial Force. At my age the best thing they can do with me is to run the officers' mess, especially with my catering knowledge. I have had my time at the front being shot at and living rough. I am happy doing what I do, keeping young men like you fed and looked after."

"I think you do an excellent job, Corporal Ely," said Freddy, "Have you ever been to Padua to visit family?"

"No, never had the chance, and to be honest I see no need. England is my home and has been good to me and my family."

"Are you married, any children?"

"Not married, and no children, as far as I know!" joked Ely, "Never had the time, and it is probably too late now. At least there is no one to grieve for me if I die, my brother might be upset for a while, but my parents have gone, and besides work I have no other responsibility."

"Are you worried about dying?"

"No, not really," said Ely, "I have made my arrangements and if it happens, then it happens."

"Well, I am a little worried about it. You know, I have never been with a woman, not even kissed one. I do not want to die without knowing what having a wife is like."

"I have known a few women in my time, but none of them would have been right for me. My father told me that when I met the right woman I would know, somehow, but I never had that feeling or knowledge. You know, many men live very happily without the company of women, like priests, so I would not worry too much, sir. When the right girl shows up just be ready to know it."

"I feel a lot better now, that milk has settled my stomach. I think I will try to get some sleep now. Goodnight, Corporal Ely, and thank you."

"Good, goodnight sir." Ely replied and left the room.

The next morning Freddy was back to his normal self, and rose early. His duty that day was to take a wagon forward to the gun line with ammunition and other supplies. Once the wagon was loaded and the drivers ready, Freddy mounted his charger and they set off. It was another fine September day, and the late summer heat encouraged a leisurely ride. Freddy mulled over the events of the previous days, deciding to avoid seafood except when he could be assured it was fresh, and despite his distaste for hard drink he was sure that Benefer's concoction had been effective. He also thought about what Ely had told him. Being chased out of your home and having to set up a new life in another country would be a great challenge, where, how would you start? He thought back to his home life. The Scotts had been at Saddlebow for generations, and the lanes and fields that he had explored as a boy had been the same for his father, grandfather, and how many generations, exactly? Papa had never said, but he suspected that they probably went back at least three hundred years. How many generations would that be? Papa was thirty when George was born, so say each generation was thirty years on average, then there were probably ten generations of the Scotts born, and died, in Saddlebow.

Brother George showed no signs of marrying, neither did Edwin, and he, Freddy, at twenty, was too young to be thinking or worrying about finding a wife. Though, he had to admit, he had started to worry about it. Walter Mann dying like that, at a similar age to Freddy concerned him. While he believed, in fact was absolutely certain, that he himself would not be killed, Walter getting shot made him start to lose that certainty.

And that girl in the barn, Roselyn, another person dispossessed of her home. Seeing her naked like that, the first woman that he had ever seen without her clothes, roused unfamiliar emotions in him. Guilt, curiosity, desire? He had seen plenty of men without clothes, at school, in the army, at the public baths, and felt no emotion at seeing them. But, Roselyn had sparked something in him. She was naked and vulnerable, but defiant and assertive at the same time. His assumption, if there had been one, was that a woman surprised and naked, in the presence of several strange men, would be coy and ashamed. In fact the girls that he knew were reserved. But Roselyn was not, and he found that fact surprising and stimulating at the same time.

They arrived at the gun line. The drivers and gun teams started unloading the boxes of shells and bags of supplies, including post and another delivery of comforts from the Lynn Ladies.

Buster was at the gun line and saw Freddy, and came over. "Feeling better now young Freddy?"

"Yes, much better, thank you, sir, right as rain." replied Freddy with a smile.

"I am glad I caught you. It seems a casualty clearing station has moved into the division rear and surprise surprise, Florence Mann has been sent out as an attendant. She sent me a message asking me to let you know she was there and that she would like you to visit, when convenient."

"She is certainly a game old bird," said Freddy, "it can't be easy for a lady of her age living in the field. I wonder why she wants to see me."

"I think they have the nurses set up in a school so it won't be too rough for her. I assume she wants to know more about Walter."

"I could go over tomorrow afternoon, sir, if that would be all right with you. I have another supply run to do tomorrow morning, but should be free after that."

"Yes, all right, let me know for certain when you leave. She wants to see James Newman as well, you could go over together, perhaps. She probably has some news for James from her brother."

The next day, after his duties were complete Freddy went over to the casualty clearing station. James Newman was on duty at the forward OP, so Freddy went alone.

The casualty clearing station, in army terms a CCS, was well signposted and Freddy found it without problem. He reported to the guard post saying that he had come with information for Miss Florence Mann of the nursing staff.

After a delay of a quarter hour Freddy saw Florence approach in her uniform. "Thank you for coming, Freddy," said Florence with a warm smile, "I hope that you are not missing important duties?"

"No, Buster has given me the afternoon off, Miss Florence. Is there anything particular that I can help you with?"

"There is a cafe in the village, let us walk down there and we can talk." said Florence, taking Freddy's arm and moving in the direction towards the village.

As they walked the quarter mile they exchanged pleasantries, asking after each other's families and how things were at home, and on the front. Florence also told Freddy that Constance wanted to know how the Scott boys were doing and that she would write to Constance and tell her that they were all well.

In the cafe they sat at a table.

"My brother has asked me to thank you in person for writing to him after poor Walter's death. He is sorry for not writing to you himself, but I fear that he finds it too distressing to think about. In a way it has changed him. I think that he had always assumed that Walter would one day take over from him, and now that future has gone. Constance is too young, but I rather think that it would be impossible for her to run the business. In any case she has no real desire to do so. As I have no children, there is no-one in the family to take it all on. It is very distressing, for all of us, going from one certainty to another."

Freddy listened politely, Florence had always been a severe figure to him, and he was not used to talking to her in such a personal and open way.

"I felt that it was the right thing to do, write and tell you about Walter, as I was with him at the time. If the circumstances had been reversed I am sure he would have written to my father and mother."

A thought came into Freddy's mind and immediately onto his lips, "Maybe Constance will marry a suitable man, someone who could join the business?"

"Yes, that is possible, I suppose," said Florence, "but she has no beau yet and she is still very young. If she were to marry then that may make things clearer for my brother. All the eligible young men are in uniform now, and any marriage plans will have to wait until the war is over. Walter's death has made us all realise how fragile things are."

"I think we are all feeling a little vulnerable at the moment."

"In your letter you said that Walter died quickly and was not in pain. Is that true? I have heard that some wounds can be very painful and men take a long time to succumb."

"Miss Florence, I can assure you that Walter did not suffer unduly. Please be assured of that, it was all so very quick, and unexpected."

As they walked back to the CCS Florence thanked Freddy for coming over, and said that he should come over whenever he was free. She also asked Freddy to ask James Newman to visit her, saying that she had some things for him from her brother that he wanted James to give his opinion on, probably about the contract the works had to assemble French aeroplanes.

They parted and Freddy returned to the wagon line.

December 1915.

Kit Chilvers sat in the room that served as an office for the brigade, in a partially ruined house in the village, with BSM Barry Evans.

"I am concerned for the men, sir, it is getting colder now and we have already had snow. The greatcoats that we have are not really suitable for the gun teams, they soak up the wet, and get in the way when we have to take post for firing. We also need more materials to improve the shelters for the men, those at the wagon line have barns to sleep in, but the gun teams have very poor protection from the wet. We have been ordered to build new gun pits nearer the trenches ready for the attack next week, and we don't have any revetting or materials for overhead cover. Can we put in for some better building materials and some warmer clothing, sir?" said Evans.

"I discussed this subject with Colonel Howard, and he says no, he says that we have to make the best of what we have. In any case, I understand that there is a general shortage of all sorts of things which the War Office is trying to change, but nothing much seems to be in prospect as yet." replied Kit.

Buster and James came in and joined in the conversation, "God, it's cold out there, and we can't even have a fire in case the Hun sees the smoke." said Buster.

"BSM Evans and I were just discussing the same subject, Buster. We have to do something to improve things for the men, but Colonel Howard is not supportive, maybe because he has a warm house to live in." said Kit.

Buster said, "I think we need to take the initiative. James here has found out that the Engineers have plenty of defence stores at a dump near Sailly, and just up the road from there is a cavalry division Ordnance store. They have those handy short greatcoats that the donkey wallopers wear. What we need is a way to break in to the stores, or something we could barter with. Any ideas?"

"In my opinion, sir, the best currency would be a plentiful supply of whisky, or brandy at the least." said Evans.

"James, can we get hold of a few cases of the hard stuff?" asked Buster.

"If you can get the whisky, sir, I can arrange an exchange, I think it would be better if this was dealt with on a warrant officer to warrant officer basis. We old sweats have ways of getting this sorted among ourselves." said Evans.

"Yes, Mister Evans, you are right, we will get the liquor and leave the rest to you, let me know what you will need in the way of transport to get the stuff back here and when." said Buster.

148

"Colonel Howard won't be happy if he finds out, Buster." said Kit.

"I am not going to tell him, and I am sure you won't either, will you, Kit?" said Buster, giving Kit a stare, then a smile and a wink, "I think forgiveness is easier to get than permission, in most cases."

With that the group dispersed. Two days later BSM Evans received his cases of whisky, by which time he had come to an arrangement with the warrant officers in the Engineers and Ordnance dumps, and in dead of night wagons returned to the battery with a fresh supply of materials for the gun pits, and enough British Warms for half the battery, and goatskin jerkins for the other half.

Freddy was given the responsibility for building the new gun pits just behind the village in preparation for the attack. The weather was clear, bright, and cool. He and his men had been working on the position for two days when a German aeroplane flew over the village, circled, and then flew off back towards the German trenches. A few shells from an anti aircraft battery in Sailly exploded in the sky, but nowhere near the German plane. When it had gone the men went back to work.

Later, there was a sudden bang, bang, bang as shells burst over the village and a shower of shrapnel bullets flew into the field where the work was taking place. Freddy felt the whizzzz as one of these bullets flew past him. He heard a shout from one of the pits, and ran over to see what was the cause. There, in the bottom, which was by now a mere three feet deep lay Bombardier Baldwin, on his back, moving his head from side to side, his face screwed up in pain. At first Freddy could not see any wound, then noticed blood seeping from the area around Baldwin's right side. Other men arrived and jumped down into the pit. One of them shouted, "Get him out of here!" while another shouted, "Don't move him!"

Freddy was momentarily stunned into inaction, his mouth moved, but no sound came. A man shook him by the shoulder, "Sir, sir, what do we do?" Freddy looked at him without seeming to hear him. All Freddy could hear was the sound of his own blood in his ears, and he started to tremble.

A sudden intake of breath, a shake of his head, and Freddy came to. "Get a stretcher!" he shouted at no one in particular. A man ran off to find the stretcher, which no one had thought to bring along on the work party as none had been needed before.

"We can use some hessian to carry him, sir," said Bombardier Reid who had arrived from across the field, "Brown, go and cut a length of hessian from the bundle in the next pit and bring it here. White, go and see if you can find a wagon in the village and bring it back here. Go!" With that Bombardier Reid jumped down into the pit and started to unbutton Baldwin's shirt, pull his braces off his shoulders, and expose Baldwin's abdomen. Freddy saw the exposed flesh, or what had been flesh and was now a raw red mass with blood welling up and running down over Baldwin's side. Reid tore off part of Baldwin's shirt and stuffed it into the hole in Baldwin's side and held it there. Freddy saw that the blood flow lessened a little. Baldwin had become pale and had stopped moving.

The hessian arrived and Bombardier Baldwin was lifted into it and brought out of the pit, carried across the field towards the road that passed by into the village. No wagon had arrived, so the men carried their burden along the road until they came to the infantry RAP where they handed Bombardier Baldwin over to the medics there.

Freddy and the men returned to the field and started working again, though their enthusiasm was diminished.

That evening Freddy was back at Brigade reporting to Kit on progress at the gun position. He dined in the brigade mess and met Gregory Fitzgerald. "I understand you were there when Bombardier Baldwin was injured," said Gregory, "How is he?"

"We took him to the Norfolks RAP," said Freddy, "he looked in a bad way, lost consciousness, and bleeding a lot."

"I will find out how he is tomorrow," said Gregory, "Kit may know the situation, and I am going to the CCS tomorrow to visit some of our sick, so I will see if Baldwin is there and see how he is. Are you all right yourself?"

"Yes, I'm fine," lied Freddy, "right as rain."

"Did you take my advice with the pipe?" asked Gregory, "It will help, you know."

"Not yet," replied Freddy, "well, I tried it once, but I did not like the taste, though I must admit that the smell is nice, but the smoking of it is not easy."

"Being a soldier at war is a dangerous thing, you know, Freddy, and we all need a way to help us deal with our worries. Smoking may not be for you, but it helps me."

"I think my main worry is about being killed before I have been able to marry and have children."

Gregory had filled his pipe and put it to his mouth, struck a match, put it to the bowl, drew breath, and sucked and sucked again to get the tobacco to flare. He looked at Freddy through the lenses of his spectacles for a few seconds, then said, "In a marriage there are two people to consider, at least initially, a man, and a wife. Getting married now could be seen as a selfish act. What would happen to your wife if you were killed? She would be a widow, and might have to bring up any children on her own. In war it can be better to stay unmarried."

Freddy nodded, taking in what Gregory had said, "You are probably right, and in my case there is no one for me to marry as yet. I have not met any girl that would make me a good wife." He smiled, as if this were an amusing statement.

"Or you would make a good husband for." said Gregory in reply. With some insight he then added, "It is usual for young men, in situations such as we find ourselves, to consider the pleasures of the flesh. While marriage was ordained that these desires are directed aright, there are other outlets for a man's natural inclinations, you know. I would advise you to seek out the company of one of the young women who offer these services in the towns and cities of France. Their young men are also at war, and facing the same perils as you, and have the same dilemma."

"Have you ever..?"

"That is for me to know, and God to judge!" said Gregory, "We each must make our own decisions, it is for your conscience to decide whether it is best, in the circumstances, to seek a permanent or temporary outlet for your desires."

Freddy, a little confused, and not entirely clear what Gregory was talking about, asked, "I am not very experienced with the ladies, I have never been alone with a girl, and am not sure what to do."

"Follow your instincts, they will be your guide." said Gregory, knocking out his pipe and standing. He put a hand on Freddy's shoulder, and said, "I think you are a good man, Freddy, better than most. Think things over and come to a conclusion. But do not think for too long. None of us know what lies in the future."

Freddy stood, as Gregory left him, then sat down again. His thoughts turned to Roselyn, he conjured up the vision of her naked body, smooth, rounded, and defiant. He recalled the look in her eyes and her manner. She was not cowed or submissive, she was alert and asserting her will. He found the images to be stirring, and was feeling the effects in his groin. He had not before given much thought to this warm fullness down below, no-one had ever explained its meaning or purpose to him. Could it be associated with thoughts of the fairer sex? And what was the meaning of Gregory's advice? Was he saying that Freddy should visit a brothel? He knew of these, of course, the men spoke of them and joked about them, but Freddy was not sure he really understood what they were for, and certainly did not want to risk embarrassment by admitting this ignorance to anyone.

In the absence of any conclusion he said goodnight to the other officers and went to bed.

The new gun position was completed and on the orders of General Trubshawe a major trench raid was planned on the Germans opposite. An entire battalion of the Norfolks was going over that night to enter the German trenches, gather what prisoners, maps, and any other booty they could find and then return across no-man's land to their own trenches. The task for the guns was to be ready to fire on the SOS target, to bring down fire into the German trenches and no-man's land once the raid was complete, to prevent the Germans from following the raiders back or counterattacking.

Freddy was to be in the forward OP during the raid, his task was to look out for the signal flares, and order the guns to fire the SOS if needed, and to take action on his own initiative if events needed him to.

All the preparations were complete, the guns had an extra issue of ten rounds per gun, twice the normal daily allowance. Telephone lines had been tested, checked, and the anticipated orders practised until everyone was satisfied that they knew what was expected of them, and what they would need to do in all circumstances.

The infantry who were going to make the raid had been in reserve for two days, rehearsing and preparing. As dusk fell they proceeded along the communication trenches into the first

153

line. Their colour sergeants brought round a good tot of rum, and they settled down for the final hour before they were scheduled to start the raid.

At one fifteen, in six different positions from the trenches, nine hundred men with blackened faces climbed their ladders, went over the parapet, and laid down on the ground in pre-arranged positions. Designated men went forward with wire cutters and cut lanes through the German wire.

At the OP Freddy looked through the slit out into the country ahead, but in reality he was not able to see anything in the gloom, but he felt that it was right for him to be alert and on the ball. This was especially so as General Trubshawe had joined him in the bunker, and was clearly excited and wanting to make sure everything went well.

At one forty, the first groups of infantry went through the gaps in the wire and rushed the German trenches. After five minutes they re-emerged, dragging with them prisoners, with some also carrying what German equipment and documents they had been able to find in the dark, including a complete machine gun with its tripod and ammunition boxes.

By 2 o'clock men were streaming back over into the British trenches, not a shot having been fired so far.

Freddy checked his watch, he should be getting the signal soon to fire the SOS, he told Hastings to check the line yet again. Trubshawe listened while he looked out of the slit.

The Norfolks CO gave the order to fire the SOS signal, green, red, green flares shot into the sky. Freddy saw them, and gave the order to fire guns at the German trenches now vacated by the British.

Back at the gun line the gunners had been at their posts from before midnight, and were cold and fed up, but as the order to fire came down to them, they went smoothly through their actions, and forty shells whizzed off towards the German lines.

At the post operation analysis General Trubshawe declared himself happy with the conduct and results of the night's raid, and planned to carry out more in future.

The British were not the only ones to realise the potential of the trench raid. The Germans had felt the need to respond to the change of foe opposite them, and after the first large trench raid decided to retaliate with one of their own.

At a little after three in the morning a few days after the British raid the troops in the British trenches to the south of Hebuterne became aware of noises and movement to their front, in no-man's land.

The company commander was alerted and he telephoned to his Brigade HQ. Three batteries of artillery were ordered to take post and ammunition was prepared. The guns were laid on targets in no-man's land and on the German trenches.

The infantry stood to, and prepared to receive a raid. James Newman was at the forward OP, and he had his signaller test the telephone line.

The Germans came on, and the British were ready for them. As the raiders emerged from the British barbed wire defences moving towards the trenches they were met by a fusillade of rifle fire. A few Germans did reach the British trenches, but were immediately shot, bayoneted, or captured. The German commander, realising that his attack had failed signalled the withdrawal, and his men started to return across the four hundred yards of no-man's land. The German guns opened up to cover the withdrawal, but due to an error of survey, or mapping, their shells landed short, among their own men.

James saw the German signal lights, knew what they meant, and sent his fire orders down the telephone. The British guns opened up and their shrapnel shells rained bullets into the retreating German survivors.

Finally all was quiet, with the exception of groans from the wounded, and occasional shouts of men out in front.

The next morning the German stretcher bearers were out in no-man's land seeking for and collecting their wounded and dead. Corporal Rippingill took it on himself to shoot at these angels of mercy until stopped by his platoon commander, Stephen Sansom.

The Germans were, from that moment on, allowed to collect their casualties without further hindrance.

General Trubshawe also declared the night's action to be a success, but decided that the British needed more notice of German raids, and ordered the construction of listening posts further out in front, to be reached by tunnels dug from the front line trenches out a hundred yards or so and to be camouflaged by day and occupied at last light until after stand to in the morning.

When the first of these had been completed, Trubshawe notified Major Watson, the company commander, that he would go out to the listening post on the first night, to satisfy himself of the practicality of the arrangements.

On the night the small group of men prepared themselves, waiting for the general to arrive before going down the tunnel and manning the listening post. The next morning they all returned after dawn stand to. General Trubshawe expressed himself happy with the arrangements, handed each of the men he had spent the night with a bar of chocolate, or a packet of cigarettes, according to their tastes, thanked them, then left the front line well satisfied.

Major Watson asked Stephen Sansom how he felt the night had gone. Stephen replied, "All was well, sir, it was a little intimidating to have a general along with us, but he was all right, actually. He did his share of the sentry duty, and did not get in the way at all."

Freddy had been at the forward OP during the night, with express instructions to stay alert and make sure that if the Germans tried to interfere with the listening post to make sure he fired the SOS in double quick time. As Buster said to him, "We cannot afford to lose a general!"

On the way back General Trubshawe visited the OP and talked to Freddy, with the intention of inspecting to see if the listening post was visible in daylight. He declared himself happy with the camouflage arrangements. Freddy suggested that a telephone line be laid between the listening post and the OP, so that any information gathered could be communicated back to the artillery brigade quickly. Trubshawe explained that there was already a line back to the company HQ.

Freddy was relieved mid morning by James Newman, and made his way back through the tunnels to the village with the intention of riding over to the gun line before getting a late breakfast at the wagon line where he was due to command the resupply run that afternoon.

As Freddy approached the gun line on his charger, his mind was drifting to thoughts of the previous night's activities and breakfast. The route to the gun line was well established and did not involve too many twists and turns to avoid observation from the German lines. What Freddy had not seen was that the Germans had brought an observation balloon into use a mile or so behind their line, and even now the observer was looking for suitable targets.

Freddy's horse walked along the familiar path, with Freddy not having to guide him. As they entered the end of the shallow valley leading to the gun line Freddy could almost taste the bacon that he knew Corporal Ely would have waiting for him.

Suddenly a shrapnel shell burst overhead, and Freddy heard the bullets swishing away to his right, into the field, followed by the slight noise of the gun firing some miles away. "Bloody Germans!" he thought, and unconsciously turned his horse to the left to get closer into the rise in the ground that might give him a little shelter.

Crack! Another shell exploded overhead.

Freddy urged his horse into a trot, thinking instinctively that he could put some distance between himself and the line of fire. There was no other target anywhere within a quarter mile of his position, so the Germans must be just firing randomly to give us a fright, he thought.

He was by now nearing the gun line and as he approached he could see no-one around. He assumed that they must have heard the German shells and decided to take cover in the gun pits.

He reached the horse line at the rear of the battery position, dismounted and secured his horse. He then walked towards the far side of the position where his section's guns were positioned. Just as he passed the first gun pit, another shell exploded, this time a little short of the position, sending its bullets flying across the field. Freddy felt a pressure wave as one of them passed by his head, and he saw several bullet strikes on the ground to his right. He broke into a run with the intention of seeking the safety of the nearest gun pit. As he reached this another shell exploded. More bullets flicked up the ground around him. He ran around the rear of the pit. He jumped down into it. He was a little breathless. His stomach was empty. He felt nauseous.

It was standard practise for every gun to be left loaded and laid on the SOS target, with a gunner in attendance at all times, and Freddy expected therefore to find at least one man in the pit with him. He looked around, and the pit was empty of crew, no-one to be seen.

He registered this as strange. He stayed in the pit for a few minutes, no further shells arrived. He decided to get to the next pit, and then on to his section. All was quiet, so he climbed back up the steps at the back of the pit and into the open. He started to walk to the adjoining pit, some twenty yards away.

Crack! Another shell, and more bullets sped him on his way. This time he dived into the pit head first, landing in a heap on the floor. He smelt the damp soil under the duckboards, and the familiarity of the odour calmed him. He could feel his heart racing. He was sweating despite the coolness of the day. Again there was no-one in the pit. He was alone. He sat on the gun layer's seat, and took deep breaths.

Had he missed something? He thought back to the orders group the previous evening, but going through his memory of the sequence of orders came up with nothing. "Why was the position unoccupied? Had something happened? Was he missing something? Should he go outside again, or stay where he was for a while?"

He noticed that he was shaking a little, and put this down to the exertion of running and getting into the gun pit. He felt the urge to laugh, but that did not make sense. He lifted himself up a little and looked out of the front of the pit, through the camouflage net. He could see no-one, just the usual grass and, in the distance a fence along the edge of the field.

Five minutes passed. No further shells. He decided that staying there made no sense, so he climbed up out of the pit and looked around him. Still no-one in sight.

He made a dash for the next gun pit in the line, and rushed down into it. He could feel his heart pumping and his legs were shaky. No shells exploded, all was quiet. No one in the pit, so, he left this one and ran to the last in the line, and descended a little more slowly than before. Again, an empty pit. "What on earth is going on here?" he thought. He went to the steps at the back of the pit and climbed far enough that he could see across the position.

At the far side he could see a group of men coming toward him. As they came closer he could see that it was the gun teams, and they were laughing and jostling each other. Sergeant Leman was in the lead. "You gave us a good laugh, sir, you were jumping and running like a hare in spring? I didn't know you were so nimble." said Leman.

At first Freddy felt angry and prepared to give the men a telling off, but realised this would only make things worse, so, he smiled sheepishly, and said, "Yes, I thought it would be a good chance to show you how to behave under fire! Did you pick up any hints?"

He could feel his spirits starting to rise with the presence of the men that he knew so well. Bombardier Reid came up to him and said, "We were worried for you, sir, we had to clear out just before you came along. The Boche have been sending a few rounds over now and then all morning, and Major Webb told us to clear off until it had stopped, especially as we have not had any calls for fire today. I am sorry, sir, if you are upset about us laughing at you, but I think most of us are glad you did not get hit."

"Thank you, Bombardier, it's all right, I just feel a little faint from not having had breakfast yet. I came down here to see if everything is in good order. Maybe I should have gone for some food first. Never mind."

Freddy spent a half hour inspecting the guns in his section, counted the ammunition, and left instructions for the work to be done for the rest of the day.

Later, in the mess Freddy was finishing a late breakfast. James Newman was there filling in some reports. James looked up from his papers and said to Freddy, "Have you heard, leave has started to come through. Married men will be first to go, so you and I will have to wait our turn, but at least it has started."

"I suppose it is right for men with families to take priority, but we could all do with some time back home. It will be nice to see my parents and sister, though, when the time comes."

They fell into silence for a few minutes while Freddy finished eating. He then went over to the table at which James was seated.

"James, have you ever thought about marriage?"

James looked up at Freddy, then smiled, "My father would like it if I did get married, but the opportunity never really presented itself. I think that I am getting a bit too old now, and in any case I am not sure that I could afford it. Why?"

"I don't know, really," said Freddy, "but I have had a few close shaves since we came out here, and if I were to be killed I think I would like to believe that there will be someone to grieve for me. I have really not seen much of life yet, and I don't want to die before experiencing what it is to be a man."

"You have a loving family, and I am sure they will grieve for you if you do get killed. My father would probably think it was my fault if I died." said James.

"I know they would, but it must be different if I had a wife, wouldn't it?"

"I have no idea, really, and am unlikely to be able to find out. My father has ideas for me which I do not think I will ever be able to realise."

"Have you ever found a woman that you wanted to marry, James?"

"Yes, one, but it is impossible, for all sorts of reasons. I am sure that I will die a bachelor, and that is it. You at least have a family business that you will probably go into when the war is over, and you will be a very eligible young man. You should have no problem finding a suitable girl to marry."

"I was thinking of now, not the future. You know I was there when Walter Mann was shot, and I have had a few narrow scrapes since then. What if the war does not end soon, and I die before it does."

"If you die then you will know nothing more, so it does not matter, really."

"I suppose so, but I am alive now, and want to do more. Do you believe in Heaven and the afterlife, James?"

"Not really, it's just a story, a fabrication, to make little children obey their parents, and behave."

"But you are a Christian?"

"Yes, a nominal one. My father was born a Jew, but converted when he came to England. I was brought up as a Christian, baptised and all that. Father thought it would make us fit in better, he wanted to put the past behind him, but in England your family background is important, it affects the way your life turns out."

"Well, Disraeli was a Jew who converted, and he did all right."

"Many fail, the one succeeds." quoted James.

"Tennyson?"

"Yes."

"Mm. James, have you ever, um…, been to a brothel? The padre has suggested that I should consider it, but I am not sure what it all means."

"Why do you ask?"

"It is silly, really, but that girl Roselyn, in the barn. You know, I had never seen a woman in the altogether, and I keep thinking about her, she keeps going through my mind, over and over."

"Ah, the vision of her naked body is what keeps going through your mind!"

"Well, I must admit it does, but not just that. I think she looked very, how do I say, striking. But the way she acted is what I keep thinking about. Somehow I always thought that girls were ashamed of their bodies, and would not dare be seen by men without their clothes. My sister being one, for instance. She has always dressed before leaving her bedroom and I am sure she would be devastated to be seen naked. But Roselyn had…., I am not sure, but she had a strength, really, in the circumstances, she put everything aside to try and protect that lad she was with. I want to find a girl like her."

"There is a lady who I would like to think of as a possible wife, but I know it will never happen. Her family would never consider me to be suitable. I have little money and no position in society, it is a futile hope." said James.

"Does she know?"

"I think so, but I can't be sure."

"Why not just tell her?"

"It's impossible, just impossible. If anyone knew then she would be destroyed."

"Well, when I find the one, I am going to tell her, make no mistake about it!"

"Just be careful, Freddy, act in haste, repent at leisure."

Buster came into the mess with Kit Chilvers and asked Corporal Ely to bring them coffee. "There you are, young Freddy Scott, I have good news for you. You are on the first draft for leave. Ten days, be ready to go on Thursday. You will be OC leave party, so make sure that the boys behave themselves and don't cause me to get bad reports from the transport people." said Kit, smiling.

"Goodness, I thought that married men would go first, Kit?"

"Yes, but we need an officer to take charge and everyone else is doing important things, you are the only subaltern that we can spare." said Kit, in jest, "Just enjoy your good luck and tell the people back home that we will be following soon."

"Thank you, I will."

Chapter 13

April 1916, Hebuterne, France.

By the time that Thursday came around Freddy had received many requests to take messages to family at home. James had also asked him to take some papers to Florence that he said were for her brother. James explained that the works had won more contracts for casting shells and William had sent the contracts for James to read through and comment on.

Freddy had to take the men on leave back by wagon to the divisional rendezvous point which was very close to the CCS. The party arrived early, with a half hour to spare before the omnibuses were due to leave for the railway station in Arras from where they would travel on to Boulogne.

Freddy went to the CCS and asked to speak to Florence. She was expecting him and soon came to meet him. They walked into the village together, as before.

"Here is the portfolio of documents from James Newman for your brother."

"Thank you, I will send them on to him. How are you, Freddy?"

"Bearing up," he replied, "and looking forward to being home for a few days. It will be good to see my parents again, and maybe I will look up a few old friends. I suppose many of them will be away at the front, but there should be enough of us to have some time together."

"Do you have a lady friend in King's Lynn?" asked Florence, "or over here in France?"

"No I don't." said Freddy, "I have not had time for that, too many things to do and Buster keeps us hard at it!"

"You should find one, then Freddy. I have seen many young men, just like you, come through the CCS. Some of them will not be going home, ever. It is sad to see so much potential being wasted. Find a girl, and make the best of things."

"I would not know how to find and persuade a young lady, persuade her to consider me, that is."

"Trust your instincts, Freddy. I am sure that by now you have seen many things that frighten you, or situations where you could have been wounded? What saved you was probably instinct, not a conscious thought, but reacting automatically, without thinking. Well, that will be the way to win a young lady's heart, act instinctively, when the time is right you will know what to do."

Freddy thought for a few moments, then said, "Am I to understand that you feel that you should have acted before, and now regret that?"

"Yes, precisely. When my sister-in-law died, when Constance was very young, I was interested in a young man. In due course we would probably have become engaged and married. But, my brother needed me more. He had Walter and Constance to consider, and I felt my duty was to them all. I have been very fulfilled bringing them up for William, but now my chance of happiness has passed. Do not make a mistake, Freddy, as I did. If the chance comes along, take it. It is better to have loved and lost, than never to have loved at all."

"Is it because of Walter?"

"Yes, partly, he was a fine boy, and I have seen many like him come through here. Such a waste, even those we put back together will not be the same."

As they reached the gate on their return, Florence asked Freddy to wait while she went to fetch some papers for her brother, apologising for forgetting to bring them with her before.

As they parted, Florence hugged Freddy, and kissed him on the forehead. "Bye Freddy, be good."

Freddy went off to round up his men, located the omnibus and they left on the long journey home.

At Folkestone a train was waiting to take them to London. On the next train from Liverpool Street to King's Lynn Freddy felt the effects of the journey and slipped into a slumber while the train rattled and swayed along.

Arriving at King's Lynn Freddy dismissed the soldiers, wishing them well and telling them the date and time to be back for the return journey. They dispersed to the corners of the town and beyond.

Freddy was preparing to find a cab for himself to take him out to Saddlebow when he heard the horn of a car which drew up alongside him. To his surprise Sissie was in the driving seat, smiling broadly. She was wearing goggles and a topcoat, her hair loose.

"Jump in, Freddy!" she laughed.

Freddy opened the passenger door and put his valise on the rear seat, and took the other front seat. Sissie set the car in gear and opened the throttle, blowing the horn again as she turned the car out of the station and onto the road.

She steered the car around and between the horse drawn vehicles, and within five minutes they were roaring down London Road and out of town. Freddy was pleased to recognise the familiar route out to Saddlebow, and felt relaxed and at home, as he, indeed, was.

"So Papa has trusted you with the car, Sissie?"

"Yes, he showed me how to drive and I have been practising up and down the village, this is the first time I have been as far as town. It is really exciting!" said Sissie, as she swerved to avoid some sheep crossing the road from one field into another, the shepherd waving to her, or at her. Freddy could not be too sure which, so he waved back in what he thought was a friendly way.

"Papa and Mamma are looking forward to having you home for a few days, Freddy, it has been very quiet since you all left."

"Do they have anything planned?"

"No, not as far as I know. All the young men have gone and many of us young women are doing voluntary work, or are in the Mann Works making aeroplanes or munitions and are too tired to socialise. I am afraid that you will have to make do."

They arrived at Saddlebow and drove up the short driveway. The house had been lived in by the Scotts for generations, each one improving and adding to it so that it no longer was the building that was attacked and occupied by the Roundheads during the English Civil War. The damage had been repaired, and in each period had been added to and made more suitable to the conditions of the time. It was a mongrel of a building, but it was his home.

As the car turned to a halt the gravel rattled and Sissie once more tooted the horn.

The front door opened, and Mamma came out to meet them, smiling, in a weary kind of a way. Freddy noticed that she was looking older than he remembered, but the warmth of her character was still there for him. She always referred to him as 'my baby', which used to annoy him when he was younger and trying to be more grown up like his siblings. He had become used to it now, and accepted the compliment without comment.

"Welcome back, my baby, how was the journey?"

"As good as three days in a train, a ship, and more trains can be, Mamma. I see you have allowed Sissie to drive Papa's car. That is very brave of you."

Mamma's smile slipped a little, "Yes."

"Let's go in and have a cup of tea." suggested Sissie, as she removed her goggles. They went in.

"Papa will be back early, he is looking forward to hearing all about France. Have you seen George and Edwin?" asked Mrs Scott.

"I see Edwin most days, but I haven't seen George for a couple of weeks. He spends a lot of time at his brigade headquarters. The brigadier has taken a shine to him, so he does not get to the front very often. Edwin is well. Colonel Howard gives him a lot to do, and he is not an easy task master, but you know Edwin, he keeps his chin up."

More small talk followed. Freddy felt out of place after a while. This was his boyhood home, but somehow he started to feel wrongly positioned. While Mamma continued to talk, he fell to merely grunting replies to her questions, and his mind wandered.

"Are you keeping clear of loose women and strong drink?" he heard Mamma ask, followed by Sissie, "Don't ask questions like that, Mamma, Freddy is a man now and has to do what men do when away from home, don't you, Freddy?" she said, nudging him.

Freddy recovered from his reverie and looked at Sissie, then at his mother, "Yes, I have done as you wished me to do, though I have taken to smoking a pipe." he said, reaching into his service jacket pocket and producing his pipe, though in reality he had only used it once, and had rejected it as a comfort. He retained it, though, as it seemed to be an appropriate thing for a man to have about him.

"Well, a pipe is better than the other things. Have Edwin and George been doing as I wish as well?" his mother asked.

"Of course they have," Freddy responded, hoping that this was true, "Though I am not my brothers' keeper, you know, you will have to ask them yourself. Leave is coming through now so they should be home soon."

Freddy's father returned and shook his hand. Though he also asked the same questions, Freddy felt that his heart was not in it, and after a few minutes Papa made his escape into the room that served as his office at home.

They dined as well as usual and Freddy turned in early. He slept deeply, in the bed of his boyhood, with his familiar toys and books around him.

He woke early, before his family, dressed in uniform, as was the required regulations, and wandered into the garden. He sat on the bench on the back lawn and looked out into the fields beyond. The house had been built on a slight rise, and from the lawn Freddy could see out across the fields and orchards. His thoughts turned to his new life in the country, another country, so different from this one. He had become used to the sounds and smells of men at war. Not so much the sounds of battle, but the sounds of men at work. The sounds of digging. The shouts. The rattle of harness and wagon wheels. The sound of horse teams dragging their wagons from place to place. A never ending stream of materials flowing from factories in England, across the channel, along the railways of France, into dumps and then on to the front.

He noticed that the fields within his vision had been ploughed in neat rows, in one field the light green of winter barley was showing, while the fruit trees in the distance were still bare and stark. The next time he would visit the field would be bare again, and the fruit gathered in. He was not sure whether he took comfort from this or was disturbed by it.

Sissie called to him that breakfast was ready. He went in to the house, breakfasted with Sissie and his mother.

"I will go into town today, I think." Freddy suddenly announced.

"Why?" asked Mother.

"I need to go to the bank." said Freddy, "The manager wrote to me and asked me to see him when I am in town, about my account. I also have some papers to hand over to

William Mann from his sister. You know she is out with the VADs?"

"I suppose that is important enough to take you away, but be back as soon as you can, I have invited some of my ladies around and they want to meet you, to let them know that their comforts are being appreciated by the boys. And you can let us know what else we can do for you out there."

"I can drive you, if you like, Freddy, would you like that?" asked Sissie.

"Yes, can we go soon?"

Sissie and Freddy left the breakfast table, and met up again a few minutes later outside the house, got into the car and left for town. As they drove Sissie asked, "Have you driven yet?"

"No, I never have. Where we are there aren't many suitable roads and driving is left to specialists, not ordinary soldiers like me."

"Would you like to try?"

"Maybe tomorrow."

"After you have been to the bank and seen Mr Mann, can we go and find some of my friends? They will be thrilled to meet a real soldier, and things have been very quiet socially since the men left. All we have in town are old men and young boys, and most of them are working around the clock and are too tired out to have fun." .

"Yes, let's do that, I don't know how you can stand to be at home by yourself with Mamma and Papa, the place seems so quiet and empty."

"I think that if I left as well Mamma would not be happy. She misses you boys, and reads the casualty lists in the paper every day, though we have not seen many local men there. Of course we know about Walter, but things must be very quiet on your part of the front."

"It does get a bit noisy occasionally," said Freddy, "but we are used to it, and we have been very lucky, so far, none of our lot have been killed."

"Connie told me that you wrote to her father to tell him about Walter."

"Yes, it seemed to be the right thing to do."

"Was it awful?"

"Yes, it was."

Sissie drew the car up outside Freddy's bank and sat there during the half hour that it took Freddy to resolve his meeting with the manager. He returned to her, and they drove off towards the Mann Works.

The factory was in full production. They had a branch line from the railway, and a row of wagons were lined up on it behind a gently hissing shunting engine. Large boxes were being loaded from horse drawn wagons onto the railway wagons. Older men were working in gangs to complete this work. Sissie drove past the siding and stopped the car in front of the office building. "Do you have anything to give to Mr Mann?" Sissie asked.

A puzzled Freddy replied, "To give him, like a present you mean? All I have is this bundle from Florence, she asked me to bring it back and hand it over to him."

"No, I was thinking about Walter's things, none of his personal possessions have come back yet, as far as I know. I thought that maybe his battalion may have given them to you to bring to his family."

"I have nothing at all, I assumed that the usual system would have arranged that, will it be a problem, do you think?" Freddy said, looking a little discomforted, realising that he had not really prepared all that well for this visit.

"I am sure he will just be pleased to see you and hear whatever you can tell him. Come on Freddy!"

They went up to the entrance, the door of which was ajar, pushed it fully open, and Freddy stood aside to let Sissie pass through first. Inside was a long corridor, which receded darkly into the distance as it ran directly away from them. They were not sure in which direction to go or how to proceed.

As they took tentative steps forward a middle aged woman emerged from a door to their right. "May I help you?" she said.

"Yes, thank you," said Freddy, none too confidently, "We would like to speak to Mr Mann, please."

"May I tell him the nature of your visit?"

"Yes, of course. Please tell him that Sarah and Freddy Scott would like to see him. I am sure he will understand why we are here."

The woman said, "Please wait here and I will tell Mr Mann that you are here." and turned briskly and strode through the doorway. Freddy looked at Sissie, hoping for a sign, but she just smiled back at him.

William Mann emerged from a door a little further along the corridor, walked up to them, held his hand out to Freddy and they shook hands, he nodded to Sissie. Freddy saw that William Mann looked a little shrunken, more stooped than he remembered. As this observation flitted through his mind he dismissed it as irrelevant to this meeting.

"Thank you for coming to see me, it is very kind of you. Please come this way to my office and we can have a cup of tea while you tell me all about things at the front, Freddy." He turned and walked to enter his office, held the door open while Freddy and Sissie went in, then closed the door and indicated that they should sit at chairs placed in front of his desk.

As they settled themselves to sit the woman came in with a tray of tea which she placed on the desk and quietly left again.

"I apologise for coming to see you on spec." said Freddy, "I have brought these documents which Miss Florence asked me to deliver to you. I assume they are important?" He handed the foolscap sized bundle of documents, which were tied up with a blue tape, across to William Mann.

"Thank you, yes, I was expecting something from my sister. She sends me her writings on what she thinks we need at the front, either for me to raise with the War Office, or for me to pass on to her Ladies Committee. She thinks I have more influence on the War Office than I in fact do, but I appreciate that it helps her to do as much as she can for the boys at the front. How was she when you saw her, Freddy?"

"She was in top form, actually, sir. Her hospital is not far from divisional HQ and I get there from time to time. I often pop in to see her for a cup of tea or coffee and a chat. I think she is enjoying her work, if that is the right way to describe things, though I am sure she would rather be here than looking after the wounded."

"Yes, the wounded!" said William, "We have seen a few of them back in town, the ones that are too bad to go back into the line. I have a few of them in the works now, though it is difficult for them to do a full job of work with some of the injuries they have. But, I suppose at least they are alive and able to be with their families."

"Yes," said Freddy, "can I answer any questions about when Walter was killed? I imagine that there are many things that are unclear?"

"For me it is clear enough. He was doing his duty and was in the wrong place at the wrong time, do I need to know more? No, that is sufficient. I rather think that knowing more of the details will make it worse for me, but thank you for offering." said William.

"If you change your mind I will be happy to come back. I was there with him, and can assure you that he was a good officer and soldier, and his men respected him. One thing you may not be aware of is that the German marksman who killed

Walter died two days later. One of Walter's NCOs found him and killed him." said Freddy, without bidding.

"I am not sure that is a comforting thought, Freddy. For another young man to die, not that I would wish him well, but revenge is a strange thing, and never positive. As an industrialist I am clear that what I do, what we make here, is involved in killing Germans, but I do this with an uneasy conscience, to be truthful. I have responsibility for my workers, and allegiance to the King. I would rather be able to carry on as before, making boilers and so on, rather than aeroplanes and shells, but needs must...." said William, his voice trailing off as he spoke and looked away towards his office window.

"I am sorry to have mentioned it, in that case," said Freddy after a few seconds, "I just thought that you might like to know that Walter has been avenged, but I take your point."

William turned back to Freddy, "Who was the NCO who killed the German? Is it someone I might know?"

"Corporal Rippingill, I don't think you would know him, he was a gamekeeper's son, comes from West Newton, I believe." said Freddy.

"The name is a familiar one. Does he have family?"

"I think so, I could find out for you. I can go to his drill hall and let you know."

"Please do, I would like to send something to his wife or other family as thanks."

"I am sure they would appreciate that, sir."

"Constance may wish to know more of Walter's passing, Freddy, would you and Sarah be willing to go to see her? Perhaps you could leave details of Rippingill's family with her?" said William, "And if you will excuse me, I must get back to my work, once again thank you for taking the time to come and see me, it is much appreciated. Please give my regards to your mother and father, they must be pleased to have one of their sons with them, if even for only a few days. Goodbye."

William said as he stood and prompted Freddy and Sissie to do likewise. He shook their hands as they left.

Freddy and Sissie found themselves outside the works again and stepped into the car. "I feel really sorry for him," said Sissie, "his only son gone and all this work to do, and no wife to help him. He must be a very lonely man."

"Yes, I suppose so. Would you mind taking me to the drill hall and I will see if I can find out about Corporal Rippingill's family?"

"Yes, and we will go to see Connie afterwards, if you like. I haven't seen her for a few days and we have things to talk about before we meet the other ladies. Will that be alright?"

The sounds of industry faded as they drove away from the works and threaded through the streets of the town to the Norfolk Regiment drill hall on Purfleet Quay. While Sissie sat in the car Freddy went in, reported to the adjutant and asked for the information on Corporal Rippingill. The adjutant was pleased to give Freddy the written address of Mrs Rippingill, and then wished him well for his return to the front.

Freddy returned to join Sissie and they then continued to the Mann's house in Gaywood, drove up the short gravel drive, and stopped the engine. Sissie skipped to the front door and rang the bell, just as the door opened and Constance Mann appeared, having seen them arrive.

Constance kissed Sissie's cheek, and embraced her, and held out her hand to Freddy with the intention of shaking hands. Freddy instead on an impulse made a bow, took her hand, and kissed the back of it, as if in the French manner and said in a mock French accent, "Mademoiselle, je suis a votre service."

Constance at first surprised, then in on the jest, took him by the shoulders and kissed him on both cheeks. Freddy blushed.

They went in to the house, Constance motioned Freddy into the room next to the front door, while she and Sissie went off further into the house, Constance saying as she left, "Tea Freddy?" without waiting for his reply.

He went to the window and looked out. He saw the car, the garden, neatly kept in a strict state of order, and the road beyond where occasional traffic was passing, mostly horse drawn vehicles of various types, and an occasional motor lorry or car. The sky was blue, with a few white clouds lazily drifting. In the distance, in what Freddy calculated must be towards The Wash a grey cumulus cloud was visible. Freddy pondered how calm and orderly, how normal, the scene before him was, and how different to what he now knew of France. Though the weather was unremarkable, here he felt less on guard, more relaxed, perhaps. Though as he had not been in this room before he did not feel fully at ease. He could hear the voices of the two girls somewhere deeper in the house as they chatted and laughed.

Freddy looked around the room, at one wall was a piano, as was usual in most houses. Pictures on the wall were of sombre tones and sombre subjects, nothing bright or visually attractive caught his gaze, though one or two were of pastoral scenes with what Freddy assumed were Mann agricultural devices featured in their natural settings. The furniture was upholstered in substantial fabrics, with little of what could be described as ornamentation purely for aesthetic appeal. Freddy thought that this room was probably where William Mann expressed his temperament - unfussy, practical, down to earth. There was no sign of any religious items, at all, something that Freddy noted in passing.

Sissie came back into the room and said, "Come along Freddy, we will have tea in the garden room." and left again, assuming that Freddy would follow and know where the garden room was within the house. Freddy lost sight of Sissie as she rounded a corner, but made his way in the direction of the rear of the property reasoning that was where a garden room would be, to be proved correct.

When he arrived the two young women were already seated at an iron table, and on this was a tray with tea making requisites and a cake with side plates.

Sissie was sitting at the table facing Freddy as he came in, her fair hair was, as usual for her, slightly awry. Though she had brushed and pinned it before her breakfast, strands and wisps of hair had escaped their bounds and were projecting from her head. Her face was animated and her green eyes sparkling as she chatted with Constance. Seeing her, Freddy was reminded how much he loved her.

Constance had her back to him as he came in, holding a cup in both hands. She was dark haired, and her attempts at control were more effective. The nape of her neck was exposed above the collar of her blouse, and as Freddy passed behind her to take his seat he had a passing thought that this part of her was very attractive.

He sat down, the girls continued to talk, and as he was not part of their conversation he poured himself a cup of tea and leaned back in his chair and half listened to them, the other half of his attention mused on other things.

Freddy did not feel left out, rather he felt at his ease. He was conscious that he had Rippingill's address in his breast pocket, and he should remember to pass this to Constance before he left the house. His mind wandered to Rippingill's face, a face that betrayed his place in society, the face of a countryman, weathered by his trade. And yet, Rippingill had a softer core. Freddy mused how a man who could be so loyal to one man, Walter, could be so brutal as to literally kill another with his hands. As Freddy was considering the act of killing that Rippingill had carried out, and William Mann's reaction when Freddy had told him of it, he flinched involuntarily. His hand jerked, and his foot struck out and contacted the table leg, causing a jolt, which was felt by the two girls.

Sissie stopped her conversation and looked at Freddy and said, "Freddy, what on earth are you doing?"

Freddy blushed and apologised, "Sorry Sissie, I must have been nodding off."

Constance turned to him and put her hand on his arm, "Sorry, Freddy, have we been ignoring you. You must think that we are such bad company, especially for a brave soldier. We should make more of having a real man with us as all the other boys have been away for such a long time. We are not used to male company, I am afraid. Just female chatter."

"No, it's all right, really. Please carry on, I am enjoying not being the centre of attention, off duty, as it were. Just ignore me and I will try not to interrupt again."

Constance patted his arm and smiled at him, turning her attention back to Sissie. Freddy returned to his musings. He felt warmed by the feeling as Constance had touched him.

William Mann had surprised him, maybe Freddy had unconsciously assumed that he would be content, if not exactly happy, that Walter had been avenged, but he seemed to be saying that two wrongs do not make a right. When Rippingill went out into no-man's land, did he consider that he was doing a wrong, or doing the right thing? Probably neither, maybe he was just acting from instinct. And, if he had done that before the war, would he now be in a court of law, answering to a crime? What was acceptable in war was not acceptable when not at war. Had Freddy killed anyone? Well, not with his hands, but as an artillerymen he had been part of the organisation that sent lethal missiles into action against the Germans. He had initiated that fire on occasions when he had been at the OP. Did that make him a killer, or just a soldier doing his duty?

Freddy decided that he could not really answer the question, in fact, he was becoming less certain of what the question was.

He did feel, though, that he was now an adult, and had adult responsibilities, and in any case, he had no option but to continue.

He realised that as he was daydreaming he was looking at Constance, rather he was looking in her direction, but not seeing, until he came to this realisation. As the girls were still absorbed into their conversation and paying him no attention, he felt able to study her features. Up to now Constance had been taken by his mind's eye as a whole person, a familiar yet unexamined character in his life.

Now, he found that he was looking at her in a new way. She was very attractive to him. He liked the way she moved her head as she talked, using it to communicate emphasis to her words. He noticed that her ears were quite small, and her eyes were expressing emotions as she spoke, and reflecting Sissie's words when it was her turn to talk.

Neither Sissie or Constance seemed to be aware that he was staring. Freddy looked at Constance's hands. They were perfect, small, smoothly skinned, yet somehow confidence inspiring, though he could not work out why he would come to that conclusion.

His mind wandered to Roselyn's hands, rougher, bigger, but when used to remonstrate with James Newman in the barn that night she had used them to great effect. Freddy had the thought that maybe hands were more than utilitarian parts of the body, maybe, possibly certainly, they had more meaning and were more effective than he had previously considered. Then his thoughts drifted to Roselyn's body, the first, the only, woman's body that he had seen naked. He recalled the sight of her breasts in the barn, and that unexpected smooth dark triangle. While other women in his life had always been careful to conceal their bodies, Roselyn did not seem to have any reservations when surprised by Freddy and the others.

Freddy surfaced from his reverie, and realised that his gaze was on Constance's chest, which, though fully clothed and concealed beneath a complexity of layers and devices that Freddy could only imagine, held his gaze. Her blouse moved as Constance talked and changed posture. The swelling shape of her breasts held his gaze and interest.

Freddy blushed as he realised that he was being very rude, staring as he was, yet the girls did not seem to notice. He became aware of that same fullness in his trousers that he had experienced before when remembering Roselyn and the barn. He felt light headed in a way that he had not experienced before, his head was spinning, and he realised that he was sweating a little.

Freddy adjusted his posture in his chair, trying, unsuccessfully, to remove the thoughts of Roselyn's breasts from his mind.

"Are you all right, Freddy?" he heard Sissie say, "you look peculiar."

"No, I'm all right, thank you, Sissie, I think I must have a chill, or maybe I am a little tired from the travelling. Another cup of tea should sort me out."

"Of course, Freddy." said Constance as she poured from the pot into his cup. She put her hand onto his hand, and said, "You have been very patient with us." Freddy felt his heart thump in his chest as their hands touched.

"I think I might be better with a little fresh air."

"We can go, if you like, Freddy, we can take a drive into the country." suggested Sissie.

"Before I go, Connie, I have an address here which your father asked me to leave with you. It is the address of Mrs Rippingill. Her husband, Corporal Rippingill, was with Walter when he was shot and your father would like to contact her." said Freddy, taking the slip of paper from his pocket and giving

180

it to Constance, their hands touching again as he did so. His heart jumped again.

"I will put it on his desk in the morning room, thank you, Freddy, you were with Walter as well, weren't you? Thank you for writing to Father, it was kind of you." said Constance, smiling.

"I was in the line, but not at the same spot as Walter, but I did speak to him a few minutes before he was shot." said Freddy.

"That is a comforting to know, that he was with friends, and not alone. That would have been worse, much worse."

Freddy considered this for a few seconds, and decided not to explore the subject further. He had a sudden thought, brought on by the realisation that most of the men in his battery, possibly the whole army, sent and received letters from loved ones, wives or girls, and he, Freddy, only received them from his mother and sister. "Connie, may I ask a favour of you?"

"Yes, what is it?"

'Would you permit me to write to you, as a friend? All the men in our battery seem to be writing every day and getting bundles of letters when the post arrives. All I get is from Mamma and Sissie."

'Yes, of course you can, Freddy, and I will write to you as well. All my friends seem to have a boy at the front, except Sissie here, of course, I think it will be a good thing to do, yes. Please write to me and let me know how you are doing." Turning to Sissie, Constance laughed, "Or do you have a boy at the front!"

Sissie shook her head, "Only my brothers, and they do not count!"

The three of them smiled, and Constance led the way to the front door, opened it and Sissie and Freddy passed out into the daylight. Constance kissed Sissie's cheek, and then moved as if to kiss Freddy in the same way, but Freddy was not expecting it and stepped onto the gravel. "Freddy Scott, come back and let me say goodbye properly!" said Constance, her eyes smiling.

Freddy blushed again, and went back to the door and exchanged a sisterly kiss with Constance. Freddy's heart thumped yet again. He recognised this and wondered what it meant. He and Sissie waved to Constance as the car pulled away and turned towards the gate and went out onto the roadway.

Sissie drove out into the country, taking the road towards the coast. They stopped at Wolferton and walked into the woods, enjoying the quiet and the smells of the ground and foliage awakening to the early spring. Sissie held Freddy's arm as they walked.

"I think Constance is very fond of you, Freddy. And Edwin and George, of course. She is putting on a brave face, I think, but misses Walter terribly. She was very attached to her brother. You will do a good thing by writing to her. I think it will help her, especially as her father is always at work and does not have much time for her. You will write to her, won't you, and please write to me as well, and if you have any boys with you who do not have a wife or girl, let me know and I will ask for girls from my circle to write to them, anything to make them feel good."

After walking for an hour they returned to the car and drove back into town. Freddy asked to be dropped off in the High Street so he could do a little shopping, and Sissie then drove off back to Saddlebow, telling Freddy to be home by the early evening as she had some lady friends coming who would love to meet him.

Freddy walked along, glancing into occasional shops, with no real purpose, he was adjusting to life at home. There were a few soldiers and sailors in uniform, and he returned their salutes in a routine manner. Just as he was beginning to think about having lunch a voice called out to him, "Freddy Scott, my, you do look well!" He looked towards the voice and saw a familiar face, though for a moment he did not connect a name with the visage. Being well brought up Freddy did not let his lack of recognition stop him being welcoming. He held out his hand and said, "It's nice to see you again, how are things with you?" to the young man in front of him.

"I am just running some errands for my father, Freddy, will you come back with me to the shop and we can have a chat?" said the youth, who had a brown paper parcel under his left arm, and held out his free hand to shake Freddy's.

"Yes," replied Freddy without thinking too much about it, "that would be nice."

"You look good in your uniform, Freddy. I have enlisted and am waiting for the call up to arrive. My time in the OTC should get me a commission. Can you advise me which regiment to apply for?" said the young man leading the way along the High Street until they arrived at a milliners shop. On the name plate was the inscription 'Rivett & Son Purveyor of Fine Wool and Fabric' and Freddy suddenly remembered who this was, Ted Rivett, who had been two years below him at Fishers.

Ted pushed open the door of the shop and walked in, motioning Freddy to follow. Inside were a couple of women looking through ribbons and other materials. Behind the counter was an older woman. Ted waved his hand in the direction of the woman and walked through the shop to the back, where a small room served as an office and storeroom. Ted pulled out two chairs and indicated for Freddy to sit. "Tea?" he asked. Freddy nodded.

Ted went out and returned minutes later with two cups of tea.

"So, Ted, which regiments have you considered?"

"The obvious one is the Norfolks, but I am not sure I am up to all that marching."

"Do you ride at all?"

"Yes, I do."

"Riding would be better than marching, I think. The army has many needs other than infantry, how about one of the corps? The ASC are very important, they keep us fed and supplied."

"I was thinking about the artillery, actually, would you recommend it?"

"It depends on where your interests are, really. Conditions for the gunners are better than for the infantry, but both are close to the front lines most of the time so are a bit risky. Some of the corps rarely get near the danger so would be safer, but not as exciting."

"When I go I do not want to be safe, I want to do something really useful. I want to feel that I have done my bit. You know women have started to hand out white feathers? I have not heard of it happening here, but I want to be like you, in uniform, so they won't think me a coward. My father's factory has a contract to make woollen puttees, and I could claim a scheduled occupation. Father would like that, but I want to do more than make uniforms. I want to fight for my king and country."

"I can't speak for the other regiments, but I am sure that if you applied for the artillery you would be accepted, it would probably help if you wrote to my Brigade Commander, Colonel Howard, and tell him you would like to serve under him. He would put in a good word for you. At least you would be serving with men from around here rather than complete strangers. They are a good crowd, and they are very good at the job. I will write down Colonel Howard's address if you like."

"Yes, thank you."

The two young men continued to chat for a while until Freddy made his excuses and left intending to find lunch at a restaurant in town. He later returned to Saddlebow by cab.

The rest of his leave passed without incident. Mamma's lady friends made a fuss of him, and though he was sure he should have enjoyed the attention from them, he did not. For the sake of Sissie, he made polite small talk, and none of them, he felt, really wanted to know about what it was like at the front. In any case, he was not sure that he wanted them to know.

Freddy spent time walking in the fields and orchards around the village. The house felt empty as his brothers and father were absent to different degrees. His mother made him welcome and comfortable, but Freddy knew that he had changed, and family life was no longer enough for him. He had never once felt homesick while he had been away in France, but he now felt homesick in a different way, though. He was homesick for the Brigade. The army was his home now.

Chapter 14

April 1916.

When the time came to return, Freddy surprised Sissie and his parents with the eagerness of his departure, they rather expected more reluctance on his part.

The journey was uneventful, though no less tedious and drawn out than before. He reported back to Brigade and went to the mess awaiting instructions to rejoin the battery. There he met Kit Chilvers.

"How was your leave, Freddy?"

"Very good, thank you, Kit, though the travelling was the worst part." replied Freddy. "I did get to the drill hall to see how things were with them. The second line brigade has been sent to Salisbury Plain, and will be coming over with their division in the next month. I could not find out where they would be sent, but I imagine they will come down here in the south somewhere, what with a push starting later this year."

"Yes, I heard that as well. I understand that they are now recruiting a third line brigade, though volunteers are running low. The rumour is that they will be bringing in conscription soon. The Military Service Act has gone through Parliament, so it cannot be long."

"Sergeant Bowles said that he has a number of younger men who were not allowed out with the second line who would like to join us, do we have any vacancies? Sergeant Leman's nephew is one of them, he is only seventeen, but very keen and wants to come out to be with his uncle in First Battery."

"He has already sent me a request, actually, Freddy. The artillery is being reorganised and each battery brought up to six guns so we will need another twenty or so men in each battery. There will be some shifting about of individuals, with promotions and so on, but yes, we can take some extra men in anticipation of the changes. I asked Colonel Howard and he has approved a draft coming out in a month. I will let you know when all the paperwork has been sent out and when to expect them. It will be on orders soon so keep an eye out for them."

"Should I speak to the BSM to make sure that Sergeant Leman's nephew definitely comes to my section, Kit?"

"Not absolutely necessary, but it might be a good idea to keep him in the know."

"I also met an old school chum while on leave, a chap called Ted Rivett. He is not sure which regiment to join when he is called up. I suggested he might like to write to Colonel Howard and request a place in this brigade, could you keep an eye out for his letter and make sure that the colonel approves it? I think he will fit in well, and if we are getting more guns we will need a few more officers in the brigade, I would imagine."

"Righto, good work, will do."

Robert Benefer came in while they were talking, and at this point went up to the adjutant, "Kit, I am a little worried about one of the men. Gunner Hastings has reported sick three times this month, but I cannot find anything wrong with him. I don't think he is malingering, but something is not right with him."

"What should I be doing about him?" asked Kit.

"Not sure, but I suppose I am just letting you know that I have concerns, I suppose. For the moment I am sending him back to duty every time, but we may need to consider something else if he keeps reporting sick."

Freddy, hearing this, said, "I think Hastings is on the next draft for leave, a few days at home will probably sort him out. He has always been on the ball when he has been with me, a good man. Why not see what he is like when he gets back? Hopefully leave and time with his wife will put things right."

Kit and Robert agreed.

Freddy left the mess and went to find a horse to get him back to his battery. On arrival he went to find the BSM who was inspecting a wagon full of ammunition that had arrived on the daily resupply run.

"Excuse me, BSM, can I speak to you for a few minutes, please?"

"Yes, sir, how may I help."

"I have just come back from leave and while in town I went to see Sergeant Bowles at the drill hall. He has some chaps who were too young to go off with the second line, but who might be coming out to join us. One of them is Sergeant Leman's nephew, Gunner Bernard James, and when the drafting order comes through I would like him posted to my section so he can be with his uncle. Will that be in order?"

"Of course it will, Mr Scott, I will make sure he comes to you. At least I will know that one of the new men has someone to look after them. Sergeant Leman will be pleased, have you told him yet?"

"No, I have only just got back, I wanted to make sure that you knew first and would approve. Thank you, BSM, I had better get on back to my section." said Freddy, then added, "That looks like a lot more ammunition than we normally get."

"Yes sir, if I had to guess there is an attack being planned. Instead of a handful of rounds per gun they are sending us hundreds. We can only hold so many in the gun pits, so I am setting up dumps around the gun line. We are not firing much at the moment, but I am sure that once the staff think we have enough ammo we will get orders to use it, so a push of some kind is in the wind."

"Let's hope the fuses are better as well, we are still getting a lot of duds and it seems a big waste of time and money to fire shells that do not explode correctly. I will leave you to your work then, BSM, cheerio." With that Freddy went off to see how his section was faring, to be welcomed back with a few ribald comments.

He noted that a few men were missing and Sergeant Leman told him that leave was regular now and another draft would be leaving in a week or so. Leman was also very pleased when Freddy told him that his nephew would be posted to his section, promising to take care of the lad.

Later that month a battery of heavy guns arrived and took up a position just behind the village. The gunners spent a long time digging enormous pits for these guns and troop shelters. Then ammunition wagons arrived daily to fill the dumps surrounding the guns. At first they did not fire at all, but remained silent and under cover.

In early May a draft of reinforcements arrived at Freddy's battery. As predicted by Kit there had been a reorganisation and each battery in the Brigade had two extra guns to man, and this draft was a mix of reservists, returning men who had been sick, and a few new men from the second line. In this group was Bernard James.

BSM Evans was responsible for organising these new arrivals into the battery, a few experienced men were moved to the new guns, while the new men filled in the gaps left. Bernard James was a farm worker and had experience of working with heavy horses, and Leman put him as a driver. His role was to load ammunition at the wagon line and then drive the wagon to the gun line and then unload the ammunition and prepare it for use.

The wagon teams were kept busy as ammunition started to arrive in increasing quantities, it was becoming clear to all the men that a push was in the offing. The infantry battalions were being withdrawn in turn and spent days being trained in new tactics, equipment and methods.

At the beginning of June the field batteries, including Freddy's were tasked with wire clearing. After the trench raids of the winter period both the Germans and the British had thickened up the quantities and types of wire in front of their trenches. These now presented significant obstacles to any movement in no-man's land, and even General Trubshawe's expeditions became more limited. Reconnaissance continued, though. In addition to observation from trenches and OPs, were aerial photography by the Royal Flying Corps, and observation balloons which now rose in numbers behind both lines of trenches each morning. Aerial raids then started on a daily basis where both sides tried to shoot down the other's balloons, often achieving this with spectacular results as a successful attack often resulted in the balloon falling to earth in flames, the crew parachuting to safety, if they were quick, and lucky, otherwise meeting an unpleasant demise.

The observers in the British balloons were officers of the Royal Flying Corps. Their role was to observe what the Germans were doing, and pass information and locations to the medium and heavy guns, these having the range and weight of shell, so that they could shoot at and destroy whatever the observers had identified.

The role and performance of these balloons became the subject of discussion among the officers of the battery.

"Would you go up in one of those balloons?" Freddy asked Edwin, "They look interesting, if I were to get the opportunity to try it I think I would."

Edwin looked at his younger brother, then looked away shaking his head, "You must be crazy, Freddy, they are far too dangerous to be up in. I am sure the observers can see more than we can down on the ground, but you can see that as soon as they go up in the morning the Hun does his damnedest to get rid of them. My advice is to keep your feet as far underneath the ground as possible!"

"Well, if I get asked to do it, I will. I never knew you were windy. It must be worth trying at least once, just imagine the view you get, they must be able to see for miles."

"And just imagine who can see you, every German for miles will be after you. Let me know when you are going up and I will have all your money and kit off you, because you will not need it any more!"

"Stop that, you two youngsters, " said Buster, "we have more important things to think about. Orders are coming through for the big push. Our job is to cut the German wire, that is why so much ammunition has been sent up. From tomorrow morning we will be firing all day every day, and I want you to make sure that every shot is observed and made to count. When the infantry have to go over the top in a few weeks our job is to make sure they have no obstacles to get in their way or nasty surprises. We will have two observers in the OP every day, and we will be firing from first light until last light, and then the guns will be laid on the SOS target. So, we are going to be very busy. James Newman is drawing up a rota for OP duty and make sure you get to see it and are ready on time."

"How long before the push starts?" Edwin asked Buster.

"The end of June is what I am being told at the moment, the exact date and time will be communicated later." Buster explained, "And you will need to keep your gun teams on top form. They will also be working long hours and the pressure will be on them."

Freddy went out to the gun line to see how his men were doing and how the extra gun team in his section was settling down. He went to each gun in turn and spoke to the men there. "I have never seen so much ammunition before, sir." said Sergeant Leman, "Where will put it all is getting harder each day. When will we be firing some of it to make some room, do you think?"

"We will start firing tomorrow, and when we do start there will be no let up for weeks. We will be firing all day, and will have to lay on the SOS target at night. With the short night times you will have to arrange rest periods and so on very carefully so the men do not get unduly worn out. How is young Driver James, by the way, settling in all right?"

"Yes sir, very well, thank you. He is my sister's boy and she has given me strict orders to look after him and keep him out of trouble. He is very keen to please and learns quickly. He is back at the wagon line at the moment bringing more ammunition up this afternoon. He has done very well with the horses, he seems to have a natural gift with them."

Freddy moved on to the next gun and spoke to the team who were also working hard to store away all the ammunition.

That evening the firing schedules were issued. The guns started firing at the German wire the next morning. Freddy was on duty with Buster on the first day. Buster wanted to control the first shoot to get an idea of how well the guns performed. He ordered the guns to fire individually a minute apart so that he could more accurately see where the shells from each gun were exploding and the effect on the wire. Over the days of June the wire in front of the German trenches was systematically degraded and large gaps opened up where the shrapnel bullets hit and broke individual strands of wire.

A week before 'Der Tag' as the British had taken to refer to the day the push was to start, General Trubshawe decided to take a patrol out into no-man's land and see the extent of broken wire for himself.

He returned safely and had plotted where further wire cutting was needed and had also identified strongpoints in the German line which had not previously been seen. He ordered his artillery batteries to deal with these obstacles.

The heavy battery behind Hebuterne had been reserved for just such an eventuality. Its heavy high explosive shells were effective against reinforced parts of the line, such as Trubshawe had found. Five days before the day of the push the heavy battery opened up to smash these strongpoints. They would continue firing throughout the days and nights left before the battle was to commence.

On the first day a problem was observed. Some of the shells fired by the heavy battery were failing to explode. Occasional shells were exploding before they struck the target area. It was surmised that the fuses were to blame. A similar problem had been seen with the 18 pounders, though the fuses used in shrapnel shells, and those used in high explosive shells, were different.

Because of the risk to our own troops from a shell exploding prematurely while it travelled overhead, all troops were warned to stay below ground whenever our heavy guns were firing unless their duties required them to be in the open.

Three nights before the big day Sergeant Leman's gun team were stood down for four hours in order to get some sleep. Driver James was with the gun, and when the order to stand down was given, he and another young gunner, instead of retiring to the relative safety of the troop shelter which had been constructed to the rear of the gun line, decided to take their blankets and sleep in the open to the side of the gun pit. The night was warm and humid, and the gunners were tired from working hard all day serving the guns of the battery. Each gun had fired seven hundred and forty rounds, followed by an hour cleaning and maintaining the guns ready for the following day. They would have to be up and about before dawn when more ammunition would arrive.

Freddy was on night duty at the wagon line when a call came through for him to go to the gun line, there had been an explosion, and he was needed to find out what had happened and report back to Brigade.

Freddy found his horse and mounted it, and made his way as quickly as he could, taking a half hour to cover the ground from the wagon line at Sailly to the gun line at Colincamps. He arrived with dawn just starting on the horizon. He heard voices over by Sergeant Leman's gun, and dismounting and securing his charger he walked quickly over.

Sergeant Leman was sitting on the ground, his head in his hands, and Freddy could hear him sobbing. Bombardier Reid came over from somewhere behind Freddy, "Right, Sarge, we have got them away, let's get this mess cleared up. Oh, Mr Scott, sir, I didn't know you were here."

"What has gone on here?" Freddy asked of Reid, ignoring Leman for the time being.

"It's young Bernard, sir, I mean Driver James, sir, he has been hit, badly. Gunner Black too, though he is not as bad. We have got them away to the RAP in one of the ammunition wagons."

"What was it that hit them?"

"We're not sure, sir. There have not been any other shells hitting the position, but the heavies were firing when we heard the explosion, it must have been one of theirs dropping short, or a premature, more like."

Just as he said this they heard the sound of the heavy battery firing again and heard the rush as the shells passed not far overhead. Freddy ducked instinctively, then straightened up as he realised the other men had not reacted to it, being used to the sensation.

"Have a look around and see if you can find any pieces of the shell, it might prove one way or another whose shell it was." ordered Freddy, a feeling of dread coming over him.

The men did as Freddy had bid them, Reid stayed with him, though. "It's Sergeant Leman, sir, he has been like that ever since we found Bernard here. What shall I do with him?"

"Try to get him away and get him a cup of tea or some rum." said Freddy. Bombardier Reid went to speak to Leman and got him to stand and walked him away from the gun pit towards the troop shelter. Freddy called after him, "Bombardier Reid, get Sergeant Leman to the RAP so he can be with his nephew, and you had better take over as number one."

"Yes, sir." Reid replied over his shoulder as he walked away with Leman.

The other gunners had found some of the fragments from the shell, and on one of the larger pieces they saw that there was paint remaining, and that paint was the same green colour used on British shells. Freddy took the pieces and told the men that Bombardier Reid would be number one until Sergeant Leman had returned. He then went off, found his horse, mounted and turned its head towards the track leading to Brigade HQ.

On arriving there he went to find the adjutant. He handed over the shell splinters as evidence, wrote a brief report describing the events, and left.

That evening the preliminary bombardment continued. Freddy was at Brigade and went into the mess for dinner. Benefer and Fitzgerald were there, also eating their meal.

Fitzgerald said to Freddy, "I understand that you had two casualties last night, I went to see them at the CCS, I am afraid that young Driver James has passed over. I am sorry."

Freddy replied as he sat down, "Yes, I heard that as well. In a way it was his own fault, he should not have been out in the open, but he has not been here long and I suppose he thought that he knew better than the rest of us. You know that he was Sergeant Leman's nephew?"

"Yes, I understand so," said Fitzgerald, "How is Leman?"

"I have not been able to get to see him yet, but I would imagine he is not at all happy. He will have to write to his sister and tell her what happened. That will be very difficult, he was supposed to be looking after the lad."

"If it is any help, I don't think the boy would have felt much pain, he was hit by a small fragment in the chest, and he bled to death within minutes, probably before they got him away from the gun." added Benefer.

"I am a bit annoyed, to be truthful," said Freddy, "the men, including Driver James, had been told to stay under cover, and I lost sleep having to deal with it, sleep I needed badly. The shell that got him was one of ours, you know, from the heavies behind us. Why can't they supply us with reliable fuses, it seems a small thing to ask for!"

"There will be a reason for this, you know, it is just that we can't always perceive what God intended. I have to admit that it does seem to be a tragedy for the lad to die so young and from our own hands, as it were."

"God's mysterious ways?"

"No, rather God's indifference more like." replied the padre, "How are you getting along with the pipe?"

Freddy was rather taken aback and hesitated for a second, "I have not really tried it much, I am not sure I like the taste."

"Well, as I told you before, persist with it, I think you will find it a comfort when you need one. Have you got it with you?" Freddy nodded. "Hand it over then, and I will fill it for you, and I want you to smoke it now."

Freddy handed the pipe to the padre, who deftly filled the bowl with tobacco from his pouch, handed it back to Freddy and lit a match for him. Freddy sucked on the pipe, breathed in the smoke, and choked.

"Gently, gently, don't take it down so quickly, Freddy, just take it into your mouth, hold it, then breathe it out, try again."

Freddy tried again, and this time did not choke. "Just remember to keep the bowl lower than your mouth," said the padre.

"Why?"

With that the padre put his finger under the bowl of Freddy's pipe, and pushed it up until the liquid in the stem ran into Freddy's mouth, Freddy snatched the pipe and spat the foul taste from his mouth. "That is why!" said Fitzgerald, and Benefer smiled.

Fitzgerald then said, "A baby at the breast is at its calmest, it is comforted and soothed. A pipe is a good substitute when you are a grown man. Just imagine you are at your mother's breast, close your eyes, and suck away."

Benefer looked a little taken aback by this, but said nothing. Freddy said, somewhat also taken aback by what the padre had said, "I don't remember suckling, that was before my memory began, but it sounds a bit, how shall I say, peculiar, to think of suckling my mother's breast when smoking a pipe."

"You may not be conscious of it, but the memory is there in the back of your mind, and if the thought of your mother does not register with you, think of suckling at the breast of a young woman. That might be better for a young man like you. You must have many fillies to choose from, just choose one and imagine that you are with her when you smoke. Believe me, it will work."

Benefer raised his eyebrows and looked at Freddy. Freddy was not sure how to take the padre's words, but thought he might try what Gregory had suggested.

After dinner Freddy had to take a resupply to the battery. On arrival at the gun line he found that Buster and Fitzgerald were there with Sergeant Leman. Freddy joined the three men as they stood behind Leman's gun pit.

Sergeant Leman seemed, to Freddy, to be back to his normal self, and the conversation that he joined was of the normal type that happened every day except for the presence of the padre.

The heavy battery started firing, so those men above ground quickly returned to their pits. The visitors left the gun line and went elsewhere out of the line of fire of the heavies, the danger having been all too recently acknowledged.

News came through that the start of the big push had been delayed by one day, and all preparations would now be co-ordinated to fit in with the infantry going 'over the top' on the morning of Saturday 1st July.

The night before the attack Freddy and Edwin were tasked with manning the forward OP during the assault on Serre. At last light on Friday 30th June they went forward with supplies to last them for 48 hours, including victuals, spare cable and telephones, and a host of paraphernalia needed by the artillery. The Royal Engineers had added another facility to the tunnel complex and had built a funk hole below the OP which could be used if the Germans were shelling the OP with heavy artillery.

All was set. The front trenches filled with infantry during the night, and the smell of rum and sweat filled the air. The scheduled artillery fire rose in intensity as dawn approached. The German artillery were responding, but not in any great strength and all seemed well for the attack.

As the light of dawn crept from the northeast Freddy looked out of the OP towards their objective, but saw little. The half mile or so of ground was filled with a swirling mass of smoke and dust. Through occasional gaps in this maelstrom Freddy could see where he calculated that the village of Serre was to be, but saw nothing that he could recognise as buildings or trees.

At 7.20 a.m. the intensity of the British artillery fire increased on the German trenches. The ground shuddered, more than either of them had known before. Later, they learned that an enormous mine had been exploded beneath a German strongpoint a mile beyond Serre.

Freddy saw the twinkling of bayonets in front of our trenches, and the khaki figures passing through our wire to line up beyond, then start to cross no-man's land in perfect formation, and disappear into the clouds of smoke and dust on the dot of 7.30.

Then a second wave of infantry followed, and they also disappeared into the murk, and Freddy then saw a third wave emerge from the trenches and form into line.

The German artillery responded and their shells started to fall on the British first line and the communication trenches. Some landed close to Freddy's OP. He saw small parties of infantry crossing open ground between the second line and the first line trenches, assuming they felt that this was safer than going along the communication trenches. He saw one party of about six men disappear as a heavy German shell landed among them, earth and debris scattered in all directions. There was no sign of the men.

The cloud of dust in no-man's land cleared a little, and Freddy could see the glint of bayonets as men went into the German first line. He saw one or two khaki figures running and jumping then the dust obscured his vision again. He reported back what he had seen, saying also that he had seen some of our men crossing from the German first line towards the second, but could not confirm that either trench was captured entirely. The barrage from the British guns had advanced beyond the German second line, but the Germans were firing shells into no-man's land and onto the British trenches, so the dust and smoke clouds were no better than before.

Later in the day the German artillery fire lifted from the British trenches, and were landing around Serre, so Freddy assumed that these were in the possession of the British, and reported this to Brigade. He received information from Brigade that the infantry had advanced beyond the German second line and to look out for signs to confirm this and to identify German counter attacks and report these back to Brigade so that fire could be brought down.

Freddy was unable to see or confirm cithcr of these, so was restricted to being a passive observer rather than an active participant in the battle that was before him.

In the late afternoon a call came through from Brigade, James Newman was coming forward and when he arrived Freddy was ordered back to the wagon line to organise a resupply run. James arrived, and Freddy collected his things and left. He travelled along the tunnels to the rear and emerged in the village. The German artillery fire had slackened, as had the British, and the level of sound was more bearable.

As he left the cellar at the end of the tunnel he came across several wounded men sitting against a wall, being attended to by a medical orderly. These were lightly wounded men, but they all showed the effects of the battle. They were dirty and dishevelled, some had torn uniforms, and all had a grey pallor to their faces.

There were several ambulance wagons waiting in the orchard behind the village and stretcher parties were moving towards these with khaki figures on them, and having delivered their cargo other parties were moving back to the line with their stretchers folded. Medical orderlies and doctors were moving around inspecting the wounded and writing labels which they tied to the men. In one corner of the orchard Freddy saw a pile of what looked like logs, but which when he passed more closely he saw was a row of blankets tied up at both ends, which he realised must be dead men ready for burial.

He hastened away as he had duties to perform, and as he progressed further away from the village the noise level reduced, though he was aware of banging, which he realised was inside his head rather than outside it.

Early the next day Freddy was back in the OP. News had come through that the attack on Serre had failed, and the Germans were back in occupation of what was left of the village. As dawn broke he looked out onto the battlefield through his binoculars. He saw dead out in the open, many in front of our wire, others in small groups in no-man's land, and many in front of the German first line.

While he was scanning the zone in front of him he saw movement about half way across between the British and German trenches. Concentrating his attention he came to see that it was an arm waving. As he was watching he also saw a puff of dust close to the arm, and realised that it must be a wounded man and that a German sniper was shooting at him. Anger rose in Freddy, he turned to Edwin, who was with him in the OP, and pointed out the waving arm and what he had seen. Edwin focussed his binoculars on the waving arm, and he also saw the evidence of the German sniper.

The two officers decided that this was not cricket, and determined to identify where the sniper was firing from. A message also came through on the telephone that Brigade had information that some of our men were still in Serre. A sergeant from the next division had managed to get through the German lines and report this fact. Edwin looked in that direction, but could see Germans crossing a section of trench that had been blown down, and reported this back to Brigade.

They also received information that though the attack in this section of the front had failed, further south had been more successful and the Germans had been pushed back beyond their original support line.

Edwin concentrated on locating the sniper. After more than an hour of searching the German side of no-man's land he spotted the sniper, seeing a puff of smoke or dust as he fired a shot. Edwin requested permission to fire and was given approval. He and Freddy adjusted the fall of shells into the area where they knew the sniper to be, then ordered five rounds per gun to be fired. The shells arrived, exploded sixty feet in the air and the entire area was covered in dust as thousands of shrapnel bullets struck the ground and, they hoped, the body of the sniper.

No further shots were fired from the sniper's location.

Freddy and Edwin discussed the situation with the wounded man waving. Between them they decided that Freddy should go to find the infantry HQ and report what they had seen. Freddy did this and was thanked by the commanding officer, who assured him that they would send out stretcher bearers to that area that night. He said that they had already recovered many wounded from no-man's land, and would continue to search for them when conditions allowed. Freddy returned to the OP and told Edwin how things had gone with the infantry HQ.

The battle continued on the following days. While the attack had failed up in the north where Freddy and his comrades were, results further south were better. No further attacks were planned for Hebuterne, but many more developed further along, and in August Freddy's brigade left their positions and were sent to take part in the Australian attack on Mouquet Farm and the final assault and capture of the village of Pozieres.

Following this they were withdrawn and sent to rest out of the line.

The whole division was billeted near Doullens, and all ranks were allowed to visit the town. The officers of Freddy's battery, along with some from Brigade and other units decided to explore.

They wandered around the small centre, Freddy with Dobbin and Matthew Holt, Edwin with Buster and George. Men and officers from many units were in the town and because it was far enough away from the front line, there was no sound of gunfire and the civilian population was intact.

Freddy's group entered a hat shop. Dobbin Holt, a large framed man with a high forehead and little hair decided that he should buy a hat. Why this should be was not clear, but Matthew and Freddy went along with this as a reason to spend some time relaxing and watched Dobbin as he tried on various types of headgear. He finally settled on a lady's bonnet which Dobbin insisted would fit his mother who he said had an equally large cranium.

In the early afternoon they found a cafe and settled down to drink coffee and eat cake. Edwin's group came past, saw them, and joined them. A little later Stephen Sansom came past with a group of officers from the Norfolks and the party grew further. Someone produced a bottle of brandy, which was quickly consumed, and another was sought from the patron of the cafe.

Soon after four o'clock a woman came rushing into the cafe and pronounced, "Le Roi d'Agleterre vient a Doullens a quatre heures et demi." Hearing this the whole party of British officers went outside onto the pavement, where many locals and soldiers were lining up to welcome the king.

They heard the crowd fall silent along the road as the King's parade of motor cars appeared and motored through the town. The officers, slightly dishevelled and unsteady, on the order given by Buster saluted as one as the king passed, he looked at them and returned the salute, with a smile on his lips. Dobbin wore his recently acquired bonnet.

They returned to the cafe. They sat around the tables chatting and in good spirits. Buster proposed a toast, 'to all of us, brothers in war, one for all, and all for one.'

The toast was drunk, and the officers fell to talking in small groups. Dobbin proposed that they should all swear an oath, that if any of them were to fall in action, the remainder would meet to drink their health. This was loudly acclaimed, until Ralph House, who up to this point had concentrated on drinking rather than talking, suggested that whoever fell would leave all their money to pay for the drinks, to another round of applause and approbation.

Stephen Sansom produced a Kodak and suggested that a group photograph was needed to record the event, and the patron was persuaded to take the picture. Dobbin, being of a playful nature, again wore the bonnet that he had bought earlier in the day.

Edwin and Freddy found themselves on the same table, by a wall, and out of the centre of noise. Freddy asked of Edwin, "What would you do if I was killed?"

Edwin, somewhat perplexed by the question replied, "I am not sure what you are asking."

"I mean, I have thought that there are so many things I have not done yet, and if I am killed then my life will have been wasted. There is no one to follow on from me. Will you make sure that I am not forgotten?" said Freddy.

"How do you mean?"

"Fulfil my life, get married, have a son, and call him Freddy."

Edwin, trying to gather his thoughts through the alcohol nodded, then said, "Yes, all right, and if I die, will you do the same? Only call the boy Edwin, obviously."

"Let's swear on it."

But, before they could do this Stephen Sansom stood up and said to the group, "Let's go and find a house of ill repute, it will be a good way to finish the day!"

Edwin and Freddy looked at each other, neither exactly sure what was intended, but not wanting to single themselves out by showing their uncertainty or ignorance.

Buster, Edwin and others declined, but Freddy was swept up by Dobbin and off they went to find a brothel.

Sansom obviously knew what he was looking for, Freddy formed the view that he must be familiar with the ladies of the night.

It was early evening. Sansom led them to a dingy part of the town and after speaking to three women who stood in doorways, he indicated that they should enter the fourth such building. Inside was a scene that Freddy was not familiar with. He could hear music being played on a gramophone somewhere to the rear of the house. He could smell some kind of perfume, but not the sort that he had smelled on his mother or sister, or, indeed, any other female of his acquaintance. Sansom lead the way into a side room. Here the curtains were closed and the only light was an oil lamp. In the gloom Freddy could make out that there were sofas and soft chairs, and on these were four women. At least he assumed this as they were only partly clothed and they were not wearing the type of clothes he was used to in male circles. As his eyes adjusted to the gloom he realised that they were in their underwear. He tried, without complete success, to avoid looking at them.

Stephen said to Freddy and Dobbin, "Take your choice, gentlemen, pay the lady over there five francs and you can have a half hour of pleasure. Let's meet here before we leave."

With that he put something into the hand of the woman at the door, put his hand out to one of the women on the chairs, who rose, and they left the room. Dobbin also seemed at ease with the situation, and reached into his pocket, drew out some banknotes, selected one, gave this to the woman at the door, made his selection, and also left the room, leaving Freddy alone with the woman on the door and two women sitting.

He felt awkward, and not sure what to do, he had never visited a place such as this, and had never been alone with a woman before. Stephen and Dobbin seemed to be familiar with what was expected, but he, Freddy, was not. In actual fact, he was not sure that he wanted to be there at all.

The woman at the door looked at him, and smiled, and indicated with her hand that it was his turn to pay. Freddy hesitated, then reached into his pocket and took out money, and paid the woman five francs. She then pointed to the two remaining women on the seats and smiled again. Freddy looked at them, but could not decide what to do next. One was fair, the other darker haired. He blushed, he started to sweat, then decided he must do something. He reached out to the nearest woman, the one with the dark hair. She took his hand then led him out of the room. The other woman, with the fair hair, shrugged.

Freddy's chosen partner took him into another side room down the corridor, the room was dim and bare, just a small bed on one side. She smiled at Freddy. Freddy smiled awkwardly back at her. His heart was pumping, he could not decide what to do next. He recalled what he had seen in the barn back at Papillon Farm but that did not really help him, it just confused him. What did men and women do in bed?

A sudden idea came to him. He said, "Je suis fatigue, tres, tres fatigue." and lay down on the bed, on his side, facing the wall, and pretended to go to sleep. He was, of course, wide awake, but his eyes were firmly closed. He heard nothing from the woman, but felt her hand gently shake his shoulder once, twice, thrice. He then felt her climb onto the bed behind him. She put her free arm loosely around his waist, then she was still. His mind racing, Freddy was not sure what would happen next. Nothing did.

The woman let Freddy 'sleep' for his half hour, holding him gently to her. Freddy could feel the warmth from her through his uniform and onto his back. It felt good to him, and in five minutes he was relaxed enough to actually start dozing.

Freddy fell in to a dream. He was in a farm, running away from something, he went into a barn, and there was a hay loft and a ladder leading up to it. He climbed the ladder and there was a naked form, breasts and legs exposed just behind the straw. He could not see the face. He stepped further into the loft to see who it was. Though he saw where the face should be it did not resolve into anything he recognised.

He awoke as the woman was gently shaking his shoulder, and to his surprise he was weeping.

Freddy was confused and disorientated.

The woman climbed off the bed and sat on the edge. She produced a handkerchief and offered it to Freddy indicating for him to dry his eyes. She stroked his forehead and patted his shoulder, then left the room.

Freddy lay there for a minute, collecting his thoughts. He had already forgotten the dream, but felt disturbed by it nonetheless.

He got off the bed, stood up, straightened his uniform and stood still for a few minutes, then pulled the curtain back from the doorway and found his way back to the first room. Dobbin was there with a glass in his hand. As Freddy came in he looked up and smiled and winked at him. Freddy smiled uncertainly back.

Stephen then came back into the room, seemingly pleased with himself, and the three men left. Freddy took out his pipe, filled it with tobacco, lit it, and drew on it as he walked along.

In the evening he met up again with his brothers and returned to the brigade.

They never discussed the episode in Doullens.

Some days later the division was called back into action. By November they were in a position in the village of Mesnil Martinsart overlooking the Ancre Valley, looking across at the German line between Beaumont Hamel and Thiepval Chateau.

The guns were emplaced behind the village with the forward OP in Mesnil Chateau itself. The wagon lines were two miles further back near the village of Englebelmer.

Freddy had to bring up a resupply from the wagon line to the guns. In any normal position this would be fairly routine, and could be completed without undue danger or alarm. Mesnil was different.

The Germans knew that the Chateau overlooked many of their key positions, and therefore the British would invest the area with many OPs and guns. They also knew that there was only one usable approach route to the village from the rear. The Germans regarded continual and irregular artillery fire on the village and the areas around it were vital to disrupt British attempts to interfere with German defences.

Mesnil was a very unpleasant place for the British to be, and whereas the OPs and the various headquarters in the area were well protected in underground bunkers, tunnels, and dug outs, those whose duties required them to travel overland to bring supplies of ammunition, food and defence stores to the area were constantly exposed to random and highly frightening shellfire.

As the loading of the wagons was being finished off Freddy went around each of the seven wagons inspecting the security of the loads, the condition and tackle of the horses, and the state of morale of the men.

He spoke to the corporal who would be the NCO on the leading wagon. "Are we ready, corporal, we need to be off in five minutes."

"As ready as we will ever be, sir, but not that willing to be honest. We are very exposed up there, six feet in the air on top of the wagons. Just the right height to get a shell splinter in the arse!"

Freddy was also reluctant, but his position as an officer meant that he was unable to show it.

"It could be worse if they put one right into the wagon, though you wouldn't feel a thing."

"That's true, sir, at least there's the chance of a Blighty one as long as the shell is far enough away when it lands."

Freddy called together the drivers and reminded them of the need to keep one hundred yards between wagons, especially as they approached and passed through the village of Mesnil itself, this being the most usual spot for the Germans to intervene with a gift of high explosive or shrapnel.

The wagons set off. The drivers were used to this task, they sometimes did three runs or more in a day, to keep the guns supplied with shells. The days of having a few shells to fire had gone. Now a hundred in an hour was not unusual, and on occasion many hundreds of shells per gun were required every day. They all had to come up on these wagons.

The first part of the journey was usually straightforward and the men were able to relax a little, but as they approached the village they would start to tense. By the track was the evidence of past disaster, broken wagons, dead horses, sometimes the dead men were still there, or parts of them, before they could be cleared away and dealt with properly. It was an unhealthy place.

Freddy was at the head of the column, and as they neared the village he looked back to check the spacing of the wagons. It was good, so he turned to the front again and rode on. As they reached the first broken house of the village Freddy had to stop and send each wagon into and through the village on his judgement as to whether it was safe enough, or sensible, to. This was a task he hated, as the arrival of the German shells was unpredictable, and Freddy had to remain exposed at the worst point for longer than any of the wagon drivers. Such is the responsibility of command, he thought.

Freddy halted his horse at the usual position and waited for the first wagon to reach him. It was quiet, no shell fire, so he waved them through straight away and the driver urged the horses from a walk to a trot, the fastest speed that was possible for these nags to achieve and for the drivers to remain in control.

The wagon passed and followed the path that they knew so well in the direction of the gun line. The next wagon reached Freddy, he halted it, waited a minute, then waved it on, the driver needed no urging to break into a trot and pass through quickly.

The third wagon reached Freddy, and he was starting to think that today would be different and they might get away without hostilities. He waved the third wagon forward.

Just as the fourth reached him shells landed in the field behind where the last wagon was halted, waiting its turn. The horses flinched, but remained in position. Freddy reasoned that if the guns were laid plus of the village there was time to get this wagon through before more shells arrived, so he waved the wagon through, it sped off as fast as it could, the driver needing no urging.

The next volley of German shells arrived, but closer this time, nearer to the village and between the sixth and seventh wagons. "The Germans are creeping back to the village, time to get a move on." thought Freddy.

He waved to the last three wagons to get moving, and to hurry up. The fifth was already trotting as it passed Freddy, the sixth had closed up when it passed, and the last one was almost in a gallop as it rushed past, just as the third volley of shells landed around Freddy. He heard nothing, but he felt a rush of heat on his right side and tasted brick dust and explosive. He felt a blow to his head, and barely kept his position in the saddle. He saw stars. His horse bucked and reared, he instinctively regained control of the beast and of his wits. He urged his horse to follow the last wagon up the remains of the street. He shook his head to clear it, but still he heard nothing. His heart was racing, and he felt his bowels moving. He caught up with the last wagon. He slowed to a trot behind it. They reached the side track that would lead them to the gun line and turned up it. His pulse still raced.

The last few hundred yards of the journey went without incident. No further shells had landed in the village. Freddy felt the need for a smoke.

On arriving at the gun line, the drivers drove up beside their guns and the gun teams and drivers immediately started to unload. The last wagon went from gun to gun unloading sandbags and other defence stores for the gunners to use later to improve their gun pits.

Freddy halted by the command post. Edwin was on duty there, and Freddy saw him speak, but heard nothing. He held a hand to his ear and shook his head and shouted, "I can't hear you!"

Edwin laughed and came up to Freddy. He brushed Freddy's shoulder and a cloud of dust was produced. Freddy looked down and saw that his uniform was covered in dust, and brushed his jacket and trousers without much effect.

BSM Evans came over, and also seemed to be speaking to Freddy but he heard nothing. "You seem to be missing your helmet, sir." was what Evans said, but Freddy was oblivious, until Edwin pointed to Freddy's head and held his own tin hat and indicated his head. Freddy reached up and realised what was being said. He smiled, and said, without hearing, "The Germans almost got me in the village." Edwin smiled and nodded, turned and asked one of his signallers to fetch a mug of tea for his brother. Freddy continued to try and remove the dust from his uniform, took off his jacket and brushed it as best he could. The tea arrived, he thanked the signaller, and drank the beverage. He found his pipe, filled it, and lit up.

His hearing started to return. The wagons had been emptied, the gun teams were storing away the new supplies, and the wagon drivers were preparing their vehicles for the return journey.

Freddy asked Edwin and the BSM if they had any special requirements for the next supply trip, took notes, mounted his horse, and turned its head towards the village. The wagon drivers followed.

They passed through the village, well spaced out under Freddy's control, with no incident. As Freddy passed the spot where he had had the close encounter with the shell he dismounted and searched for his helmet. He found it by a ruined wall at the side of the street. The rim on one side was bent, the dome dented. He placed it on his head and then followed the wagons along the track towards the rear, and the next resupply run.

Later in the month, Freddy was on duty in the OP at Mesnil Chateau during the final assault on Beaumont Hamel when the British finally captured the position that had resisted all efforts at its capture since the first day of the battle.

Most of the firing was on a timed schedule, so there was little for the officers at the OP to do other than observe and report what they could see to Brigade.

Hastings was Freddy's signaller during the attack. "What is the name of the place that we are attacking, sir?" he asked.

"Beaumont Hamel." replied Freddy, looking through his binoculars at the mayhem across the valley.

"Does it mean anything, sir?" Hastings asked.

"It means that the Germans are there and we want them to leave, so we are going to take it from them."

"No, I mean the name of the place, sir, do the words mean something in English?"

Freddy lowered his binoculars, looked down for concentration, and then said, "I think it means hamlet by the beautiful mountain."

"It's not a good name then, sir. It's not beautiful, I do not see any mountains round here, and the village is just rubble, there is nothing left. Perhaps they will change the name when we are finished."

Freddy looked at Hastings for a while, then returned to his observations, and said, "Hastings, you are thinking too much, it's not good for you."

Chapter 15

25th July 1987, Arras, France.

The next morning we drove down to the village of Hebuterne. Freddy had told me that he was stationed near there for a year up to the big battle, the Battle of the Somme.

He wanted to visit another cemetery, in the village. We found the signs and ended up on a farm track where the entrance to the cemetery lay. We went up a set of steps and along a grassy path to the cemetery proper. The scent of farmyard was in the air.

Being now familiar with the routine I found the register and asked Freddy who we were looking for. We went to stand by the grave of a lad called Driver Bernard James of the Royal Field Artillery.

"Tell me about him, Freddy."

"There's not much to say, really, I hardly knew him. He was a relation of one of my sergeants and came out to join us just before the battle started. I think he was still underage, but was very keen to join us."

"Why is he important enough for us to visit the grave, then?"

"He was the first of my men to be killed. In fact, I think he may have been the first in the brigade to be killed in action. It wasn't the Germans that got him, though."

"What killed him, then, if it wasn't the Germans?"

"One of our shells exploded too soon, prematurely. He was in the way. It happened, sometimes. Quite a few men were lost to disease as well, especially towards the end of the war. Mainly Spanish Influenza. We lost some down in Italy with that. A few survived the war and died later back at home, a year or two after the war, from wounds, or conditions they acquired from their service."

"Were there many more men killed here, after Driver James, that is?" I asked.

"Actually no, not here, in this battle. We were in the thick of it from the off, but were remarkably lucky, really. Certainly compared with the infantry, they took a hammering, but somehow we got off lightly. We lost a few later on in the battle, and we will see them later today, in Aveluy, not far from here. Up near Ypres, in Belgium, where we were yesterday was the worst. You remember all those graves at Vlamertinge?"

"Yes."

"Well that was about half of the people we lost up there, the others are scattered around in other, smaller, cemeteries."

"You were involved in the battle, though, weren't you? It says so in your diaries."

"Oh yes, from the first right through to the end. The official battle ended in the November, but the fighting didn't stop, of course. It just got impossible for either side to attack. So we just looked at each other across the mud and threw shells and other things at each other until the spring weather improved ground conditions."

"Where to next, Freddy?"

"We need to find a village called Mesnil. Not far from here. It has special memories for me."

After going to Mesnil, Aveluy, and the Thiepval Memorial we found lunch at a nearby restaurant. In the afternoon we toured a few other places that Freddy had mentioned in his diaries, and at each he gave me a potted history of why it was significant for him.

As the evening approached we motored the hour or so back to our hotel.

As we drove Freddy told me what happened after the battle and over the winter. He said that his brigade was sent further

215

south, over the River Somme, to take over positions from the French and again met up with his friend Armand.

He told me that the French had made much better progress at the beginning of the big battle, and had advanced several miles in that area. The British had agreed to take over more of the front line so shuffled (his description) to the right and took over territory that the French army had won so that they could send more of their troops to another part of the front.

He said that at first it was a quiet sector, but very cold. Whereas the British tried to keep the battlefield as tidy as possible, the French tended to leave debris where it was, especially if it was beyond further function or usefulness. The area they took over was, according to Freddy, liberally littered with broken equipment and dead horses, which his brigade spent much time and effort in clearing away.

He also said that they really thought the war was going to end that year. They had reports that the Germans were short of everything, particularly food, and that the war might have to end to prevent the population of Germany from starving to death. In April the Germans suddenly withdrew and the British advanced very quickly, thinking that the Germans were going home. It turned out to be a false hope, and they were only withdrawing to a more advantageous position.

We dined again at Sebastian's restaurant. I was not sure if I wanted to go there, not sure if I wanted to see Sebastian again. I was certain that if I told Freddy of my reservations he would have allowed me to choose another restaurant, but I did not, and so we went back.

I had not packed for smartness, so had to choose my best pair of jeans and a top, but put on a necklace and tied my hair back so as to be reasonably presentable. Freddy was complimentary, of course, and we walked arm in arm to the square.

Sebastian seemed pleased to see us, and showed us to a table at the rear of the restaurant, beyond the bar. He brought us a bottle of wine and three glasses.

After Freddy and I had eaten Sebastian joined us while the restaurant staff looked after the other customers.

"Did you see everything that you wanted to see?" he asked, more to Freddy than me.

"Yes, thank you, Sebastian, and thank you for the food and wine. You are very generous." said Freddy, to which I agreed.

"You were here, in the first war?" he said to Freddy.

"Yes, only briefly, but yes, I was here. It looked much the same as it does now, except there are fewer soldiers, of course. It was before the big battles later in the war." said Freddy.

"I spoke to my father but he is unable to join us this evening. He told me where his photographs were and I have some of them to show you, please wait." Sebastian left the table and went through to the back of the building.

While he was out I said to Freddy, "It will only be polite to look at the photos, won't it, and we have all evening, don't we?"

Freddy sat back and smiled at me, "Yes, all evening. He is a nice young man. I think he is keen to let us see something that his family have kept for a long time, so let's see."

Sebastian returned and had a photo album under his arm, leather bound and looking old and well used.

He sat down again, then produced glasses from his pocket and put them on. He looked more serious, studious, perhaps.

Opening the album he flicked through the first few pages then pressing it open he turned it round and pushed it across the table so Freddy and I could see the pictures. They were very small, just a couple of inches square. Pointing to one of them he said, "This was my grandmother and her father before the war. They lived on the square, and that is her at about ten years or so. A pretty girl I think."

"Yes," I said, "very pretty." in a polite English way, as in reality the picture was too small to make out the features of the people.

"Her father was taken away by the Germans when they arrived in 1914. She never saw him again. We never found out what happened after that, he did not return."

Freddy was silent, just looking at the photos.

"That is very sad," I said, "what did her mother do?"

"She died before that photo was taken, we do not have any pictures of her. My grandmother was brought up by her aunt, her father's sister." said Sebastian, with no sign of emotion.

"Poor girl!" I said, thinking about a little girl without a mother.

"That sort of thing was very common, you know, all over." said Freddy, looking at me, "Many children lost one or both parents back then. If they had family who could look after them, so good, if not, a neighbour would look after them. It was quite normal, and no legal documents were needed."

"Yes, many children lived that way, especially after the war." said Sebastian, "She had a good upbringing, actually. During the war the shelling here in the city became worse and most of the civilians were sent away into the countryside or other parts of the country. My grandmother went with her aunt to live in Brittany, then they returned to Arras after the war had finished. Her uncle was a carpenter and was not able to serve in the army because he had a problem with one of his legs, he wore a metal brace. In any case, they were safe in Rennes, and after the war there was building to be done here, so they returned. He had many years of work in Arras rebuilding the damage."

"Interesting story." said Freddy.

"Many people in France had similar experiences, I think." said Sebastian, "by the time she came back she was, perhaps, twenty years, and helped her uncle with his work. Then she married and had three children, boys, my father was the youngest. Her husband was in the resistance during the second war. His name is on the wall of the citadel, the Germans shot him, here is a picture of him." and Sebastian turned the pages until he found another picture, a larger one, showing a man, a woman, and three boys. "That is my grandmother, and that is my father." he said, pointing these out on the picture.

"Before the war?" asked Freddy, meaning when the picture had been taken.

"Yes, before that war." confirmed Sebastian.

"So your family lost men in both wars even though they were not soldiers?" I asked.

"Yes, we French have been unlucky in the neighbours we have. At one time it was you English, the Spanish, or the Dutch coming here and fighting us, then it was the Germans. For centuries we have had to live with these facts. This square, Place des Heros, is named for the resistance fighters shot by the Germans, at the citadel."

"I am sorry." I said, not really knowing why I did so.

"It is not your fault, Kate, at least now things are better. You English are lucky, you have been able to decide when to fight a war. My grandmother used to say 'thank God for the English.' She always had a great respect for the English, unusual for a French woman, I know. She used to say that the English were the luckiest people in the world. I think I know what she meant, and why she said it." said Sebastian.

"I think she was a wise lady." said Freddy, "I wish I could have met her, she sounds like my kind of girl."

Sebastian showed us more pictures from his album. Many of them were of his grandfather's work in rebuilding Arras.

We continued to talk late into the evening before Freddy and I returned to our hotel, having bid farewell to Sebastian. On an impulse, and maybe because of the wine I kissed Sebastian on the cheek as we parted.

The next morning Freddy and I left Arras. It would be some time before I returned there.

We drove to the town of Peronne where we stopped for an early lunch.

Freddy explained to me that this town had been occupied by the Germans at the beginning of the war, and that he had spent a cold winter looking down at it from the hills above. He said that it was one of the hardest winters he had ever had, cold and being gassed by the Germans almost every day. He also explained that in early 1917, just when we were hoping that they were going to pack up and go home, the Germans left Peronne, and many other places. They were not going home, though, just pulling back a few miles to a better position, which he said was called the Hindenburg Line.

Freddy spent some weeks after this in a quiet part of the line before his unit was sent up north to Ypres, where they made a big attack, a push as he called it, that autumn. Most of the graves we had visited in Vlamertinge were of men killed in that battle.

Freddy then said that, at the end of the battle, just when they expected to be sent into the attack again an order came through for them to go to Italy to help the Italian Army to stop an attack by the Austrians. He said that our next stop would be in Italy, in a town called Marostica.

While Freddy was in the gents I looked at the road atlas in the car, but I couldn't find where Marostica was.

When Freddy returned to the car he showed me where it was. "It's a long way, Freddy, how long will it take us to drive there?"

"We can take our time, we will drive towards Switzerland tonight and complete the journey tomorrow. We should be there by nightfall tomorrow."

Chapter 16

February 1917, near Peronne, France.

It was cold, it was very, very cold.

Freddy was stamping his feet as he and Ralph waited in the lee of a ruined farmhouse for their French guides to meet them and take them to see the positions that they were to take over.

"I say Freddy, it's mighty parky here, isn't it? How long before the Frenchies turn up, do you think?" said Ralph, his greatcoat collar turned up and a scarf across his lower face.

"Soon, hopefully." was all that Freddy could say through chattering teeth, his gloved hands buried in his topcoat pockets.

The two men were not wearing respirators despite the air being thick with lachrymatory gas. The cold air meant that the eyepieces misted up making the limited vision through them much worse. Most opted to leave the helmet off unless mustard was sent over. The Germans had perfected, if that is the right expression, the art of mixing high explosive and shrapnel shells with lachrymatory and choking gas shells. This was what the British called the 'Kaiser's Cocktail.'

Just when they were thinking they were due a trip back to the transport waiting along the track and over the hill to get a warming cup of tea, two light blue uniformed figures came out of the gloom.

Freddy immediately recognised Armand Chaleyer. "Armand, is it really you? Good God, man, I thought you would have found a cushy billet somewhere in a deep funk hole!"

"Freddy, why, Freddy, it is good to see you again. Come with me, and I will find a place for us to sit and get warm again." said Armand, and after shaking both Englishmen by the hand,

and introducing his companion, he turned and waved his hand to indicate for them to follow him.

Armand was taller than Freddy, as tall as Ralph, and stepped out quickly, leaving Freddy, with his shorter legs, to try to keep up. Freddy was forced to do a kind of half run and half walk.

The new arrivals noticed as they went along the track and across the ground to one side towards what they hoped would be a very deep and very warm bunker, that the entire area seemed to be littered with debris. Smashed wagons, dead horses here and there, piles of shell cases and boxes of all shapes and sizes scattered around randomly.

After perhaps fifteen minutes Armand found a trench and jumping down into it pulled back a curtain of heavy grey material and went down steps. He turned and indicated to Freddy and Ralph to follow him.

The steps led down thirty feet or so, round a corner, through another curtain of similar material, and then into a room lined with wooden revetting. There were chairs and a table. While Armand went into a corner and found a bottle and glasses, Freddy and Ralph sat down without removing any of their clothing.

Armand gave a glass to each of the Englishmen and poured brandy into them, and into his and his assistant's.

"Sante!" he said as he held his glass up and then downed the contents.

"So, Freddy, you have been sent to us again. How were things for you last year?"

"Not so bad really, thank you, Armand."

Armand raised an eyebrow, but did not pursue that line. He knew how the English were, unemotional, understating things. In any case, he reasoned, he was just being polite in asking. No one had had a good time last year.

"When you are warmed up I will take you to see the area."

Freddy looked at Ralph, "Ready?"

"Yes, let's go before it gets too dark."

They went out through a tunnel and arrived after some time in another bunker.

"This will be your home when on observation duty. From here we can see right into Peronne. The Germans are in trenches about a half mile down there, just this side of the river. Our trenches are on the forward slope, so moving over the top is not to be recommended during the day. They send over shells of different sorts all the time without any pattern, so my advice is to keep all movement underground whenever possible, even at night."

Armand then spent time explaining things on the map and pointing out key places on the ground through an observation slit.

"You must have seen many targets in the German rear." Freddy said to Armand.

"Yes, we have a good position here, but the Germans know it and shell us heavily from time to time. We are very exposed here and can only move around during the night time. The infantry have it worse, of course. They are on the hill above Biaches, and are trapped in the trenches during the day. It is very hard on them, especially as they do not have very good dugouts down there. It is difficult for them." said Armand.

While they were in the OP the Germans sent over some shells, they exploded way over to the right in an open area.

"The Boche, they have many ways to upset us." said Armand, "and many different types of shells. Which ones do you dislike the most, Freddy?"

"I hate them all, Armand, though the Little Willie is the most surprising because it is so fast you do not hear it coming. When I am in the infantry trenches, of course the Minnie is really bad, because you can see them coming and they seem to

223

know where you are and chase you along the trench." said Freddy.

"Yes, I agree," said Armand, "The 4.2 is a strange shell, it always seems to land somewhere else, but my worst is the 5.9. It comes slowly, you hear the gun fire first, a long way off, then the sound of the shell arriving. Even a dud shakes the ground, and one that explodes can destroy a deep dugout if it lands close enough. That is my worst one, the 5.9."

"I wonder which of ours the Germans hate the most, Armand?"

"Who knows, perhaps we should ask the next prisoner that we capture?" said Armand with a smile.

"By the way, Armand, thank you for the pinard that you left for us in Hebuterne, the men enjoyed it."

"Did you not enjoy it, Freddy?"

"I did try it, but it was not to my taste, but thank you. Will you be leaving any behind this time?"

"Yes, there will be plenty for you and your men. Personally I think it is terrible stuff, but there is always lots of it around and after a few days without good wine it becomes more attractive. The poilus drink a lot of it, but they are mostly country boys and would not know a decent wine from a bad one."

"My lads will drink anything with alcohol in it."

"Ah, yes, the English are famous for their drinking. Do you have a special girl yet?"

"One that I write to, and who writes back? Yes, a friend of my sister back home."

"And how special is she to you?" asked Armand, becoming serious, "A soldier needs a special woman to give him the desire to fight. We have to fight for something. We French say we fight for the Republic, but in reality we do not, we fight because we have to, it is a duty. You English are different, you come to fight, maybe to help us French or Belgians, but I think you fight for something more than your king and country. You fight to protect your women, and you fight because you enjoy it, am I right?"

Freddy thought about it for a second, "I think that you fight with your heart, and we fight with our heads."

"That may be so, Freddy, but you English also have hearts. Have you found a girl to open your heart to yet?"

"No, not yet, I am not sure how to go about it. My father has never told me how to win a lady's heart and her hand. Apart from my sister and her friends I have not had much contact with the fairer sex."

"I must guess that all your schooling was with boys? The English are very strange, you know, they keep the two sexes apart for much of their life, then expect you to know how to do things. It is a wonder that the English people have managed to survive!"

"Your wife is English, isn't she? How did you woo her?"

"A woman needs to feel special, and to be needed. I made Elizabeth feel both of these things."

"How would I do that? How would I know a girl was the right one for me and how to make her feel special?"

"Ah, that is the secret that you will know only after you have achieved it. Every woman is different. You must know many of them before you can really know who and how. It is an enigma, that is the truth of the matter, but trust me, Freddy, it only makes sense looking back. Follow your instincts." Armand said, looking directly at Freddy, "Every man knows only what he has experienced himself, there are no books on the subject of affairs of the heart which can help more than going with your instincts. Have courage, my friend. When you have the feeling, act!"

Freddy nodded and smiled at Armand, "I will." he said, and they went back to discussing the scene before them on the battlefield.

They later returned to Brigade and discussed the schedule for the relief of the position. That night the British would come in and the French would leave.

The relief went to plan, and the French were clear of the position by first light. Armand stayed with the brigade for a further day, as before, to make sure everything his British comrades needed to know was in order.

That night, as Armand prepared to leave, Freddy sought him out and gave him a bottle of whisky. "This is to thank you for all your help and advice, and the pinard, of course."

"That is very kind of you, Freddy, good luck with your mission." Armand replied, with a wink, "This whisky will be excellent for keeping me warm."

The weather continued to be very cold. The Germans were not very active, and generally contented themselves with sending over shells at regular times, sufficient for the British to be safely underground when they arrived.

Freddy was on duty at the OP, Hastings was on telephone duty with him, and in the funk hole below the OP Ralph House was taking a nap in between duties.

Freddy turned to Hastings and said, "How is the line?" Hastings turned the handle of the field telephone, mumbled to someone at the other end then replaced the handset. "Through, sir." And then he huddled back down with his hands inside the flaps of his greatcoat. Freddy noted that Hastings had been quiet recently, a normally ebullient man, ready to take on any task, he had become morose and withdrawn.

"How are your family, Hastings, had any letters from them recently?"

"My old girl writes me every week, they be all right." said Hastings, with no enthusiasm.

"You have children, don't you, how many?"

"Three." Came the curt response.

Freddy thought about it for a minute, and decided that Hastings must be coming down with a fever, as many others had.

"Hastings, you are not yourself at the moment. When we get off duty go and report to the doctor. I don't want you to go down with trench fever like young Kent and the others did. I need you to be on top form." said Freddy.

"Yes, sir." came the reply.

"I am worried about you, you know. You are not yourself at the moment."

"I am all right."

"I don't think so, is something worrying you?"

"No."

A pause while Freddy pondered about his signaller's condition.

"Do you smell burning?"

Hastings sniffed, looked around, sniffed again, "Yes, sir, there's smoke coming from behind us!"

Alarmed, Freddy told Hastings to stay there and pulled the curtain back from the entrance and was met by a wall of hot smoke. "Bloody hell!" then, "Ralph! Ralph." realising that the smoke was coming up from the room below.

Just then he heard coughing and Ralph's head appeared up the steps, waving his hand in front of him and wearing his repirator. Freddy knew it was Ralph as he had his surname inked across the forehead of the mask, as they all did now, to aid identification.

Freddy reached forward, grabbed Ralph's arm and pulled him into the bunker.

Ralph pulled his respirator to one side exposing his mouth and nose, breathing deeply. "Sorry, sorry, it's all right now."

"What!"

Taking another deep breath Ralph calmed down. "Sorry, Freddy, I lit a fire to get warm and boil a brew but the stove fell over and set fire to the gas curtain. It's out now."

"Bloody fool, you bloody fool." said Freddy.

Hastings just raised his eyebrows and muttered to himself, "Fucking officers." He seemed a little brighter.

Before dawn the next day Freddy and Hastings handed over duty to Edwin and his signaller and returned for breakfast and to get some rest. As they reached the wagon line Freddy reminded Hastings to report sick, and he himself went off to the mess. There Ely had a cup of coffee waiting for him, which Freddy downed with relish, smacking his lips, "Thank you Corporal Ely, how are things with you?"

"I am fine, thank you, sir, but this cold weather is getting me down. The water is frozen, and I have to break the ice every time I need some. Even the food is frozen by the time it gets to us, roll on spring!"

Buster came in, rubbing his hands and shrugging his shoulders, "It's brass monkeys out there, oh, hello Freddy, how were things last night?"

"Very routine, Buster, nothing going on, really, except for some fires and smoke on the far side of Peronne, I reported it to Brigade. They think the Germans must be all a bit like Ralph, setting fire to things to keep warm."

Buster made no comment about Ralph, and continued, "We have some good news, there is a draft coming up in a few days to replace the men we sent down the line with fever. One of them is a friend of yours, Ted Rivett. Can you take him under your wing for the first week or so as your understudy?"

"Of course, Buster, it will be a pleasure to see a fresh face after all these long'uns."

"We are all getting a bit tired of things, I suppose, but at least it is better than the mud we had at the end of the year.

Spring is not far away, and a young man's fancy lightly turns to thoughts of….." said Buster.

"Love?" added Freddy quickly.

"Yes, love." confirmed Buster.

"Fat chance of that out here," said Freddy.

"Not from the Hun in any event, or even from our own masters." said Buster.

"I suppose with the spring will come more action, another big push," said Freddy, "Though the last one turned out to be a bit smaller than we expected."

"Take heart, Freddy," said Buster, "This is going to be a decisive year. There is a rumour that after the battle at Verdun and up here on the Somme the Germans are running out of everything, including enthusiasm. We are expecting that they will want to straighten the line and pull back, when they do we will chase them up and keep them moving. The war could be over by summer, take my word for it."

The doctor, Benefer, came in with Padre Fitzgerald. Corporal Ely served them coffee.

"Thank you, Corporal Ely," said Fitzgerald, and to Buster he said, "Robert and I have been talking. I think we need to do something about the state of the men. A lot are getting sick with fever, and morale seems to be low at the moment. I am worried because the amount of grousing is a good indicator, and many of the men have stopped complaining, not a good sign, Buster."

"Is it just us, or is there a wider problem?"

"It is throughout the brigade, and beyond. I just hope that the generals do not decide that a big push is the antidote. We had a lot of casualties last year, and as you know we have had just as many sent down with fever this year." said Fitzgerald.

Benefer added, "Yes, I have a long queue every sick parade, some of the men have trench fever, but some are just malingering."

Freddy asked, "Hastings should have reported sick this morning, Stephen, have you seen him?"

"Yes, but I think he may be one of the malingerers. He has no signs of fever, but there is something not right about him, but I can't put my finger on it. Keep an eye on him, Freddy, and send him back to me if you think he needs attention."

"I will," said Freddy, "It could be trouble at home, perhaps?"

James Newman came in holding a bundle of letters, "The post is in, the BQMS gave me these to bring along."

He handed Freddy three letters as he doled out the post to those present, "There are two for you and one for Edwin, can you take his and let him have it later on?"

Freddy looked at his letters, one was from his mother, and one from Constance, he decided to read Constance's first. As he put Edwin's letter in his pocket he noted that the writing on it was the same as his, Constance had been busy writing to both of them.

He opened the envelope, and unfolded the paper inside. He caught a slight odour of Constance's perfume. The letter read:

My Dearest Freddy,

I hope that you are well and the cold weather is not causing you too much distress. It has been cold here at home but at least we have a roaring fire to sit before and warm ourselves.

The news we are seeing from the front is good, the papers are saying that the blockade is causing the Germans much trouble and that they will be ready to stop fighting if food becomes more scarce.

Father continues to spend most of his time at the works. He has signed several contracts with the War Office and without James Newman to help it is very difficult for him.

My aunt has written to me to tell me that there are many cases of fever and other difficulties for the men at the front. She is well in herself, and I imagine that she is much happier now that she is close to the front and able to help in a practical way. She has told me that you Scott boys come to see her when you can. She asked me to tell you that she values these visits and knowing that you are all well.

Freddy, you are a very special person to me, I look forward to your next leave when we can spend a little time together.

With much affection,

Connie

Freddy, read the letter a second time then folded it and placed it into his breast pocket, smiling.

Three days later Buster told Freddy that General Trubshawe was planning to lead a patrol into no-man's land. As Freddy was on OP duty that night he would be responsible for keeping watch and calling down artillery fire if the patrol got into trouble. Apparently there had been intelligence reports that the Germans were up to something, and the general wanted to see for himself.

For several days there had been explosions and smoke all over Peronne and the countryside beyond it. The patrol would be led by Stephen Sansom, and he and Sergeant Wilf Baker were in the room when Freddy arrived for the briefing. General Trubshawe arrived a little later with his chief of staff and his intelligence officer.

Trubshawe was wearing his usual mackintosh without any rank badges showing. On removing the top coat Freddy could see the row of ribbons above Trubshawe's left breast pocket. His greying and thinning hair and moustache betrayed his years, but his bearing was upright. The way he carried his spare frame confirmed that he was still a man in his prime, and well inured to the military life. Trubshawe took off his haversack and hung it over the back of a chair.

Freddy idly wondered whether the old boy had brought along his usual bars of chocolate and packets of cigarettes in the haversack.

Trubshawe said, "Good afternoon gentlemen, please smoke if you wish to, and we will get on with this evening's patrol."

Freddy took out his pipe and filled it with Erinmore and lit it up. He had become adept at smoking now, though he had to admit to himself that he was still not sure that he enjoyed it. Others who smoked seemed to get some satisfaction from tobacco, and Freddy felt that also being a smoker helped him to fit in.

Trubshawe explained that he believed that the Germans were thinning out their line and preparing to pull back to a more defensible line. Their positions around Peronne were under direct observation from the British lines, and he felt that they may be moving their main position back beyond the high ground on the far side of the town.

He wanted the patrol to enter the German trenches, see what the state of manning there was, and if possible bring back a prisoner. The signals for Freddy to fire the SOS and other targets was agreed, and the timings for the patrol to leave and return were communicated.

The group then dispersed, the infantry to go off and brief the men and prepare their equipment, the gunners to go off and calculate the possible fire missions and prepare the guns and ammunition.

At the appointed hour for the patrol to leave, Freddy received a call on his field telephone confirming that the patrol was about to depart.

While the patrol was out in no-man's land Freddy, though alert, was thinking.

Armand had advised him to act on his instincts, but he was not sure what his instincts were. He had been brought up to act rationally, using logic to examine issues, work out possibilities, then choose a course of action that would produce the optimum results. How would he recognise instincts? If he could recognise them, could he trust them? A thought occurred to him, he needed more information, and that might mean talking to more men who had the right experience. He said, "Hastings, you're a married man, aren't you? Would you mind if I asked you a few questions?"

Hastings replied, "Yes. sir, what about?"

"You have a wife, and children, so you must have been single once and decided to get married, and that your wife was the right girl for you. How did you know she was the right one? I mean, you must have known a lot of girls, but you chose one, so how did you come to make that choice?"

Hastings looked a little perplexed, then said, "I did not choose her, really. We lived next door to each other. We grew up together, and it just seemed natural that when we were of age we would get married. All the lads in The North End do the same."

"Would you say that you are happily married? Is she the right one for you?"

"I suppose so, we are no different from anyone else, really. I have never thought about it much. I love her, and she loves me, and we both love our young'uns."

"Do you miss them, being out here?"

"Of course I do, I miss them like mad, but my family are looking after them. I have one sister left at home who keeps an eye out for them, and my dad is around when he is not at sea. My mum and dad live next door, so I know they are all right." said Hastings, a little brighter than he had been of late.

"Thank you, Hastings."

"Are you having girl trouble, sir?"

"No, not really, but a lot of us out here have a wife or special girl, and I don't."

"Don't worry about it, sir, until your next leave. There must be a lot of girls back home without men, a young gentleman like you will have a lot to choose from."

"Mmm." said Freddy, just as a shot rang out from no-man's land. Freddy lifted the binoculars to his eyes, but all was dark and still out towards the Germans. Freddy continued to scan while he lifted the receiver of the field telephone and reported what he had heard.

Freddy looked at his watch, it was about time the patrol returned. He heard and saw nothing.

A half hour later he was still watching when the telephone rang. Brigade informed him that the patrol had come in and therefore any movement in no-man's land would be by the Germans and he should report it.

Freddy and Hastings continued their watch until dawn when they were relieved and made their way back to the battery and then Freddy went on to Brigade HQ. He arrived early for the debrief, so he went to the mess for breakfast.

Corporal Ely was ready with hot coffee for Freddy, and he received it with grateful thanks. Buster came in and also had a cup of Ely's coffee. Buster, who had been on duty at Brigade the previous night, asked Corporal Ely for whisky, and poured one for himself and one for Freddy. "I don't normally drink in the morning, Buster, thank you, in fact I am not much of a drinker at all." said Freddy.

"Get it down you, Freddy, it will warm you up and I understand this is a celebration. I heard that the patrol last night found the German trenches empty, apart from a couple of dozy buggers in a bunker. One of them made the mistake of resisting and they had to shoot him, but the other one came back with the patrol. It seems that the Germans are going home, and that means the war is over, or will be soon!"

Freddy was not sure that Buster was right in his assessment, but supposed that Buster had better information and experience than him, so took the glass and sipped at it.

General Trubshawe came in with Stephen Sansom. Corporal Ely somehow knew they were arriving and had two more cups of coffee waiting for them.

Buster said to the general, "I understand that things went well last night, General."

"Yes, thank you Buster, they did. You will hear all about it at the conference, but we have confirmed what we suspected. The Germans have gone, their trenches were more or less empty. They have done a bunk. Intelligence are interrogating the prisoner, but I understand German a little, and he was babbling about them having gone. The front is wide open. We will be planning a general advance, so I want your guns to be ready to move forward for mobile operations by tonight."

"That sounds like very good news, General." opined Freddy, emboldened by the whisky.

"In my opinion, and experience, no news is as good or as bad as it first seems, young man, so we still need to be prepared for anything. What is that you are drinking?" said Trubshawe.

Freddy looked around and saw that Buster's glass had disappeared, and he was the only one to have a glass and not a cup in his hand. "It's whisky, General."

Trubshawe looked at Freddy and said in a tone that his father used when Freddy had transgressed, "You will not find comfort in the bottom of a glass, young man, it is not a good thing to start drinking at this early hour!"

"No sir, sorry sir." Freddy mumbled and put the glass down.

The advance started that night. Firstly infantry patrols went out all along that section of line and found the Germans had departed. The patrols advanced as far as the river Somme, then the Royal Engineers came forward with bridging materials.

Once on the other side of the river the troops fanned out and entered the town. There they found that the Germans had destroyed everything. Trees were down and laying across the roads, many buildings had been blown up and burned, wells had been poisoned. It was clear that the Hun was living up to his reputation for abominable behaviour.

Buster and Ralph were standing outside the entrance to a German built bunker in the centre of Peronne, pondering what to do next.

"Should we go in, do you think?" Ralph asked Buster.

"I am not sure, Ralph, I think we should wait for the sappers to inspect it first. The Germans have left traps and trip wires all over the place."

Freddy arrived with more men. "Is this the bunker for us to set up in?" he said to Buster.

"Yes, but I want us to wait for a while until we can get it cleared."

"Where should I go, then, Buster?

"Settle down over there for a while." said Buster, indicating a pile of rubble on the other side of the road. "I will let you know when this is all right to use. Ralph, put a sign board up by the entrance claiming this bunker for our brigade so no one else bags it, will you, please? I am off to find the colonel and see what's what."

Buster left and Ralph chalked up the sign and then went to the rubble pile to sit with Freddy and his men until further orders arrived.

One of the signallers had searched around and found some scraps of wood and had started a fire to boil water for a brew.

"Is that wise do you think?" Freddy asked of Ralph, "the Germans might see the smoke."

"Relax, no-one is going to notice the smoke. There are entire buildings on fire all over the place, this will make no difference and a warm drink will be just the thing while we wait." said Ralph, his age advantage of a year over Freddy giving him added gravitas, despite his habits of taking very little seriously and getting into trouble constantly.

Freddy acquiesced and sat down on the remains of a wall, took out his pipe and filled it, waiting for the water to boil.

One of the signallers said, "Look, sir, over there, those buggers are stealing our bunker!"

And sure enough a group of soldiers, infantrymen, had turned up and were in the process of entering the bunker despite Ralph's sign outside.

Ralph stood and shouted across the road, "I say, you, that bunker has been taken, it's ours. Bugger off and find another one!" as a sergeant, his rifle slung over his shoulder was talking to another soldier and three others were going into the entrance.

The sergeant looked across the road at Ralph and put his hand to his ear as if he did not catch what Ralph had said.

Ralph took one step forward, then was blown backwards onto the rubble pile, landing on Freddy's lap.

Picking themselves up Freddy and Ralph stood and saw that the road was covered with debris, bricks, wood, and bodies. They went over to see if there was anything they could do, but there was nothing to be done for the sergeant, for the bundle of rags they found in the middle of the road had been that sergeant. Or at least part of him.

Freddy was laying in the undergrowth at the edge of a wood, looking out over a field towards a low hill. He could see the rooves of a village just beyond.

Over the previous week he had been involved with daily advances of about a mile, followed by rearguard actions by the Germans which required quick bombardments by his battery. The infantry would probe forward, and once again find that the enemy had gone.

The weather was warming with spring, and the constantly withdrawing enemy helped to raise morale.

"Check the line again, Hastings. The infantry will be going forward in five minutes and I want to be sure we can get through to Brigade if they need some shrapnel." he said.

"Yes, sir." Hastings turned the handle of the field telephone, listened then said, "Through, sir."

"Thank you."

"Is the war going to be finished soon, sir?" Hastings asked after a while.

"Possibly. Hold on, there they go." Freddy said as he saw infantrymen come out of the wood and start to cross the field. "Tell Brigade that the attack is going in."

Freddy watched as the infantry made it across the field and disappeared over the top of the hill. No reaction from the Germans. "It looks like the Boche have gone. Time for us to pack up and move on, Hastings."

"We have not moved forward for three days, now, have we?" James said to Freddy while they were drinking coffee.

"No, the Germans have stopped. Maybe they are enjoying the sunshine." said Freddy, drawing on his pipe.

"There was a new draft yesterday."

"Yes, we have a new subaltern, Ted Rivett. Buster has asked me to look after him until he has learned the ropes. He was keen to join our brigade. He was at Fishers when I was there and has been through the OTC so should fit in. There are a couple of men returning from hospital as well, but most of them are new men, conscripts. We will have to see how keen they are on their new way of life."

"I think that the war will be going on for a while yet. The Boche still have some fight in them." said James.

"I'm afraid you are probably right." said Freddy, tapping out his pipe.

The brigade were out of the line as spring was turning into summer. General Trubshawe was on one of his frequent visits to the gunners.

He asked for the officers and senior NCOs to be assembled for a briefing. They sat around on the grass in a semicircle as the general stood before them.

"I can tell you that the Americans have declared against Germany. We can expect to see their troops arriving here, in France, soon."

A burble rose from the assembly.

"While we are waiting for them to arrive and lift the burden from our shoulders, or at least share the burden, we have things to do. As you will know by now our attacks at Vimy and Messines have gone well. Well done to the Canucks. A new battle has just started at Arras, and early indications are that progress is good. We may be needed to assist up there, but for the time being we will be moving to new positions in a quiet sector. We should have at least a month there, so make the best you can of the weather and the opportunity to bring your equipment and training up to the best that it can be. The better weather has reduced the trench fever. The doctor will be inspecting everyone in your brigade to make sure that you are in good health. The chief of staff will be issuing detailed orders for the next move, and I will keep you informed of developments up north as I have them. Gentlemen, are there any questions?"

Buster asked, "Is there any information on the state of the Germans, sir. We have been told that they are on their last legs."

"It is safe to assume that if they are, they seem to have more legs than is normal. Please assume that they are just as resolved as we are to win. My view is that they will not give in for a long while yet. I am sorry if that is not what you would want to hear."

"Thank you, General."

After a few more questions the general handed the parade back to Kit and left. The officers and NCOs were dismissed and broke off in small groups to return to their duties.

"What is that town over there, sir?" Hastings asked.

"Cambrai, why?" said Freddy, as he and Hastings sat in the OP, keeping watch.

It was warm, and there had been no firing to disturb the sounds of nature around them for several days.

"No reason, sir, just wondered. Is the war over?"

"No, not yet, soon though."

"The Germans are quiet, sir, have been for days."

"They are all up north, with a bit of luck, that is where the war is at the moment." said Freddy.

The two men fell into silence again. Freddy opened his breast pocket and took out his latest letter from Constance. He read it again.

"That looks like a woman's writing, sir, who's it from?" asked Hastings.

"None of your business, Hastings." Freddy said, without feeling.

Ignoring this statement Hastings continued, "You have a lady friend now, sir, do you?"

"No, she is a friend of my sister."

Hastings looked at Freddy, raised an eyebrow, and smiled.

The mess was full. It had become the habit over the last few days, it being quiet, for the officers to gather at breakfast for eggs. While bacon was supplied by the army, eggs had become a rarity. That was, they had been a rarity until Sergeant Leman had somehow acquired some chickens which he kept at his gun. They clucked and pecked while the gunners sunned themselves and polished and oiled their guns and stacked and re-stacked the ammunition that seemed to be irrelevant to the war.

Sergeant Leman became a popular man. In return for a few eggs he was able to swap duties with other NCOs, and acquire supplies for his crew that would otherwise have been in short supply. He always made sure that the officers' mess was well supplied with eggs and the occasional chicken carcass. Every morning the officers were able to enjoy scrambled eggs, or omelettes with their coffee and bacon, as also were the sergeants in their mess.

"Football again this afternoon, then, James, who are we playing this time?" asked Buster as he helped himself to another cup of coffee.

"The Norfolks, B company I think." replied James, "but I may be wrong on that detail."

"This is just like peacetime, isn't it? Just like being on annual camp."

"It won't last, of course." said James.

"No, it won't."

Dobbin came into the mess and seeing Buster went over to him. "Buster, Brigade have had a message from Ralph at the OP. They want you to go along and give your opinion on something he has seen."

"Righto, all right, I'm off then. See you all for lunch." Buster put on his helmet, buckled on his Sam Browne and haversack, and left.

He was in a good mood as he wound his way to the OP, a country gent out for a stroll, he mused as he approached the OP.

"Tell me what I should be looking at, Ralph. It had better be good, you disturbed my breakfast."

"Well, Buster, we saw a flashing light about two miles away, over there, towards Cambrai. It looks like the Boche are using a heliograph, but it might be something else."

Buster went to the front of the OP and looked out, his binoculars ready in his hand. stayed there for five minutes. "No, nothing seen, Ralph, point it out to me again."

Ralph moved forward to be beside Buster, just as Buster saw a light flashing. "Wait, I think I've got it. Is that it, there?"

Ralph looked in the same direction, "Yes, that's it."

Buster watched for a while until the light stopped. "I think you are right, it is probably is a heliograph. They must be communicating with a position somewhere nearer to us. Lets plot the direction and see if we can estimate where they are."

Ralph took a compass shot and plotted it on his map. "How far do you think, Buster?" he asked.

"A couple of miles. What lies on that line on the map at that distance?"

"There is a farm there," Ralph said, pointing to a position on the map, on the side of a hill. My guess is that is where it is."

Buster looked at the map and sat thinking for a minute. "Yes, I think you are right. Let's report it to Brigade and see what they want to to with it."

The signaller turned the handle on the telephone and handed the receiver to Buster. He reported the information. Colonel Howard came on the line and decided to fire at the target.

Buster sent orders to his battery.

At the gun line the gunners were kicking a football around, preparing for the match against the infantry later that day, when the order came down to 'Take Post!'

They all ran over to their guns and took their positions. Two of them went to the ammunition stack and pulled back the canvas cover and exposed the rounds which had been unboxed and laid out for easy selection of the type of shells that were to be loaded and fired.

The order came. Three guns were to fire HE, three guns were to fire shrapnel. Direction and range were passed to the guns and the layers set their sights. The time setting for the shrapnel was calculated and set on the fuses. The shells were loaded, the numbers one checked that direction and range had been set correctly.

D sub gun was designated as adjusting gun, and Buster proceeded to bracket the target with shrapnel shells. When this was achieved to Buster's satisfaction he gave the order to fire five rounds per gun.

The gunners had not had a fire mission such as this for many days and were keen to exercise themselves.

The gun teams competed to see which gun could report 'rounds complete' first.

Ted Rivett was at the gun line as section commander for the day, understudying Dobbin. As Ted was doing well, Dobbin had decided to join C Sub as layer.

As the third round on C sub was being fired the breech exploded, sending pieces of metal flying around the gun pit. Most of the breech passed by and missed the number one, but the breech lever flew sideways striking Dobbin. His left humerus was shattered, and the ribs on that side of his body broken. His left lung collapsed and he was sent flying away from the gun, landing in a heap on the floor of the gun pit. He lay there, writhing in pain.

Ted froze, his mind blank as to what to do. Sergeant Leman, hearing the explosion immediately shouted, "Stand Fast! Cease Loading!"

While the gun teams remained at their posts Sergeant Leman ran over to C Sub and took in the situation. The gun team were also concussed by the breech explosion, and unable to collect their thoughts.

Leman went to where Dobbin lay and put his hand on his undamaged shoulder, and reassured him speaking softly in his ear.

Ted was shaking, his voice wavering, but he managed to tell two gunners to get the stretcher from the troop shelter at the rear of the position. They put Dobbin onto the stretcher, and Ted ordered four of them to take the stretcher back to the RAP, some half mile further behind their position.

Buster, hearing what had happened over the telephone immediately ordered the end of firing, left the OP and hurried back to the gun line. Ralph was left at the OP.

Later, in the mess, Ted sought out Freddy. "I am sorry about Dobbin, there was nothing I could do."

"I know, Ted, these things happen. We have had problems with the ammunition before but never a breech premature. I understand that Dobbin is in a bad way, let's hope he pulls through all right."

"It was so sudden, the day was perfect, then that has to happen."

Freddy put his hand on Ted's shoulder, "Ted, it was not your fault, there was nothing you could do to prevent it."

"I know, but I just froze when it happened. I didn't know what to do. I am not sure I am cut out to be an officer. I should have been in charge, and I just froze." Freddy saw tears forming in the corners of Ted's eyes.

"Come away from the others, come with me." Freddy took Ted by the arm and led him away and out of the mess. When they were outside Freddy said, "Ted, these things happen, we have all had doubts from time to time, but you will get used to things, just hang on. Believe in yourself. The first casualty is the worst, over time you will get used to it, I promise." Ted looked at Freddy, and tried a weak smile. Freddy could see that Ted was struggling to control his face, which looked as if he would burst into tears. Freddy patted him on the shoulder and said, "Let's walk around for a bit, the air will do you good."

They walked around for a long time while Freddy talked and Ted stayed quiet, just grunting and nodding from time to time, with an occasional sob escaping.

They came to the farmhouse that served as sleeping accommodation for the mess, Freddy told Ted to go to bed and get some sleep. Ted was due on OP duty that night, but Freddy told him that he would do his duty for him. Ted did as he was bid, and Freddy went back to the mess, spoke to Buster about doing Ted's stag at the OP. Buster agreed.

The next morning Ted seemed to be much better, and resumed his duties.

Leave rosters were announced. When his turn came Freddy went to see James Newman to see if there were any papers to go to William Mann, but there were none.

The journey home was no less tedious and long, but in due course he arrived at Lynn railway station. Once again Sissie was there to meet him and take him to Saddlebow.

As he went to open the front door it opened and his mother was there. She smiled and hugged him, for a little longer than was her habit. His father was out. The four of them had dinner together, and without thinking Freddy asked for wine, forgetting that his mother forbad anything other than sherry in the house. He settled for a small glass of sherry.

The next morning he woke early, put on his uniform and, without breakfasting left the house.

Freddy walked the two miles into town in under the hour, and went to the South Quay. Here he found a low wall to sit on and watch people passing by. It was a warm day, and a soft breeze came across the river towards him, bringing with it the reassuring smell of spring.

Many thoughts passed through his mind as he sat there. People passed by on their errands and business. Few glanced in his direction, and none tried to speak to him.

Though Freddy was in a safe, peaceful, familiar place, he felt unsettled. Remembering Fitzgerald's advice, he smiled to himself, pulled the pipe from his pocket, filled it and lit it. He calmed.

His thoughts turned to France, and the things he had seen there. He thought of Walter, and seeing him die. He thought of the hundreds, thousands of men that he had seen leave the relative safety of the trenches and advance across no-man's land, many never to return. He thought of the waving hand that he and Edwin had seen, and felt a little satisfaction in knowing that he had probably helped to save that man, though he had to participate in the death of another, the sniper, to achieve that. 'An eye for an eye' was a fleeting thought, Old Testament? Yes, Old Testament he decided, is that how we are meant to think, and to act? Or, New Testament, forgiveness? Not sure. What would William Mann say if he knew?

He thought of poor Dobbin, a friend who had been just like Freddy, who in an instant had been reduced to a statistic and was now buried under six feet of French soil in Grey Villas.

Was he, Freddy, lucky, or unlucky? He decided that he had been lucky. So far. How long would his luck hold out? What would Walter, or Dobbin, tell him from their graves? Would they give him advice, would they want to? Would he follow their advice if he were to receive it?

Something that the padre had said came into his mind, and also Armand. They both said act on your instincts, if only he knew what instinct felt like. Looked like? How would he know?

He thought back to the time in Doullens, they had all sworn brotherhood. He and Edwin had promised to fulfil the other's destiny if they were killed. If he were to be in a position to fulfil the promise he would need to find a wife. He still did not know how he could achieve that. Where to start?

'Act on your instincts' stuck in his mind.

He stared out at the river flowing slowly past, at a blackbird pecking for its breakfast. He lit another pipe of tobacco and continued to think.

Fitzgerald had said that a pipe was comforting because it recreated the act of suckling at your mother's breast. He was right, it was soothing at least.

He found the thinking of his mother's breasts impossible, it was not the way to think about your mother. His thoughts turned to Roselyn. She was the opposite of what he had been led to believe a girl should be. His own sister, Sissie, had always avoided showing her body to her brothers, she seemed to be ashamed of it, yet Roselyn was completely oblivious of her nakedness in the barn.

A decision suddenly came to him, he must find a wife, on this leave, today. He must know what it is to have loved as an adult. He must not pass over, leaving nothing behind but fading memories in others. But who would be the chosen girl? Constance! Of course, had she not written to him in very affectionate terms in her letters. Had he missed this before? Had he not returned her affections?

He would go to her, today, and ask her to marry him. It had suddenly cleared in his head, he was meant to marry Constance, the truth had been in front of him all this time, and he had been too stupid to see it.

He knocked out the pipe and put it in his pocket as he stood with new purpose.

A ring! He would need a ring!

He strode off towards the High Street, he knew there was a jeweller there. He had often passed by on his way to the town centre.

He walked in and said to the old man behind the counter, "I would like to buy an engagement ring, please."

The man nodded and opened a cabinet which had a couple of dozen rings in trays. "What did you have in mind, sir?"

Realising that he was on uncharted territory, and that he had not really thought this through enough, Freddy replied, "I am not sure, what would you suggest?"

"Well, it rather depends on the lady's likes and dislikes, sir. What is your intended's preference? Her birth sign, perhaps?" the man said.

"I have absolutely no idea, I am afraid." said Freddy, realising his rashness.

"May I suggest, sir, that it would be better if you were to find out from your intended what her preferences are? I think that would be best, don't you, sir?" said the man in a kindly manner.

"Yes, yes, you are right, thank you." said Freddy, realising his mistake, but excited in a strange way, to be doing something like this. He left the shop and with new impetus strode off towards the Mann's house in Gaywood, to see Constance.

He arrived, marched up the drive and knocked at the front door. He heard movement inside the house, then the door opened, and there was Constance standing on the threshold.

"Freddy!" she said, "we were not expecting you today. How nice to have you visit, and so early, please come in."

Constance stepped to one side and held the door open for Freddy to pass inside. "May I offer a cup of tea or coffee?" she asked.

"Er, um, yes, please, coffee, please."

Constance smiled at him, put her hand on his arm and said, "It really is very good to see you Freddy, please come through." She led the way to the garden room at the back of the house.

While Constance went to make the coffee Freddy stood in the garden room, pacing around as if trying to make up his mind what to say.

When Constance returned with the tray of coffee Freddy watched her, still standing. "Won't you sit?" said Constance as she sat down.

"No, I would rather stand, Constance. I have something rather important to tell you."

Her face flinched, as if she thought this could be bad news. Sensing this Freddy went to her and put his hand on her arm. "Constance, it's all right, it's not anything bad. In fact, it's something rather good that I want to tell you." He was close enough to her to smell the lavender perfume that she wore. He felt the warmth of her skin beneath the flimsy sleeve of her dress.

"Whatever can it be?" she said, a little relieved, but unsure of what was to come next.

"Constance, I have been doing a lot of thinking lately. Many things have happened and I am conscious that I have not always written fully and honestly to you in my letters."

Constance lost her smile and looked more seriously at Freddy.

"I think that I may be guilty of overlooking the true meaning of your letters to me." he said, and then knelt down, and said to her, "Constance, I want you to be my wife, I would like to ask for your hand in marriage." And without waiting for her response, for there was none as he had caught her completely unawares, he continued, "I know that I will have to speak to your father to ask for his permission, and my own parents, of course, but I know that they will agree. Please say yes."

Constance was not smiling. She looked down at her hands, "Freddy, this is very sudden, but no, I can't marry you, it is not right."

This was not the answer that Freddy had expected. He had thought that maybe she would delay, or hesitate. He carried on, without apparently hearing what she had said. "Some of my friends have passed over, and they have lost the chance to be married and have a family. I want to make sure that does not happen to me. If I am to be killed, then I must leave something tangible behind."

Constance looked at Freddy full in the face and said "Freddy, Freddy, no, I can't marry you."

Freddy did hear this. "Why, why not?"

"Because I am not ready to marry anyone, Freddy, and I think your reasoning is wrong."

"Why are you not ready?"

"Well, I am too young for one thing, and I should wait until the war is finished, for another."

"The war is almost finished, Constance," he said, "the Germans are on their knees and they won't last much longer."

"Freddy, my answer is no. Please do not be angry or disappointed. I want to be friends with you, but I won't, can't, agree to marry you. I'm sorry."

Freddy, crestfallen, looked away. He had another thought. "Is it because I am younger than you?"

"No, Freddy." Constance replied, with a smile, "You are a good man, and a good friend, but I do not think of you as a husband. I do not think you are ready to be a husband for any girl, really. You have time to find a wife, but wait until the war is really finished. If you were to marry now you may leave behind a widow if you are unlucky enough to be killed. Or what if you are badly injured, how would you look after a wife and family. I am not saying it would be selfish of you to marry now, but think about what it would mean for your wife, to be left alone, worrying about things and not knowing if you would be coming home."

Freddy had visibly sagged, his plan had not worked, and he felt, and looked, deflated.

Constance realised she had disappointed him, and tried to cheer him up. "Freddy, all is not lost. You will make a good husband for some lucky girl, some day, just not now. You will be a good catch for someone."

Freddy remained silent, so much so that Constance felt impelled to add: "Freddy, we can still be friends, can't we? I still regard you, and your brothers, as my brothers. Please don't think that I do not love you, just not in that way. Shall we just pretend that you never asked me that. I am just not in a position to think of being promised to anyone, but if I were, you would definitely be on my list of suitors."

Freddy brightened a little, the hope of a possible future, deeper, relationship with Constance brought him some comfort.

He sat down.

"Constance, I would like to continue for us to write to each other."

"Of course, of course we will, we must, Freddy." she said, "Now, you must tell me all about what you and Edwin have been up to, and George, of course!"

The conversation continued for another hour as Freddy told Constance a sanitised version of what he had seen, done, and experienced over the previous year, filling in a few more details than he had felt able to in his letters. By the conclusion he was feeling better about things. On the way back to town, and home, he did not feel able to revisit the jewellers shop, but held the hope that he would be able to at some point in the future.

For the remainder of his leave he spent time with Sissie, out of the house as much as possible. His parents, being Methodists, did not condone drinking at home, so Freddy and Sissie often went to the Duke's Head Hotel in town to find refreshments. Sissie expressed concern at Freddy drinking more than she thought sensible.

"Freddy, you are drinking more than before." Sissie said.

"I know, it's how things are now."

"Mamma would not be happy if she knew."

"I think she does know, but ignores it."

"Papa would be angry, he has never touched alcohol." she said.

"Neither had I until I went to war. I know Grandad's family were against it and built the chapel in the village to try to stop the farm hands drinking, but everyone in the army drinks. It has just become a habit, I suppose, like the pipe."

He filled his pipe and lit it.

"I am still worried for you, Freddy."

"I know, I know. But I never drink to excess, to be incapable."

That night Sissie drove back with Freddy slumped on the seat beside her, sedated by a combination of alcohol, disappointment, and the thought of the return journey to the front.

Sissie helped him out of the car and into the house, putting him to bed, where he slept soundly.

The next morning Sissie told her parents that Freddy was suffering from a chill and she would nurse him back to health, though, of course, his real malady was a hangover.

Freddy went back from leave to the front with a degree of relief. At least he was entirely familiar with the ways that things were there. The affairs of the heart had remained a mystery to him.

He arrived back at the brigade just as they were packing up to move to a different sector. They had been relieved from the front and were laagered in their old haunt at Sailly-au-Bois.

On arriving he reported to Kit Chilvers at Brigade HQ. "I have some bad news for you, Freddy." said Kit, "both your brothers have been wounded and evacuated. They will probably be on their way to Blighty already. George was shot in the leg, and Edwin got a shell splinter in his back. They should be all right, though. The doctor says that they both were lucky to get Blighty ones. A few months in hospital with pretty nurses should sort them out and they will be back with us by the end of the year, he thinks."

Freddy was taken aback by this news. He had been feeling that returning to what he now knew best, soldiering, especially with his brothers, would counteract the disappointment he had experienced at home, with Constance.

"So they are going to be all right? You are being honest with me, aren't you, Kit?" said Freddy.

"Yes, yes, of course I am Freddy. I know the news is not what you would want to hear, but at least they will both be safe for a while." said Kit. "Unlike Colonel Howard. He was killed by the same shell that got Edwin. I have had to write to his widow to tell her what happened, not a pleasant experience, and Trubshawe has done the same. We had to make sure our stories tallied so Mrs Howard did not get too distressed by knowing what really happened. It was strange, really, as you know Colonel Howard was not too keen on being at the front. He preferred to lead from the rear, as it were. In fact, I don't think he had been anywhere near the gun line for ages. He and Edwin were there to look into how we were storing the ammunition. Apparently some staff officer had heard that the gunners were letting the shells get dirty and left all over the place - total rot of course - and Howard thought he would go down there and see what was happening. Just as he was leaving the Huns threw over some HE and caught him as he was mounting his horse. It took his head clean off, they found it twenty yards away. Anyway, we will be getting a new CO when we get to our new position."

"Bloody hell!" breathed Freddy, "You said Edwin was there with him?"

"Yes, Edwin was a bit behind the colonel and had not got on his horse. She took most of the splinters and the vet had to put her down, so Edwin was lucky, in a way." said Kit.

Freddy sat down.

"I am sure you will have more questions, Freddy, and I am happy to answer them as and when, but for now we have to get ready for the move. You will probably have to fill in for Edwin for a while until we can sort out reinforcements. Ted Rivett will take over your section."

"Right, where are we going next then, Kit?"

"Somewhere up north, around Wipers, exact locations will be given to us before we get there. It seems a big push is on the cards. Oh, another thing you need to get involved with. We have had problems with your signaller, Hastings. He has been threatening to go AWOL. He has been reporting sick again, and the doctor says there is nothing physically wrong with him. Can you have a word with him and the doctor and try to get to the bottom of the problem. Hastings seems to get on with you and we are going to need everyone on top form if we get involved with a push up north."

Freddy went to the wagon line and found James Newman. James commiserated with Freddy about his brothers, and asked about conditions at home. Freddy said that he had seen Constance and that she said her father was working hard but seemed a little brighter than before. The works was busy with war contracts, but that the general opinion was that life was on hold until the war ended.

James did seem to be in a better mood than was normal, but for no obvious reason, Freddy thought, but shrugged this off.

He went on to the gun line to see how Ted was getting on with his new responsibilities. He seemed excited, "We are off for a big push, Freddy!" was Ted's opening statement.

"I think I would prefer a small push!" replied Freddy.

Chapter 17

October 1917, The Ypres Salient, Belgium.

Battery Sergeant Major Barry Evans stood beside a shattered tree a hundred yards from Hell Fire Corner. It was early evening, and the rain had started again. It was unseasonably cold, and as he breathed out clouds of vapour slowly drifted away into the mist.

While he waited for the latest draft of reinforcements he thought back over his life.

He felt the pain that his father inflicted on him when he had tried to protect his mother from the drunken rage. He remembered arriving at the orphanage in Cardiff after his mother's death. He remembered the cold and the hunger of being a waif and stray in the workhouse. And the beatings.

He recalled the day he enlisted as a boy soldier to escape.

The Army had been good to him. It had become his family. It had cherished him. It had let him grow into manhood. And he loved it in return.

The rain dripped from his tin hat onto his shoulders and his boots squelched in the mud as he shifted his position.

He could recall stepping ashore in Durban in March '79 to serve in the Zulu Wars. As a 15 year old trumpeter he saw action at Ulundi. This had been his first time in action. The first time he saw human flesh being destroyed, and where he first lost friends. Where he first comforted a man as his life ebbed away, and first saw how pathetically vulnerable a grown man can be when he exceeds his capacity to endure.

Over the years he had served in many other places, India on the North West Frontier, and the Third Burma War. His last time in action had been in South Africa again where he had served with men from Norfolk. Where he had decided that when he left the Regular Army he would go to live in that county. Where he believed that life would be better than in his native Wales, a place that held no warm memories for him.

Now he was at war again, in his fifty fourth year, when he should have been a grandfather, a status that he had found unattainable because he had married the army, and the men, boys rather, under his care were his family.

Like any father, or grandfather, he loved his children with a deep concern for them, though he was careful not to show this too often. If they knew how he loved them he would lose their respect and deference. It was better, he knew, to look after them by his actions, than by his words.

He had, once upon a time, thought that it might be good to find a loving wife, settle down somewhere, raise sons, and daughters. This dream had failed to solidify into reality. There had been women in his life, but none of them were willing, or able, to tolerate the life of a soldier such as him.

By persistence and loyalty, and doubtless by ability, he had built a career. As a warrant officer in the Royal Regiment, willing to serve wherever and whenever his monarch needed him he felt that he had repaid the debt he owed to the Army. The Army that had reclaimed him from a life that had started badly.

He knew that his position, here at Hell Fire Corner, was dangerous. The name of the place told a story, but orders were orders, and wait here he would, until the draft arrived and he could take them forward to Hill Top Farm where the gun crews desperately needed their strength.

He checked his wristwatch, the draft was late. Still he waited.

His mind went back over the last three months. The build up to the push, the roads and canals lined with stores, camps, guns, equipment. Men by the hundred thousand marching towards the Salient. The journey through the old city of Ypres, with its buildings all smashed and ruined. The journey across the canal and out into the Salient. The arrival at Hill Top Farm and the digging of the gun pits and the stocking up of ammunition.

His guns were kept out of the initial preparation shoots for the attack. Their position was so close to the front line trenches that they could hear the infantry singing and shouting to each other. They were to remain silent until the morning the infantry went over the top. To remain undetected until the Germans were too busy to counter bombard them. Where their range would be used to protect the infantry when they reached and captured the German third line, without the guns needing to move any further forward.

It all started so well. Then the rains came. And then it rained some more. The rain changed everything. Ammunition had to be brought up in harnesses on horses instead of by wagons. Even then, many horses became so stuck they had to be shot. Then the ammunition had to be brought forward by men, four shells at a time in harnesses from the dump three hundred yards and one hour behind them. The guns could not be got out, some of them sinking to their axles, despite repeated efforts to build beds for the wheels and trails.

They had lost so many good men.

Captain Newman, going forward to Mouse Trap Farm with Hastings, and Hastings returning, shell shocked and covered in blood and gore, saying that Newman had disappeared. Literally so, a shell wiping his being and his future from existence in the blink of an eye.

Major Webb, when the battery next door received a shell in their ammunition store, sending shells scattering in all directions and setting fire to our ammunition store. Major Webb had led the attempts to extinguish the fire before the shells exploded, standing at the head of the line passing water to quench the flames, and then being dismembered and his pieces flung around when the attempts failed and the hundreds of shells went up in one almighty whump.

How many bodies had he, Evans, had to collect together, identify, document, and transport back across the canal to Vlamertinge where they now lay? He had lost count, how many broken men had been sent back across the canal to be cut about and bandaged and then sent to a grim future at home as cripples, or maybe now returning to duty with this draft? Dozens.

He also recalled other events of the last three months. Young Mr Scott, eating pickled onions from a jar sent out by his mother. The jar smashed out of his hands by a shrapnel bullet, and not a scratch on the man! Though he smelled of vinegar for a long time afterwards.

It was unusually quiet. German shellfire had stopped, Evans thought that perhaps the Hun had gone for his tea, or maybe for sausages. Even the British guns were quiet.

Then he saw, through the rain, a column of men marching towards him. How many? He needed at least thirty to fill the gaps. He counted the ranks, one, two, three. So, only a dozen men, but that was better than none.

As they approached Evans recognised one of the faces at the front, it was the other Mr Scott, now wearing captain's pips, and looking fit and well. He recognised some other faces as men who had been reclaimed for the front from previously discarded bodies. Most, though, were new faces, looking young, yet with their martial ardour dampened by the inclemency of the weather.

Evans straightened up into his best authoritarian sergeant majorly stance, "Evening Captain Scott, it is good to see you, welcome back. As for the rest of you, where the bloody hell have you been, you've kept me waiting and I don't like it!"

He winked at Edwin, who extended his hand to Evans and said, "I am glad to be back, Mister Evans, how are you?"

"I am fine, thank you, sir. I think we should get going as quickly as possible. The Huns have been quiet but this is a dangerous place and it will be best to get away as soon as we can."

Edwin agreed and they started to march in the direction of the brigade, keeping to the duckboards as they went for the mud on all sides presented a clear danger.

As they moved along Evans asked Edwin, "How was your leave, sir, I imagine your parents were glad to see you?"

"Yes, they were. I was put up in hospital in Downham so they came to visit me there, and then I went to Thornham for recuperation, so it all worked out well in the end. My sister was pleased to see me, and my brother George, of course. He was in hospital in Cambridge, but we both ended up in a sanatorium at Thornham."

"How is your brother, sir?"

"Freddy should be back with the brigade, oh, you mean George. He is still back in Blighty, and likely to stay there, by all accounts. He will not be fit for active service so they have promised him a job at home, recruiting, training, or something like that. I am sure he will get a bit restless not being out with us again, but Mamma will be happier that he is safe at home."

Evans glanced at Edwin and said, "At least they know one of you will get through the war all right. The odds for the rest of us aren't so good, sir. You will have seen the casualty lists. It's a wonder any of the original brigade are left, there are very few of us, you know."

"I am aware of that, yes, it seems to have been a difficult campaign, but, not to worry too much, it can't go on much longer, can it? Winter is coming on and things will slow up then."

They fell silent, each in his own thoughts for a while. As they progressed they passed by piles of stores, rows of guns which had started banging away again, with shells arriving in the reverse direction. The flashes as the guns fired lit up the muddy fields all around them, and the rain continued to fall.

At one point they were held up as the trackway had been destroyed by a shell and sappers were replacing the duckboards. There they stayed for a nervous ten minutes, having to stay upright and vulnerable as they waited for the repairs to be completed.

"You are in a remarkably good mood, sir, for one who has swapped a warm bed and pretty nurses for this chaos." said Evans to Edwin.

"I have good reason to be, sergeant major, I have become engaged while I was recuperating. I am to be married the next leave that I get. That is something to look forward to isn't it?" smiled Edwin.

Evans thought about this, deciding not to point out the immediate dangers that might prevent Edwin enjoying his plans, "Congratulations, sir, is your intended one of those pretty nurses?"

"No, she is Miss Mann, the daughter of William Mann. I will have to ask you to keep this to yourself, though, her father does not know about our engagement and she wants us to keep it as a secret, from everyone. Her father still has not got over his son's death, and she feels he would be very unhappy for her to marry a soldier, at least until the war ends. Hopefully the Germans will throw in the towel before the end of this year and we can all go home and live happily ever after."

Evans considered this information, then said, "Your secret is safe with me, sir, but I think you are being optimistic about the war, though. They are starving and short of everything but the Germans will not give in that easily, they are a stubborn lot of bastards." He held out his hand to Edwin and the two men shook hands again.

The track was complete again and they started forward.

The gun line was a mess. The whole brigade was lined up almost wheel to wheel. The Salient was so congested that there was no room to spare between stores dumps, dressing stations, headquarters, gun batteries. The rain over the preceding months and the movement of men, horses, and wheels had churned the clay over and over until it became a stinking slippery sloppy sludge. Guns, men, everything, could, and did, disappear into the mud if not supported on firm foundations, and foundation material was in short supply.

In between firing each gun had to be dragged back up out of the mud where they sank to their axles. The gunners sought whatever they could find to put under the wheels to try to keep them above the surface, debris, wood, empty shell cases, even unused shells.

Shelters for the gunners had been constructed a little behind the gun line on ground that was a foot or so higher, and sandbags and scrap wood formed crude walls and groundsheets were improvised into roofing to keep out the rain.

Freddy, and Ted shared one of these shelters. On one particularly chaotic night the two men were snatching an hour of rest in between the constant sending and receiving of shellfire. A particularly close explosion roused them. They heard shouting close by. Ted got up bleary eyed to see what was happening and was called over to one of the shelters behind the guns. A shell had landed in the shelter and killed the men who had been sheltering in there. By the light of his torch Ted saw that the shelter had been blown apart, the wood and sandbags scattered around and the remains of the men littered the ground.

Freddy arrived soon after Ted and looked at the mess. It took a few seconds for each of them to take in what they were seeing.

Ted slumped and vomited onto the ground. Freddy, more inured to seeing death and dismemberment took in the scene quickly and ordered that the remains be collected and secured in a groundsheet, and placed away from the shelters ready to be sent off to a suitable place later.

Ted, shocked, seemed unable to respond. Once arrangements had been made Freddy suggested that they return to their shelter to get what sleep they could.

When they got to their shelter they found that their groundsheet cover had been blown to one side and all their kit and blankets were wet. They shrugged and climbed in to try to rest. Freddy felt Ted shivering next to him. Freddy cuddled up to Ted, put his arm around his middle, and for the next hour they shared their body heat.

They were roused by the BSM with a cup of coffee an hour before first light. Sergeant Major Evans seemed his normal self, dour, gruff, but kindly.

"What is the score for last night, sergeant major?" asked Freddy.

"D sub four men killed, F sub two wounded, sir, and we have three men suffering from gas, blistered around their wrists and necks. I will get them back to the doctor but he should be able to send them back to us after some ointment." said the BSM.

"Righto, Mister Evans, thank you. I will speak to the gun numbers one and make sure that they are all fettled. Can you reorganise the men to cover the casualties, please?"

"Already done, sir, each gun has four men and there are five on A sub, a bit short of the standard, but the lads will manage, I am sure. I have moved Bombardier Reid to D sub as number one, I hope that is all right, sir, and I think he should be made up to sergeant." said the BSM.

"Yes, he is ready, I will speak to the adjutant later today about that. Can you let me have a list of the casualties and any changes in rank like Sergeant Reid? I will hand it over to the adjutant so he can make sure that they get paid. It's the least we can do for them. I will see if we are getting any more reinforcements, it looks as if we will need them."

Edwin and Freddy went off to Brigade leaving Ted and the BSM to run the gun line during the morning.

They first went to see the adjutant who was in a concrete shelter just below the walls of the town.

"Ah, Edwin, I am glad you have arrived. I have good news for you, well, I think it is good news. You have been promoted to major and are to take over command of C Battery. Get your kit together and move across this afternoon. BSM Anderson is in the know and will make you welcome. There is a major fire plan for tomorrow night. The Norfolks are going over the top at last light and there will be a lot for you to get sorted to be ready for them."

Edwin looked pleased, but would be sorry to move to a battery that he knew little of. They were a Suffolk battery. The ancient rivalry between the two counties, though illogical, was real and deep.

"There is a new BC appointed to A Battery, a chap called Proudfoot. He is new to the brigade, apparently he is a sporting type, won a gold medal at the '08 Olympics. He will be along tomorrow to take over, can you show him the ropes, Freddy?" added Kit.

"What do we know about him?" asked Freddy.

"Nothing really, but he has some form. He has been out in Mesopotamia and came back with some kind of fever, and has spent some time in hospital recovering. This will be his first time in Flanders, so will be a bit of a shock for him, no doubt." said Kit.

Edwin left them and Freddy continued to discuss matters with Kit, including the list of casualties and promotions that BSM Evans had given him, and pleading for reinforcements when they became available.

Edwin was going back through the town out to Vlamertinge to the wagon lines to collect his spare kit ready to join his new battery. Once he had done that he had a little time so he went to the CCS and visit Florence Mann, on the excuse of visiting some of the men from his battery who had been evacuated there.

As he arrived he was struck by the busy scene that greeted him. A steady stream of horse drawn ambulance wagons lined the road to Vlamertinge, bringing the casualties of the previous night. There was an unloading station at the entrance where these wagons lined up and stretcher bearers and a nurse came to receive the wounded and take them to the appropriate wards. Other wagons were loaded with piles of sewn up blankets concealing the dead, these were unloaded behind the CCS in the area set aside for burials.

The other side of the CCS, which was situated in a large farm with several outbuildings supplemented by large tents in the nearest field, a line of motor ambulances were parked, waiting to take casualties back to the field hospital further back.

Edwin enquired about his men, and found their wards. Two of them had already been sent back to the field hospital, one had died, and one was in the ward for gas casualties. After seeing the man and spending a little time with him Edwin went to find Florence, who he knew to be there.

He found her in the fever ward, she signed across the tent for him to wait outside. He went out and lit a cigarette and stood for the few minutes that it took for Florence to finish bathing the man she was attending to and join him.

"How nice to see you, Edwin." Florence said with a tired smile, "Shall we walk for a while, I have a few minutes and could do with fresh air."

They walked between two tents and out beyond the CCS into a lane that ran alongside the farm.

"How are you after your time in hospital, Edwin?"

"I am fine, thank you, I still get a twinge or two from the wound, but it is entirely bearable, thank you. And how are you, it seems to be very busy here?"

"We are always busy, we just get used to it, I suppose." said Florence. "Tell me, did you see anything of my brother while you were home? His letters have been few and far between of late, and I sense that all is not as well as it should be."

"I did see Constance. She says your father spends most of his time at the works. He has been very busy on the French and War Office contracts and he never seems to get any rest. He comes home late and is up early and out to work."

"I think that Walter being killed has changed him. He has not really ever come to terms with it. He had always assumed that Walter would take over the business from him. But that won't happen now, of course. Constance has no interest in the business or any aptitude for commerce." said Florence, "I think he worries a lot now about what will happen to his business when he dies."

"Well, I may have an answer to that. What if Constance were to marry a suitable young man who does have the interest and the aptitude? Do you think that might solve his problem?" Edwin stopped and turned towards Florence and was speaking directly to her.

Florence studied Edwin's features for a second, then said, "She is too young, and in any case there are precious few young men who fit the bill and who are not in uniform. I can't see that happening just yet." She turned to continue walking.

Edwin touched her arm to stop her and said, "Yes, there is, me!" He looked into her eyes as if seeking approval.

"Edwin, if this is true it's not me you should be talking to, it's Constance, and William, of course."

"I know that your brother would never agree to it while the war is not finished, but that may be very soon if the Germans give up. I have a secret to share with you. I asked Constance to marry me, and she has agreed! The only problem is that she insisted it must remain a secret until after the war."

Florence was not sure how to respond to this news, finally deciding that it was good news. She put both her hands on Edwin's upper arms, looked him directly in the eye, and said, "Edwin, that is excellent news, and I will keep your secret. But, you must try your best to stay safe. I am not sure that Constance would be able to lose another young man. She was very upset by Walter you know, even though she tried not to show it for her father's sake."

"Thank you, Miss Florence, I promise to look after myself. And thank you for promising to keep it secret, it would be very awkward for the news to get out."

"I look forward to drinking a toast at your wedding, next year." said Florence, smiling outwardly, but inwardly regretful for the other secret she held which only one other had known, and that one other had gone. When James Newman had been killed, her dreams and hopes had also died.

The next evening the guns were firing away at maximum speed. The gunners were stripped to the waist and sweating despite the low temperature, though it had stopped raining.

The final push of the campaign had started.

Freddy was in the HQ bunker getting details for the next day's targets, he was to be in the OP when the Norfolks went over the top and he had to make sure that everything was right and ready.

The candles in the bunker wavered and occasionally went out as the pressure waves from the outgoing gunfire and the incoming detonations penetrated even to this level underground. Despite the heavy gas curtain at the entrances, the garlic smell of mustard gas was evident, as was the eye watering lachrymatory gas. Kaiser's Cocktail was on the menu again.

Freddy had to concentrate as his eyes watered, his neck, his hands and wrists stung, and the flickering light made taking down the target data from the typed forms in front of him next to impossible. A particularly heavy explosion outside was followed by the gas curtain being thrown back and several figures in respirators came in.

The curtain was replaced. The men revealed their faces and Freddy recognised Stephen Sansom, and Sergeant Rippingill among them. Stephen said, "My apologies, gents, but we need to take a breather for a few minutes, sorry to interrupt."

"How is it outside?" Freddy asked.

"No change," said Stephen, "But there are some tanks coming up the road ready for the attack and I thought it prudent to get my men off the track while they passed. I don't want to lose any more of my chaps before the attack and those tanks just go where they want. If you get in their way they will just run straight over you."

Freddy stopped his scribbling, reached down for his haversack, opened it and took out a bottle of whisky, took a swig and offered it across to the newcomers. Rippingill took it and took a swig, wiping his lips with his palm. Stephen declined, and pulled a hip flask from his greatcoat pocket and offered it to Freddy, "His Majesty's best rum, Freddy?" Freddy took the flask, and swigged from it.

"Keeps us warm, and gives us courage." said Stephen. A soldier opened the curtain from outside, looked in and said, his voice muffled and distorted by the respirator, "Tanks have gone, sir."

Stephen and Rippingill put their helmets on as they stood, and left through the curtain back out into the maelstrom. As he left Stephen gave the thumbs up, and Freddy returned the pleasantry and went back to his scribbling.

Freddy knew that where they were going he would follow in an hour or so to spend the last few hours before the attack in a forward trench hoping that the rain would not come back, or at least be lighter than of late.

The attack went in exactly to time, the infantry disappearing over the slime masquerading as a parapet. As Freddy looked out as the light faded he saw nothing but mud in front of the trench, no sign of any of the men. A good sign he thought to himself, at least they had a chance to get to the enemy trench before the slaughter started.

The attack was deemed successful, and the division was relieved by Canadians, and withdrew back across the canal, through Ypres, and back along the road to Vlamertinge.

The new BC, Major Peregrine Proudfoot had made his presence felt in the battery. He was a man of some thirty four years, tall, athletically built, with a neat moustache.

Freddy had initially got on well with Peregrine. Freddy become efficient at his duties and confident and competent in assessing situations and taking the right action. Some of the others, though, Major Proudfoot felt, were not up to scratch.

The battery was drawn up in the farmyard that served as their home for the next few days. They were a dishevelled lot. Uniforms were muddy and torn. Some had no caps, and buttons were missing from tunics and trousers. Most were suffering in one way or another. Gas blisters around their wrists and necks. Many had colds and sores. All had lice, and were trying to resist scratching while on parade, some unsuccessfully.

BSM Evans brought them to attention as Major Proudfoot stepped from the barn to begin his address and inspection.

"You have now had a good night's rest. I want you to spend the rest of today cleaning the guns and oiling them. All your personal kit will be inspected for deficiencies this afternoon by BQMS Mason. The Brigade Fitter will be arriving tomorrow to inspect all the guns and instruments and will be giving me a written report. Any major omissions or lack of maintenance on the guns will result in disciplinary action for the gun numbers one. The farrier and the veterinary officer will also be along soon to report on the condition of the horses. You are to make sure that they will find no deficiencies in the condition of the beasts. If there are any deficiencies or damage to any tackle or equipment gun numbers one must report these to BQMS Mason this morning. I want you all to be in top form by tomorrow evening, everything must be ready in case we are needed back in the Salient. Take over, Sergeant Major."

With that Proudfoot turned and left the parade.

The BSM dismissed them.

BQMS Mason had an urn of tea in one corner of the barn, and was soon surrounded by gunners, tin mugs in hand, scratching their bodies and legs, and grouching.

"What a bastard!" was heard, as was, "It's all right for him, he has only just arrived, he still has sand in his boots, not mud!"

"Pipe down, lads." said Mason, "enough is enough. Let me know what you are short of and I will get you what I can. The major is right, we have to be ready to go back in."

BSM Evans added, "I know you can do it. Just let me know what you need and we will see what can be done. We will all pull together."

The officers and NCOs tried their level best to do as he wished, but all their attempts met with the same sarcastic response from their commander, "Is this the best you can do? Well, it's not good enough." The battery were well disciplined enough to persevere, but morale was not restored in any way. Major Proudfoot acquired the nickname 'not good enough.'

Freddy had the opportunity to visit the CCS to see how the men from his battery who had lived long enough to be there but who were not so badly injured that they needed to go to Blighty. As Edwin had, he also went to see Florence Mann while he was there.

She was pleased to see him, but obviously suffering the strain of her chosen work. She looked pale. Her hands trembled a little, something that Freddy had not noticed before. He said to her, "I normally take some whisky to help my nerves, do they allow the nurses here to take alcohol?"

Florence looked at Freddy and said, "Many of the men here have nervous debilitation, they sometimes call it shell shock, but I think it is more than that. Some of them have used up all their reserves of energy and courage, and their bodies and minds are starting to lose control. Alcohol is a temporary comfort for them, but it is not a cure. Freddy, are you drinking too much?"

Freddy could see that Florence had tears in her eyes, and was on the point of crying. He looked away, as much for his sake as hers, for he knew that if she was to cry, he would have to as well.

"I hear that the Boche come over every night and drop bombs on the rear areas. Have you received any of their gifts in this hospital?'

"Yes, and we have lost nurses and patients when they do. It is not good for our nerves, Freddy, I do not know how you men at the front deal with things. It is bad here, but it must be many times worse where you are."

"At least we have a way of hitting back at them, Miss Florence. Here you have nothing to get back at them with, do you?" said Freddy, "Though I fear that many of us in the brigade will find it hard to become normal people again when the war is over."

"The chance to be normal disappeared for me a long time ago, whether the war continues or ends. I can never be normal again." she said, brushing the front of her uniform.

Back at Brigade Freddy met Edwin who was there to receive orders for a move. "I have just had orders from the colonel, Freddy. We are being taken out of the Salient and will be going a little south for a few weeks. It seems we have done our bit for the time being and will have some days in the country to rest and recover."

"Any idea where?"

"No, not yet, but we will find out for definite tomorrow or the day after. How are you getting on with Peregrine? I hear that the lads find him to be different from Buster."

"Buster was one of a kind. Any new man is going to have to set his own way of doing things. We will get to know him better in reserve when we have time to relax."

The brigade officers' mess was in a partially ruined house in the village of Vimy.

One day, a bright November one, cool but with warm sunshine, Freddy was sitting outside the mess writing up some notes and letters to those at home. Ted came over to him and said, "Freddy, I want to say thank you."

Freddy looked up from his scribbling, "What for?"

"For looking after me and not letting on that I funked it." said Ted, emotion showing in his face.

"Ted, I did nothing special. This war is hard on all of us. Are you all right now?"

"Yes, I think so, glad to be out of it for a while, of course. Freddy, I have written to my father and told him that you were very good to me, and that if I die he is to look after you when you go home."

"You should not think like that, Ted, you are not going to die. But it is a kind thought."

"Do you ever worry about dying and not leaving anything behind you?"

Freddy thought for a second, "Yes, I did once, but I have not thought that way for some time. There is nothing we can do about it anyway, so I think it is best to concentrate on our duty and not get distracted."

"Well, when I get leave I am going to find a girl, get married, and start a family, all in one week." said Ted.

"Goodness, that would be a very busy week! Do you have anyone in mind, that would be a good first step?"

"No, not yet, but my real concern is that I do not know how to, well, you know, what to do with a girl to start a family. Have you ever used one of the French girls that do, you know, that do it for money?"

Freddy thought carefully about his answer. "No, I have not, why are you thinking that way?"

"I want to find one of these girls so that I know how everything works so when I marry I do not look stupid. A wife would expect me to know and I want to do things properly, I don't want to make any mistakes."

"If it is any comfort to you, Ted, I have never been like that with a woman. It is territory that I have never explored. You might be better off talking to a more experienced person, perhaps a married man?"

"Maybe I will, but in any case, the next chance I get I am going to find a French girl and find out what I need to know."

"Maybe the doctor can help you? He is in the mess today, he must be able to teach you what you want to know?" said Freddy as he rose and went inside to the mess.

Freddy went over to Robert Benefer. "Doc, do you have a minute? I need to discuss something with you."

Robert nodded, "What is it?"

"I am still concerned about some of the men in my battery, particularly Corporal Hastings. He has been acting strangely again, particularly since that time he was out with James."

"In what way?"

"He used to be so enthusiastic and ready to volunteer for any duty. He has become progressively sullen and lethargic, though he still does his duty. I am not sure what is wrong with him."

"He has been regular on sick parade as you know, but most of the time he is remarkably fit and well in his bodily functions. It is something in his mind, probably, but I am not really sure what that could be or how to diagnose or treat it. It is beyond my competence. As you know a lot of men are suffering from all sorts of nightmares, a good rest might put him right."

Just then Peregrine arrived, "Gentlemen, we have had news of a tremendous battle in Italy. Apparently the Austrians have broken through in the mountains and the Italians are in full retreat. We have been told to prepare for a redeployment to the south, possibly into Italy itself. It seems that we are either going to stop the Italian Army retreating any further, or to protect our lines of communication to the Middle East. In any case we will be relieved by the Canadians tomorrow and all equipment and guns must be brought up to one hundred per cent by then."

Freddy said to Robert, "Italy sounds nice to me, better than the Salient. In any case I would imagine it will all be over by the time we could arrive. Do you speak any Italian? I don't."

"Never been there myself, and no, I do not speak the lingo. Corporal Ely might, ask him. Maybe we will get a good rest down there in the sunshine."

Chapter 18

26th July 1987, Marostica, Italy.

The drive to Italy was long and tiring, though I was surprised how well Freddy stood up to it.

We stopped overnight near Strasbourg before continuing on through Switzerland to Italy and to our destination, Marostica.

Freddy told me that after the terrible battle of Passchendaele his division was sent south into Italy. This was after the Austrians had broken through the mountain barrier at a place called Caporetto. He said that the Italians had started the war on the side of the Germans and Austrians, but had switched sides to join the Allies early on, in early 1915. They had been trying to persuade the Austrians to give them territory that they considered to be part of Italy proper which had been occupied by the Austrians for a hundred years or more. When the Austrians said that they would not leave the Italians had declared war on them. After two years and more of fruitless attacks the Italians had not advanced very much, then the Austrians, with German help, managed to break through the Italian front and force them to withdraw about eighty miles to set up a new front line just outside Venice.

British and French troops were sent to help the Italians stay in the war. If Italy had fallen to the Central Powers, the Allied situation would have been much worse and the war would have ended differently.

He said the journey down, by train, was quite pleasant, and a welcome change from the mud of Flanders.

Freddy and I were able to travel by a more direct route. In 1917 Freddy had gone down through France to the Mediterranean and then along the coast into Italy, then across Lombardy to an area just near Vicenza, and ended up in a camp just outside Marostica, in a village called Nove. Freddy said that this means nine in Italian, though he also said that he never found out what this referred to.

We found a hotel just outside the town in the hills above it. After freshening up we drove the five minutes into town and parked in the piazza inside the walls of the old town.

As we walked from the car Freddy pointed out to me the enormous chess board pattern made of paving slabs in the centre of the square. Later he explained that this related back to the days of the Venetian Empire. Marostica was a frontier town in those days, defending a pass down from the mountains. If invaders from the north could penetrate through this pass they would threaten the whole of the Venice region. The governor of Marostica therefore had a very responsible position, he also had a beautiful daughter. Two noblemen came courting her, and she was unable to decide which of them to favour with her hand in marriage.

The governor, a wily man, decided to offer his daughter's hand to the nobleman who would win a chess match with the other. When the match had been played, and the lucky nobleman took the young woman's hand, the governor disclosed that he had a younger, slightly less beautiful daughter who the loser was expected to marry.

Very interesting, I thought, but not exactly in line with modern thinking on women's liberation.

"How do you know that story?" I asked him.

"A man I met while I was here told me."

Freddy seemed to know his way around the town and we soon found ourselves in a side street in an old looking restaurant, small and homely, called La Madonnetta.

"It hasn't changed much since I was last here." said Freddy.

"When was that?"

"March 1919." Freddy said.

"Seventy years almost."

"Yes, a long time, but it seems only a very short time ago. I did read somewhere that Ernest Hemingway came here during the war. The name has changed, I think. When we were here in the war I don't remember this restaurant having a name."

"Did you meet Hemingway?"

"No, never laid eyes on him, as far as I know. There was a chap, an Englishman, he was in the Italian Army. I used to meet him here. He was from an Italian family, he brought us here when we first arrived, and it became our usual haunt if we were in town."

"What became of him, after the war, that is?"

"I have no idea, went back to his wife in London I should think."

"What are we going to see, tomorrow?" I asked Freddy.

"We are going up into the hills behind the town here and see where a big battle took place. It was the last big one of the war, for me at least."

"When did they send you back to England?"

"I was one of the last to leave, in 1919. When the Germans and the Austrians gave up, in November '18, there were rumours that we would be sent as an army of occupation. Just like after the Second World War the Continent was in chaos and all the empires, except the British one, of course, had collapsed. The Ottomans, Austro-Hungarians, the German empire, the Russians, they all went. Someone had to keep order. In the event, though, they all got together in Paris, Versailles. There was a big conference and they decided there was no need for us to go to keep order in Vienna or elsewhere. Being young, unmarried, and without responsibilities, I was regarded as the lowest priority for demobilisation. I had to wait until the very end. I must have been on just about the last draft to get back to Blighty."

"That seems unfair, Freddy, you had been in the army right from the beginning."

"Yes, there were men who had only a year's service who got out before me. If they had a wife, children, a job to go to, they got priority. It was just how it was, we accepted it."

"What did you get up to, after the war that is, and before they sent you home?"

"I don't know, really, it was all a blur."

Chapter 19

December 1917.

In the early evening the train stopped at a station on the outskirts of Paris. There were only four platforms, and another troop filled train sat at another of them as theirs arrived.

As the carriages jerked and jolted to a halt British railway transport NCOs appeared alongside and shouted the information that there was to be a one hour halt for food and drink.

The doors of the carriages swung open and men flooded down onto the platform. The doors of the wagons slid open and the drivers travelling with their four legged charges climbed down and went to find sustenance for themselves and the horses.

There were wooden tables set up along the wall at the entrance to the station where piles of sandwiches and urns of tea awaited the throng. Salvation Army volunteers were there to try to keep some semblance of order.

"Where are we?" asked Ted as he and Freddy wandered away from the mêlée to drink their tea in a quieter area.

"Dunno, but somewhere around Paris I would think, based on the fact we spent the last hour passing factories and housing. This must be a sizeable city, and the only one I can think it can be is Paris." said Freddy, with some logic.

"I am surprised at how slow this train is going, Freddy. At this rate it will take days to get to Italy."

"It can take as long as it likes, as far as I am concerned! Every day out of the line is a good day. Once we are clear of Paris and on the way to Marseilles it may go faster. I think up here in the north they have to fit us in with all the other military traffic. Further on there will be less, so we should be able to speed up."

Just then, with a burst of steam, the train at the other platform started to move. Ever so slowly, slowly, it gradually built speed until it moved at walking pace and passed by the men from Freddy's train who watched without much interest. It was still moving at more or less the same speed as it went round a bend along the line and disappeared from view.

"I could run faster than that!" said Ted.

"I wonder how long it would take to walk to Italy? It might be a good way to spend a month or so." mused Freddy, almost as if to himself.

After the train had gone from their sight Freddy and Ted continued walking towards the end of the platform.

A hundred yards or so along the track they saw a man standing, apparently without purpose other than writing in a notebook. As they chatted they idly watched the man. Suddenly three gendarmes appeared and grappled him to the ground, placed handcuffs on him and then dragged him away down an embankment to a roadway, where a dark coloured motor van stood. They put the man in the van which then drove off.

"What was going on there do you think?" Ted said to Freddy.

"Probably a spy, they are all over the place." said a voice from behind them, they turned to see an RTO standing there. "If I were you I would get back to the train, this is not the place for us to be."

The RTO was a man of perhaps fifty years, of decidedly unmilitary bearing, shortish with a thickened middle and a grey moustache. More like a senior clerk or bank manager thought Freddy, to himself.

"Do you get many spies around here?" asked Freddy, thinking back to his time in the barn, where the spy turned out to be a naked young woman and her AWOL man friend.

"Dozens of them." said the RTO, "The police take them away and lock them up. They have even shot some of them so I am told. Good riddance!"

Ted and Freddy did as they were bid and slowly walked back to the main body of the station where their train gently fizzed as it waited for the next stage to begin.

The transport NCOs were once again circulating telling everyone to get back on the train as it was leaving in ten minutes. The brigade went to their respective positions, and reclaimed their seats. The train groaned out of the station just as another arrived.

As the train rumbled gradually southwards the weather improved by increments. On the third day they reached the Mediterranean coast at Marseilles, and, after a halt for ablutions and food they turned eastwards and carried on parallel to the coast with the sea to their right hand side.

At Menton they halted for several hours so that officials could complete the necessary paperwork to allow them to cross the border into Italy. Freddy and Ted wandered into the town, finding the Hotel Bristol just off the seafront. They went in to enjoy a proper breakfast, one that did not arrive wrapped in paper or in a metal tin.

"My father brought me here once, when I was very small. I remember that it was owned by a German, I suppose that he is even now back in Germany serving the Kaiser." said Ted as they were tucking in to their food.

"Did you get abroad often, as a boy?"

"Yes, I did. My father comes from a Huguenot family back several generations. They came over to England two hundred years ago. We still have family in France and he used to bring me over in the summers to visit them. I only remember them vaguely, but I do remember coming here to this hotel." explained Ted.

"So you are Church of England?"

"Yes, we have become anglicised all right, though our relatives in France were mostly Romans Catholics, I suppose they must have converted to avoid the persecution."

After breakfast the two friends walked along the seafront for a while before returning to the railway station. Just as they arrived their train was leaving. They easily found their carriage and climbed up into it as the engine puffed and heaved starting its slow acceleration.

"Where have you two been? We thought you had deserted!" demanded Peregrine as they passed his compartment, which he shared with the other battery commanders and the adjutant.

"Sorry, sir," they said in unison, then Freddy added, "We went for a recce just in case the Austrians chase us back this way and we have to put in a block to stop their advance. We thought that we should use the time we had for a good military purpose, sir."

The other officers saw the excuse for what it was and suppressed smiles, but Peregrine seemed uncertain how to take this information, "Right, I suppose that was a good idea, but next time clear it with me before you go off like that Captain Scott!"

"Yes, sir, we will." said Freddy as he and Ted saluted and went off to their compartment next along the corridor, trying not to smirk too obviously. As they closed the door after them they could hold their laughter no more. Harold Kent, a little taken aback as to what they should find amusing said, "I'm glad you can find something to be happy about." Harold Kent had returned to the brigade with his shiny new second lieutenant's pips just before they had left France. Ted was pleased as this meant that he was no longer the most junior officer in the brigade.

Freddy explained what had happened and the others agreed that he had got one over Major Notgoodenough.

Harold added, "You will be pleased to know that Corporal Ely has been able to stock up on local delicacies at the last stop and has promised us a good feed this evening. He says that we are entering his homeland and that he is happy with that, in fact he looked almost cheerful. He wants us to celebrate."

"Ely is a good man, Harold, very good indeed. I look forward to dinner." said Freddy.

The railway track along the coast wound in and out around the hills and inlets. The train continued at a slow rate caused by the frequent changes in gradient and direction. At times it slowed to walking pace, and it became the habit of many men to get down from their carriages and wagons and walk or trot alongside as a way of relieving the fatigue of inactivity from their legs. Occasionally one of them would stumble and fall, or slip down the embankment, but they were usually able to regain their place with the train without much trouble.

After Genoa the track turned northwards up into the hills. At Arquata the line started to descend to the Plain of Lombardy and the speed of the train increased such that the men walking alongside had to scramble to regain their places. Unfortunately Freddy and Ted were just too slow to realise the changing circumstances. They found themselves being left behind as the horse wagons, then the flats with the guns on passed them. Eventually they saw the end of their train disappearing into the distance.

Neither man felt too distressed, partly due to the confidence of youth, and partly due to the invigorating, or rather stultifying, effects of the bottle of brandy they had purchased at

Genoa station and which even now lay empty and discarded in their compartment.

"Well, Freddy, what to do next?" slurred Ted.

"We could wait for the next train."

"But we would have to go back up the track to where the trains go more slowly, wouldn't we?" said Ted, starting to realise that they had a problem to solve.

"And Notgoodenough is going to have a fit!"

"Where is the next stop for our train? If we walk quickly we may catch it up and can get back on?" suggested Ted, sobering up.

"I have no idea, but I bet it is further than we can walk. By the time we get there they will have started off again. We will never catch up that way. I heard someone mention Milan, but how far is that? I have no clue." said Freddy, also starting to realise that this was the time for straight thinking and shaking his head in a futile attempt to clear his mind.

"Forward or back?"

"Let's toss for it." said Freddy, and fumbled in his pocket until he found a coin. He flicked it into the air and managed to catch it in his hands, then opened them to show the tail.

"Which is it, then?" said Ted, "What does tails mean?"

"We should've decided before we tossed, I suppose." said Freddy. "Choose again."

"Heads back, tails forward!" declared Ted.

Freddy tossed the coin again and missed catching it. It struck the rail and pinged off somewhere that neither of them saw. "Bugger!" said Freddy, and rummaged for another coin. He tossed this one, caught it, and showed it to Ted, "Tails again!" said Ted.

"What did we decide for tails?" asked Freddy, confused.

"Um, forward, I think, or was it… no, forwards." said Ted.

The issue being decided they started walking along the track.

A mile further on they came to a bridge over a road. "Let's lorry hop." suggested Freddy.

They climbed down the side of the bridge to the road and stood on the side ready to stop the next lorry to come along in the right direction. Ten minutes passed. Then fifteen. Then twenty. Freddy and Ted looked at each other. The brandy was wearing off and they both were feeling sober and worried. Freddy stood and relieved his bladder on the verge.

"Where are we do you think?" Ted said.

"In hot water, I should think." said Freddy, not altogether in jest, over his shoulder.

They heard the sound of a motor coming along the road, and to their astonishment and delight they saw that an Italian army lorry was coming towards them. Freddy stepped out into the road and held up his arm. The lorry skidded to a halt on the gravel. Freddy went round to the door, realised that the driver was on the other side, and then went to the correct driver's door. He looked up and saw that the driver was laughing and indicating with his thumb for them to climb in the back.

They went to the rear, and climbed over the tailboard of the lorry. Ted banged his hand on the wooden side of the lorry and they heard the driver put the lorry into gear and off they went. The driver obviously knew the route as he never seemed to brake or slow for any of the corners, of which there were many.

The journey took over an hour, and in that time they travelled many miles. Eventually they came into another town and the lorry pulled up outside a railway station, just as a train was arriving from the south. Freddy read the name plate above the station door 'Pavia.'

"Ever heard of Pavia?"

"No."

The driver came to the back of the lorry and with his thumb indicated that it was time for the two men to get down, and he pointed to the train. They saw that it was, indeed, a military train, and to their delight realised that it was their train. Suddenly happy again they jumped down, shook the driver's hand vigorously, clapped him on the shoulder, and said 'thank you' realising that this was not Italian, but not knowing what the right word was in that language.

The driver waved them away and turned back to his cab, still chuckling. Ted and Freddy ran onto the station platform as the train heaved to a stop. Their compartment was positioned opposite where they stood, and they saw the amazed faces of their friends, and Peregrine, looking out at them, open mouthed.

As one they both saluted. They then went to the carriage, climbed the steps and went to their compartment, entered and sat down as if nothing had happened. Harold woke as they came in, and grunted.

Later the next day the train arrived at a small siding at the village of Bovolone after having travelled forwards and backwards along a seemingly endless series of branch lines. The siding allowed only three wagons to unload at a time and it took several hours to complete the unloading operation. The train had to be repeatedly shunted in and out of the siding to rearrange the order of the wagons and carriages.

While this was happening the men were involved in manoeuvring the cargo from train to road and sorting everything into the correct sequence for the brigade to trek to the next destination.

The officers were temporarily redundant and stood around chatting to each other and generally keeping out of the way in order not to obstruct the work going on around them.

Freddy found himself next to BSM Evans and the two of them fell into conversation. "Have you ever been to Italy before, sergeant major?"

"No, not that I remember, but I did go through the Mediterranean on the way to India a few years back. We may have stopped off in Naples, but I am not sure. No, this is all new to me. How about you, sir?"

"No, never," said Freddy, "I am looking forward to being here rather than in Flanders. They say the fighting is in the mountains so we will not have so much mud to contend with, and the weather must be better this far south."

"We will see," said Evans, "the situation here is different, but the Italians are used to the mountains and we are not, so I am not sure who will be helping who. The rumour is that Americans will be here soon as well."

"How well do you think the men will cope with fighting in Italy?"

"They are a bit out of shape, actually, with so many new men as reinforcements. We have lost some of the old sweats and some of the NCOs are young and inexperienced. It's a good thing we have Major Proudfoot, he will get us back into shape and no mistake, just the man for the job." said Evans.

Freddy was not sure whether to agree or not with what Evans had said about the major, so just grunted his reply and proceeded to fill and light his pipe as a way of changing the subject.

When the pipe was alight Freddy said, "We will have to warn the younger men, and the older ones too, probably, about the wine and women down here. Both are unknown quantities and we are going into a country where they may be more conservative, especially about our boys eyeing up their women, don't you think Sergeant Major?"

"I am not one for foreign drink, sir, happy with beer, and if I can't get that then army rum will be enough for me. As for the ladies, well, that way madness lies. No, sir, better to stay with the beer and bacca, but you are right, we will need to keep an eye out for them."

When the brigade had finished unloading and sorting itself out into a semblance of order for the trek to their new quarters Colonel Goodson came round and gave orders. Freddy's battery was to lead, and Major Proudfoot appointed Freddy to lead the whole brigade. Somewhat daunted by this responsibility but with no option but to comply Freddy lit his pipe once more and taking his horse to the front of the column he led them off. Luckily, for Freddy, within a mile of the start an Italian officer mounted on a white horse appeared at the side of the road, and as the column reached him he took his place alongside Freddy, and reached out his hand to shake Freddy's as they rode.

"Hello, chum, my name is Simone, Tenente Simone Grossi. I have been sent as a guide to get you to Marostica." said the Italian, in a London accent.

Taken aback by this turn of events, but relieved as well, Freddy smiled and said, "Pleased to meet you Simone, you sound English, where do you come from?"

Simone smiled back and said, "I thought it might surprise you, but I was born in London, Clerkenwell, and I have only been in Italy since early '15 when I was called up."

"So, how come you are in the Italian Army?"

"My father never gave up his Italian nationality so I am Italian, but I had never been here at all until two years ago, but I do speak the language. My grandmother used to teach us kids all about Italy." explained Simone, "But I am just as English as you are, really. I suppose I could have volunteered for the British Army, but the Italians sent me my call up papers first, so I thought it might be a way of seeing my country. My family come from not far from here, near Lake Garda, and my mother put me in contact with my family over here so I have had the opportunity to meet cousins and so on that I had never met or even known about before."

"Well, well," said Freddy, "Interesting story, so how far do we have to go? Where exactly is Marostica?"

"About two days from here, we will stop tonight outside Vicenza where we have set up a transit camp, and the next day we will carry on to the end, should arrive by mid afternoon." said Simone as they rode along.

"How far away are the Austrians?" asked Freddy, "Are we likcly to have to fight them as soon as we arrive?"

"No, not all," laughed Simone, "We stopped them two weeks ago the other side of Venice. Now the winter rains have come they will not be able to get across the Piave River and all the bridges are down so we are safe for the time being. I don't think there will be any more fighting until the spring, and then we will be attacking them. You know they are starving, the Austrians? Apparently this attack of theirs was a last attempt to end the war before they have to give up, so either the war ends soon, or we will end it for them in the spring."

Freddy was impressed by Simone's confidence, but not sure whether he was right or not. They continued on their way, occasionally chatting, but mostly in silence. Freddy took a liking to Simone.

The night was spent, as Simone had explained, in a tented camp outside Vicenza. For breakfast the British had their first exposure to the delights of polenta, a foodstuff that they would soon come to love or hate.

They arrived at their final destination, another field full of tents, a mile or so outside the town of Marostica and the brigade was met by guides who took each battery to its designated area and they settled in to the camp.

Simone left his new English friends with the promise to rejoin them the following evening and show them the delights of Marostica town.

The evening came and true to his word Simone arrived in a Fiat motor lorry driven by an Italian soldier. Several officers of the brigade climbed aboard the lorry and it set off for the town. The lorry rumbled through the ancient gates at the entrance to the old city and drew up on the edge of the square. The men tumbled out of the back and stood looking around them at the town and its buildings. Simone said that he would take them to a good restaurant where they could try local food.

He led them down a side lane and they entered a building that had dim light emerging from a window. As they went in they saw a room with two heavy rustic wooden tables with bench seats along all four sides. One table had a half dozen older Italian men already sitting at it, talking loudly with wine glasses in front of each one. These men fell silent, then, recognising Simone they greeted him and he said something in Italian to them. The men rose and came across to the Englishmen and shook hands vigorously for what seemed several minutes, before returning to their table.

Simone then indicated for his English companions to sit at the empty table and he went over to a door at the back of the room and went through it. He returned a minute later with a woman in her early twenties, fair haired and of strikingly good looks.

Simone said, as he stood beside the woman, "Gentlemen, this is our hostess, Raffaella. She will look after us. I am afraid that food is a little short at the moment in Italy so there is little to choose. I have asked Raffaella to serve us with the best that she can manage, so, please relax, and food will arrive in due course."

Raffaella smiled at them and then bowed and went back through the door at the rear into the kitchen.

Jugs of wine arrived and many toasts were made and as the evening progressed spirits lifted in line with the amount of wine that had been drunk.

Freddy found himself sitting next to Simone and fell into conversation with him.

"For a man from London you seem to know your way around these parts?" said Freddy.

"I have been based here, just outside Marostica for over a year. My military specialisation is supply and there is a big Italian Army supply depot not far away. The army food is so bad that many of us come into town to dine most days except when we are sent into the mountains to resolve supply problems." explained Simone.

"Are the mountains very close?"

"Yes, one end of Marostica is on the plain, the other is in the foothills, we can walk up there after we have eaten, if you wish. This town still has its fortified walls, you may have seen them as we came into the piazza. In history the Austrians were always a threat to the Venetians and they built the town to defend the valley. One of the biggest and widest routes from the mountains comes through here, and they built this town as a castle to protect the plains, the back door to Venice. Today, the Austrians are up in the mountains again, about twenty miles away up there. If they want to get to the coast they must come through here, that is why we have our army up there. This place is very important to us. The Austrians tried to come through in '15 and we beat them in the mountains, but they will try again. They have to if they want to win the war."

"But all the fighting has been to the east from here hasn't it, on the Carso?" said Freddy.

"We have been attacking the Austrians on the eastern border because we want more territory from them. Some say that it is our right to have that territory. Did you know that the French and Austrians occupied this area, for a hundred years, and we have had to take it back piece by piece? Venice was Austrian until 1866, but the threat from them is always there. The Risorgimiento is not finished until we have all of Italy together, under one king. We will not stop fighting until we have what is rightfully ours."

After an hour the door to the lane opened again and a small group of French officers came in, and Freddy was pleased to see that among them was his old friend, Armand. Freddy rose and held out his hand and stepped towards Armand.

Armand smiled and was obviously pleased to see Freddy. He nodded to the Englishmen that he knew and shook the hand of everyone. The Italians at the other table, realising that these arrivals were French, drained their glasses, got up, and left the restaurant.

The French took their places.

Freddy introduced Simone to Armand. More drinking and talking followed.

Freddy asked Armand, "How come you are here? I did not know that French divisions were being sent down here."

"We are bringing more divisions here than you English. Did you know that at the start of this war we had to put many troops down on the border with Italy because we believed that they were going to fight on the same side as the Germans? Now they are our allies and we fight for them rather than against them. Will this change again? Perhaps it will. Be careful, Freddy, these Italians will stab us in the back if circumstances demand it. They are temporary friends only!"

Raffaella continued to bring food and wine to the table. Freddy suspected by the way that Simone and Raffaella looked at each other that there was more to their relationship. Perhaps Simone was providing the food from his supply depot?

The next day Peregrine told his officers that there was to be a conference in Padua at the Commando Supremo, the headquarters of the Italian Army, to which selected officers were being sent. This was to be a welcoming conference for the newly arrived divisions which would send deputations and get to know each other. Freddy and Ted were on the list, and at the appointed time they climbed onto the Fiat motor lorry that had been sent to transport them to the conference, and off they went.

Their route took them southwards across the Venetian Plain, following the line of the River Brenta. They arrived at midday and the lorry dropped them outside the headquarters building.

Inside they saw hordes of officers of all ranks from Italian, French, and British formations. There were even a few American officers there. The new Italian supreme commander General Diaz addressed the massed ranks in Italian. While the British could not understand the words spoken, they had no doubts about the meaning. They were there to support their comrades and it was an international effort.

General Trubshawe was there on the stage with Diaz, along with many other generals and senior officers, French, Italian, American and British.

More speeches were made.

Later Freddy's group joined the others from their division at a side room, in which was a large map on the wall showing the lines established in north eastern Italy. General Trubshawe explained that for the time being the division would remain in their concentration areas, and they could expect to be there for several weeks, until the new year at least. Reconnaissance would take place at a number of possible areas for the division to be deployed and orders for these would be sent through in due course. He instructed the officers to go back to their units and train and prepare their men for service in the mountains, for river crossings, and for mobile operations. The officers were then dismissed and allowed to leave.

By the time they left the building it was night. The city was very dark, a combination of narrow streets, winter, and the extinguishing of all exposed lighting due, they were told, to the nightly air attacks by the enemy.

They knew that their rendezvous with their motor lorry was to be just outside the city gate at the western edge of the city, but had no idea of how to reach it through the maze of streets and in the dark.

As they were pondering what to do and unable to come to a consensus they heard the drone of an engine overhead. Listening they heard an aeroplane fly across the city, then the crump as a bomb landed and exploded, somewhere to the north. Then another explosion, and the plane flew back over them and faded away. "Bloody Austrians," said a voice, "what barbarians!"

"Actually they are Germans, probably," said Simone, "They come over every night, sometimes as far as our camp. They have no culture, the Germans, they will be here many times tonight. We should go."

"I have my compass with me, we could set a direction and follow it, that would at least get us to the right side of the city." declared Freddy. "We need to head west, don't we?" he said, no-one answered, so Freddy struck a match and used the light to set his compass. "Right, let's go, follow me." he started off following the compass, the others following him.

They had walked a few streets when they came to one where there seemed to be things going on. By now the moon had come out and they could see in its dim light a number of men standing around and an occasional door opening and someone passing through going in or coming out. Freddy recognised what this meant.

Raised voices caught Freddy's attention. A man was shouting and as Freddy looked in that direction he saw a smaller figure with an arm raised as if in defence. Freddy had a feeling of deja vu, or deju entendu. The man continued to shout and make threatening gestures. "We need to go and sort that out, come with me!" and Freddy started across the street to where the altercation was happening, closely followed by Ted, Edwin, Simone and Armand.

Freddy reached the man and grabbed the arm that he had in the air. The man spun round towards Freddy and raised his other fist, but Simone grabbed this and they pulled the man away from the woman. He smelled of stale wine and was unsteady, trying to resist Freddy and Simone without much effect.

Armand struck a match and looked at the man, and recognised him as from his brigade. While Armand gave the man a lecture on how French soldiers should behave, Freddy and Simone comforted the woman. In fact they realised that she was in fact a girl of about thirteen years. Simone found out from her that she had come to this area to find her mother, who had left home earlier in the evening to come here to work the streets and had not yet returned. The girl was worried about her mother. Freddy, with Simone's help translating offered to see her home, but she refused.

Having resolved this they saw that the man had gone. Armand had told him to report to him the following day for discipline.

The group of officers continued to follow Freddy's compass and eventually reached the west gate to the city, and from there it was an easy walk to the rendezvous point where the motor lorries were waiting. They returned to camp, arriving after midnight.

Christmas came, and the division was still in reserve. Training took place, long treks in full marching order, small arms drill and firing.

Special supplies had been secured and all troops enjoyed a traditional Christmas dinner, the men being served as was usual by the officers. The officers then retired to their mess and

Corporal Ely had laid on an equally luxurious dinner for them, followed by brandy and cigars. All retired to bed happy and well fed.

At the end of December orders came through for a reconnaissance of the mountain area above them. Fiat motors arrived early in the morning and the officers and the BSM climbed aboard. They had been warned for cold weather and had been issued with packed rations for the day.

The lorries left the camp and turned towards the road leading up into the foothills. The Italian drivers were in the habit of driving at full speed wherever possible. The men in the back of the lorries became increasingly alarmed by the apparent dangers as the lorries approached the many hairpin bends at high speed and skidded round to start the next section. The process had to be repeated at frequent intervals. The danger was more apparent as there were no guard rails and the roads became increasingly snow packed and icy. The humour of the men aboard was not helped by the obvious signs of previous departures over the edge, including a number of wrecked lorries seen on the slopes of the hills.

Nonetheless they arrived after two hours progressive climbing at the village of Rubbio, the mist of the plain being replaced by a clear blue sky and icy temperatures.

They felt themselves lucky to have paid attention to the order which was for them to dress warmly.

The day was spent being shown around a defensive position occupied by an Italian division overlooking the valley of the Brenta River near Campolongo.

They ate lunch with the Italian officers and in mid afternoon were ready to return to the plain, none of them looking forward to the prospect of the return journey with the same drivers and their suicidal tendencies.

The journey started, all the men in the back of the lorries were tense. About halfway down, near the village of Crosara they came upon an accident. A lorry carrying supplies had run off the road, hit a bank of earth, and turned on its side blocking the road.

While the Englishmen stood around, stamping their feet and flapping their arms in an attempt to regain some measure of warmth the Italian drivers tried to remove the blockage. They tied ropes to the stricken lorry and the other ends to the lorries that were still upright. They then engaged their gears and pulled at the ropes. Slowly they managed to move the recumbent lorry far enough to permit passage by a carefully driven one. The drivers came down from their vehicles and a voluble discussion took place between them as they debated the merits of goodness knows what. Eventually it seems they reached the consensus that the roadworthy vehicles would continue the journey, leaving the casualty laying on the road to be recovered or further manipulated in the morning.

"I am not sure that I am up to any more riding in the back of these lorries." said Ted, "How far is it back to camp? We could walk, it would be safer."

"You walk if you will," offered Edwin, "I am going to take the lorry, how about you, Peregrine?"

"Those who need the exercise can walk, the rest of us can take the lorry, make your minds up and we will get going." said Peregrine, a little peevishly.

"Tell you what, we will leave one lorry for you where the road levels out, a couple of miles ahead. Walk as far as that and you can have a lift the rest of the way." suggested Edwin, "and we will meet up for dinner in the mess."

The more senior, older, officers got back into the lorries, while a small group of younger men decided to march back to the rendezvous with the lorry as Edwin had suggested.

The darkness of the night came upon them before they could complete their journey. The lorries reached camp near Marostica without problems, but the marchers took a wrong turn and left the road that would have resulted in them reaching the rendezvous on time. Consequently they reached the plain on a road that was not the one they were expecting to be on. After some heated discussion it was decided to continue until they could work out where they were.

In the event they reached a larger road running east west, and the assessment was that they were now west of Marostica and therefore they should turn to the left, eastwards, and follow this road which should eventually bring them to a village or even Marostica itself.

This strategy proved to be the correct one, and after three hours of walking the group reached the outskirts of Marostica. Continuing along the road they arrived at the Castello Inferiore and after the briefest of discussions decided to find the restaurant where Simone had entertained them and dine there.

They entered the piazza and turned left up the dark lane and located Raffaella's familiar restaurant with no difficulty.

On entering they saw that the same group of local men were at their table. A chess game was in progress and the two men playing did not look up. The British officers nodded acknowledgement at them and went to sit at the other table. A log fire was burning, throwing warmth and flickering light into the room. Freddy remained standing and said, "I will go and see where Raffaella is, and we will see if we have enough Italian between us to tell her what food we need." He went to the door at the rear that he had seen Raffaella come into and out of on his last visit.

He knocked gently and there was no answer, so he lifted the latch and pushed the door open. There was the sound of a scuffle inside the room and Raffaella appeared from behind the door from some inner part of the room, brushing her hair back and Freddy noted in passing that she looked a little flushed.

On seeing Freddy Raffaella smiled and waved her arm to indicate that this room was her domain and for Freddy to go back into the restaurant area. She followed him to the table and smiled and nodded to the others, said something that none of them understood and went off. She returned with two jugs of wine and glasses and set these down on to the table. She then went back into her room and was lost to sight.

The British men poured the wine into a glass for each of them and toasted each other and took swigs of the wine. They started discussing the events of the day and the wine brought colour to their cheeks and animation to their conversation. After a while Raffaella reappeared with plates in her hands and set them on the table before the men, and then returned with dishes of polenta, vegetables, and a jug of sauce.

The British dug into the food with relish and more jugs of wine appeared on the table as if by magic.

Freddy felt good, whereas a few hours ago he had been lost on a strange mountain in the cold and dark, now, after using their common sense and initiative they had reached safety and comfort. They all felt good, and this was reflected in the atmosphere at the table.

Freddy felt a hand on his elbow and turned from his conversation to see that Simone had arrived, he must have been there for a few minutes as Freddy noted that he was without a topcoat and must have taken this off after arriving.

The two young men greeted each other, and Simone went round the table and shook hands with all the British and Italian men on both tables.

Simone came back with a chair and sat next to Freddy.

"How did your visit to the mountains go, Freddy?" said Simone as Freddy filled his glass.

"Cold, very cold!"

"Soldiering in the mountains is very different, isn't it?'

"Very different from what we are used to, certainly." said Freddy. "Actually the getting up and down the mountain is pretty frightening. We saw a lot of wrecked transport on the side of the mountain."

"Yes, our drivers are very brave, aren't they, going up and down all the time, every day. We have lost dozens of motors over the side, especially when it is icy. Personally I avoid going up there, it's far too dangerous. Life is dangerous enough down here with the Austrian aeroplanes dropping bombs and the jealous husbands."

"Jealous husbands?"

"Most of the local men are away with the army or in prisoner of war camps, so the local women here have to look to the soldiers camped around for company. If any of them ever get back there will be many murders and fights breaking out. Many of the women I know have taken up with temporary husbands. If the war itself is dangerous, it is going to get even more dangerous when the war ends and the men come home!" He took a swig from his glass, "Freddy, if you ever take an Italian woman as a lover, make sure you leave the country as soon as you can before her husband returns. Believe me, it would be better that way."

"I have no intention of getting involved with the local girls, I have a girl at home who is waiting for me."

"Do you really believe that, Freddy?" riposted Simone, "Girls are the same all over the world. Even if they are married they will be attracted to the man that is there with them. As we say in England, 'absence makes the heart grow fonder, of another'."

"I am sure of her. She is not the type of girl to let a man down. When the war is over I will go back home and we will be married."

"Good luck!" said Simone.

The evening continued and spirits were high. The British officers paid Raffaella, wished her good night and left. Simone remained, and went to sit at the other table as Freddy and his comrades left to walk the mile back to camp.

They found their way easily and went into their mess tent. Peregrine and Edwin and other senior officers were there standing around with glasses in their hands.

"Where the bloody hell have you been!" shouted Peregrine as they entered.

Taken aback, the newly arrived men, still wearing their topcoats, were lost for words, until Ralph House, emboldened by the alcohol, stepped forward and said with much feeling, "Actually, Peregrine, we have been struggling to get back here for morning muster. After you abandoned us up on the mountain we have had to march all the way back. Your lorry did not meet us and we were forced to hoof it all the way. Do you know how far we have marched this evening? It must be at least a dozen miles, and in the dark and the cold! If you had done as you promised we would have been back hours ago!" By the end of this Ralph had come so close to Peregrine that the latter could feel Ralph's breath and spittle on his face. He stood back a step as if anticipating violence.

"How dare you!" Peregrine shouted back, "Adjutant, take this man's name, he is to report to me in the morning!"

Kit came over and placed his hand on Peregrine's arm, and Edwin came over to restrain Ralph, "Lets all just calm down, shall we?" said Edwin. "It has been a difficult day for all of us."

Chapter 20

February 1918, Montello, Italy.

January had come and gone. In mid February orders came through for the division to take up a position to the east, on the Piave River.

A long trek and they took over from an Italian division that had been in position overlooking the river and the Austrians opposite since the Caporetto disaster the previous year. They were to go into reserve for re-equipping and training, and to be brought back up to strength.

Freddy's brigade took over the gun line just south of the prominent hill feature known as the Montello, and the forward OP was atop the hill with a clear view across the river and deep into the Austrian position.

General Trubshawe issued orders covering an attack that had been planned between the Italian, French and British commanders. Under cover of a smoke screen engineers were going to build temporary bridges across the river. Infantry would then cross these bridges and attack and capture the forward trenches in the Austrian positions on the far bank. When the Austrians counterattacked to regain these trenches artillery fire would be brought down to kill as many Austrians as possible. The Allied forces would then withdraw across the river to the near bank.

Trubshawe visited Freddy's brigade a week before the attack was due to take place, and in a meeting with the senior officers he expressed the opinion that the attack plan was unrealistic, but that the French who were the main proponents of it were in the position of wanting to regain their pride having failed to attack on the Western Front the previous year.

In the event the attack was cancelled when heavy rain in the mountains swelled the river and washed away the bridges that the engineers had built.

The division was then withdrawn from the front and sent back in to reserve at Marostica.

During the relief when an Italian division was taking over from Trubshawe's division Peregrine Proudfoot and his batman stayed behind on the position to complete the handover. As they were leaving to rejoin the brigade a stray Austrian shell hit them and they were both killed. They were buried near the small hamlet of Giavera.

In the mess later the officers were gathering for their usual pre dinner aperitif.

"What do you make of Peregrine having gone? What do you think will happen next?" Freddy asked of Edwin.

"We have been told that we will get no reinforcements, so he will be replaced by someone who is already out here I should think. There are a couple of obvious candidates within the brigade, but they may send someone in from the other brigades." said Edwin.

"I hear the Germans are making a big push in France, do you think they will send us back up there? I was rather looking forward to spring and summer in Italy, the weather should be better down here." said Freddy.

'I am sure the War Office are considering sending some divisions back to France, we will have to wait and see. I am happy to go wherever they want me to go." said Edwin, "It's all the same to me."

"How did you get on with Peregrine? He always struck me as a bit stuffy and not one of us."

"He was all right, really. I think the battery needed a strong commander. Buster was very good, but he did let a few things slip and Peregrine was the man to get things in order again. A

BC does not have to be popular, you know, just respected." said Edwin.

"You are right, I suppose," said Freddy, "but not many of us got on well with him, not my type at all. Was he married, do you know?"

"Yes, and he had children. The colonel has had to write to his widow and explain what happened. She will have to bring the children up without him, it will be difficult for her I am sure." said Edwin.

General Trubshawe arrived, was offered and accepted a drink, and came over to speak to Edwin.

"Do we have any news on going back to France, General?" Edwin asked.

"Yes we do, Edwin. Two divisions are being sent back and will leave within days, but we are staying here in Italy. I will be issuing orders soon, I think we will be staying in reserve for a couple of weeks until the situation in France stabilises, then we will be going up into the mountains. General Diaz wants us to attack the Austrians up there and push them back into Austria so we will be planning for a major attack in the early summer." explained Trubshawe.

"So you think the German attack in France will fail, General?" asked Freddy.

"It certainly will, Freddy, the Germans have one last chance to beat us before the Americans are ready, but I think they are already out of time. The Yanks are sending troops over at a division a week, more or less, and in any case the Germans are running out of everything, food, men, supplies of all kinds. It is only a matter of time, now, mark my words." said Trubshawe.

"And we have good news from the Middle East as well." added Edwin.

"The Ottomans are finished. When they give up we can transfer all those men to France and finish the Hun." said Trubshawe.

Before they deployed in the mountains the officers of Freddy's brigade decided to have one last night out in Marostica. And so they set out for the town.

Once more they dined, and Raffaella made them welcome. As there were more customers than before she had placed another table in the room, which made the space inside more congested.

The wine flowed and the food was served. Simone was there again. Freddy said to him, "How come you are always here in Raffaella's restaurant, Simone?"

"Freddy, you are slow on the uptake! Raffaella gets most of her supplies from me, I get them from my supply depot. She makes money, she also makes me happy!" said Simone, smiling.

"But you are married, you have a wife in London!" said Freddy, shocked, and realising that the obvious truth had been in front of him all the time.

"When the war is over, and I leave the army, I will go back to my wife, and Raffaella's husband will come back from Austria. We will all be happy then." said Simone.

"Her husband is in Austria? Is he a prisoner?"

"No, he is working for the Austrians. Some of the families around here, up in the mountains, are really Austrians." said Simone, "When the war started and before Italy joined in the men had to make a choice. Some of them decided to join the Austrians, and Andre, her husband, was one of them."

"Good god, we have been eating in an Austrian restaurant!" said Freddy, shocked.

"No, we have not." said Simone, "Raffaella comes from a good Italian family, her husband's family are in the mountains and regard themselves as Austrians, it is as simple as that."

"Does Andre know about you and Raffaella?"

"I shouldn't think so." said Simone, "And if he did, he could do nothing about it. When he comes back, as he will, some day, he will just accept things as they are. I will be gone, and he will be here. At least Raffaella is not being bothered by lots of soldiers, I look after her and make sure that she is safe."

"Things certainly are different here in Italy."

"Yes, we do things differently here, because we have to. When the British go to war they do it in somebody else's country. In Italy when we fight we do it on our own territory, much closer to our homes. We have to find ways to deal with the reality of our lives. When the war is over you and I will go back to England and things will be more or less as they were before, here many things will have changed." said Simone, becoming uncharacteristically serious.

"Freddy, have you noticed in the main square, the chess board?" asked Simone.

"Yes, I think so, what is it for?"

"Many years ago, when we were not Italians here, but Venetians, the governor of the town had a beautiful daughter, Lionora. Two noblemen came to Marostica and wooed the young girl and both of them wanted to marry her. This was, of course, impossible. Only one could have her hand, and she was not allowed to choose, that was for her father to decide. So, the governor thought that the best way was for the two noblemen to play a game of chess, and the winner would marry the beautiful Lionora."

"Is that what happened, the girl married the winner of the chess match?" enquired Freddy, somewhat intrigued by the story.

"Yes. it happened that way, but what the governor did not tell the noblemen was that the loser was to marry the other daughter, Oldrada, younger but not as beautiful. That would have been a good story for William Shakespeare, would it not? Better than Romeo and Juliet?"

"Hmm, you do solve things in a different way in Italy, Simone." said Freddy, lifted his glass and drank more wine.

The next day the division started its move up onto the mountain. The weather was better and heat had started to build on the Plain. As the wagons gradually ascended the roads up to the plateau the air cooled and by the time the first British troops arrived at their destination on the southern edge of the plateau they had to don their greatcoats to keep out the chill.

The Italian division that they were taking over from had been in position for almost three years, since they had repulsed an Austrian attack which had almost succeeded in breaking the Italian line. By reaching the edge of the plateau they would have been able to descend to the Venetian Plain and thereby cut off the bulk of the Italian Army on the Carso Front.

The Italians had fought desperately, facing fearful odds and fearsome weapons. Vast areas of the wooded hills on the plateau were still bearing the scars from the fighting of three years earlier, including much of the forest which was dying due to the quantities of poison gases employed in the battle.

Since that battle, though, it had been a quiet sector. The Italians had not improved their defences and many positions had deteriorated or had been abandoned due to the shortage of men and equipment needed to defend other parts of the line.

So, the British arrived, and the Italians left. The area was marked by a number of prominent hills, many of which were heavily wooded, with deep ravines and water courses. Small hamlets were dotted around the plateau, with the main town of Asiago in Austrian hands, about two miles inside the Austrian position. However, most of the Austrian position was open to observation from the Allies on the hills. The Allied lines of supply were out of sight on the slopes of the mountains coming up from the Plain, and through clearings in the forests at Granezza, Pria dell Aqua, Carriola, and Magnaboschi. From these clearings, where large dumps of stores were positioned, tracks led to the forward trenches through the forest and which were largely unobserved from the Austrian side. This gave some advantage to the Allies in that they could generally operate, move, resupply and administer themselves free from observed interference by the Austrians. The latter had the ability only to move by night as any movement to and from or between their positions was liable to be observed and attacked by artillery.

The main weakness, though, of the Allied position was that it was positioned on the edge of the hills above the Plain, and therefore any penetration of their position threatened to descend onto the Plain and cut the lines of communication to the bulk of the Italian Army to the east on the Plain and positioned along the near bank of the Piave River.

On arriving in the position Edwin went over to meet up with the French Brigade to the British left, and Freddy went to inspect progress in the gun line and the forward OP. The Brigade HQ was to the rear in the forest.

Armand Chaleyer was the senior French artilleryman in the French Brigade, and Edwin met him in a forward trench of the French position that they had just taken over. Edwin was happy that he had someone that he knew well to discuss arrangements with.

"Armand, I think that you will find it impossible to advance from your position. There is a deep ravine in front and it is pretty well impossible for anyone to cross, it must be two hundred feet deep and has vertical sides." Edwin said after they had toured the position.

"Yes, you are right, Edwin, we have little to fear from a direct attack by the Austrians, and it will be impossible for us to advance directly against them. We will have to come through your division's position to get across the Ghelpac and then move back to the left. I am concerned that the main track to the plain comes through your position. If we attack, that crossing will be very congested, and if we get attacked the Austrians will concentrate against there. You must tell your commander to reinforce the crossing. The Italians have left this position badly constructed, and there are not enough communications here between the rear and the front and laterally. We are going to have to build more trenches and tracks so we can get reserves around the position quickly when we need to."

"You are right in every respect, Armand. General Trubshawe has told us to be ready to attack in two week's time, which is not time enough, really. He wants me to deploy my battery right forward near Cesuna so we can cover an infantry advance of up to five miles. We have a lot of work to do to get this position in good shape. If we can help you in any way do not hesitate to let me know, we will have to help each other out whether we get attacked or we do the attacking."

"I think we are finished for the time being, Edwin, I may be able to come over and see round more of your position tomorrow, if that is all right with you?"

"Let me know when you are coming and what you want to see and I will fix it up for you. Many thanks, Armand." said Edwin.

"Before you go, tell me how your brothers are, I think Freddy is still here, is he not?" said Armand.

"George is back in Blighty for good, some cushy number in London. Freddy is here, still in A Battery, and still being a silly arse! I will tell him you are over here, he will want to come and see you and say hello." said Edwin.

"George is a lucky man, out of the war. I think that Freddy has a young lady by now?" said Armand.

"Freddy? No, not as far as I know. He always seems a little shy of the ladies. George is lucky, though, and he has a choice of lady friends no doubt, with most of the young men in the army."

They parted and Edwin made his way back to his battery which as he had told Armand, was setting up its guns near the village of Cesuna, in between the first line and second line trenches.

Freddy meanwhile was inspecting preparations at his battery which was more than a mile to the rear and not far from the wagon lines.

"How are things progressing, Sergeant Reid? Do you have enough men and materials?"

"Short of everything as usual, sir." said Reid, "We had another case of fever this morning. As soon as one man gets over it another goes down with it. I have only four of us on the gun at the moment, but we will manage. How are things with you, sir?"

"Oh, all right, I suppose, but like you and your men I have more to do than I can manage, especially as the Italians have not prepared the position all that well. General Trubshawe wants some new tracks built and more line laid between the batteries and the forward trenches. I have to go up that hill over there this afternoon to see the OP. Apparently it is something to see all right. I am told it is thirty feet up on a platform between two trees. They say you can see right into the Austrian rear, beyond the range of our guns."

"What about when it gets windy? It must move around a bit!"

"I will let you know what I think after I have seen it, Sergeant Reid. One problem is that it is about a mile and a half from here, so a long journey by foot when we have to man it, and the track goes through the stores and ammunition dump at Handley Cross where it is always busy. Actually I understand that General Trubshawe is not very happy about that area. Too many things in too small a place, they need to be spread out more, but there is a shortage of level areas suitable for the stores. The main front to rear track crosses the main east west track at the same spot. They should have called it Hyde Park Corner! If we have to attack all the follow up troops and stores will have to get through the bottle neck in short order. It is bound to cause chaos, and if we ever had to withdraw in a hurry through there it would clog up very quickly." said Freddy. "Wish me luck and I will see you this evening if all is well."

On his return from seeing Armand, Edwin went straight to Handley Cross and sought out General Trubshawe at his HQ, which was in an underground cave on a track about a hundred yards east from the cross tracks. The cave consisted of several rooms or spaces that radiated from a central bunker and which had all been dug out by the Italian engineers. The side rooms contained staff officers and telephone operators, all seemingly intent and busy at their tasks. As Edwin came in he saw the general was sitting at a wooden table in the middle of the central space.

Edwin saluted, and said, "General, I have been to see the French on our left and feel I must report certain things to you for your urgent attention."

Trubshawe looked up, smiled, and indicated for Edwin to sit at another chair. He looked worried, but at the same time his features displayed a kindly welcome. A soldier brought both men tin mugs of coffee.

"I guess it is not good news that you have brought me, Major Scott?" said Trubshawe.

"No, sir, not entirely. The position to our left, where the French are, is damn near impregnable due to the ravine between them and the Austrians. To advance they would have to move right through our area and then adjust left. This would be very difficult and will need careful planning and rehearsal if the two divisions are not to get badly mixed up. Our front is better for an advance, but as you will know, sir, the main track leading to the back areas and the plain runs through our positions on the left flank. If the Austrians attack this is where they will be aiming for. They tried it three years ago, apparently, and damn near made it all the way and that would have been a disaster for our lines of communication. The trenches guarding that track are very thin and mostly in the wrong locations. On top of that we are short of manpower, as you know, due to having no reinforcement drafts for months. A third of the men are down with fever on any particular day. We don't have the manpower to put the whole position right, and not enough men to cover the front in any depth at all." said Edwin.

"Well put, major, you are completely correct in what you say, but I have other problems as well. This area outside causes me concerns. We have divisional HQ and the two forward Brigade HQs close, and ammunition dumps as well as several stores dumps all crowded together. If we need to get troops up for an attack or counter attack they have to come through here before they can spread out across the front trenches. It's a pinch point, all right, and a nasty and dangerous one. I have asked our engineers to put some more tracks in to help with the lateral and forward lines of communication, but my real worry is the ammunition dumps. The Q Branch and the ASC people are looking to disperse the dumps but that will take time, and if the Austrians land a lucky shell among all that ammunition, well, I leave it to your imagination. We need half the ammunition further forward for our attack, and some further back out of the danger area." Trubshawe elaborated.

"How far back is the reserve infantry brigade, General, could they be stationed forward of Handley Cross?"

"I am considering that, major, however there are not enough trenches to accommodate them in a way to help a counter attack across the divisional front. We are doing what we can, but as usual, time is short. Thanks for your report, though, it has been very informative. Please dictate it to one of my clerks and you will need to be getting back to your battery, no doubt." said Trubshawe and turned away from Edwin as if to end the interview.

Edwin rose, saluted, and went off to find the Chief of Staff to complete his report.

Meanwhile Freddy and Ted Rivett had finished directing work at the gun line and left the gun crews to get on with their work. They collected their kit together, grabbed some food, and then started their march to the OP on the peak of Monte Lemerle, taking Corporal Hastings with them.

It took them over a hour to reach the top of the mountain. The track led them from the valley, along several twisting and turning minor tracks, past trenches blasted into the limestone rocks, and occasional dumps of stores and equipment. They had to pass through the centre at Handley Cross behind the mountain, then ascend a steep track which wound around to the front of the mountain and up to the peak.

On arriving at the top they found a series of trenches and dugouts. The sides and top of the mountain were heavily forested, and throughout their journey they were in the shade and cover of the trees. Many areas of the forest were, though, dead. These areas had suffered from the use of explosives and poisonous gases in the previous Austrian attacks. There were Italian soldiers around, seemingly removing their equipment and supplies. Freddy went over to an officer and saluted and tried to communicate, but as there was no common language this was effectively impossible.

Needing to find where the OP was so that he could set up and familiarise himself with the territory that he could observe, Freddy lifted his binoculars to his eyes to indicate to the Italian officer what he needed.

The Italian smiled, lifted his eyes to the tree tops, and pointed to a ladder that Freddy had not noticed to this point. The ladder was between two trees, and following the Italian's gaze Freddy saw that there, about thirty feet in the air, was a platform that the ladder led to.

Freddy and Ted exchanged glances, this was something new to them. OPs were normally underground with a view point at ground level. The implications of being up in a tree when shells and bullets were flying around was not a pleasant prospect.

Freddy said 'grazie' to the Italian and went over to the foot of the ladder. He handed his kit to Hastings, and started to climb the ladder, which moved gently as the trees either side swayed in the breeze.

He reached the top rung and swung his leg up onto the platform. It was a substantial construction. Heavy wooden beams ran between the two trees, and on these were strapped a wooden floor, with wooden walls at the front and rear. There was even a sloping roof and what really impressed Freddy was the view from the front of the OP.

Though open to the elements above the front wall, the aspect of the platform gave visibility for miles, across the plateau to the mountains on the far side, some six or seven miles away. The platform itself extended about twenty feet from left to right and about eight feet from back to front. As he looked round Freddy noted that there were four chairs and a table, and a shelf running along the front wall just below the opening. Above the opening, just below the roof, pinned to a board running the length of the platform was a series of photographs of the scene before them, with buildings and topographical features noted on them.

Going back to the point where the ladder met the platform Freddy shouted down for the other two to join him.

Ted arrived first, still puffing a little after the morning's efforts, and as he entered the OP he whistled and nodded his head as he looked around, in an approving manner. Hastings arrived a few seconds later and his reaction was similar to Ted's.

The three of them stood, looking out at the plateau, silently transfixed, gazing out into the distance. Not in three years at war had any of them seen such a vista. "Bloody hell." breathed Hastings.

Freddy and Ted, as one movement, lifted their binoculars to their eyes and scanned the distance.

They could see the town of Asiago and many hamlets and villages, but no movement. Though they knew there were hundreds if not thousands of Austrians out there, they saw not one person.

"This has got to be the best OP we have ever had for visibility." said Freddy.

"Yes, sir, but what about when the shit starts to fly around, we are very exposed up here, and what if they knock the ladder down, we are stuck!" said Hastings.

"I think the powers that be will want someone up here whenever anything is happening. At least the weather should be good for the next few weeks, and if it rains we have a good roof by the look of it."

"Maybe we should get a rope we can slide down as an escape plan?" said Ted.

"Yes, that sounds good, and we must test the communications. Corporal Hastings, can you connect up the field telephone to the terminals over there in the corner and see who you can raise at the other end?"

Hastings did as he was bid and in a few minutes reported that he was through to divisional exchange at Handley Cross.

Freddy and Ted spent an hour using the panoramic photographs, their maps, and their binoculars to familiarise themselves with the ground and the features out in front. They could see much of the Austrian trenches, but they discovered that they were not able to see the British front line due to the lie of the land and the trees, but they could estimate where these trenches were. If an SOS flare was sent up they satisfied themselves that they would be able to see it.

"Ted, stay here until last light and then return to the battery when the relief arrives, I think it will be Ralph. Corporal Hastings will stay on the telephone for you," said Freddy looking in turn at the other two to confirm their understanding, "I am off back to Brigade to report on what we have up here. I think I will recommend that we lay more line direct to the batteries. This is such a good OP that if a battle starts and the line goes out we will not be able to do our job properly. Having lines to the batteries will mean that at least we can fire some of the guns."

Freddy collected together his kit and descended to the ground. There were fewer Italians around, but he saw some British uniforms and went over to find out who they were.

A captain of Royal Engineers was standing outside the entrance to a bunker just behind the hill. "Hello, old chap, moving in as well?" he said, holding out his hand.

The captain turned, smiled, and shook Freddy's hand. "Tom Cox, what are you up to?"

"Freddy Scott, RFA, we have our OP up there, Tom, great view, feel free to have a look when you get a few minutes. Ted Rivett is up there at the moment. I think we will be manning it round the clock from now on, so we will be neighbours."

"We are here to inspect the dugouts and trenches. Apparently General Trubshawe wants things stiffened up, so we are going to be busy. This dugout I will grab as my HQ while we are working here, let me know if there is anything we can help with."

"There is one thing, actually. If you are laying line you may be able to help. We only have line to division from here, I want to lay more cables direct to the four batteries in my brigade. It is a big job, but any help you could give us would be much appreciated, Tom." said Freddy.

"Let my sergeant have a sketch map of what you need and we can discuss it tomorrow, is that all right?"

"Yes, that would be very helpful. I will be back in the morning and we can see what can be done. Cheerio for now, off to Brigade." said Freddy as he left to begin his journey back.

Going back down from the mountain was quite easy for Freddy, even with all his kit on. He reached Handley Cross and found it to be a scene of much activity. The British were now busy establishing themselves. He saw columns of marching infantry passing through, rows of horse drawn wagons delivering supplies, or loading them up and taking them away to other sites. There were wagons with large reels of telephone cable, staff officers hurrying between dugouts. In the distance he saw General Trubshawe, dressed in his usual mackintosh despite the warmth of the day, in discussion with a staff colonel. Freddy made his way to his Brigade HQ which was a little way away from Handley Cross.

The Brigade Commander, Colonel Goodson, was inside the dugout standing at a table on one side of the space, with a map propped up on it and against the wall.

Freddy saluted the colonel, "Excuse me sir, I have just come back from the OP on Mount Lemerle and I need to speak to you about it."

Colonel Goodson looked up and waved his hand to indicate that Freddy should join him at the map on the table.

"Right, what do you need to say Freddy."

"Firstly, sir, I have to report that it is an excellent OP for the observation it gives. It covers the whole of our divisional front with some observation into the divisional fronts to our left and right, from here," Freddy pointed to the map, "to here. However our front trenches are not observable due to the lie of the land and the trees. We have calculated their position, but should there be action for up to a half mile in front of them we will be unable to observe from there."

"Go on." said the colonel.

"There is only one telephone line connection at the OP, to division. The OP is also a mile from the nearest battery, C, here, near Cesuna," again Freddy pointed to the map, "and two miles from A and B Batteries as the crow flies, near Carriola, here. The howitzer battery is behind Cesuna, here, as you know. I think we should lay more telephone lines to the OP from here at Brigade, and from each of the batteries so that if one line goes unserviceable we can still talk to the guns. We could consider laying a line direct to the other brigade so that we could fire their guns as well if we have good enough targets."

"Go on." said the colonel.

"There are engineers up at the OP location at the moment digging dugouts and trenches. They say they may be able to help lay line, maybe we could ask them to help out, sir. Also, it takes over an hour to get from the battery to the OP. In an emergency this would be too long. May I suggest that we find an unused dugout closer to the OP, maybe half way up the mountain. We could stock it with enough stores to last a couple of days. We can send the relief party up twelve hours before a handover so that should we need to we can add extra hands in the OP faster than otherwise would be possible."

"Is that all, Freddy?" asked the colonel.

"Yes, sir." said Freddy.

The colonel turned to a doorway deeper in the dugout and said, "Kit, do you have a minute, please, Freddy here has some business for you."

Freddy then spoke to Kit and explained what he had found while Colonel Goodson continued with his work.

At the end of the interview Kit gave Freddy a document that listed targets and other plans for the defence of the divisional position. Kit also told Freddy that General Trubshawe had ordered work to be carried out to strengthen the position including practising the bringing up of the reserve infantry brigade in case a counter attack was needed. He said that this would also enable them to familiarise themselves with the route and record timings for troop movements around the position. Kit assured Freddy that the extra telephone line would be laid as soon as the manpower became available, and suggested that Freddy get around the infantry positions so that he could see for himself the state of play and to find out who was in each sector.

In the infantry trenches forward of the village of Cesuna Captain Stephen Sansom was going round his company position with the newly appointed Sergeant Major Arthur Rippingill. He was concerned about the layout of the position, and the ability of his company to defend it as ordered by his commanding officer. "How many men answered muster today, Sergeant Major?"

"Eighty seven, sir."

"How many due to come back from sick tomorrow, do you think?"

"Not sure, sir, but as soon as we get some back on duty others report sick. I think that for the time being we should assume that the number we have is all we will have until this fever runs its course. We had another two die from it last night down at the field hospital, and there will be no reinforcement drafts at all, I am told." Rippingill said.

"All right, then we will have to be more efficient with what we have. I am concerned that the trenches the Italians have left us are in the wrong places, and there is no mutual support between them. The Austrians could infiltrate between posts and we would never know they were there until they were behind us. I think we will have to put out listening patrols a few hundred yards in front of the line at night. Can we lay some line out to two of the ruined farms out there so the patrols can report back to us without giving their position away? And we will need to put out more barbed wire to block the covered approaches, especially where we are thinnest spread." Stephen said, a worried look on his face.

"Anything else, sir?" asked Rippingill.

"Yes, there is going to be a practice tomorrow for withdrawal and counterattack. At 08.00 I want half the men to withdraw from the front trench and make their way back to the reserve switch trench behind Cesuna. The reserve battalion will be moving up at the same time from Carriola and we will join them in the switch trench. If we get attacked at any time we have orders to immediately inform division on the telephone, or by runner, and they will move the reserve battalion up to the switch. Can you pass that on to the platoons and make sure that they understand that this is a an important rehearsal? And keep an eye on the work on improving the position, I have to go off for orders at battalion now, apparently the colonel had a bit of a punch up with General Trubshawe and there are more instructions coming down the line than we can probably manage, so we need the men to keep at it, no rest today, or tomorrow, or the day after. Make sure they get plenty of rum, though, they deserve it!" said Sansom, and turned and left before the sergeant major could respond.

The work continued at a furious pace.

At last light two patrols left the front trenches. Bayonets fixed and faces blackened, they trailed telephone cable behind them as they cautiously made their way to abandoned farms some way out in front of the position. One of them was led by Sergeant Major Rippingill.

Rippingill's patrol of five men approached the building slowly, being careful not to make any noise. Though they had been assured that the Austrian line was much further out than this farm, the Austrians were known to patrol no-man's land, and they may be in the farm ahead of the British.

They used wire cutters to make a new way through the wire fence that the owner of the farm had put up to keep his goats and cattle secure, but which now was a barrier to the patrol. Rippingill knew it was better to follow an untrodden path to his objective rather than follow tracks as this would mean his patrol could better reach the farm without being detected or attacked.

He signalled for the others to lay down while he went forward to the rear door of the building. He paused for several minutes while he listened for sounds within the building which might indicate that the Austrians had got there first. All was quiet. He put his hand on the door latch and very very slowly lifted it, soundlessly. He pushed the door gently, it swung open with a low groan. He stopped again, listening intently.

Taking a deep breath, he stepped inside, his rifle slung across his shoulder, his knife in his right hand, ready for use. He stepped to the side so he was not silhouetted in the door way. He listened, he heard rather than felt his heart thumping. Nothing.

Rippingill's eyes adjusted to the gloom inside the room. He could sense that there was no-one in the room with him.

He went outside, and a low whistle brought the other men to join him.

They set up the telephone near the middle of the room, while one man stood at the rear door and one at a window on the other side, opened carefully, listening intently.

They stayed like that for two hours, then the man by the window reached out and touched Rippingill's arm. Rippingill could just make out that the man, Private Watson, bespectacled, had one hand cupping his ear, and with the other hand made a signal to indicate something outside. Rippingill moved to the window, and listened as hard as he could, but heard nothing. He looked at Watson and screwed his face up, shaking it. Watson nodded, continuing to cup his ear.

Then, Rippingill did hear something. A gentle swish swish as someone walked through long grass. They both looked out intently, trying to see anything, but it was too dark.

The swishing stopped. They heard a low murmur about fifty yards away. It must be an Austrian patrol. No time to telephone. The sound of the cranking might give them away.

If they were coming in to the building they would have to come through the back door, Rippingill reasoned, so he moved across the room to stand by it. He signed to the other sentry to be aware. They waited.

Out of the darkness a figure emerged, moving cautiously. Rippingill still had the knife in his hand, and he clenched his fingers to make sure he had a good grip.

The figure came to the doorway and standing just outside leaned forward to have a look inside. Rippingill smelt the odour of unwashed body. He grabbed the man's head with his left arm and thrust the knife upwards into the man's belly and under his ribs. The man went rigid for a second, fell to his knees, then fell forward onto his face. He made no sound because Rippingill had left his knife in the guts and clamped both his hands around the man's throat, preventing any sound escaping. He held him there, on the ground, until the man stopped moving. Rippingill let go, the man was dead. He pulled the knife out and wiped it on the dead man's tunic. Feeling over the corpse Rippingill realised that he was unarmed, no rifle, no revolver, nothing.

Minutes passed.

Another figure came to the door, and quietly said, "Andre?"

Rippingill grabbed the man by the throat, and threw him to the floor in an embrace. The man choked, then went still.

Rippingill relaxed his grip, the man was breathing. He felt for a weapon. The man had none.

Rippingill dragged the man into the room and laid him next to the corpse. He took out his electric torch and, shielding the beam, used it to inspect the man. The smell of stale sweat and tobacco had by now been augmented by the smell of faeces. "The bastard has shit himself!" thought Rippingill. The man lay quietly, eyes wide open, catatonic, though that was not a word that Rippingill would have used.

He wore the uniform of the Austrian Army, though the tunic was dirty and torn and unbuttoned at the top, he had no helmet or cap, and he had no undershirt on as far as Rippingill could tell. He was now lying in the pool of blood that had flowed from his comrade.

Rippingill stood up, went to Private Watson and said in a whisper, "Have you heard any others out there?"

Watson shook his head.

"Keep listening, I am going to report in that we have a prisoner."

He went to the telephone, cranked the handle to signal to the other end. A voice crackled through the earpiece, "A Company HQ."

Rippingill whispered into the mouthpiece, "Rippingill here, have a prisoner, am sending him back, thirty minutes, be ready."

Rippingill knew that anyone unannounced approaching the front trench was liable to be shot. Captain Sansom was quite clear on that point, shoot first, ask after.

Rippingill told two of his patrol to gag the man, and march him back to the trench, making sure that they announced themselves clearly before showing themselves. He wanted no accidents on his patrol. He needed to keep as many men on their feet as possible. The small group left, and Watson and Rippingill continued their listening watch.

When Rippingill and the remainder of his patrol arrived back at the trench at first light they made sure the sentry was aware of them, and then climbed down into it. "Bloody hell, sergeant major, you are covered in blood!" said the sentry. Rippingill looked down and saw that his right arm and the belly of his tunic were darkened by stale blood. He replied, "Yes, this is the blood of a sentry who fell asleep on duty!" and before the soldier could respond, made his way along the trench to find Captain Sansom.

Sansom wanted to have the details of the night's events, and Rippingill provided them to him. His final words were, "Sir, it's Watson we should thank. For a man who wears spectacles he has remarkably good hearing!" Sansom was not sure how to take this remark.

The prisoner had arrived safely and had been sent back to divisional HQ where he was interrogated. He was given hot coffee, a sandwich, and a cigarette.

He was clearly pleased to be captured, though the method was not to his liking. He gave details of his name, his unit, and freely answered all the questions put to him. When he was asked why he had decided to desert now, he told the staff officer that he and his brother had been told that the Austrians had been preparing for a big attack tomorrow. He said that many German officers had been visiting the Austrian lines and that they had forced the Austrians to prepare the attack. He and his brother were sure they would be killed so they decided to desert. The staff officer said that he was sorry that the man's brother had been killed. The Austrian started crying. He said that his brother, Andre, was married to an Italian woman, and he had wanted to get back to her. She had managed to get a message to him and had arranged with an Italian officer to hide them both until the war was finished.

The report from the prisoner was passed to General Trubshawe, and from him to Corps HQ and to the other French, British and Italian divisions on the front.

The French and Italian commanders considered the possibility of an attack by the Austrians, and decided that it was probably incorrect information or only a small local attack. Trubshawe alerted his units to be aware of the possibility and to make sure that dawn and dusk stand to was strictly observed in all units. Counterattack plans were to be in place and ready to be implemented.

Edwin's battery were positioned just behind the infantry trenches, between them and the village of Cesuna.

Sergeant Major Leman had transferred to the battery with Edwin. On arriving in Italy he had decided to extend his menagerie and bought some geese locally at a farm near Marostica. He had brought these up onto the position with the battery and they now wandered around the gun pits quite happily foraging on the grass and vegetation all around.

"Are those your geese, Sergeant Major?" asked Edwin when he first saw them. "Yes, sir," came the reply, "My father was a drover for a time when he was young and used to drive them to market in London. We always have a few around the place back home. I thought they could supplement the rations if supplies don't arrive up here, sir, I hope that is all right?"

Edwin assented, knowing that he relied heavily on Leman, and that the good sergeant major would be happier with a little slack.

"Right, Sergeant Major, just keep them away from my bivvy. Now, there is a bit of a wind up. Apparently a prisoner was taken last night and he says that the Austriacos will be attacking tomorrow morning. Make sure the guns are properly manned tonight as we are likely to be needed for SOS at first light. Better make sure we have plenty of ammunition in the pits, especially shrapnel."

"Righto, sir, I will get right on it. What about our attack, sir, any news on that yet?"

"No date set yet, and I think General Trubshawe will want to delay until the position is properly arranged to his liking. As soon as I know anything I will pass it on."

During the day all infantry sentries and artillery OPs were told to look out for any signs of increased activity out front. Ted was up at the OP all day and spent most of his time searching with his binoculars out across no-man's land, but the Austrians showed no signs of activity at all, which by now the British had come to regard as normal. Up to this point they had seen nothing happening in no-man's land or behind the Austrian lines. Intelligence reports were that the Austrians and Germans were not able to mount any offensive due to shortage of men and materiel. In fact, there had been reports during the previous winter of food riots across the German and Austro-Hungarian territories. The German spring offensive on the Western Front had drawn to a close with enormous losses, and it was felt unlikely that the Austrians would dare to start a fight down here in Italy.

Ralph House was at the OP, the remainder of the brigade officers were in the mess having dinner and reporting progress to Colonel Goodson, who was anxious to comply with General Trubshawe's orders.

Corporal Ely had produced an excellent meal, and the officers were relaxing for a half hour before going off to their night time duties, or to bed.

"What do you think of the reports of an attack tomorrow, Edwin?" asked Freddy.

"I'm not sure. One scruffy Austrian deserter does not seem like a very reliable source for information. Why would someone at such a low level in their army be party to secret information like that? It may be true, more likely a trench raid, no more. If a big offensive was planned we would have had more signs, wouldn't we?" Edwin reasoned.

"I have read that when the Germans attacked on the Western Front in March they were a complete surprise, some units were surrounded or bypassed before they realised the Germans were there. It could happen here, couldn't it?" said Ted.

"It could," said Edwin, "but it's unlikely. The Austrians are worse off than the Germans for everything. They just don't have the means to mount a big attack. Their morale is shaky, so they probably could not get the men out of the trenches to attack. In any case, the ground here is very different to the Somme or Flanders. We can see right behind their lines back to the rear areas, and there has been no sign of any build up. Surely we would have seen something if they were getting ready for a push? My view is that we may get a raid tomorrow morning or during the night, but nothing more. As long as the gun teams are quick with their SOSs everything should be fine. A few rounds of shrapnel in no man's land will take the edge of any warlike attitudes in the Austrians."

The others could see no reason to disagree with Edwin's assessment, and talk turned to more usual topics of soldierly conversation.

Ted said, to no one in particular, "When will leave come through, do you think?"

Freddy pushed at Ted's arm and said, "You have not been in long enough for leave, Ted, you are still wet behind the ears!"

Colonel Goodson came over, "Leave, leave you say, no chance, no chance at all. No reinforcements, either, what we have here is what we have to finish the war with. At least there are signs the fever is easing off a little, we have more men fit for duty today than for several weeks."

Kit Chilvers added, "At least supplies are getting through pretty reliably. There was post delivered today which should help morale, and the weather up here is better than down on the Plain. I was in Marostica yesterday and the temperature is up in the nineties, and very close. We can breathe better up here, can't we?"

"And drink well!" said Freddy, raising his glass of whisky and sucking on his pipe. "Here's a toast to those we have left behind!" he added.

The others raised their glasses and toasted, "Those we have left behind!"

"We will have been at war for four years, soon, Edwin. I wonder how Mamma and Papa are getting on with us being away for such a long time." said Freddy, suddenly maudlin.

"George must get home from time to time, and they have Sissie, though she must be going mad having them to herself. No news of any beau in her life. Must be the shortage of young men in Blighty. All the good ones are in uniform and doing their bit, like us." said Edwin, equally maudlin.

"Do you feel that our best years are leaking away, Edwin?"

The other officers had drifted away to another part of the hut that served as a mess, leaving the two brothers in a corner.

"Not really," said Edwin, "The war will not last long now. We will be home soon."

"You were saying that this time last year! We are still out here, in fact, we are further from home with no chance of leave, and men are dying from fever all the time." said Freddy.

"This year is different," said Edwin, "there are definite signs that Germany has shot its bolt. I bet we will be home by the end of the year."

"Well, you can't make any plans yet, can you?" said Freddy.

"Not with any precision, no, because when we win the war we will not all be able to go home at once. There will be a lot of clearing up to do, and so on, but I am already preparing for peace. I have someone waiting for me, and when I get back we will get married and make up for lost time." said Edwin.

"Have you asked her yet?" said Freddy, "As far as I can see no girl is going to want to agree to marry until she can be sure her man is safe and coming home in one piece."

"Freddy, can I ask you to do something for me?" said Edwin.

"Yes, of course you can Edwin, what?"

"Sometimes I get a strange feeling that I am not going to survive the war. Do you remember that day in Doullens when we all swore brotherhood to each other? Well, some of those there that day are no longer with us, they are six feet under. I worry about being the next one." said Edwin, emotion showing in his face.

"Don't be silly, Edwin, you and I are lucky, we will both get back all right." said Freddy.

"If I die, will you please look after things for me?"

"Like what?"

"Make sure that Mamma and Papa know that I did my duty, of course. And look after my charger." said Edwin.

"Is that all?"

"And look after Constance for me, I want you to promise to look after her." said Edwin, more emotionally, the alcohol making him more maudlin than ever.

"Constance? Constance Mann? Why her?"

"Because she and I were engaged last September."

Freddy was taken aback by this news. He shook his head as if trying to take in this surprise. "You never said. Are you sure she said yes to you?"

"Of course she did!" said Edwin.

Freddy realised that Edwin had managed what he had been unable to, Constance was not his, but Edwin's. Confused, and his head befuddled with drink Freddy did not at first know how to respond. His heart was sinking even as his pulse accelerated. He resented the fact that Edwin had succeeded where he had failed. He felt cheated that the girl he thought of as special to him was promised to another, his beloved brother.

While Freddy remained silent, Edwin continued, "Freddy, if I am killed, or am so badly damaged that I cannot be a man, a proper husband for Connie, I want you to promise me that you will look after her. I want you to marry her in my place!"

Freddy was taken aback by this, again. He could see the obvious advantage for him to be able to marry Constance, but if that were to happen it would mean that Edwin was gone. Or, he might be there, but so bad as not to be able to be a man. To be able to get what he wanted, Constance's hand, Edwin had to die, or worse.

"All right, I will promise to do that, but what if Constance does not agree? You know I asked her once, but she refused me. She might not go along with your plans." said Freddy.

"You asked Constance to marry you? She is mine, how dare you!" said Edwin, half rising from his chair.

"Yes, I did! You never told me you were sweet on her! How was I to know? She never said anything about you and her being engaged!" said Freddy, starting to shout.

"In that case, forget what I said. If I am killed she will never be yours, I will write to her to tell her to ignore you. I will find a more loyal man to do the job for me!" shouted Edwin, now risen from his chair and standing over Freddy, his fist raised as if to hit him.

Ted rushed over and pushed between the brothers. "Hang on, that's enough, enough, Edwin." Colonel Goodson and Kit Chilvers looked across the room, alerted by the raised voices.

Ted pushed Edwin towards the door, "Sorry, Edwin, but you do yourself no favours." Ted said.

Kit, seeing the tensions, and aware that there was work to be done announced, "Gentlemen, it's time we all went to our duties. The bar and the mess are closed until breakfast.

Edwin grabbed his helmet and left. Freddy drained his drink, and rose as Ted came across to him.

"What was that all about, Freddy?" asked Ted.

"Nothing, just a difference of opinion. Let's go." said Freddy, a little confused about what had happened, but sobering up as he stepped outside. "We are due up at the OP for stand to in the morning Ted, I am going to get some sleep now. I will ask Corporal Ely to wake us at two with breakfast so we can be up at the OP before first light."

"I am going up there straight away, just in case the Austrians come across. I know Ralph is up there already, but I want to make sure I am there if he needs help. I can get some sleep in one of the dugouts if I am not needed." said Ted.

"Right, Ted, see you in the morning, then." said Freddy as he went off to get a few hours of sleep.

Chapter 21

15th June 1918, Asiago Plateau, Italy.

At two o'clock the next morning Freddy felt Corporal Ely shaking him. "Get up, sir, get up. The Austrians are shelling us, you need to get up, sir."

Freddy was awake in a second, sat up, looked at his wristwatch. "Right, thank you, Corporal Ely, I will be right with you." as Ely passed him a tin mug of coffee and left.

Freddy was in the habit of wearing his pyjamas when he was able to sleep in a proper bed in the mess. This was no exception. As he pulled back the blanket covering him there came a loud explosion and a pressure wave, which blew out the candle that Ely had left. Freddy felt for his tunic jacket, found his matches, struck one and relit the candle. He sniffed, and tasted the smell of lachrymatory gas, which he instantly guessed was Austrian. He quickly put on his uniform over his pyjamas, pulled on his boots, and went outside into the mess room.

Corporal Ely gave him another mug of coffee in exchange for the empty one that Freddy had in his hand. He also gave him a sandwich, which Freddy bit into and tasted the egg and bacon inside. Freddy hastily ate the sandwich and downed the coffee. Ely pressed a paper package into his hand, which Freddy knew was another sandwich that he had prepared for later consumption. He thanked Ely, put on his respirator, and went outside checking that he had his compass, binoculars and maps in his haversack as he started to march to the OP.

He realised that he was not wearing his tin helmet, but decided to leave this detail to luck.

As he walked there were explosions on every side. They seemed to be coming at random, to his trained gunner ears there was no pattern to it. The early morning was cool, and a mist was wafting through the forest, reducing visibility and muffling sounds. He marched as quickly as his legs would carry him. His heart rate increased, and he could smell the familiar odour of the inside of the respirator. The eye pieces misted over, he wiped the outside of the lens with his hand to clear his vision, but there was mist on the inside as well. He took off the helmet and took a sniff. The lachrymatory was not too strong here, and for the sake of better breathing, he left the respirator off, slinging it over his forearm for quick return if that were to be needed. No mustard must mean that they were attacking, they would not want to attack into an area full of mustard gas.

His way lay uphill on a slight gradient. He started to sweat, his breathing was deepening, taking traces of gas into his lungs. His airways burned a little, but he had experienced this before and he knew that if the gas stayed at low levels he would be able to continue without the helmet.

The bombardment continued, Freddy heard the crump of high explosive, the thud of lachrymatory shells as they landed, and the crack of shrapnel shells overhead, but all these seemed always to be a hundred yards away from where he was. He seemed to be in a protective bubble as he continued. A stretcher party came by with a lifeless form on board, then was lost in the mist. He passed the entrance to a dugout, and heard a low murmur from inside. There was shouting from somewhere off to his right.

He estimated that he should soon arrive at Handley Cross. The shell fire seemed to increase in volume as he approached, and the smell of the tear gas also strengthened. Still no mustard. He went on.

Freddy turned the final bend in the track before he came up to the level area between two mountains and two valleys that the British had named Handley Cross, after a fictional English village. It was a scene of concentrated military activity. Groups of soldiers were moving purposely from place to place, a few wagons and horses were scattered around bringing or collecting stores, and the ammunition and other dumps, though reduced in size, still existed in close proximity to the tracks. Freddy continued to trudge on his route, he knew that he was now about halfway to the OP. He put his respirator back on, partly in response to the increased level of tear gas in the air, and partly to disguise his identity.

He reached the far side of Handley Cross and found the track junction that he would take to climb further up the mountain to reach the OP.

He was thrown forward onto the ground, and landed ten yards into the forest narrowly missing the trees. He heard nothing, but a pressure wave of hot air had been the cause of him being tossed into the undergrowth, and it continued to flow over him as he lay face down on the soil.

He was dazed, staggering to his feet, holding on to a tree. He looked back and saw that a large fire was burning a hundred yards behind him. In the light of flames he saw men running away from, and some running past, the fire. Soldiers had come out from the various dugouts and were standing watching as the fire burned. Freddy could see boxes, wooden ammunition boxes, laying all over the place. The Austrians must have landed a lucky HE shell right in an ammunition dump, he thought briefly as he breathed deeply and tried to collect his wits.

"There's nothing for me to do here." he thought to himself, and walked back to the track whence he had been tossed and turned up the track leading to the OP.

He found that his respirator was missing, it must have been lost in the explosion. He continued without it.

Realising that the Austrian attack must be in progress and that he would be needed at the OP he started to jog run up the track, but slowed again to a fast march when his lungs and heart could not sustain the effort.

Gradually as he passed along the track and it curved around the side of the mountain the flickering light from the fire faded and he came back into semi darkness. A pale light was showing in the east, above the mountain. Dawn! The Austrians would be coming now, maybe they were already here. He marched as fast as he could.

He reached the top of Monte Lemerle. He leaned against a tree to catch his breath.

Wheezing still, he went over to the foot of the ladder and started to climb. The thirty feet took an age, his legs were shaking, his lungs burned, and his heart was thumping away in his chest.

There were sounds of battle, but not close. There were explosions all round in the distance, and in between he heard a new sound, the tat tat tat of a machine gun. That meant infantry on the ground! The Austrians were assaulting, but where?

He reached the platform, and with a great gasp threw himself onto the floor and lay there, his chest heaving. "I am bloody useless, a chance to have a crack at the Austriacos and I am lying on the floor like a baby!" he thought to himself.

He felt footsteps coming up to him on the wooden floor. "Hello Freddy, nice of you to join us!" He heard Ted's voice, and opening his eyes he saw Ted's hand reaching down to help him up. He heaved himself upright.

"What's going on?"

"I have no idea, Freddy," said Ted, "We can't see a damn thing at the moment. We can hear the shelling, of course, but there have not been any SOS flares yet, so the infantry must be all right. I have heard some machine gunning, and smaller explosions, like grenades, out in front, but nothing that we can fire at."

"Have you been on the telephone to Brigade or Division? What do they say?" asked Freddy.

"Yes, we are through to division, they have no more idea than we have. They said to keep watching and report if we see anything, so that is what we are doing, isn't it Ralph?" said Ted, turning his head towards Ralph who was sitting at the observation slit with his binoculars to his eyes.

"Dawn is just coming up and there is a little light, we should be able to see something soon." said Ralph.

Freddy looked around and he saw Corporal Hastings sitting at the rear of the platform with the telephone to his ear.

Freddy went over to the slit and looked out. He could hear explosions and the sound of shells passing overhead, and the rattle of small arms somewhere out in front. But he could see nothing to focus on. He turned his head to one side and looked down slightly, as if this would help him to discern more from the sounds, but no.

Then the telephone rang, Hastings answered it, in the dim light Freddy could see Hastings listen, then pass the handset to Ralph. Ralph listened intently, and made notes on his notebook which was on the table next to him.

Ralph handed the telephone handset back to Hastings.

"That was Brigade. They say they think the Austrians are in our positions. They have lost contact with A Company of the Norfolks, and C Battery near Cesuna, and we are to look out for signs of Austrians coming across no man's land and to engage them with shrapnel. Also, we have to report anything that we see that indicates how far the Austrians have penetrated, but not to engage in case our own chaps are still there." said Ralph.

Freddy and Ted went to the observation slit and lifted their binoculars. Freddy said, "Let's split up the zone and we can each keep an eye on our section. We can change around every now and then, and keep talking so we all know what each of us can see."

337

The light was now enough to see the outline of the countryside, but not the details. They heard the rushing sounds of shells passing by and felt a thump on the platform. Ted left his position and went to the ladder to see if anything vital had been hit, and saw that a rung of the ladder was missing. He went back on to the platform. "Careful if you go out for a pee, they've taken out a rung of the ladder." and continued to observe.

As the light grew further Freddy continually scanned his section, which included the point where the north south track crossed the Ghelpac river, and where if the Austrians were coming they would have to pass that way. It was out of sight behind the trees, but Freddy felt that by looking at where the crossing was, even though he could see only trees, he might discern something that would indicate what was happening.

The sounds of small arms fire, the rattle of machine guns and the pop pop of rifles, could be heard quite distinctly now.

"Hastings, ring Brigade, I am going to engage, tell them I want the three batteries on the same target." ordered Freddy.

Hastings cranked the handle of the telephone, once, then again, then a third time. "Line is down, sir!" he shouted.

"Bugger!" Shouted Freddy. "Do we have any other lines laid in yet?"

"Yes, sir, we have the line to A Battery, I will try that one." said Hastings as he quickly uncoupled the line to division and connected up the one to A Battery. He cranked the handle, listened at the earpiece, and said, "Through to A Battery, sir."

"Tell them to take post and ready twenty rounds per gun, shrapnel, target location to follow." Freddy ordered.

Ralph looked across at Freddy, "What are you going to do?"

"If the Austrians are attacking, they have to come along that track from the river crossing. I am going to put down shrapnel onto the track a hundred yards in front of where our chaps are. It will do no harm to our men, but if the Austrians are there they will be in the open and the shrapnel will stop them dead. It's better than sitting here doing nothing, isn't it?"

And with that Freddy ordered the guns to fire the shrapnel at the track. He could see some of the rounds exploding in the air above the trees, but could not see the results. In the meantime, Ted and Ralph had enough light to see out far into no man's land. Targets started appearing, and the three officers took turns to control the battery, firing mission after mission throughout the day.

At about the time that Freddy had decided to fire at the track leading to Cesuna, Sergeant Major Rippingill was checking his section of trench to make sure that none of his men, other then the dead ones, were left. It had been a misty morning, and the Austrians had infiltrated the position before first light, quietly moving through the forest and between the isolated British positions. Before they knew what was happening the British found themselves fighting at close range, being fired on from the side and from the rear.

Captain Sansom had been one of the first to go down, caught in the open between the trees as he tried to move between posts to warn his men.

The Austrians had bombed and shot their way through the position, leaving only a few British soldiers alive. Rippingill had gathered together as many survivors as he could into one section. Every attempt by the Austrians to get to them had been repelled, until the Austrians had decided to leave them alone, bypass them.

Once the shooting had died down and the Austrian assault troops had moved on further along the track, Rippingill had decided to move his survivors back to the switch trench closer to Cesuna. He had found a route the previous day that took him through the forest and away from any assault route of the Austrians.

Out of his company of eighty or so men, Rippingill had with him a bare twelve survivors. They followed him as he ran through the trees towards the temporary safety of the switch trench.

He knew that if he could just reach that trench he would have to hold out for perhaps two hours, until the reserve battalion could get up. He knew that C company would be there, and if they were still more or less intact there would be enough men to hold the trench for the two hours.

He raced through the trees, occasionally looking behind him to check that his disciples were still there.

Sergeant Major Rippingill's small group reached the switch trench safely. He immediately got the men down into the trench, told them to wait for him, and he moved along the trench hoping to find other soldiers there. British soldiers, hopefully, who could tell him what the state of play was. After a hundred yards he came across men in khaki. Before approaching them he shouted from around a corner who he was and for them not to shoot. They shouted back for him to come forward. He cautiously put his head around the corner and advanced, his rifle and bayonet in front of him. He knew all the men in C Company, but he did not recognise these men.

"Sergeant Major Rippingill, A Company, who are you?" he said with the customary authority of someone who expects obedience.

"Sergeant Major Leman and Sergeant Reid, C Battery, Norfolk Brigade RFA." came the reply.

"Where are your guns?" Rippingill asked.

"Out there somewhere," said Leman, "we were overrun and Major Scott told us to withdraw to this trench and keep the Austrians away. They were on us before we knew what was going on. I have had a count and there are forty three of us from the battery, but no officers. Major Scott stayed on the position to check for stragglers, and he hasn't come in yet. We have our rifles, and some ammunition."

"There should be plenty of ammunition, we stocked this trench with some yesterday. I will find some for your men. Do you know who is further along the trench?" said Rippingill.

"There are some of your lot, they told us to come along here and hold this bit of trench. There is a howitzer battery about five hundred yards behind us, I have sent one of my men back there to them to see if they can help us if the Austrians attack again. He should be back in a minute to let us know what they can do." said Leman.

"How good are your men on musketry, sergeant major?" Rippingill asked Leman.

"We have not had much practice since we got to Italy, and some of the lads joined us in Ypres last autumn so we have never seen them shoot rifles."

"Best to use the young 'uns as runners and ammunition carriers, then." said Rippingill.

The two sergeant majors organised the gunners and the infantrymen into sections each under an NCO and briefed them on what was expected of each of them.

Just then a shout came from further along the trench, "They're coming, stand to! Staaand Tooo!"

Rippingill carefully looked over the parapet, and there before him, four hundred yards away where the edge of the wood opened out to the field in front of the trench he saw Austrians skirmishing, dashing forward, dropping down to fire their rifles, then rise again and dash forward in short rushes.

"Right, lads, put one up the spout, safety catches off! Set sights at one hundred. Aimed shots, pick your target when they take cover, then shoot them when they get up again, on my order, wait for it, wait until they are a hundred yards out, wait for it…., wait…., wait…., Fire!" said Rippingill.

A hundred rifles fired as one. Some men had rifle grenades and these joined the fusillade and exploded among the Austrians. A lone Lewis gun stuttered further along the trench.

Austrians fell, but more came on. They came closer, and closer, their ranks thinned, but the ragged horde came on.

Rippingill shouted, "Prepare to repel raiders! Make sure your bayonets are fixed! Make every bullet count!"

The Austrians were now within fifty yards, then Whoomp! Crack! and four 4.5 inch howitzer shells exploded over the trench, two thousand shrapnel bullets shot forward and into the Austrians. Four gaps were opened in the Austrian line.

"Bloody hell, what was that?" came a young voice from along the British trench. "Howitzers!" shouted Leman, "The boys behind have got their eye in!"

Thirty seconds later another set of shells arrived and did similar slaughter on the Austrians.

A few had got closer to the trench and through the shrapnel bullets, but were so few that they were easily cut down by Rippingill's men. The remaining Austrians started to run, the few survivors running or limping away. Some could be seen on the ground, moving, obviously injured. Three, close to the British trench, knelt with their hands up in surrender.

"Stop firing!" shouted Rippingill. A few lucky Austrians were still to be seen running back into the wood.

"Let those three in." Turning to one of his soldiers he said, "Get out there and bring 'em in. Watch out for tricks." The soldier gingerly climbed over the parapet and went forward in a crouch, grabbed one of the Austrians and led him back to the trench. He then went back out for the other two.

Rippingill ordered each man to count his ammunition and make sure he had at least one hundred rounds. He ordered half the men to clean their rifles, while the others remained on watch.

"They will be back. Let's be ready for the buggers. Stay sharp and you will stay alive!" Rippingill shouted as he toured the trench.

"Your gunner friends were bloody welcome." Rippingill said to Leman, "We owe them a beer or a bottle of wine. Remind me when all this is done, sergeant major."

"Yes, they were pretty effective weren't they?" replied Leman, smiling.

The Austrians came back three times more during the morning, each time with less enthusiasm and fewer in number. The last attack, just before midday, barely happened. The Austrians advanced a hundred yards from the wood, but the first salvo from the howitzers put an end to it. The survivors retreated to the woods and were not seen again.

At eleven o'clock the reserve battalion had arrived in any case, and they brought with them their Lewis guns and three Vickers machine guns, and plenty of ammunition for them. The position was secure.

Following the last failed Austrian attack the British infantry rose from their trenches and advanced across the field, passing hundreds of Austrians in various stages of dismemberment. Some were still alive, but none offered any resistance. The infantry swept through the woods and regained the first line trench, abandoned earlier in the day, capturing odd groups of Austrians, wounded and whole, as they went.

At the OP Ralph, Ted, and Freddy had been having a good time. Despite losing part of the ladder, and shells landing around them, they had continued to fire throughout the attack.

Freddy had fired the battery on the track leading to Cesuna, stopping any Austrian reinforcements reaching the spearhead of their attack. The Austrians had tried to progress by avoiding the track, but every time they tried this they came into view, and the guns were tasked to fire at them. The result was that the Austrian attack had failed in this sector.

In the afternoon, after the Austrians had failed to get to Cesuna, Freddy saw groups of Austrians withdrawing. There were wagons with clear red cross markings, and stretcher bearers carrying away the injured. He brought his battery to bear on these and took delight in firing at them every time they appeared.

Corporal Hastings realised what Freddy was doing, and said, "Sir, you are shooting at wounded men. Those are stretcher bearers, we should not be shooting at them!"

Freddy turned to Hastings and said, "We are just returning the favour. The Germans shoot at our stretcher bearers and wounded men, I have witnessed it, so have you! If we get them now, while we can, at least they won't be able to come back tomorrow!" He continued to observe and pass firing orders to Hastings.

After a while Freddy realised that Hastings was not responding to his instructions. Freddy turned to face Hastings, who was sitting looking at the floor. "Hastings, I just gave you an order for the guns, have you passed it to them?" he said.

Hastings remained silent.

Freddy went over to Hastings, grabbed his arm, shaking him. "Hastings!" he shouted, "Hastings!"

Hastings did not move or respond.

"Hastings, pull yourself together man!" and Freddy pushed at Hastings harder. Hastings pushed Freddy's arm away, but said nothing.

"Ted, we have a problem with Hastings, here, can you come and have a look?" said Freddy, by now more puzzled than angry.

Ted came over and looked at the signaller. He put his hand on the rim of Hasting's helmet and lifted it so that he could see Hastings's face. It was expressionless, Ted bent down to take a close look at Hastings. His eyes were open, but he was not seeing. Ted shook Hastings by the shoulder, he remained where he was, neither moving nor reacting.

"He's out of it, Freddy. Maybe we should get him downstairs, in any case, seems he's no use to us at the moment. What do you think?" said Ted.

"Leave him there, we can work the telephone between us, take turns. Is that all right with you, Ralph?" said Freddy, turning to face Ralph at the far end of the platform.

Ralph looked across and nodded, "Yes, I will take over from him for a while, I could do with a break from looking through these glasses."

Ralph came across and took hold of the telephone and moved it a little away from Hastings, sat down on the floor, and opened his haversack which he had left on the floor. "Time for some grub as well." he said, as he opened the haversack, put his hand inside, and came out with a package, "Corporal Ely's best." he said, opened the package, and offered the contents to Ted and Freddy.

The rest of the afternoon found the artillery officers seeing fewer targets, and by nightfall all opportunity to fire at the Austrians had gone. The battlefield was apparently empty, though they knew that out there were many men, most of them making their way to safety back in the Austrian lines.

As night came on the three officers contemplated what they should do next. There was not enough work for the three of them, and Hastings was a problem, still sitting without responding in any way.

And there was the ladder to consider as well, Ted had been out to inspect it before the light faded and had found that two rungs had been removed, presuming this to have been by a shell.

Ralph offered to stay in the OP until they could send up a replacement, so Freddy and Ted set to work to find a way to descend the ladder.

Luckily the engineers under Tom Cox were working nearby and after they had stopped laughing at the plight of the artillerymen they rigged up tree branches and ropes to provide a safe way down from the platform.

After thanking them Freddy and Ted started their way down the mountain.

Freddy recalled the explosion he had experienced on his way up that morning, "I wonder how things are at Handley Cross." he said almost to himself.

"Why do you say that, the Austriacos didn't get that far, did they." said Ted.

"When I went through there on the way up they must have hit one of the ammunition dumps. It went up with an almighty bang and there were bits all over the place, and fires. They almost got me, I was just through the junction when it went up, I am surprised you did not hear it." said Freddy.

As they walked along the track around to the rear of the mountain and towards the area they passed parties of soldiers engaged in a variety of tasks. They continued to chat as they walked.

"We had a good day, didn't we, Freddy?" said Ted.

"Yes, we must have helped, done our duty, the colonel should be pleased with us. What do you make of Hastings? We will have to get him down somehow, maybe he will sort himself out and Ralph will be able to get him down." said Freddy.

"I think we have earned our pay today, for certain. Yes Hastings condition is a puzzle, I've not seen anything like that before. Do you think we should get him to report sick? He did not seem to be injured, just mesmerised." said Ted.

"I have seen something similar before, one of our men just jumped up one day when the gun line was being bombarded

346

and ran off. He came back after a half hour and seemed fine after that, but I have not seen anyone go blank for more than a few minutes. If he gets some sleep and food he will probably be all right." said Freddy.

They turned the bend in the track and approached Handley Cross, which was a shambles. Fires were burning left and right of the track, and groups of men were trying to extinguish the flames. Others were moving stores around, wagons were dotted about, and they passed small groups of officers and men standing around apparently discussing things.

Two wagons came past with red crosses on their tilts marking them as medical wagons, the horses plodding forward. Outside the medical dugout a small number of bandaged men sat around, apparently waiting for transport to take them further to the rear at Carriola or beyond to the plain and the field hospital. All in all they looked cheerful, though two were on stretchers and motionless.

Large sections of the trees were either down, or burnt, giving witness to the power and extent of the explosion.

They went to the Brigade HQ dugout and enquired from Kit whether they should report to Colonel Goodson. He advised them to go off to the mess and get some food and drink inside them, the CO would be along later to speak to them. Gratefully they left the HQ.

Freddy and Ted plodded on, the excitement and energy of the day declining as they advanced. By the time they reached the mess they were exhausted. Corporal Ely was waiting for them, with mugs of coffee in hand, which they wordlessly took from him and drank.

They went inside the mess and Corporal Ely had the table laid out and was in the process of plating up food to bring to them. He also brought across a bottle of whisky and glasses, which he set before them. "Can I get you anything else, sir?" he asked.

"No, thank you very much for this, it's very welcome." said Ted.

"What do you think Colonel Goodson will want to talk about, Ted?" said Freddy as he drank some whisky and started eating.

"He probably wants to tear a strip off you and Edwin for the fracas last night. He is a stickler for proper behaviour, isn't he?" offered Ted.

"We will just shake hands and it will all be over." said Freddy, taking another swig of whisky.

Colonel Goodson arrived, accompanied by Kit and padre Fitzgerald. As they came in they glanced at Freddy and then exchanged glances with each other. Goodson came over to the table. Freddy stood up, "Good evening colonel."

"Freddy, I need to speak to you, can we go outside, please?" said the colonel.

"If it's about last night, sir, Edwin and I are very sorry. It won't happen again, I promise." said Freddy.

Goodson took him by the arm and led him to the door.

They went out. "Freddy, I have some bad news for you, I am afraid that Edwin is no longer with us. I'm sorry." said Goodson.

Not grasping the point immediately Freddy said, "Where has he gone, colonel?"

"Freddy, Edwin is dead. I'm sorry."

Freddy still had difficulty taking the news. He looked blankly at the colonel, then made to speak, his lips moved, but no voice came. He continued to look blankly at Colonel Goodson.

"We found him this afternoon when the Austrians withdrew. He was in one of the gun pits. His revolver was out of its holster, and he had used all his ammunition. There were quite a few dead Austrians around, so he probably went down fighting. I have spoken to General Trubshawe and we will be putting him in for an award, an MC probably, or a DSO. You can be proud of him." said Goodson, gently.

Freddy did not answer but walked back towards the mess, just as the padre came out. Gregory stood in the doorway and took Freddy by the arm and led him away from the mess. Fifty yards away he stopped and leaned on a tree, took out his pipe, filled it, and lit up, indicating for Freddy to do the same.

Freddy did so, absentmindedly. Gregory watched Freddy as he lit his pipe and took a couple of draughts from it.

"Does that help?" asked Gregory.

Freddy replied, "Not really, should it?"

"Men die in war, don't they? And most of us, if we are going to die, would want it to be in battle, doing our duty, and being heroic. Edwin has all those things, doesn't he?" said Gregory.

"Yes, I suppose so. But we had an argument last night, and we never had the chance to put it right. Now it's too late."

"Do you believe in the afterlife, Freddy?"

"Yes, of course I do." Freddy replied.

"Then you must accept that Edwin will know that your argument was not serious. He will be forgiving you as he stands before Saint Peter, just as I am sure that you forgive him."

"Yes, I do."

"You must write to your parents and let them know what has happened and do it straight away before they hear from anyone else. That is a duty for you." said Gregory, continuing to puff at his pipe.

"And his fiancee,"

"Oh, I didn't know he was to be married. Yes, you had better write to her as well, Freddy, she will be very upset. How well do you know her?"

"Very well, her family and ours were close. In fact, I was sweet on her as well. Still am, in fact. Edwin asked me to look after her if he was killed or badly injured." said Freddy.

"Will you?"

"Will I what?"

"Will you do what Edwin asked of you?"

"I'm not sure, I will need to think about it. I once asked her to marry me, and she turned me down, said it was not the right time, the war and all that. Then Edwin asks her and she agrees. Up to last evening I would have jumped at the chance to marry her, now I am not sure. Edwin would always be there, in the background, wouldn't he?" said Freddy.

"It depends," said Gregory, "but whichever way you decide to go, you will not know what the other course would have led to, would you? The road not taken."

"The road not taken?" queried Freddy.

"It was in a poem I read recently, about coming to a fork in the road, and you can only take one way, how do you decide."

"I have not read that one," said Freddy, "how should I choose?"

"Basically it's up to you, Freddy. Take some time, it needs a lot of thought, and tobacco. At least a three pipe decision. If you need to talk it through I am always available, but it must be your decision, not mine." Gregory said, putting his hand on Freddy's shoulder, "I think you should go and see Edwin before they bury him. It will help, believe me, and get busy afterwards. Being busy will help." Gregory led Freddy back to the mess.

His fellow officers offered their condolences and patted his shoulder as he went in. Ralph had arrived by this time, and came over carrying a bottle of whisky, and said, "Let's all drink to Edwin, gone, but not forgotten!"

They sat down at the table and Corporal Ely brought more glasses. Freddy stood, went to a corner of the mess and brought another chair to the table. "This is for Edwin, he is here with us in spirit if not in the flesh." The others nodded agreement, and raised their glasses towards Edwin's chair as they toasted 'Absent friends!'

The next day Freddy did go to see his brother's body. The dead from the battle had been brought back to a small field just outside Cesuna, at Magnaboschi. They were laid in rows, the Austrians in one long line, and another, shorter, line for the British. A pioneer company had been sent in to recover the bodies and repair the damage, as well as salvage the debris from the battlefield.

Edwin's battery had gone back to the gun line and found their guns intact. The Austrians had no opportunity to damage them or carry them off. They had removed the breech blocks before abandoning the guns. Under Sergeant Major Leman the gun line was soon back in good order and ready for duty again.

Freddy had picked some wild flowers on the way to the grim prospect of seeing his dead brother. His way led him past the battery position. The gunners there recognised him, and called Sergeant Major Leman over. Leman went to speak to Freddy, "We are all very sorry about your brother, sir, he was a good man, a good officer, we all respected him."

"Thank you, sergeant major, thank you. Who found him? I would like to know more about how he was found." said Freddy.

"I did, sir. I found him in C sub pit, he was laying on his back, and he looked quite peaceful, really. He had a bullet in the chest, and he must have bled to death. He was just laying there, his eyes were closed, like he was asleep, no sign of being in pain, you know."

"Is that the truth, sergeant major? I can take the truth, you know." said Freddy, more forcefully than he intended, and then burst into tears.

Sergeant Major Leman took Freddy by the shoulder and turned him away from the sight of the men and led him a little way away. He put his arm around Freddy. "Everything I said was the truth, sir. He did not suffer at all, as far as I could see."

Freddy sniffed and took his handkerchief from his pocket and wiped his eyes. "Thank you, Sergeant Major, I'm all right now. It's all just a shock, you know."

"Of course, sir. I think it would be better for you to go off to see him up there, I will let the men know you were here." said Leman.

Freddy went off and found the dead laid out. He spoke to an older officer who seemed to be in charge of recording the details, He checked his papers and directed Freddy to where Edwin lay.

Edwin had already been processed and covered with a blanket, ready for sewing up and transport to the cemetery.

Freddy pulled back the edge of the blanket, and saw Edwin's face, pale, grey, drawn, his lips pulled back with the shape of his teeth plainly visible. Freddy knew it was Edwin, but it did not look like him. He pulled the blanket further back to see the chest, and there it was, a small hole where the bullet had entered with a small stain of blood, dark against the khaki of Edwin's tunic. He saw the back of the tunic at Edwin's shoulder, and there it was black with what Freddy assumed was congealed blood. "At least he was shot from the front." thought Freddy, "A hero cannot be shot in the back."

He knelt beside Edwin for a long time, deep in thought. He took out his pipe, and filled it with tobacco, lit it, sucked on it. When that one was finished, he filled another pipeful and lit up.

He pondered on what the padre had said to him, and started a dialogue in his mind with Edwin.

Firstly he apologised for the argument. Then he said that he was working on the assumption that Edwin forgave him. Then he asked Edwin's advice about Constance. Was he serious about Freddy looking after her? Did that mean be her friend, or offer to become her husband? If he did offer, and she accepted, would Edwin be happy, or would he be angry? What about being William Mann's son-in-law? How would he respond? Would he have to go into the Mann business? He knew nothing about the Works, or how to make things, but would it be expected of him to become William Mann's successor as Walter Mann would have been?

All this depended, of course, on Freddy surviving the war. Many dangers persisted. The Austrians, though they seemed to have shot their bolt, they still had guns. Men were still dying, from fever, and there were other ways to die. Who would look after things if he were to pass?

After a half hour of musing, and three pipes of tobacco Freddy had his mind made up. He said, "Goodbye old chap, you can rely on me." He gently replaced the blanket to cover Edwin's face, stood up, and placed the flowers on the blanket. Then he changed his mind and pulled the blanket back and put the flowers on Edwin's tunic, and again repositioned the blanket.

Having decided, he felt more cheerful, and actually started whistling as he returned to the mess, passing once more through Handley Cross, looking with a more cheerful frame of mind than the day before at the damage and mayhem that even now was being organised into operational efficiency.

Back at the mess he met Robert Benefer, "Hello Doc, how are you?" Freddy asked cheerfully.

The doctor was surprised by Freddy's good humour, assuming vaguely that he would have been more mournful. Putting that thought to one side he said, "Freddy, you knew Corporal Hastings didn't you, he was in your battery, wasn't he?"

Freddy did not notice the past tense in the doctor's question, "Yes, he's my usual signaller, why?"

"You obviously don't know then. He was found dead this morning."

"Dead? How? Where? He was alive the last time I saw him, a bit dazed, but alive, and the fighting had finished."

"He was found this morning. The engineers on Monte Lemerle found him behind their position. Apparently one of them went for a dump, and found Hastings laying on a rock. He had his rifle between his legs and a bullet had gone through his throat and took the top of his head off. We think it was suicide."

"Suicide? I know he was a bit strange at times, but we all are, occasionally. Why do you think it was suicide?"

"You know he had reported sick quite a lot, especially since we came out to Italy. I had concerns about his state of mind. He kept saying that he thought he had the clap, but when I checked him out I could not find any signs of it, or any other disease. He was perfectly fit." said Robert.

"As far as I know he never went with the other men to brothels, he always told me that he was a married man and wanted to keep himself clean for his wife." said Freddy.

"That fits. He had no signs of venereal disease at all. He had the usual bouts of fever and so on, but we have all had those, or most of us have. I think it was all in his mind."

"When I last saw him he was with Ralph House at the OP, he was a bit dopey, but thinking about it he was acting a bit strangely. He just went into a sort of dream. We put it down to fatigue, and left him with Ralph while we came back here after the Austrians had been sent packing. Have you spoken to Ralph? What does he say?"

"Ralph says that after you and Ted had left and Harold Kent arrived as relief that Hastings and he left the OP and they walked back together. Hastings wasn't very chatty, but seemed normal otherwise. Ralph says they parted at Brigade HQ where Hastings had his bivvy." said Robert.

"Bloody hell, what a shambles! I should have been more alert, I suppose, but I didn't see this coming. What do we do now, Robert?"

"There will have to be a court of enquiry, of course, and I will have to prepare a report. I suppose it will be put down to some sort of unbalanced mental condition, and that will be that."

"Will someone be writing to his wife? What will we say about him?" said Freddy, realising the implications for Hasting's wife.

"Kit will do that. I am not sure what he can say. If he wants to be kind he will say that Hastings died in battle, which I suppose is true to a point. Or the truth, which would be harder for her to have. What would you do, Freddy?"

"Tell the usual lie, I suppose, a hero, died doing his duty, painless death etc etc."

"Yes, that would be best, I think."

"I will write to her as well." said Freddy.

General Trubshawe came into the mess, and came straight over to Freddy. "I was very sorry to hear about your brother's death, Freddy, it came as a great shock to all of us. I know that you were both very attached to each other, please accept my sincere condolences. I will be writing Edwin up for a medal, of course, he deserved one for what he did, holding the line and making sure the Austriacos could not turn the guns on us."

Freddy straightened, "Thank you General. I will pass your good wishes on to our parents when I write to them. Edwin was a good soldier and brother, and son, of course."

355

Chapter 22

March 1919, Nove, Italy.

Freddy, Ted, and Barry Evans were sitting in the mess tent on the site of the former Italian airfield, at Nove, a village near Marostica. They were the last officers of their brigade to remain in Italy. The division had been steadily demobilising since the previous December, after the armistice. The final draft of British soldiers to be repatriated from the division had been assembled at the camp on the airfield. Tomorrow morning they would be taken to the railway station to start their journey back to Blighty. Freddy was the officer in charge of the draft, while Ted had been appointed as his adjutant. Regimental Sergeant Major Barry Evans had volunteered to stay with the vestige of the division, even though as an older man his points had entitled him to return to Blighty much earlier.

"Is everything ready for tomorrow?" Freddy asked Ted and Evans, "Do we have any problems to sort out before we can get a clean chit?"

"No, Freddy, we have everything buttoned down, don't we, RSM?" answered Ted.

"Yes, sir, all the men have been documented and medically inspected, and all the kit has been handed over. Reveille will be at four, and we will march out at five." stated Evans.

"Excellent! Shall we drink to tomorrow, and all that the future will bring?" said Freddy, standing up to fetch a bottle of whisky and glasses.

Freddy poured three drinks and handed them to the other two men. "Here's to the future!" toasted Ted.

"And absent friends!" said Freddy.

Freddy and Evans raised their glasses in acknowledgement and drank the whisky straight down. Freddy refilled the glasses.

"What does the future hold for you, RSM?"

"I am not sure, sir. I understand that the Brigade is being dissolved, so I expect that I will be out of a job, unless I can find a position with the army of occupation. I think that the War Office will regard me as too old for peace time service, though they were happy for me to serve in the war. Maybe I will settle down somewhere. I will have a reasonable gratuity if I leave, and an annuity, so I should be able to get by."

"Where is home for you, RSM?" asked Ted.

"I don't have one, really, sir. The army is my family, always has been as far as I can remember, and if they no longer need me I will have to make the decision where to live for myself. I am not sure how to do that, yet, but I am sure that I will. I might settle down in King's Lynn, maybe buy a small holding and breed geese. The war has shown that we need to produce more of our food at home, so getting into the food game might be the right thing for me. People will always need to eat, and geese more or less look after themselves, don't they?"

"That sounds like a good plan, RSM, but there will not be another war like this last one, will there? We have always had to trade overseas to put food on the table, I am sure that the ships will even now be ploughing their way across the seas to get our trade back to where it was before the war."

"The bastard Boche will be back, mark my words, sir. They may be beat now, but even with the Kaiser gone they will still want to fight for their place in the world. We have all learned important lessons in this last war, and we will have to make sure we do not forget them. We are sure to be at their throats again before long. Next time, though, they will have to do it without my help. I am willing, but I will be no use on the scrap heap."

"If war does start again, will you volunteer, Freddy?" asked Ted.

"One part of me says no, and the other says yes. There are many things to want to forget, but there have been good times as well, haven't there? At least in one way things at war are very easy. Events happen, and we just react to them. There are few decisions to be made by the individual. That is a good thing. But, I suppose it depends on what I do when I get home, what sort of a life is open to me. My brother George will probably take on the business from Papa, so I may be able to make a go of it on my own."

"What about settling down?" asked Ted, "Is that likely?"

"I will ask Constance Mann when I get home. You know she was engaged to Edwin before he was killed. We took an oath to live the life of the other, didn't we, if any of us were to be killed? So, I will ask her if she will take me in Edwin's place, and if she agrees, then I suppose that we will become a family in due course."

"But will it be as easy as that?" asked Ted, "won't she be mourning for Edwin? Do you think she will be open to a proposal from you?"

"I have always been on good terms with Connie, I will have to see. You know I once proposed to her, and she turned me down, in the nicest way. It was when I was on leave, but she said that it was the wrong time, due to the war. Then she accepted Edwin, in secret. Maybe now, or soon, will be the right time, who knows?" said Freddy. "Constance and I have been writing to each other since the start of the war, and more since Edwin passed over. From her letters I think she will be open to me when I get back."

"There are many uncertainties in the future," said Evans, "but at least we know with more certainty what is in our past. You have both done well as young officers, if I might say so, sirs. There were many difficult times, but you both acquitted yourselves well. There were some that did not."

"Like the Italian pilots at the parade for King Victor Emmanuel and the Prince of Wales. And the French battery, they were certainly drunk as hell, and clearly had no respect for royalty. I suppose it is because they got rid of their own a hundred years or more ago." said Ted.

"Yes, they put up a merry old show, didn't they?" said Freddy, "Though I am glad we did the spit and polish for the parade, our battery looked the best at the show, and I think Prince Edward was pleased. He certainly seemed to brighten up when they came to inspect us. They say he is a bit of a ladies' man, likes the fillies."

"People in his position have a different way of seeing the world than we do." said Evans. "He is entitled to his life, a young man should be allowed to spread his wings before the call of duty traps him. He has done his bit in the war, and his private life is his to know."

Freddy nodded at this comment, and the room was silent for a few moments. A breeze disturbed the flap of the tent, as if an unseen visitor had entered.

"What do you make of what happened to Hastings?" asked Freddy.

"Robert Benefer said that he must have had some kind of mental aberration. Apparently he kept reporting sick but the doctor could find nothing wrong with him. He was obsessed with having caught the clap, but said that he had not been with a woman since leaving home. He was worried about passing it on to his wife when he did go home." said Ted. "Whatever the cause it was a great tragedy for him and his family. He was your regular signaller, wasn't he, Freddy? Did you ever notice anything strange about him?"

"He was always a bit closed off, like many from that part of town," replied Freddy, "and a bit ancient to be here with the youngsters, but he always did his job well. I had no complaints about him, though, and I never saw him as being mentally deficient. We were both with him the day before he shot himself, did you see anything unusual in him then, Ted?"

"I did not know him as well as you did, but he seemed normal to me up to the time he went quiet." said Ted. "RSM, what do you think happened to the Austrians? After the mid summer attack they seemed to lose heart, and when they gave up in the autumn they seemed to be a ragged lot, nothing like as smart or disciplined as us."

"They had lost confidence in themselves and their officers, Mr Rivett. A soldier can bear terrible things as long as his morale is solid, but once he loses confidence in himself, or the reasons he is there, then he is lost. They were poor starving wretches in the end, but when they went to war in '14 they had their tails up and were sure they were going to win. The main problem for them, though, was that they were not their own masters. They needed the Germans for all sorts of reasons, and the Austrian Empire could not sustain itself for food and supplies. They over reached themselves and have paid the price. Their empire is finished, they will never have the same power again." said Evans.

"What about our empire?" asked Freddy, "Are we headed the same way, do you think?"

"Maybe." replied Evans.

"I personally do not feel any sympathy with them, or the Germans." said Freddy, "They started the war by invading Belgium, and anyone who starts a war cannot be expected to be able to determine how it ends."

"It was clear that you had no regard for them, Freddy, when you fired at that bunch of them when they were trying to surrender. Did you not see the white flag?" asked Ted.

"It was a trick, they had no intention of surrendering as far as I am concerned. They still had their rifles and were a threat so I did what any good artilleryman would do, I gave them some shrapnel to squash their ardour for battle. It stopped them in their tracks. I gave them what they deserved, as far as I am concerned."

"Nasty things happen in war, I think you did the right thing, Captain Scott, but another man might have acted differently. It is for you, and you alone, to decide if your conscience is clear." said Evans.

"Well, they killed my brother and did not show him any mercy, did they? He was surrounded, and his revolver was empty, no threat at all, but they shot him anyway." said Freddy, with emotion showing in his face.

"None of us knows what actually passed that day. There are no witnesses, but it is likely that your brother refused to surrender. Maybe the Austrians had no alternative? Is that possible, sir." asked Evans.

"I am sure that Edwin would not surrender, he would have never done that."

"No, I am sure that is true, sir, but not surrendering is a decision, and your brother had to take the consequences of that decision. He died a hero, and we are all proud of him, but he died nonetheless."

"Well, Freddy, if it's any comfort to you, I think Edwin was a hero, unlike some of the others." said Ted. "I am very grateful to you, though, I am not sure I would have got through things without you. I will always be in your debt, Freddy."

"You did well, Ted, and we both came through it all right."

"And you will both have to do it again, some day. I have been in several wars and campaigns. The first is the hardest, after that it gets easier and easier." said Evans, almost to himself.

"It got a bit sticky for poor old Trubshawe, though." said Freddy. "He did all that was expected of him, and more, and they binned him. Sent him packing. Why did he have to take the blame? After all, we kept the Austrians out and killed a lot of them. We were back in our positions within a day, and as far as I can see that means the Austrian's attack was defeated, and yet old Trubshawe had to go. It seems unfair."

"It's the way it is, Captain Scott, General Trubshawe had to pay a price for the failure of others. He will not get another command of course. His career is finished, and, like me, he is over the hill. One of the best generals I have served under, and I have seem some good ones." said Evans.

"Let's have another drink." said Ted, and refilled the glasses with the remains of the whisky bottle, then raised his and toasted, "To absent comrades, let's never forget them!"

The draft left on time in the morning. The men were in high spirits as the train left the station on its way to the coast and the troopship that would take them home.

Freddy's draft arrived at Lynn railway station mid morning. Sissie was not there to meet him. He dismissed the soldiers, wishing them well, with much back slapping and cheerful farewells. He shook hands with each one, and said his goodbye to Ted, arranging for the two of them to meet up in a few days once they had settled back into civvy street.

He hailed a cab, and directed the driver to the Mann's house.

During the journey from Italy Freddy had much time to think and mull over what he had experienced, and what he would do. There were periods of animated conversation with Ted, and times where they both felt comfortable to be in their own thoughts. They discussed many things, but foremost in Freddy's thoughts were what he should do about Constance. Should he propose as soon as possible, or should he bide his time and see how things developed?

On Ted's advice, he resolved to act at once, and as the cab drove the couple of miles to the Mann's house Freddy's energies reached a level he had not experienced since that day atop Monte Lemerle, when he had the scent of battle in his nose, and he had known exactly what to do.

When he arrived at the house he paid the fare and, shouldering his valise, he walked quickly up the driveway. Though it was mid morning he noticed that the curtains were still drawn, and there was a wreath on the front door. Freddy drew back the brass knocker and let it strike the door to announce his arrival.

The door opened, and Sissie stood there. Freddy had not expected to see his sister, and was stuck for words while he cleared his mind.

Sissie put her finger to her lips and whispered to Freddy, "Come on in, but be quiet, Mr Mann is resting and he must get some sleep."

"Is he ill?" whispered Freddy in reply, a questioning look on his face. This was not the scene he had imagined as he travelled back home to Blighty.

"No, but he has taken to his bed, he is very distraught still." whispered Sissie.

"Still? What has happened? Is it his sister?"

"Didn't you get my letter?"

"The last one I received was a week ago, saying that all was well except for the Spanish flu going the rounds. Has something else happened?"

"Oh, Freddy, you haven't heard. I'm sorry. It's Constance, she caught the fever and died last week."

Freddy felt a wave of nausea rise from his gut, and fell over in a dead faint.

Chapter 22.

28th July 1987, Cesuna, Italy.

I drove the car along the gravel track that led from the village of Cesuna up to the cemeteries at Magnaboschi. Freddy was quiet as we drove along. I parked outside the Commonwealth War Graves Cemetery, opposite the Italian military cemetery that shared that part of the wooded valley.

As I helped Freddy out of the car I was struck by how peaceful the place was. Surrounded on three sides by trees, and with no through track and thus no passing traffic, it seemed perfect. The smell of pine sap, cleansing and fresh.

We walked slowly up the short slope from the car to the cemetery entrance, swung open the gate, and looked for the brass plate in the wall that would contain the register. Opening the door Freddy took out the green covered book and opened it and found the entry for Major Edwin Scott. Freddy read it out to me. "Scott, Major Edwin Leonard, DSO, Norfolk Brigade Royal Field Artillery. Killed in action 15th June 1918. Son of George and Sarah Scott of Saddlebow, Norfolk. Plot 1. Row B. Grave 6."

We found the grave and stood in front of it, looking down at the white headstone, engraved with Edwin's name. At the bottom another inscription read, "Our Son, Our Brother. Fidus et Audax."

Freddy had tears in his eyes. I looked away to spare his feelings. "I forgot the flowers, Freddy, I will just get them from the car." Freddy did not reply, lost in his thoughts and leaning on his stick.

I returned from fetching the flowers and stood next to Freddy and offered him the posy. He made no motion, so I bent and laid them in front of the headstone.

I stepped back a few paces to let Freddy complete his thoughts. I looked to the other graves, and saw other names there, Hastings, Sansom, Baker. All with the same date, 15th June, that must have been the big attack that Freddy had talked of earlier.

I heard a match being struck, and saw that Freddy had lit his pipe and was holding it to his mouth. His lips were moving as if in prayer, but I heard no sound from him.

I wandered off to look around the other graves. I knew that Freddy would need some time to spend with Edwin.

Freddy had told me all about the big attack that he had helped to stop. How Edwin had died a hero. And how the war had drifted to a conclusion down here in Italy. He had told me about the swarms of ragged, starving, and rebellious Austrians who had given up in their thousands.

We had even been able to find our way up to the top of the hill where Freddy had been during the attack, though there was not much to see nowadays. Just trees and rocks, and an Italian monument.

He told me how the men of the brigade got home and went back to their lives, back to their families. He said that a few had been unable to settle into normality, and some had rejoined the Territorials when they started up again in the 1920s. Some even served in the next war.

I looked around and saw the headstones. Every one marked where a young man had given his life. Freddy had convinced me that the lives of these men had not been wasted, but spent. Spent to buy a better future for others, for us, for me.

I resolved at that point that I would honour them by living my life to the full. To fulfil my future, for Edwin, for Freddy, for Constance.

Chapter 24

24th December 1992, Arras, France.

When we returned from Italy Freddy asked to come to stay with us in Saddlebow, which he did. We spent many hours together working on his memoirs. He told me that had he always kept a place for Edwin at his table in the flat.

He gave me away when I married.

He was happy when I fell for my first child, and that I named the boy Edwin. That pleased him, a lot.

His last days were peaceful. Then, he left us.

It has been a year since he passed away.

And now, my belly is swelling with my next baby. If he is a boy, we will name him Freddy. If she is a girl, Constance.

I will tell my children about Freddy, and the times that I shared with him.

We always set a place for him at our table.

Freddy's Glossary

Adjutant. A military officer, usually a captain, who prepares and distributes orders and plans for a more senior officer, especially in an artillery brigade, cavalry regiment or infantry battalion. Our brigade was lucky in that our adjutant was Kit Chilvers, a man with plenty of the right sort of experience and who knew how to sort out all sorts of difficulties.

ASC. Army Service Corps. This was the part of the army responsible for storing, moving and delivering all sorts of necessary supplies, from Blighty out to the front.

Battalion. An infantry unit commanded by a lieutenant colonel and having around one thousand officers and men.

Battery. The basic unit of the artillery, having four or six guns and the men and horses to operate them in the field. My battery was 1st battery, but it was renamed A Battery in 1916. I was lucky enough to serve in the same battery throughout the war, and I was privileged to command it in the 1920s.

BC. Battery Commander, the officer, normally a major, in command of an artillery battery. Our first BC was Phillip Mount, a bit of an arse, actually. He was over the hill and was not allowed to serve overseas. Buster Webb was the next BC I had, an excellent man and great friend of our family. Unfortunately he was killed at Hill Top Farm and we were sent another difficult man, Peregrine Proudfoot. He was also killed soon after we went to Italy.

Bombardier. An artillery NCO equivalent to an infantry corporal. I was lucky to have some really sound men as bombardiers in my section, really good men of the best sort.

BQMS. Battery Quarter Master Sergeant, a senior NCO responsible for supply, storage and catering arrangements in an artillery battery. We had Staff Sergeant Mason from the beginning to the end. He never let us down, and shared the difficulties and dangers with us. He had a wicked sense of humour and could always raise a laugh even when we were worn out.

Breech. The rear opening in a gun barrel that has to open and close so that ammunition can be loaded and then is sealed for firing.

Breech Block. A metal device that seals the breech of a gun after the ammunition is loaded and which ensures that propellant gases are contained when the ammunition is fired. A gunner should never abandon his guns in a usable state. If we did have to withdraw and could not get the guns away, we removed the breech blocks and took them away or hid them. That way the guns were useless and could not be fired at our own troops. I think that Edwin was checking that this had been done properly in his battery when he was killed.

Brigade. In the artillery, this is a grouping of two or more (typically 3 or 4) batteries. In the infantry or cavalry, it is a grouping of three or four regiments or battalions. Our brigade was a Territorial brigade, most of us were civilians, with a few Regular Army officers and senior NCOs to keep us on the straight and narrow. By the end of the war, though, we had a lot of Kitchener men and conscripts who came as reinforcements to replace our casualties.

British Warm. A brand of thigh length woollen top coat worn by British military officers. Jolly useful bit of kit, especially if you had to travel by horse in the winter.

BSM. Battery Sergeant Major, the senior NCO in an artillery battery, responsible for discipline and other matters. Barry Evans was our BSM. A real old sweat, he served in the Regular Army since Adam was a lad. A tower of strength to all of us.

Bunker. An underground construction of strength that permits military activity at ground level, such as operating weapons or for observation. And we were jolly happy to have them, especially when the Boche were slinging their shells at us.

Cable. Insulated wire used for connecting field telephones or other communication devices. We had miles and miles of the stuff and had to lay it from HQ to the guns and to the OPs. It often became cut and had to be repaired by our signallers, a very dangerous job, even when the Boche were quiet.

CCS. Casualty Clearing Station, a military medical facility that is close to the front line but normally out of artillery range. This is where casualties are taken and receive treatment to stabilise them before they are sent on to hospital. Our injured men were sent to our division's CCS once we had given them first aid. Florence Mann was working at our division's CCS from early 1916.

Charger. A military officer's horse. Mine was called Peter, a fine looking chestnut. I had to leave him behind in Italy after the war and he was sold off for meat, a great shame as he was a wonderful character, and always looked after me.

Chit. Army term for a receipt or other paper document to certify something. The army ran on chits. If the Germans had destroyed our paper supplies they would have crippled our war effort!

CO. Commanding Officer, a senior officer responsible in all respects for an infantry battalion or cavalry regiment. Normally a lieutenant colonel. Our first one was Colonel Howard, a local solicitor. Really he was too old and kept himself out of harm's way most of the time. He was killed in 1917. Colonel Goodson then turned up, a Regular, and he really knew his stuff. A great officer.

Company. A sub unit of an infantry battalion, commanded by a major, and having about two hundred officers and men.

Direct Fire. A military term where a weapon is fired at an target that is in the sight of the men firing the weapon. See also Indirect Fire. Before the war this was the usual method for artillery, but early in the war we lost men and guns because if we can see the enemy, they can see us, and shoot at us. We learned the hard way to keep our guns out of sight behind a hill or wood, so that indirect fire became the normal method. Except at Cesuna when our howitzer battery helped stop an Austrian attack with direct fire shrapnel. That really sorted the Austriacos, took all the fight out of them.

Division. A military formation of about twenty thousand men commanded by a major general, and which is composed of units from several arms, such as infantry, artillery, and engineers, organised into brigades. Robert Trubshawe was our division's commander up until the time he was sacked in Italy. He was a very good officer, always in the front line, and handing out chocolate and cigarettes to the men. I never saw him smoke or eat chocolate himself, though. He often went on patrols into no man's land. I would have followed him anywhere.

DSO. Distinguished Service Order, a medal awarded to senior officers for meritorious acts during battle. Edwin was awarded one of these.

Field Telephone. An electrical device that can be connected to cable and is portable, such that soldiers in the field can communicate back to their headquarters.

First Light. Dawn, a traditional time for an attack. Also the time for changeover at the OP.

Flanders. The region on the border of France and Belgium that is on the North Sea. Lots of mud and the smell of dung everywhere. Lots of flies as well.

Funk Hole. An underground construction where troops can rest when not on duty, or retire to when under shell fire. Very useful, and a place to brew up or sleep during battle.

Fuse. A mechanical device that is fitted to an artillery shell to keep it in a safe condition until it approaches the target, and explodes or activates the shell to a predetermined time or event, such as striking the ground. The early ones were very poor, with many failing to go off properly. Later some went off too early, but eventually they became much more reliable.

Gas Helmet. A cloth hood that protects soldiers from the effects of poison gas. Unpleasant to wear, and impossible to tell who was who when wearing them. Quite effective, though.

Greatcoat. A heavy woollen ankle length top coat worn by soldiers in cold weather. Soaks up the water and becomes very heavy, but keeps you warm. Can also be used to sleep in as a blanket.

Gun Line. The position where artillery guns are placed when in action. Also includes the men and organisation needed to operate the guns in action. The beating heart of any battery, and where the hard work is done. A great bunch of men, especially in my section!

Gun Number. The crews of guns have specific duties that are detailed in drill manuals. Every member of each crew will be able to carry out several of these duties. The crews are organised according to each set of duties. For example the Number One is usually a sergeant who commands the gun, the Number Two lays the gun for elevation. Number Three lays the gun for direction. Number Four loads the gun. Numbers Five & Six prepare and fuse the ammunition. Numbers Seven Eight & Nine are ammunition handlers, unboxing and stacking and moving it around. Number Ten is Coverer or second in command. My gun crews were the best in the battery, and my battery was the best in the Brigade. Very quick into and out of action, and very accurate laying of the guns. Our infantry were very appreciative of the support we gave them.

Gunner. The most junior rank in the artillery, and a general term for all artillery officers and soldiers.

HE. High Explosive, used for a type of artillery shell that is designed to explode when it strikes the target. Our HE shells were too light to really do the job, we mostly used shrapnel shells. For a really good explosion to destroy anything it was best to use a medium or heavy gun. They had a heavier shell with more explosive, and the shells came down more vertically and that was better for penetration.

Heliograph. A communication device that uses light to transmit messages. Not used much.

Horse Lines. A military term for the location that horses are kept when not required in action, or, out of the line, where the horses are stabled or rested.

HQ. Head Quarters. A location or part of a military organisation where the officers and men who originate orders and carry out central command functions are located. We usually tried to put our HQ in a building or bunker. The mess would usually be close by.

Imperial Service, IS. Before the war Territorials were enlisted for service in the UK only. A few volunteered for service worldwide, and received extra pay and badges to reflect this. After the war started the law required Territorials to volunteer for IS before they could be sent to France. Most agreed, but a few refused to do so. I signed up as soon as I was asked to do so.

Indirect Fire. A military term for the arrangement where a gun is fired at a target that cannot be seen by the men firing the weapon. This usually requires an observer in a position that they can see the target and communicate information to the guns by field telephone or other means. This became the normal method for the artillery. I spent a lot of time at the OP looking for targets that could be fired at by our guns.

Kaiser's Cocktail. British army term for the German habit of mixing various types of projectile, HE, shrapnel and poison gases, during a bombardment. Very inventive is the Boche, but we soon copied him. I wonder what he called our cocktail?

Lachrymatory. Tear gas, normally delivered by artillery shell. It was designed to impede the operation of troops by forcing them to wear gas helmets which were tiring to wear and obstructed normal vision and communication. I found that you could get used to it very quickly and often left my gas helmet off if the lachrymatory was not too strong. The Boche used it often, especially in areas where he wanted to attack as it did not linger and prevent his own troops from operating.

Last Light. Dusk. Just the time when all sorts of things started to happen, working parties, patrols and so on.

The darkness brought a kind of safety, but it could still be jolly dangerous.

Line. Telephone cable, or a trench system, such as front line, second line, reserve line. May also be used to refer to an objective during the planning of an attack. We had all sorts of lines!

Lorry Hop. Get a lift from a passing motor vehicle. Frequently used by soldiers going to the local town or returning from a night out. Very useful, especially as the drivers knew more about where to go in the district.

MC. Military Cross. A medal awarded to officers for acts of bravery in action.

Mess. The place where officers or senior NCOs eat and relax.

Muster (Parade). Military parade before daily routine starts, where men are accounted for and duties are allocated and orders are communicated. Usually we had a muster parade every day if we could.

Observation Post, OP. A position be it a bunker or just a place on the ground, where an observer from the artillery or other military arm, operates by observing the enemy or the ground. In the artillery it is where the forward observer communicates target information back to the guns. A system developed where nearly every officer in the brigade took turns of duty in the OP, sometimes we had more than one for each battery. Some OPs were in the front line trenches with the infantry, sometimes on an elevated spot where the visibility was better.

Open Warfare. A phase of war where neither side has taken up fixed positions, manoeuvre warfare in other words. We trained for this, but the nearest we got to it was in the spring of 1917 when the Boche withdrew several miles. Then we went back to trenches again, the opposite, positional or static warfare.

OTC. Officers Training Corps. Military training organisations at universities and public schools which train pupils in military skills and prepares them for military service as officers. I trained at the OTC in Fishers school, as did both my brothers.

Parapet. The low mound running along in front of a trench, that faces the enemy, and is intended to prevent the enemy observing into the trench. Sometimes this had gaps where shells had landed, and you had to be careful when moving along the trench in case a Boche sharpshooter took a pot shot at you. We also used gaps in the parapet to use periscopes and look out points to keep an eye on the Boche.

Pinard. Rough red wine issued to French troops as a daily ration. Rough, very rough. I could not stand it, but it became popular with my men when they could get their hands on some of it.

Platoon. An infantry sub unit of a company, comprised of an officer and about fifty men.

Poilus. French slang word for an ordinary soldier, equivalent to the British Tommy. The name means 'hairy ones.' And they certainly were. They never seemed to shave in the trenches and all the older men had walrus moustaches.

Premature. Artillery shell that explodes before it was intended to, often caused by faulty fuses. Very dangerous to our men. One of these killed Driver James and another got Dobbin Holt.

Puttees. Strips of woollen cloth wrapped around an infantry soldier's lower legs as part of uniform, designed to act as a gaiter. Later they were issued gum boots in the trenches as puttees were not much use in the mud and wet.

RAP. Regimental Aid Post, part of an infantry battalion's medical organisation when in action. This was where we tried to get casualties to as soon after they were injured as possible, for first aid. The battalion medical officer was usually there with his orderlies, and the padre would spend a lot of his time there as well helping out. The casualties would be taken back to the advanced dressing station and then to a casualty clearing station further back for more comprehensive treatment, if they survived that long.

RFA. Royal Field Artillery, the part of British artillery that is in direct support of infantry. My brigade was part of the RFA. The artillery also had other parts to it. The Royal Horse Artillery supported the cavalry and had better, faster horses than we did. The Royal Garrison Artillery manned the heavy guns that had bigger shells and were used on longer range targets.

RSM. Regimental Sergeant Major, the most senior NCO in a battalion or regiment, holding the Royal Warrant.

RTO. Railway Transport Officer, a military officer responsible for rail transport of men and materiel. Usually retired officers brought back into uniform, a bit officious usually, but they kept things running efficiently.

Section. In the artillery, a sub unit of a battery, normally with two or three guns and their crews. My section was the best in the brigade, if not the whole division!

Shrapnel. Artillery weapon that uses a specialised shell containing hundreds of lead balls similar to musket balls. A time fuse explodes the shell in the air above the target and sends the lead balls forward fast enough to kill a person. Jolly unpleasant when you are on the receiving end! Designed in the Napoleonic Wars, but a modern version for our modern guns.

SOS, SOS Target. An artillery term. When guns are not actively firing they are loaded and aimed at the position that, should the enemy attack from there suddenly, our troops would be most at risk. If an attack does occur, the guns can be fired immediately, bringing fire down to protect our troops. Sometimes this involves our infantry sending up flares to a known pattern to visually indicate the need for the guns to fire. Every time we were stood down from a firing task the guns were loaded and aimed at the SOS target. One man would be left on every gun 24 hours a day so he could fire the gun and we could have shells on the way within seconds.

Stand To. An order used in the infantry or other unit where all the soldiers man their battle positions at full alert and fully equipped. Routinely ordered at first and last light in case of surprise attack by the enemy, or when an attack is expected.

Sub (Artillery). The men manning a single gun, standing for sub-section. My section consisted A sub and B sub. When we expanded the battery to six guns I had three subs, so C sub became part of my section.

Switch Trench. In a defensive position this is a trench behind the main front line trench and usually connected to it where the defenders or other troops can retire to contain a penetration of the front line trench. This is often placed at an angle to the direction of the main trench so that fire at attackers will be from a flank rather than head on. Luckily we had a switch trench behind the position at Cesuna and some gunners from Edwin's battery helped our infantry to defeat the Austrians.

Take Post. A military command, especially in the artillery, for the men to stop whatever they are doing and man the guns. Similar to Stand To in the infantry.

Trek. A journey over time and distance, from the South Afrikaans for 'pull', as in pulling wagons and guns. These could be long and dusty in the summer, or long and cold in the winter, and often wet as well. Always long, though, and a change from the routine in the line.

Verey. Brand name for white or coloured illuminating and signal flares shot from a Verey Pistol, the main type in use in the British Army.

Wagon Line. Military term for the place where wagons and spare transport is laagered when not required to be used, such as when in a defensive position. This is often more than a mile behind the guns, but needs to be close enough to enable resupply runs and so on. Usually the administrative parts of an artillery brigade will be located here as well. We often had our wagon line close to Brigade HQ if possible. I had to take duty at the wagon line which involved loading stores and taking them forward to the gun line or the OP. Sometimes also bringing back casualties to the CCS.

Wind Up. Slang term for nervous, panicked, excited. Some officers suffered from this quite regularly, though others never did. Our men, though, never seemed to suffer from it.

Wire. Barbed wire, which comes in several forms and has stakes, knife rests, and other fixtures and fittings to make it an effective barrier to the movement of and penetration by attackers. Collectively these are known as wire. Often used to funnel attacking troops into killing zones covered by machine guns or artillery fire.

Author's Notes.

As a young(ish) officer in the Royal Artillery, I once spent a
night in the officers' mess of my Territorial Army battery in
Whiteladies Road in Bristol. Not being able to sleep, I found
some diaries from the First World War among the books on a
shelf, and decided to read the contents. I was drawn in
immediately, and read with great interest the personal stories
of the men and officers who had served with the
Gloucestershire Volunteer Artillery in the Great War. Many of
the names of places and battles meant nothing to me at that
time, but over the succeeding years I have researched them all
and have uncovered a story that is fascinating to me, and I
hope will have been to you as well.
All the main events of the First World War in this story really
happened. All the locations are real, I have visited them all,
and more, and relived in my mind the events of a hundred
years ago. The only difference is that I have made new names
for each of the characters, and mixed events and dates around
somewhat to make more of a story. I have imagined the
meaning between the lines of the diaries, for the Edwardians
who wrote them were not given to disclosing their emotions,
and I have had to imagine what they were really feeling during
their war. I have changed the names as the experiences
recounted were not always to the same character. Please accept
this as a work of fiction based on real events and real people.

I have read many books and personal accounts of the First
World War, but none of note about the Territorials, and few
about the Gunners. In part I want to put that right by telling
the tale of Freddy and Edwin Scott, Thomas Hastings, Harold
Kent, Arthur Rippingill, Joseph Leman, the Mann family, and
the others, who fought the Kaiser War and endured to triumph
over the King's enemies.

67860201R00209

Made in the USA
Charleston, SC
24 February 2017